Breathless for You

About the author

Elizabeth Anthony discovered historical novels early in her teens. After graduating from university she worked as a tutor in English Studies, but always dreamed of writing. Her ambition was fulfilled with the publication of an eighteenth-century thriller received with great acclaim in the UK and US and translated into nine languages. She has also written several historical romances. Elizabeth lives with her husband in the Peak District.

ELIZABETH ANTHONY

Breathless for You

HODDER

First published in Great Britain in 2014 by Hodder & Stoughton
An Hachette UK company

1

Copyright © Elizabeth Anthony 2014

The right of Elizabeth Anthony to be identified as the Author
of the Work has been asserted by her in accordance with the Copyright,
Designs and Patents Act 1988.

A CIP catalogue record for this title is available from the British Library

Paperback ISBN 978 1 444 76897 8
Ebook ISBN 978 1 444 76898 5

Typeset by Hewer Text UK Ltd, Edinburgh
Printed and bound by CPI Group (UK) Ltd, Croydon

Hodder & Stoughton policy is to use papers that are natural, renewable
and recyclable products and made from wood grown in sustainable forests.
The logging and manufacturing processes are expected to conform to
the environmental regulations of the country of origin.

Hodder & Stoughton Ltd
338 Euston Road
London NW1 3BH

www.hodder.co.uk

Prologue – Madeline's story

I was born in the first week of February in 1904, just as all the church bells of Paris began to strike midnight, and my nurse Babette used to tell me that the snowflakes danced outside the windows to celebrate my birth. 'You were so pretty, Madeline,' she loved to say. 'You were a winter baby, with blue, blue eyes.' But when I was seventeen, the church bells tolled for my mother's funeral, and within a month of her death, an English duke became my guardian. Although I was afraid of travelling to a foreign land, I agreed to do so because I was even more afraid of my past.

People were envious – 'You will live in London, Madeline!' And so I did for a short while, but the shadows of my past pursued me. I took temporary refuge in my guardian's country home, Belfield Hall, but even there I wasn't safe; because I met a man who worked on the land, a man who obsessed me, until I, who'd vowed to guard myself, became his in every way. He seduced me, I think, with his first smile.

He made me beg for his love, and I did so. I gave myself to him freely, because I guessed that he understood my need. I remember that I saw the shadows of his own damaged past in his eyes as he stripped me bare and took me fiercely, proudly, rousing me to a desire and a fulfilment that I had not believed possible. Other women wanted him badly, but he laughed at my jealousy, saying, 'How could I look at anyone else, when I have you? You are mine, Madeline. Mine.' I replied again and again that yes, I was his; I surrendered myself to him as he made love to me in ways that were dark and blissful, in ways that I hadn't been able to imagine.

I was young, you see, and I was a fool. My childhood should have taught me to trust no one, but I trusted him. I was an exile, I was an orphan, I was shunned by society. I thought that in him I'd found what I wanted – what I needed.

But I'd also discovered that my guardian the Duke – perhaps the kindest and best man I'd ever known – was in danger of losing the love of his life, who'd once been a servant at Belfield Hall. I realised that the Duke had enemies who were also my enemies – the old Duchess of Belfield for one, who hated the fact that he had inherited her former home, and Lady Beatrice, who'd once wanted him for herself. And I found myself having to make almost impossible choices, because if my guardian was to be reunited with his Sophie, then I had to be prepared to sacrifice my own dreams. I knew that I did not deserve happiness – but the Duke and his Sophie did.

My story begins on the day I arrived at Belfield Hall, three years after the war ended . . .

Chapter One

November 1921

'Welcome to Belfield Hall, ma'am,' said Mr Peters the butler, holding open the door for me as I stepped down from the Duke's big Daimler. 'We hope you will be very happy here.'

Thirty or more servants were waiting out in the freezing cold courtyard, and I think I tried to smile as the housekeeper led me past them listing their names, which I repeated, though I feared I would never remember each one. 'Welcome,' they all said. 'Welcome, ma'am.'

I had travelled to Oxford by train with my companion, Miss Kenning. A servant called Eddie had driven us from the railway station, and in the back of the car Miss Kenning whispered, 'Oh, Madeline. To think that we are actually going to be living at Belfield Hall – I believe it is a *treasure house* of art and antiquities.'

I remember that I felt guilty, because the servants all had to stand outside like that in the cold wind, bowing their heads or curtseying to me in turn; the footmen in the Duke of Belfield's livery, and the maids in black, with starched white aprons and caps. Their servitude reminded me of my childhood: of the big house in the rue Saint-Honoré where the footmen had carried trays of wine, and my mother had made me go round with a dish of little honey-cakes, curtseying and lisping to her guests in French: *My name is Madeline, and what can I do to please you? What can I do to please you,* mesdames et messieurs?

'Ma'am? Are you ready to go inside now, ma'am?' The voice of the housekeeper, Mrs Burdett.

'Of course,' I said. 'I'm so sorry. Of course.'

So Mrs Burdett led me inside, with Miss Kenning hurrying behind. 'It is unfortunate, ma'am,' Mrs Burdett was saying to me, 'that the Duke of Belfield himself could not come with you.'

I remembered saying goodbye to my guardian, and how I'd tried desperately to hide my panic. All wrapped up in my winter coat and hat, I'd been standing outside the Duke's beautiful London house while his chauffeur James was loading my luggage into the car, and I felt terribly alone, because my guardian had told me he had to go away, to his estate in Ireland. Perhaps the Duke saw my fear, for he said quickly, 'I will, of course, come to Belfield with you if you wish, Madeline.'

I'd shaken my head firmly. 'I really will be quite all right, Your Grace.'

He'd looked at me gravely with his clear blue eyes. 'I'm so sorry that I have to go to Ireland. It's a matter of business and duty, I fear.'

'I understand,' I said quickly. 'Please don't worry about me.'

'I'll write to you regularly.' He touched my hand. 'And you've got my telephone number, haven't you? You must ring me, whenever you wish, and when I next get to Belfield we shall discuss your future again. I'm only sorry that London didn't suit you.'

'I'll be happier in the countryside,' I said. 'I'm sure of it.'

'I hope so. Write to me in Ireland, Madeline. Ring me.'

I'd nodded, the lump in my throat almost choking me. And now I could only feel dismay at the sight of this vast cold place to which my life had taken me, miles from anywhere, with the trees all bare and the skies growing heavier by the hour.

I remember that a footman called Robert carried my luggage upstairs, and Mrs Burdett showed me my accommodation. As well as a bedroom, I had my own bathroom, and a small parlour where a fire had been lit; but I still shivered as I took off my heavy travelling coat and saw that the rain was starting to lash against the windows. Miss Kenning was taken to her own smaller apartment just along the corridor, but as soon as the housekeeper had left, she came rushing in to me. 'This house is truly astonishing, Madeline,' she said in an awed voice. 'I believe there are paintings here by Rembrandt, and the ceiling in the Great Hall is by Verrio. Oh, I cannot wait to explore it.'

Miss Kenning had been my governess and companion for nearly two years, and I was pleased that she at least would be happy here. As for me, I hoped that my past might be forgotten. I hoped that I might be safe.

People asked me, in that first week at Belfield Hall, if I was homesick for Paris, and I would reply, 'A little,' because that was what they expected of me. I was fully aware of the servants, as they scurried about their business, casting furtive glances at me. 'She's an orphan, poor thing,' I heard the housemaids whispering. 'The Duke's ward. She's only seventeen, and she's so far from home.' Several Oxfordshire neighbours called to visit within the first week, and cards were delivered inviting me to afternoon teas and luncheons; but I told the butler, Mr Peters, to inform them all that I was still recovering from my journey.

Every morning at a quarter past nine, a service would be held in the Hall's chapel. The chapel was very ornate, and had wooden and stone carvings that dated back to the seventeenth century – Miss Kenning told me this. The local vicar, who walked over from Belfield village each day whatever the weather, came up to me after my first attendance there, and asked if I wished to be put in touch with a priest. 'I'm assuming,' he said, 'that you are a Roman Catholic, Miss Dumouriez? I could arrange for Father O'Ryan from Oxford to—'

'No,' I interrupted. 'There's no need.' I could tell he was puzzled by me, as most people were.

'But I heard that you were educated in a convent. Surely—'

'I don't need a priest. Thank you.' I was aware of the servants watching me and holding their breaths, as I walked with Miss Kenning out of the chapel.

One fine, crisp afternoon at the end of November, Miss Kenning and I went for a long walk up into the woods. There must at some time have been pheasant shooting here, I realised, for a mile or so from the Hall we came across an old cottage in a clearing, and close by were several pheasant coops made of woven willow laths. But the coops looked as if they hadn't been used for years; the cottage too looked deserted, and I wondered if perhaps the gamekeeper who might have once lived here had gone away to the terrible war and had not come back.

Whenever it was fine, I walked and walked, in the grounds, or in the woods. When it rained – as it so often did that winter, I remember – I wandered around inside the vast house, but there were so many rooms that I frequently got lost; indeed sometimes a servant would find me and would, with a mixture of puzzlement and pity, I think, guide me gently back to my own small parlour. One day, a long letter arrived for me from the Duke in County Wicklow, describing the Irish country-side, and his visits to nearby Dublin, and the weather. A few evenings later, he telephoned me. 'Are you all right, Madeline?' he asked. 'Are they taking good care of you?'

'Yes,' I replied, shutting my eyes for a moment, pictur-ing his face. 'Everyone has been very kind, Your Grace.' It was around then that I learned from the Duke's stew-ard, Mr Fitzpatrick – who lived in Belfield village, and managed the Duke's estate – that my guardian had in fact been requested by the Home Office to be part of a commission that was involved in settling Ireland's future. I felt stupid for not knowing this; for not know-ing that his duties there were so important.

When December came, with its so-short days and freezing nights, I nevertheless hoped my guardian might ring to say that he would soon be on his way to Belfield Hall, but instead he wrote, asking me if I would like to come to London for the festive season. 'If you decide to do so,' he said, 'I shall make sure that I get there myself, for a short while at least.'

Only that morning Mr Fitzpatrick told me, with an anxious frown on his kind face, that the Duke had been asked to stay on in Ireland over the Christmas period as a matter of urgency, because the announcement of a new treaty between England and Ireland was imminent. 'He's a much-respected figure there,' Mr Fitzpatrick told me, 'and his opinions are highly valued.'

I wrote to my guardian, and said I was happy to remain at Belfield; but after I'd given Mr Peters my letter to be posted, I twisted the emerald bracelet I wore on my wrist, as I did when I was disturbed. The Duke was so very kind, and I could not bring myself to tell him how terribly alone I felt, here in this vast house where the silence was broken only by the sounds of the clocks in every room; the wretched wall clocks and grandfather clocks that ticked and chimed to mark the slow passing of time for me in my solitude.

Christmas came, and there was a service in the chapel followed by a special dinner in the servants' hall for all the indoor and outdoor staff. Miss Kenning and I ate roast beef and plum pudding alone, in the huge dining room that Robert the footman had valiantly tried to make festive with candles and wreaths of holly. In the evening the Duke rang to wish me a merry Christmas, and to say that he wished he could be there.

By then, I'd grown accustomed to the routines of Belfield Hall, but the staff were by no means used to me. For instance, I had not brought a maid with me from London. Mrs Burdett had been astonished when I told her I didn't really need one; she had pressed her lips together, and said that perhaps we could discuss the matter again shortly. In the meantime, various house servants came to bring me my tea or to draw my bath, and to see if I needed any help with my hair, or my clothes.

But I was used to managing by myself, and the few clothes I had were plain and serviceable enough for winter in the country: cream blouses, long serge skirts, and gowns in navy or brown, into which I changed for dinner at half past six – they kept old-fashioned country hours at Belfield Hall. I had no need of a maid to lace me into heavy corsets, because I didn't wear them, nor did I wear pretty silk underwear, as many girls my age did, preferring instead a cotton brassiere that laced up the side and flattened my already small breasts. My long dark hair tended to be unruly, so I would brush it hard, as if I was punishing myself, and tie it back with a plain ribbon.

One of the maids, Nell, whom I found the kindest of them all, said to me once, when she was laying out some newly laundered clothes for me, 'Oh, ma'am. You should be wearing pretty gowns and going to parties. I don't know why His Grace the Duke—' She broke off, her cheeks aflame.

It's not the Duke's fault, I wanted to say to her. *It's mine. It's mine.*

I wore only one piece of jewellery: the bracelet I've already mentioned, which was a band of gold set with small emeralds fastened tightly around my wrist by a serpent's-head clasp. 'It was a gift,' I used to say in London when the Duke's friends asked me why I always wore it.

'Oh,' they would breathe. 'How beautiful. It looks so – *old*. What a lovely present.' But if they had looked beneath it, they would have seen that the sharp-edged bracelet had made livid scars on my white skin.

There was a frequent visitor to the Hall around that time whose name was Lottie Towndrow, and I was told that she was a historian. She rented a cottage in Belfield village and often rode over on her bicycle, because she had permission to visit the library here whenever she wished. She was writing a history of the landed families of Oxfordshire, Mr Peters told me, and one day he took me to meet her – he perhaps thought that she might be a friend for me.

As Mr Peters led me into the library, Miss Towndrow was sitting at a table writing, with her spectacles perched on the end of her nose, and her long red hair coiled tightly at the nape of her neck. She was only a few years older than I was, and appeared almost severe in the way she dressed, though her plain clothes suited her slim figure very well. She had the pale but perfect skin that some redheads possessed, and she looked up at me curiously with her clear green eyes.

'So you've recently become the Duke's ward, I take it, Madeline? That must have meant a sudden elevation of status for you.'

I was as surprised by her casual use of my first name as I was by her implied insult. 'Not particularly,' I said.

'My father was a baron with estates in Normandy, but he died when I was two. My mother died last year.'

She nodded. 'In a motor-car accident, I heard. And the Duke was your mother's cousin – were you pleased, to find yourself in his care?'

In fact I'd not known at the time of the Duke's existence. I simply said, 'His Grace has been most kind to me.'

'So you have a duke for your guardian, yet here you are at Belfield Hall, all on your own. What on earth do you *do* all day?'

I muttered something about reading books, and taking walks in the grounds.

'What an incredible waste,' she said. 'Especially as you speak English reasonably well, though I don't suppose you had much of an education. By the way, do call me Lottie – we've no need to use the antiquated formalities of our elders, don't you agree?' Quite clearly, though, she wasn't offering me her friendship, since she straight away turned back to her studies, making it plain that I was no longer welcome.

Later that day I happened to come across some of the staff talking about her. 'That Miss Towndrow,' a young footman was saying. 'What she needs is a man to sort her out.'

'She's a suffragist,' said one of the maids importantly.

'So? That's the trouble with all of her kind. They frighten the men away, when really all they need is a good . . .'

Then they saw me, and hurried silently on with their tasks.

Those winter afternoons grew dark so very quickly. One January day after I'd been for a walk, I returned to my sitting room to find that the electric light wasn't working, and since I was still too shy to ring the bell for a servant, I made my way down to the basement where the kitchens and pantries were, hoping to come across someone who could help me.

When I came to the servants' hall, the door was open, and I could see that they were all sitting down to have their afternoon cup of tea; I turned to go, not wanting to disturb them, but I'd already been noticed.

'Ma'am,' someone exclaimed, and they all jumped to their feet. A housemaid knocked over a teacup, then set it straight with an even louder clatter.

My cheeks burned and I twisted the tight emerald bracelet on my wrist. 'I think I need a new light bulb, in my sitting room,' I said. 'That is all. There's really no hurry. Only when you've time.'

I turned to go, but Robert the footman was already holding out a chair for me. 'I'll see to that in a moment, ma'am,' he said. 'You should have rung. But now that you're here, please do come and join us.'

It might seem unusual that they welcomed me there, but I think they'd been glad to find that I did not put on airs and graces; in fact I didn't really know how to give them their orders, and I think they felt sorry for me, as well as being deeply curious. I sat very hesitantly, and someone pushed a cup of tea towards me, then silence descended. I tried to smile.

'Well,' I said, my heart sinking to my shoes. 'It is so lovely to be here, in your beautiful English countryside. And I do hope that I'm not making too much extra work for you all . . .'

The silence continued, and I felt the old fear. *They saw. They saw.* But then one of the housemaids looked at me eagerly and said, 'Oh, ma'am. You speak English so very well. Do all French people know as much English as you?'

So though I still felt sick with tension, I explained that I'd been taught a little English at the convent where I was educated, and then – thanks to Miss Kenning – I'd learned to speak the language reasonably well.

'More than that, ma'am,' marvelled one of the scullery maids. 'You talk like a grand English lady!' She'd been gazing at me in wonder ever since I'd sat down. 'Please – will you tell us about Paris?'

'Yes,' urged the others. 'Please, tell us about Paris.'

So I lied to them about the city where I was born; I made up stories about the parties and the theatres and the *couturiers* that they assumed would have been part of my life before I came to London last spring. Lies, lies: my whole life was built on lies.

And as the days went by, I felt as though I was hidden away from the world.

Miss Towndrow, the researcher from Oxford – Lottie, as she'd asked me to call her – continued to visit the Hall regularly. Miss Kenning was awed by her. 'She is so very, very clever,' she would say to me. 'So independent, and she knows so much.'

I realised that Miss Kenning often sought Lottie out on the pretext of asking her opinion on some aspect or other of Belfield Hall's history, and I guessed my curious companion was probably a nuisance to her. As for me, I would speak to Lottie with the barest civility if our paths crossed, for I didn't like the way she looked at me, as if she saw much more than I wanted her to see. But on one occasion she trapped me by asking me to come downstairs with her to one of the storerooms; where, she told me, there were some documents in French that she wanted me to translate.

Since I thought she was the Duke's guest, I didn't feel I could refuse, so I followed her down to the windowless basement rooms. Lottie, as confident as ever, had asked for some coffee to be brought to us as we worked, and she already had the documents laid out on a big oak table. 'It will make a change for you, Madeline,' she said breezily as she pulled a chair out for me, 'to be doing something useful. What you usually find to fill your days, I simply cannot imagine.'

She'd said this before, of course. She thought me shallow and stupid. This time I didn't respond – I don't think she expected me to, and anyway, she was already pushing the first of the papers towards me. It was a letter, I realised, in exquisite but faded handwriting. I translated it aloud, carefully. '*My love,*' I read. '*I dream of you at night. I dream of your fine body . . .*' I stopped.

I think she gloated over my confusion. 'That letter,' she said, 'is over sixty years old. It was written by the fourth

Duke of Belfield's young French wife to her lover, Giles, who was a footman at her parents' chateau in Lille. After her marriage, and her move to England, she claimed unbearable homesickness and went back to Lille as often as she could – to see her parents, and Giles as well, presumably.' She shrugged. 'The poor girl – she had to have *some* compensation for her husband's lack of interest in her. Coincidentally, the Duke's lover was also a young footman, here at the Hall . . . Do carry on, Madeline.'

I said calmly, 'Your research is clearly going to be of a personal nature. Does the Duke know precisely what you are writing about?'

'Oh,' she said, 'he must surely have every sympathy with the disastrous love affairs of the nobility. After all, he had a mistress who was once a scullery maid here, and now she's a popular singer.' Contempt coloured her every word. 'It's hard to say which occupation is the more demeaning, really.'

I felt a pulse drumming in my temple. 'I met her,' I said. 'I met Sophie in London, and I thought she was very beautiful, and very kind.'

'Really? But you didn't actually stay with the Duke in London, did you? I heard that he packed you off to live with a well-connected family in Mayfair, so he would be free to indulge himself with his low-born mistress—'

'He was thinking of *me*,' I broke in. 'He thought I would enjoy London more in the company of other young people.'

She lifted one eyebrow. 'Clearly, you didn't. Since you find yourself here.' She pushed the letter towards me. 'Please continue.'

So I did. '*I dream of your tongue,*' I read, '*pleasuring me in the place you love to call your own. I dream of your seed –*' I hesitated only slightly '*– spilling itself deep within me. During the long lonely nights away from you, I toy with my breasts, and I think of you, my magnificent lover . . .*'

I paused, as she scribbled away. 'Are you managing to keep up?' I asked her politely.

'Oh, indeed. Your English vocabulary is – excellent.' Lottie let her green eyes rove up and down me casually. 'What a good thing it is for us, Madeline, that you're no shrinking innocent. Or so I've heard.'

I froze. *What did she mean? What did she know?* But already she was calmly pouring us both coffee, saying, 'Shall we move on to the next page?'

I continued to translate, capably and coolly. I played her at her own game. Afterwards I went up to my room, knowing that she'd been trying to disturb me – even to arouse me. But she would have to try harder than that.

I was safe here, I kept telling myself. I was safe.

February arrived, and with it came my eighteenth birthday. Cook baked me a cake, and my guardian sent me a beautiful little gold locket, and wrote saying that he hoped to be back in England shortly. But that afternoon I met Mr Fitzpatrick, who drove over to the Hall every week to check that all was well in the Duke's absence; and he told me that he feared the Duke was likely to be detained in Ireland for a while longer. 'I don't suppose you have much chance to follow the news, Miss Dumouriez?'

'I sometimes look at the newspapers,' I told him. *The Times* was delivered daily to Belfield Hall, and Robert or Richard always ironed it before placing it in the library. 'I try to read about Ireland, but I find the situation difficult to understand. Please will you explain to me what the Duke is doing there, and what this new treaty will mean?'

'Well, now,' he said, 'it might take a while.'

'Please,' I begged.

He looked at his watch. 'I have time enough to spare, if you do. Will you come to the library with me, Miss Dumouriez?'

'Of course.'

Once in the library, Mr Fitzpatrick went straight to the bookshelves and lifted down a weighty atlas, which he spread out on the table in front of me. He was meticulous and kind; he pointed out Dublin and Belfast, and sketched an imaginary line with his finger across the country, to show me where a new and permanent boundary was in the process of being created by treaty between the north and south.

I shook my head in bewilderment. 'So they're dividing the country? But why?'

He gave a small sigh. 'Basically, Ireland has been split for a long time – between the Catholics, who live mainly in the south and who want to be free of British rule, and the Protestants in the north, who want to remain part of Britain. This treaty means that the south – the Irish Free State – is to have its own government, based in Dublin.'

'But why is the Duke so involved in all this?'

'Because he's been contributing to the negotiations as

to where the boundary should be drawn – partly because, like many of the English nobility, he has property in the south, in County Wicklow, to be precise.'

I still didn't understand. 'The Irish people must surely resent a group of Englishmen drawing up the terms of their independence?'

'Most of the men who've been drawing up the final treaty are Irish politicians,' he explained. 'But the Duke – and other Englishmen – have made the same point as you, and in fact His Grace has already said that he's quite willing to give up his Irish estate, since he hardly feels entitled to it. "It's like owning a piece of foreign land," he told me once. Though saying *that*, of course, has made him rather unpopular with the other English lords who hold castles and great swathes of land in Ireland.'

I wished my guardian had told me something of all this before he went away, because I'd never guessed; I'd had no idea. 'But why, if there's a treaty, are people still arguing?'

'Because the leaders of the Republican Army want *all* of Ireland, north and south, to be united, and they feel that the new government of the Irish Free State has given way to British demands too readily – for example, by allowing British naval bases to remain in Irish waters. The Republican Army claim that they've been betrayed.'

'An army? Do you think that the Duke is in danger?'

'Oh, bless you, no, he's safe enough, at his Wicklow estate or in Dublin. But the Treaty Bill has only just been presented to the House of Commons in London, and there are Irish tempers to be soothed, Irish politicians to be appeased. The Duke telephoned me last night, and said that he cannot come home until his work's done. He asked after you, of course – he always does. He will be here as soon as he possibly can, I'm sure.'

I nodded. Again I gazed at the map of Ireland – all those beautiful names: Limerick, Tipperary, Kinsale . . . 'There were Irishmen fighting in France in the war, weren't there?' I asked him suddenly.

Mr Fitzpatrick looked sad. 'Yes, many an Irishman fought in the war. But those who wanted to be free of British rule *didn't* fight, you see. And there's bad feeling still, between both sides, but our Duke is most highly regarded there. You have His Grace's telephone number, don't you? You must ring him any time, if you need to – he won't see it as an imposition at all.' He smiled at me, put away the heavy atlas and left, but I stayed there, turning the pages of that day's newspaper, until I saw the headline, NEWS FROM IRELAND. And I read: *The Catholic bishops have implored all the people of Ireland to accept the peace treaty, and to make the best of the freedom it brings. But the Irish Republican Army vows to fight on . . .*

Fighting? I read a little more, then slowly put the newspaper aside and left the library. But the afternoon had grown colder for me, and my thoughts darker.

The next day, I wrote to my guardian to thank him for my present, and to say that I was quite happy here. I gave the letter to Mr Peters and went out for my usual walk, wandering around the bare shrubbery gardens until the gathering dusk made it almost impossible for me to see my way, then I returned to my sitting room to find that Miss Kenning was there.

I expected she'd come to enthuse over some painting or sculpture she'd found, but instead, she held an envelope out to me. 'Dear Madeline, a letter has arrived for you – from London! It must be from one of your young friends there – perhaps a belated birthday greeting.'

I'd made no friends in London. She handed it to me, waiting for me to open it, but I didn't, and her face fell. 'Well,' she said, 'we've almost an hour before dinner, so I shall get back to the portrait gallery – I've discovered four Constable sketches in there. This place is full of wonderful surprises.'

I waited until she'd shut the door before I opened my letter. I read it, then put it down. For a moment the room swam around me; because my old life was catching up with me at last.

I fastened on my leather walking shoes and wrapped myself in a shabby fur coat that I'd found lying forgotten in a side room. 'I think it belonged to the Duchess,' one of the maids, Betsey, had told me when I asked her about it. 'We weren't sure whether or not to send it on to the Dower House, for that's where she's moved to, ma'am, her and all her cats.'

'Her cats?'

'Oh, yes, at least a dozen. What a one for cats the old lady is. If I were you, I'd keep that fur coat, ma'am – you need something warm for these English winters.'

The coat had a large, deep pocket in the lining, and

after I'd put it on, I slipped an oblong leather case into the pocket, then left the house by a back door and headed across the now dark park towards the woodland path that I'd climbed some weeks ago with Miss Kenning. In less than half an hour, I'd come to the clearing where the old pheasant coops were, and the disused cottage. Reaching carefully inside the Duchess's fur coat, I took out the leather case, laid it flat on a big tree stump and opened it.

In the moonlight, my small pistol gleamed.

Down below in the valley, I could see the lights of Belfield Hall. Dinner would have been announced by now, and Mr Peters would have set all the footmen roaming around the house looking for me. The maid-servants would be chattering excitedly. *What has she done now? What has* mam'selle *from Paris done now?*

Mam'selle from Paris was afraid again. Even more afraid, when there was a sudden crashing in the under-growth and I swung round to see two huge black Labradors bounding towards me – followed by a roughly clad man with a shotgun over his shoulder.

Chapter Two

I snatched up my pistol and aimed it straight at the man with the gun. 'Stay away from me,' I called out. 'Do not come any closer. Do you understand?'

He took one glance at me, then whistled the dogs sharply to his side. 'Here, Sam. Here, Georgie.' They stood close while he ruffled their heads, then he turned back to me. 'Please don't point that pistol in my direction, *mam'selle*,' he said.

Only then did I realise that in my panic I'd spoken to him in French. Had he understood? I didn't know, but I stammered in English, 'I – I thought your dogs were going to attack me.'

'My dogs don't attack humans,' he said. 'But your fur coat must smell of something. That's why they're so excited. I'd say it smells of – cats.'

I closed my eyes briefly and lowered the gun. *What a one for cats the old lady is.*

'So it *is* the coat?' he asked sharply.

For some reason – perhaps because he'd moved nearer and the moon shone full on his face – I found my mouth was so dry that I couldn't speak. He was wearing a battered tweed jacket, with cord breeches and well-worn leather boots. His hair was light brown and curling

and a little too long, which softened some of the hard
angles of his face; his eyes were dark in the moonlight,
and the way he was looking at me made me feel pinned
to the spot. He'd leaned his shotgun against the wall of
the derelict cottage. Who was he? Was he a poacher?
Why did I feel an unaccustomed heat trickling down my
spine at the sight of him? Fear. It must be fear. My first
instinct was to move away, but in stepping backwards I
stumbled against one of the pheasant coops – and I
dropped the pistol. He strode forward and scooped it
up, looking furious.

'It's all right. The safety catch is on,' I said quickly.

'Even so. Even so . . .' He weighed it in his hand and
appeared to be trying to calm himself. 'It's a Ruby,' he
said at last. 'Used by the French in the war.' He looked
up at me, frowning. 'And what exactly you're doing up
here, in charge of a lethal pistol, is beyond my compre-
hension. Do you even know how to handle it safely?
What on earth were you intending to do with it?' His
eyes darkened almost to black. 'I assume that you're the
Duke's French ward – and I very much hope you
weren't thinking of harming yourself, *mam'selle*.'

My pulse jerked and faltered. 'You're letting your
imagination run away with you,' I said. 'I have this gun
for self-defence – is that such a ridiculous notion?'

'It is when you've no idea how to use it.'

'Please give me my pistol back.' I was trying my hardest to keep my voice steady. 'Or I shall report you for
trespassing on the Duke of Belfield's property.' I was
aware even as I spoke that my attempt at defiance
sounded utterly foolish.

He gave a cold smile; he was still casually weighing my pistol in his hand. 'Trespassing? Now, I could make a strong case against the entire notion of trespassing, and property, by claiming that the aristocrats of England have, over the centuries, built up their wealth by stealing the land that once belonged to the ordinary people.'

I drew a deep breath. 'The Duke is an excellent land-owner. He cares about the people who work for him. He feels true responsibility for them—'

'It's easy to say that, when you've got a full stomach, several well-staffed mansions and an income beyond most people's wildest dreams. Isn't it?' He strolled across the clearing to carefully lay my pistol back in its open case, then he turned to me, and his eyes suddenly gleamed. 'Bring on the revolution,' he said softly. 'My name's Nathan Mallory, by the way. The information might help you, if you decide you want to report me to your esteemed guardian, the Duke.'

I wasn't tall, and he towered over me. I also realised that his body beneath that battered tweed jacket was solid with muscle, and my legs felt unsteady again. 'Two of the Duke's footmen are waiting for me at the bottom of the hill,' I lied, 'and soon they'll be up here looking for me . . .'

'No, they won't,' he interrupted. 'You came up here alone. I saw you. And it's my guess that you're probably still upset over being banished from London.'

I stepped forward, an exclamation on my lips.

'Not going to defend yourself, *mam'selle*?' he taunted gently. 'Against the gossip that you tried to seduce your

24

highly eligible guardian in London and failed, so he packed you off here as punishment?'

My heavy fur coat kept sliding off my shoulders, and I hitched it up, wishing I'd never set eyes on it. 'It appears that you and the gossips have judged me already. I asked to be sent here. I hated London.'

His eyes widened a little. 'So it wasn't a question of not getting exactly what – or who – you wanted there?'

'I hated London,' I repeated in a low voice.

'Then perhaps you're not as stupid as I thought. And I must compliment you on your English.'

I gazed steadfastly up at him. 'I'm only sorry,' I said, 'that I haven't yet acquired the English vocabulary that I would like to use in a situation like this. But I know the French.'

I proceeded to insult him with a series of fluent French gutter-words, and he laughed – in the moonlight I saw that his teeth were white and even, and his brown eyes were dancing. 'Bravo, *mam'selle*.' He leaned closer. 'Now, I can enlarge your English vocabulary, whenever you like. I can teach you – all sorts of things.'

I felt myself beginning to tremble – but suddenly I realised he was pointing to the night sky above us. 'Look up there, for example,' he was saying in a different sort of voice. 'Not at the moon, but at the stars. You don't see sights like that in London, or in any city in the world for that matter – there's too much smoke, too much artificial light. Listen a moment. What can you hear?'

I was so astonished I did exactly what he said. Who was this man? Was he half-crazy? 'I hear the stream,' I said. I thought it safest to play his game. 'And twigs crackling in the frost. And – owls?'

'No. Not owls.' Taking my arm, he pointed in the direction of the shrill, perplexing calls. 'That's the sound of foxes, mating.'

Oh. My breathing quickened. His hand on my arm was doing something to me, even through the sleeve of my coat; his fingers, I saw, were well-shaped and strong.

'They come out here,' he went on, 'when the moon is bright. As soon as the vixen's in heat, the males fight over her and the victor comes to claim her. She's aroused by the fighting, she's aroused by the victor's strength and she prepares to copulate with him. That's what you're hearing right now. The sound of life. No shame or embarrassment about it – the sound of sex, pure and simple. Do you know about sex, *mam'selle?*'

That was when I pulled myself away from him and whispered, 'You are being unspeakably insolent, Mr Mallory.'

He shrugged again. 'I'm just trying to open your eyes, and your other senses, to what's going on around you. You'll be used to fine city ways – to the company of men who've stolen from the poor for generations and who think nothing of it. You French had a revolution over a hundred years ago, didn't you? – though your nobility didn't take long to claw everything back. They always do. But the rich don't know about the foxes, or the other creatures of the wild. They don't know, for example, that in the early days of spring, the hares – usually solitary creatures – gather near the crest of the hill where the pine tree is, and dance on their hind legs beneath the moon. And look – look here.'

He stooped to probe at the half-frozen leaf mould at his feet and pointed out a small seedling. 'It's an oak,' he told me. 'Do you see it?' I saw him almost tenderly firm the earth around it, then stand tall again in the moonlight. 'In a hundred years' time,' he said, 'you and I will be mouldering in our graves. But this oak will live on. The moon and those stars will still shine as brightly. The hares and foxes will still be mating and calling out their desire. Think on it when you next try your snares on some rich, grasping lord.'

I could hardly breathe. I glanced again at my pistol in its open case nearby and whispered, 'As I said before, you are very free with your insults.'

His hooded eyelids half closed. 'Perhaps I'm trying to help. Indeed, as *I* said before, I could teach you a thing or two, *mam'selle*. I'd make a bet on it.'

My heart had begun to thud once more, but before I could even think what to say, he'd taken my hand in his, and he bent his dark head to press a single kiss on my upturned palm. His tongue touched my skin – *his tongue*. Its tip slid from between his curved lips and caressed me there, on the sensitive flesh at the base of my thumb; all my nerve endings prickled with danger, but there was something else. Something dark and forbidden, coiling softly at the base of my belly; something I fought against, with every instinct I possessed.

I snatched my hand away, but not quickly enough – my coat sleeve had fallen back, and he saw my emerald bracelet gleam in the moonlight. Grasping my wrist, he held it up. 'It's too tight for you,' he exclaimed. 'That bauble's cutting into your skin – it must be marking you, for God's sake—'

He broke off, because I'd leapt away, dived to get my gun from its case and was pointing it straight at him. I heard him swear.

'Put that thing down,' he ordered harshly. 'Even though you say the safety catch is on, it's still damned stupid to point it at someone. *Put it down.*'

I didn't move – but Nathan Mallory did, so swiftly that I wasn't forewarned. He'd taken three strides towards me, and even as I tried to grip the pistol tighter, he knocked it and sent it flying from my hands.

It went off. *It went off.* There was a terrible silence after the explosion, followed by the sound of all the birds in the woods flying up from their roosts in terror. I stood there shaking.

He had me in his arms. 'Jesus Christ,' he swore, and his voice was thick with tension. He carried on swearing under his breath, but he held me. 'Are you all right?'

I tried to nod my head. 'The safety catch . . .'

'Must have been faulty. They often are, on those things—' He broke off as I let out a sob. I heard him draw a deep, ragged breath, then he gave a small sigh. 'I'd guess you've had a difficult time lately,' he said at last. 'But using a gun – for whatever purpose – isn't the answer. You've got spirit, I'll give you that. You've got courage. Show your enemies what you're made of, *mam'selle.*'

He laid one finger beneath my chin and tilted it gently up. By this time I could scarcely breathe. *Was he going to kiss me?* The wayward pulse at the base of my throat began a rapid thudding beat; once more I felt a surge of dangerous heat low in my belly and my skin prickled with tension. Somehow I pulled myself away, but as I did so, that heavy and over-large fur coat slid completely from my shoulders and dropped to the ground. I hugged my arms across my chest in utter despair. *Nowhere to hide now, Madeline. Nowhere to hide.*

His eyes narrowed. 'I think you'd better get back to the Hall. And as for your fur coat . . .' It had fallen into the mud; he picked the thing up and let it drop again. 'You can't wear that. It's filthy. But you'll be cold without it—'

'It doesn't matter.' I was quite distraught by now. 'It really doesn't – I must go.'

He watched me a moment longer before saying suddenly, 'Here. Wear my jacket.' He was already taking it off and wrapping it around my shoulders. *'Mam'selle,'* he went on, 'it's not my place to say it, but you're clearly in some kind of predicament. I thought the Duke, whatever his faults, would be more attentive to his young ward.'

I cut him short. 'I don't like to ask him. He's in Ireland, and I don't like to trouble him.'

I heard the hiss of his indrawn breath. 'You've come up here in the night with a quite lethal pistol. Something's clearly very wrong. Yet – *you don't like to trouble him.'* He paused a moment, then he said, 'Before you go, let me fetch you something.'

He moved towards the coop that I'd stumbled over. It lay on its side, its wicker door hanging open, and he bent down to set it upright, then came back to me and pressed something into my hand. I realised it was one of the wooden pegs that were slotted through leather loops to close each cage. Longer than my hand and with a hole pierced in one end, the peg lay smoothly against my palm and gleamed in the moonlight.

I jerked my eyes up to his. 'Why are you giving me this?'

'I thought you might be interested.' His eyes never left mine. 'The gamekeepers used to take great pride in carving these.'

'Are *you* a gamekeeper?'

'Of sorts.' He closed my hand around the wooden peg, and the pressure of his fingers jolted my senses. 'You can see, *mam'selle*,' he went on softly, 'that the gamekeepers decorated them with their own marks, and some of them are perhaps over a hundred years old. They're treasured as talismans by the country folk, because they're supposed to bring good luck and good health. In fact, I'd keep that particular one close if I were you. You'd be surprised at what it can do.'

He withdrew his hand, but I was sure that I felt his fingers feather my wrist. I said sharply, to hide my disarray, 'You won't tell anyone? That I've been up here tonight?'

He shrugged. 'Why should I? But for God's sake, don't roam around the woods again with a loaded gun, will you? And now – as you say – you really should be going home.'

'But I need my pistol . . .'

I saw him glancing over to where it still lay after he'd

knocked it from my hands, and I knew that he'd hoped I'd forgotten about it. He said, 'You're quite sure?'

'*Yes*. I must have it.'

His mouth tightened, then he went to swiftly check it over and put it carefully back in its case before handing it to me. And so, with the strange wooden peg in one pocket of the gamekeeper's jacket, and my pistol case in the other, I hurried down the path, my mind churning – *Who was he? What was he doing up there? What would I do or say, if I met him again?*

And so confused were my thoughts, that it was only when I reached Belfield Hall that I realised I'd lost my emerald bracelet.

What had happened to it? Oh God, I must have dropped it; I would have to try to find it again, *somehow*. But my immediate quandary was to get into the house without being seen, so I pulled off the gamekeeper's jacket and thrust it deep in some bushes, then hurried in by a side door. But my luck had deserted me that night, because Harriet the housemaid caught sight of me.

'Ma'am,' she whispered, aghast at my tangled hair and my torn stockings. 'Whatever's happened?'

'So foolish of me,' I said with an effort at lightness. 'I went out for a walk, and I got lost. My coat became caught in a bramble thicket, so I left it behind.'

'Oh, ma'am.' Her eyes were very wide.

'Harriet,' I said quickly, 'please don't make a fuss.'

'You've missed your supper, ma'am.'

'I'm sorry. Perhaps you could bring it to me in my room?'

'Of course – Cook's kept it hot for you. And I'll just say you went out for some fresh air, shall I?'

She spoke in a whisper, as if we were in an exciting conspiracy together. I nodded. 'Yes, some fresh air. Thank you, Harriet.'

I went quickly up to my room, where I sat on the edge of my bed. The gamekeeper – Nathan Mallory – was probably laughing about me even now, as he strolled through the woods with his dogs and his shotgun. 'I met the French *mam'selle* from the Hall tonight,' he might boast to his friends later at the local inn. 'I could have had her in the woods, just like that. She was hot for it . . .'

I reached to twist my bracelet, then remembered it had gone – the old scars gleamed naked on my wrist. I tried, I really tried to eat a little of the supper that Harriet kindly brought to me on a tray, but I felt dizzy and unwell.

The gamekeeper.

Miss Kenning called in on me, but I told her that I had a slight headache, so she left me to return to her own room and her beloved art books. I looked at the unsigned letter from London again – the writing was stark and clear. *I met your mother in Paris. Her name was Celine Dumouriez. Like you, she was beautiful. Like you, she was a whore.*

I sat with that letter in my hands, gazing out into the darkness beyond my window. Then I locked it away in the desk in the corner of my room and hurried out through the back of the house and into the shrubbery, to bring the gamekeeper's jacket up to my bedroom.

From its pocket I drew out the case containing my pistol and hid it in my wardrobe. Killing myself was one way to escape my past, but – as Nathan Mallory had pointed out – I wasn't exactly proficient with a gun. Doubtless I would make a mess of suicide as well. Distractedly, I wondered where to hide the jacket – *his* jacket; the fabric was rough against my fingers and smelled of woodsmoke, reminding me of that clearing, and of him. *Like you, she was beautiful. Like you, she was a whore.* I caught sight of my face in the looking-glass – I saw my blue eyes, my full mouth, my pale clear skin and dark hair . . . *Who had sent that letter?* Suddenly I buried my face in his jacket, and only then did I recall the wooden peg, and I reached for it.

It was several inches long and made of polished oak, smooth with age and use. I ran my fingers over the hole in the thicker end, where I guessed it would have been attached to the coop by a thong of leather, and I realised that the gamekeeper had been right – its maker had etched an image into it: a bird of prey, a falcon. And I felt that the bird's eyes were slanting wickedly up at me.

I turned out my light, remembering how the gamekeeper's arms had felt around me; remembering how he'd kissed my hand and let his tongue flicker over my palm. I imagined his tongue on my lips, on my nipples; I lay down on my bed hugging his tweed jacket to me, my breath coming thickly now, my pulse thudding, and I rolled the wooden talisman against my breasts, trying to soothe them with its hardness.

I hated him. I hated him for doing this to me, for arousing feelings in me that I had fought for so long. In the darkness I unbuttoned my blouse and pulled down my brassiere and I rubbed the rough tweed of his jacket against my breasts until they were aching with need. Then I put the talisman between my legs and I stroked its dark length up and down, up and down against my tender core until an acute and almost painful crisis overwhelmed me, making me shudder and cry out. I imagined his lips on my mouth and on my breasts, and I was riven with fear.

He had known what I craved. He had seen how I was scarred, both in my body and in my mind. I lay there panting, my womb still throbbing from my release, my skin lightly sheened. I reached to turn on my light again, because sometimes the darkness terrified me.

Chapter Three

You must not be afraid of the night, my nurse Babette used to say when I was very small, and I believed her, because I loved everything about her, especially the bedtime stories she used to read me about princesses and palaces. But one night, there were no stories – because after my mother's maids had bathed me and put me to bed, Babette hadn't appeared.

I waited with childish trust and impatience – I was only five. Then I got out of bed and wandered towards my door in my nightgown and bare feet, saying her name. 'Baba?' That was what I called her. 'Where are you?' I went to her room, where a light was shining beyond the half-open door. I pushed at it slightly.

And I saw, as I froze there in the shadows, that she was with a friend of my mother's, the Marquis, whom I did not like at all – he had a black moustache and cold black eyes, and I'd thought Babette disliked him too. 'He is very proud,' she had said to me one day.

'Proud like the evil king in my storybook?'

She'd hesitated. 'Yes,' she'd said. 'Yes, he is.' She'd held me close, and rocked me. But now Babette was letting him do things to her that I thought must hurt her, and I was very frightened.

'Please,' she was moaning to him. '*Monsieur*, please.'

They couldn't see me, for I was in the dark beyond the doorway. But I could see that Babette was on her bed, on her back with her legs wide apart, and the Marquis lay on top of her, resting the weight of his upper body on his arms. He kept pushing at her hard, and I saw that he had one of her breasts in his mouth and her face was flushed and desperate. *What was happening? What was he doing, to my Babette?*

I remember that I turned, almost senseless with fright, and ran back to my room, where I curled tightly in bed with my doll. Later, Babette tiptoed in.

'Madeline? Are you asleep, Madeline?' Then she gave a little gasp and reached out to touch me. 'You've been crying. Oh, what is it, *ma chérie*?'

I'd whirled round to her, still clutching my doll, my eyes swollen with tears. 'I saw you with *him*, Baba. You – you were letting him hurt you.'

She had the merriest face in the world, I used to think, but at that moment her eyes grew wide with shock and distress. She held me close, she cradled me. 'Oh, Madeline,' she whispered. 'Oh, *ma chérie*. One day, you too might meet a man for whom you'll do *anything* . . .'

I didn't understand, of course, and I sobbed again. She'd sighed, and stroked my dark curls, until at last I'd become calm and slept.

But I'd wept bitterly the next day, when my mother ordered Babette to leave her house – the house that I later learned the Marquis owned. 'You are a slut,' I heard my mother raging at her, 'you are a whore,' and though the words meant little to me at the time I realised later that my mother was enraged because *she* was the Marquis's mistress, but Babette had temporarily engaged his attentions. I'd been afraid when Babette had to leave, just as I was afraid again here in the dark stillness of Belfield Hall; because of the letter. *I met your mother in Paris . . .*

My sleep was often ravaged by nightmares, and now I expected them to return with renewed intensity. But after my walk up into the woods, something happened. I thought it an aberration, but the next night and the next, I dreamed about the gamekeeper. I was unable to recall exactly what those dreams were when I woke; yet I couldn't help but believe that they were somehow connected to the talisman he'd given to me, which I'd started to keep under my pillow.

You'd be surprised, the gamekeeper had said softly, *at what it can do.* Why had he given it to me? Because he'd guessed how I'd felt, when he was near to me? Because he'd guessed how my blood had darkly raced, when he'd kissed my palm with that wicked caress of his tongue?

Sometimes I would wake to find that as I lay curled in my half-dreams, I was holding the polished wood between my thighs, using it to caress that warm, so-sensitive place that I could hardly bear to touch even when I was bathing myself. I would clutch it tighter, until my blood coursed sweetly through my veins; I would put it in my mouth to moisten it then stroke it against myself, while desire pooled in my belly and my skin heated with need until I reached my crisis, rolling my hips up to meet its hardness and biting my lip to silence my low cries.

Then I would hold the talisman against my breasts until sleep returned; but I would dream again of the gamekeeper, and I woke from those dreams flushed and restless and disturbed.

Harriet the housemaid usually came to my rooms in the late afternoon to prepare my clothes for me before dinner, thus making herself the nearest I had to a lady's maid. I would have preferred Nell, who was quiet and gentle, but I guessed that the more assertive Harriet had probably insisted that she be the one to regularly attend me. One benefit of Harriet's lively presence was that through her chatter I'd learned much about the upper servants – Mrs Burdett, the efficient housekeeper who had lost a brother in the war, and Mr Peters the butler, who took his responsibilities very seriously and was rarely seen without a long list of tasks for his minions to carry out. Harriet also told me about Eddie, who was in charge of the Duke's motorcars at Belfield Hall.

'Eddie hates it when His Grace is in London,' she confided, 'because then he can only drive the Daimler on special occasions, like collecting you from the station, ma'am. Otherwise he's supposed to use the Ford for everyday errands.' She had her sights set on Eddie, I think.

She went on to describe the footmen, including Robert, who was too big for his boots – a phrase that puzzled me, so she had to explain it. To be truthful, I only half-listened to much of Harriet's chatter, until she told me one day that the marriage of Nell to Will, one of the footmen, had been postponed yet again.

I'd been gazing out of my window at the rain that had been falling all day. 'Their wedding, what a to-do,' Harriet exclaimed as she brought out one of my old gowns for dinner. 'It's been put off so often, ma'am, that we're wondering if it will ever actually happen.'

I turned to her and said, 'Is Nell a little unsure about their marriage, then?'

Harriet was busily patting my gown with a velour pad to remove any specks of dust, but she did it with a slight air of distaste – I knew she was disappointed that all my clothes were so very plain. 'Oh, my goodness no,' she said, 'it's Will. Shall I help you take off your blouse, ma'am, before it's time for you to take your bath?'

Swiftly I pulled the sleeve of my blouse down to make sure it covered the old thin scars on my wrist. *What had happened to my bracelet?* 'No,' I said quickly, 'thank you, I'll leave my clothes on while you see to my hair. Is Will having second thoughts?' I went to sit at my dressing table, and Harriet followed me to brush out my long hair, then pin it up so I could keep it dry while I bathed.

'Oh, ' she said with a shrug, 'Will's always been ready to end it, if you ask me. He was desperately in love, you see, with a girl called Sophie who was a maid here. But she was a bit above herself, sticking her head in a book whenever she got the chance – and she spoke like she was gentry rather than one of us. Then off she went to London, to be a dancer and a singer, on stage! And there – Harriet picked up my hairbrush '– she landed the Duke himself. Well! We just couldn't believe it, you can imagine—'

'I've met her,' I broke in. 'I met her when I arrived in England last year, and I thought she was quite lovely.'

I could see Harriet registering that she would have to be more careful. 'Well, ma'am,' she said, 'that's as may be, but now – she's gone to New York. Gone to be a singer there, no doubt because she realised it wasn't right *at all* for her to marry the Duke.'

I remained silent as Harriet chose some hairpins from an enamelled box on my dressing table and started to pin up my hair.

'Though we heard,' she went on, 'that he might well have followed her to America – oh, he'd fallen for her badly! Some folk claimed he was *determined* to make her his bride, ma'am. But then – then—'

'He had to go to Ireland,' I interrupted. 'He has important government duties in Ireland, as well as an estate there.'

'Yes, indeed,' she said. 'But we don't believe, downstairs, that the Irish business would have stopped him from going after his Sophie, sooner or later. At least, not until . . .'

'Please go on, Harriet.' A sudden premonition chilled my skin.

'Then, ma'am, he began to realise his responsibility to *you*.'

And it all came out in a rush. 'Indeed,' Harriet said, 'he feels that he's got to do his duty by you, and see that you make a good match, begging your pardon, ma'am. But if he marries his Sophie, then there's a lot of rich folk who won't want their sons even to *think* of marrying you, because it will mean having to associate with her. A singer, who makes her living on the stage.'

My lips were dry and my throat was tight. 'But times have changed, Harriet. And if they were actually married, people would have to accept her, surely?'

'There's many will *never* accept her, ma'am,' said

Harriet – and clearly she was one of them. 'The old Duchess, for example, she was heard by Robert saying that marrying a former scullery maid would be like – like spitting on the family name, if you'll pardon the expression. And anyway the matter's settled, because His Grace has come to realise that for *your* sake, ma'am, marriage to his Sophie simply will not do.'

I reached for my bracelet, but of course it wasn't there.

'All done!' Harriet exclaimed, tucking up the last coil of my hair with a pin. 'You're ready now, for your bath – I'll just go and start running it for you. And while you take it, I'll go downstairs with the shoes you wanted to wear tonight. Robert was supposed to polish them earlier, but look at them – they're a disgrace! I'm going to get him to do them again . . . ma'am? You look pale. Are you all right, ma'am?'

I nodded. 'Yes, thank you, Harriet, I'm quite all right.'

'Then I'll be back soon, with your shoes,' she promised. Noticing that my curtains were open, she went to close them. 'Oh, this rain, is it ever going to stop?'

And she left.

After my mother's sudden death last year, I'd been afraid when I was told that the Duke of Belfield, whom I'd never even met, was to be my guardian. I'd written to him that I was happy in Paris, and I'd lied that I was being safely cared for, but then the Duke came to France to visit me, and all my fears had vanished, because he'd been so kind. My hopes, my foolish hopes, had even started to rise.

After swiftly turning off the bath taps that Harriet had turned on, I went over to the desk in the corner of my bedroom, in which I'd locked away my old diaries, then I searched almost frantically for the pages I'd written during my last months in Paris. *The Duke of Belfield is to be my guardian, and he came to see me today. They say he was burned in an aeroplane crash in the war, and I saw the scars on his hands* . . . Into that diary I'd also folded some letters from the Duke, and I pulled the first one out. *My dear Madeline, I am so looking forward to your arrival in London. I appreciate the extent of your loss, and it is my utmost hope that I can provide you with a true home* . . .

I tore up his letters, and the pages of my diary too, throwing all the pieces on the fire. There were photographs as well, that I'd stolen from his house in London – portraits of my handsome, blue-eyed guardian that in my foolishness I'd kept even when I'd realised, almost straight away, that there was no one for him but his Sophie; for yes, the gamekeeper had been right to accuse me of dreaming uselessly of my Duke. My guardian had decided to give up Sophie because of *me?* This could not be. It could not be. And finally, I threw upon the coals the unsigned letter that I'd been sent about my mother. *Like you, she was beautiful. Like you, she was a whore.*

The last scraps of papers were turning to ashes when Harriet came hurrying back into my bedroom with my newly polished shoes. 'There, ma'am – oh! What have you been doing to the fire? I thought you were taking your bath!'

'I was putting on a little more coal. I was cold, you see.' I moved quickly away from the fireplace.

'I would have seen to the fire, but never mind. Now, these shoes of yours look so much better, don't you think? That Robert, he should have done them properly in the first place, he's growing so lazy . . .' She was still talking when someone knocked at the door of my sitting room. Harriet hurried to open it. 'Robert. Whatever is it now? *Mam'selle* is about to take her bath. A phone call for her? A man? Did he say who he was? No? Well, can you ask whoever it is to ring later?'

'No,' I called quickly. 'No, Harriet, I'll take the call. I'll be there straight away.' Clearly it wasn't my guardian – but who else would ring me, here? I pulled a cardigan on over my skirt and blouse and hurried downstairs to pick up the receiver in Mr Peters' office, aware that my hand was trembling slightly. I whispered, 'Hello?'

'*Mam'selle*,' the man's voice said. '*Mam'selle*, is that you?'

I remembered the rough feel of a tweed jacket against my skin, and the scent of woodsmoke. I thought of the talisman, and the things I'd done with it. It was Nathan Mallory, the gamekeeper.

He carried on talking as though we were casual, everyday acquaintances. 'I realise you won't be able to talk very much,' he went on. 'I imagine that everything you say will be overheard. But I wanted you to know that I've got your emerald bracelet.'

My heart thudded. 'You – you found it?'

A moment's silence. Then: 'I stole it,' he said calmly. 'And today I took it to a jeweller in Oxford, to get it valued. Did you realise how very much it is worth, *mam'selle*?'

I tried to say something, but my throat had closed up.

'*Mam'selle*? Are you still there? I think it's best if we

talk properly about all this. And since the rain has stopped, can you come up to my cottage, as soon as possible?'

'Your cottage?'

'In the clearing.'

'Very well,' I whispered at last. But I think he had already put the phone down.

I pressed my hands against my hot cheeks. He must have somehow unfastened the bracelet from my wrist, but how could I not have noticed that he'd done so? How could I not have realised that the cottage I'd thought derelict was his?

I left Mr Peters' office, and because I was hardly looking where I was going, I almost bumped into Lottie Towndrow. 'So you've finished with the telephone? Good,' she said in her clipped voice, 'because I need to make a call—' She peered at me more closely. 'Goodness me, Madeline, you look quite overwhelmed. Who have you been talking to?'

I pushed past her without saying a word and went back up to my room, where I had to dismiss Harriet, who was as eager as Lottie to know who my call was from. I never did take that bath. Instead I quickly pulled on an old coat and my lace-up shoes, but before leaving my room I pushed the curtains back a little. The rain had indeed stopped, and I saw that up on the hillside, close to the clearing where I'd met the gamekeeper, a small fire dimly burned.

I hurried out of the house and towards the path up into the woods.

Chapter Four

It had stopped raining, yes, but I almost had to fight my way through the wet bracken that grew in a tangled mass across my path, and all the time I was rehearsing what I was going to say. *You stole my bracelet. You stole my bracelet.*

I rebuked myself for my stupidity in not bringing a torch. I must have taken several wrong turnings, but just as the moon broke through from behind ragged clouds, I reached the clearing at last – and he was there. At first he didn't see me, because he had his back to me and was tending his fire, whistling softly. Then he moved towards one of the wicker coops, and brought it just a little nearer to the fire's warmth.

A lantern hung from the low branch of a tree, and by its light I could see that he wore a flannel shirt loose over his breeches, and a sleeveless leather jacket and boots. He was bending to reach inside the coop to stroke some small animal there, and I could see his hands – so strong, yet so gentle. Then he stood up and slowly turned round, as if he'd been aware all the time of my presence. He regarded me steadily.

'*Mam'selle,*' he said. His shirt was unfastened, and for a moment I wasn't aware of anything except his muscled chest and abdomen. I felt renewed fear at this reminder of his physical strength, because this man had calmly admitted that he'd robbed me. Then I realised he was holding something – a tiny creature that lay trembling in his big cupped hands. 'Oh.' I let my breath out in a little sigh. 'What is it?'

'A leveret,' he answered. 'A young hare. When I found him, his leg was broken – caught in a trap some fool had set up. And he was trying to gnaw himself free but only making his own misery worse. Like you, *mam'selle.*'

I could barely speak. 'Like me?'

'With that bracelet of yours.' He watched me a moment, then nodded at the hare. 'You'll see that I've splinted his leg, and I've been keeping him in the coop so the foxes can't get him. He'll soon be running around again.' He looked at me. 'I'm glad that you're here on time. And you'll want your bracelet back, I suppose?'

I watched him as he lowered the baby hare so gently into the cage and fastened it. My heart was hammering. I said, 'No. I don't want the bracelet back.' He turned to look at me, his eyebrows raised, and I went on, 'You told me it was valuable. I – I'd like you to sell it for me, please.'

'To sell it?' His eyes were searching me, burning into me. 'You know, you could always get it altered, so it doesn't hurt you so—'

'I want you to sell it. I really do. I don't want it any more. I'll give you half the money . . .' My words were coming out in a choked rush.

He came towards me, and quite calmly put his arms around me. 'There. There,' he soothed. He was stroking my tangled hair. 'Has this bracelet of yours got anything to do with your pistol, I wonder?'

I tried to speak, but I couldn't. He simply carried on stroking my hair, while his other hand at the small of my back held me so close that my face was pressed against the warm skin of his chest and I could hear his heart strongly beating.

'Look at me,' he said. 'Listen to me.' He tilted my face up by cupping my chin, and I saw that his brown eyes were as steady as ever. The glow of the fire softened his hard cheekbones and jaw, which were stubbled with dark beard. He smiled just a little, and my heart bumped raggedly against my ribs. 'You're rather alone in the world, I take it, *mam'selle*. But shouldn't your guardian, the Duke, be aware that you're in some sort of difficulty?'

He stroked one firm finger across my lower lip, and I felt that delicate touch all the way through my body. 'He's in Ireland,' I said. 'He has important work to do there, for the government.'

'More important than looking after his young ward?'

I sprang to my guardian's defence. 'He writes to me. And he would come here, I know he would, if I asked him, but it's not fair to trouble him with my stupid problems.' I'd already cost my Duke his Sophie. I could not – *must not* – do him any more harm.

He was silent a moment. 'Didn't you miss your bracelet? Didn't you guess that I'd taken it?'

'I thought that I'd forgotten to fasten it properly. I thought it was lost, on the hillside . . . Why didn't you sell it?' My voice was starting to break again. 'You could have sold it and kept the money – I would never have known.'

He didn't answer at first, but his dark eyes never left me. At last he said, 'I was going to sell it. But then, I had second thoughts – for one reason and another.' He lifted my wrist and pushed back my sleeve so he could gently finger my scars.

I tried to speak, but his fingertips on my wrist sent something flickering into life deep inside me. I thought of the talisman, which I'd put in the deep pocket of my coat because I didn't want anyone to find it in my room – *oh God, if he knew what I'd done with it . . .*

After a moment he gestured towards the cottage. 'The bracelet's in there. I'll sell it for you, if that's what you really want, though I don't need paying. You must come inside. It's warmer, and we can talk.'

'I should have brought back your jacket . . .'

'Some other time,' he said. 'There's no rush.'

He never doubted, of course, that I would follow him. 'Where are your dogs?' I asked him, suddenly afraid again.

'Safe round the back, in their kennels.' He'd turned to answer me. 'Like all dogs they howl at the full moon, so they're best kept locked up. The moon does strange things to animals as well as to people.' He gave his smile, unfastened the door and beckoned me in.

His cottage was unlit except by the moonlight coming in through the open doorway. Inside was a single large room, sparsely furnished, and in the corner I could see a bed. I tore my eyes from it, saying, 'You rang me. Yet you haven't got a telephone.'

'Oh, there's a telephone not far away that I can use.' He was watching me. 'Take your coat off, will you? It's damp from your walk.'

I did so, and he hung it carefully over the back of a chair, but fresh apprehension began to claw at me, because he was saying, 'I've left my lantern out by the coops. I'll go and fetch it.' And then he was going through the door again; he was already outside and letting it swing shut, plunging me into the suffocating darkness, and I cried out, 'Mr Mallory. Nathan—'

He hauled the door open. 'For God's sake. Whatever's the matter?' He strode closer. 'You're afraid of the dark – is that it?'

Please don't leave me in the dark. I'll be good, I promise I'll be good. The voice of a child, a terrified child – I moistened my dry lips and I even tried to laugh. 'Yes,' I said. 'Yes, so absurd of me . . .'

'I'll light the fire,' he said. He knelt and set a match to the kindling and wood that were already laid in the hearth – the flames leapt. Then he came back to me; his arms were around me and I leaned quite helplessly against him. Something had broken inside me; I was still shaking, but this time not with cold. *I can't want this man. I can't.*

He gazed at me with those dark brown eyes, and I struggled to control myself. 'I'm sorry.' I tried so hard to sound calm. 'Please sell the bracelet for me, will you?'

He took my wrist to gently run his fingertips over the old scars again, and this time the feelings that tore through me, the longings, were almost unendurable.

'Madeline.' His forefinger traced the worst of those scars. 'Why did you keep it? Why did you wear it? Do you like pain, *mam'selle?*'

I went rigid.

'Do you like pain, mingled with pleasure?' he went on softly, patiently. 'Many women do. It's nothing to be ashamed of.' He caught up my hand, and kissed my scars very carefully. Then he lifted my fingers, drew the middle one into his mouth and bit on it; lightly at first, then harder. I cried out and he steadied me.

'Sex is such a mixture of extreme emotions,' he murmured, lowering his head to press his forehead against mine. 'Power and submission. Pleasure and near-pain. Young as you are, I would guess that there is a great deal of your past that you have no intention of telling me. And I would hope – very much – that you're not trying to punish yourself for something in your past, *mam'selle*. Are you?'

He let his fingers trail over the scars on my wrist again, and waited. When I didn't reply, he cupped my face with one hand and with the other pushed some stray locks of hair behind my ears. 'Well,' he said softly, 'perhaps I've asked you enough questions for now. Perhaps it's my turn to confess to you that I've by no means told you everything either. Yes, I stole your bracelet to sell, because I thought it was doing you no good. But I also hoped that you might come up here looking for it again. Looking for – me.'

My heart was hammering.

'You don't have to ask why,' he said quietly. 'Do you, *mam'selle?*'

And his mouth came down softly on mine, feathering my lips with light, sensual touches. At first pure shock tore through me and my instinct was to push him away, to defend myself. But then, as the tip of his tongue gently parted my mouth, my body betrayed me. My hands stole up with a will of their own to clasp his shoulders, and the feel of his rock-solid muscles beneath my fingertips made me moan under my breath.

He must have heard. Suddenly hauling me closer against the hardness of his body, he was kissing me properly, a deep, sensual kiss; his tongue was tangling with mine, his teeth were nipping at the vulnerable inner flesh of my mouth.

And I panicked. I tried to push him away. I was familiar with my body's shameful cravings, yes, and I was deeply afraid of them – but oh, he was so strong. His firm jaw was rough with unshaven beard, but his kiss was silken and soul-wrenching. This should have felt wrong, and yet I could not remember anything having ever felt so right. *The gamekeeper and his kiss* – what was he doing to me?

I clung to him, shuddering beneath another kiss so intense that I was scarcely aware of him lifting me in his strong arms and lowering me onto his narrow bed, while his tongue thrust steadily, masterfully inside my mouth as I wound my arms around his neck, letting his caresses thrill me. Being lost and lonely did not feel like *this*. Did not make my heart pound so fiercely that I felt my ribs actually hurt with it. His lips, his tongue, his teeth, were ravishing me, until I thought I might faint from the sheer pleasure of it.

And yes, there was pain, as he'd hinted. I was lying on his bed now, and he was arched powerfully over me, still kissing me, but also nipping sharply at my lower lip; not enough to make me cry out or to draw blood, but enough to heighten my senses so that I kissed him back, moaning with raw hunger and twining my tongue urgently with his. He cupped my breasts with tenderness, but he squeezed my nipples between his fingers as well, in a way that made molten desire rush down to my abdomen, to *there*, making me soft and aching for him, and by then he'd eased himself fully onto the bed beside me. I clutched blindly at his heavily muscled shoulders, I drew my legs with delight up against his, and at the same time I realised his hands werc splaying themselves over my bottom and pulling me taut against his powerful frame, until I couldn't help but feel his thick member pressed against my belly. I let out a low gasp. *'Oh . . .'*

'You like that?' Nathan growled softly down at me as he tore his mouth from mine and eased himself up on one elbow. It was the voice of a fiercely aroused man; his eyes were dark and burning, the sharp edges of his cheekbones were taut beneath his skin. And I was aroused too – incredibly, frighteningly aroused; I felt a jagged raw hunger tugging deeply.

'Please.' I was begging wantonly for more. 'Please . . .'

He was already exploring the buttons of my blouse, unfastening them with expert skill and sliding the garment off my shoulders; then his fingers started work on the tight lacing of the ugly cotton brassiere I wore to flatten my breasts, but soon he was pulling the thing apart. He held me close, and because his own shirt was loose, my naked breasts were pushed against the warm skin of his chest. My nipples were tight and burning; a sweet, low pulse throbbed through my blood, and I was on fire for him, clutching at his muscled body as if it were my only reality, my only safety. He rolled me onto my back, arching himself over me with one thigh between my legs while he rested his weight on his forearms and gazed down at me with blazing eyes. 'I want you, *mam'selle*,' he breathed. 'But I need to know. You're not an innocent, are you?'

My breath caught in my throat, and for a moment the sounds and scents of my mother's *salon* in the rue Saint-Honoré were all around me. 'No,' I breathed. *No.*

He smiled again, darkly. Then he took my breast in his mouth, suckling, pulling, and I writhed beneath him, panting for him. My hands roved over his back and I reached to tangle my fingers in the curling brown hair at the nape of his neck, wanting him to kiss me again, but he had other ideas. Suddenly pinning my hands on the bed either side of me, he moved steadily down to kneel between my thighs. Then he let go of my hands, and began to run his palms down my flat abdomen.

And I gasped, for his fingers were pulling aside my panties, his fingers were *there* – I burned with shame, because he would feel how wet I was, how ready for him. But by then I was writhing helplessly, because he'd pushed one finger then two deep inside me, probing, exploring, until he looked up at me and softly smiled. 'So ready,' he breathed. 'So deliciously ready.'

Before I even had time to think, he was holding my knees wider apart, and his mouth was there, his tongue was stiffened and thrusting, his stubbled jaw rasping hard – pain again, the warning of pain – but it only heightened the pleasure that was threatening to consume me, as his lips and tongue worked their way into my secret flesh, licking, tantalising. I grasped his shoulders, I wrapped my legs around his strong back; I was trembling, I was about to explode, and—

Suddenly he stopped what he was doing. *No. No, Nathan, you cannot stop. You don't know what this means to me, how I've never willingly . . .*

'I'd like you to beg, *mam'selle*,' he said softly.

What? 'What do you mean?' I was afraid again.

'I mean just what I said.' With *that* smile, he eased his way up to me again – oh, his body was so strong, so deliciously heavy with muscle. Carefully he tucked a stray strand of my hair behind my ear – the scent of him, the good male smell of skin and woodsmoke and the outdoors, was intoxicating – and he went on quietly, 'I want you to tell me how very much you'd like me to carry on with what I was doing.'

'But you know I do.' I could hardly speak for the desire that was burning me up. 'You can see. You can *tell* . . .' Wasn't my body laid bare, laid open for him?

'I'm still waiting for you to say the words, *mam'selle*. I want to be sure, you see.'

Sure of what? I didn't understand, and for a moment I was frightened again, more frightened than I'd been when he talked about pain. But I couldn't bear to wait, that was the truth of it; I simply could not bear to wait any longer for the extremity of pleasure that the gamekeeper was promising me.

I drew a harsh breath. 'Please, Nathan. Please continue to . . .'

'To what, *mam'selle?*'

I was desperate. 'To – to make love to me. To kiss me, as you were doing. To make me feel the – the longing.' I sensed tears burning at the back of my eyes now; I could scarcely bear any more of this, but his body pinioned me, so I jerked my head to one side as a tear trickled down my cheek.

He tenderly kissed that tear away and said, 'Madeline. Have you still got the gamekeeper's talisman I gave you?'

What? What games was he playing now? What else did he plan, to complete my humiliation? I was in despair. Did he want it back? Why?

'Yes,' I said. I closed my eyes again. 'Yes, I have. It's in my coat pocket.'

His eyes glinted with something I didn't even want to guess at, then he left me – oh, I missed him – and came back with the talisman in his hand. 'Magic powers,' he said softly. 'Healing powers. To cure you of wanting your Duke.'

'No,' I breathed. 'I've told you. You're so wrong . . .'

'No need to feel guilty about it,' he interrupted. 'Better by far to deal with it.' He knelt between my legs, rubbing the polished wood slowly between his fingers, and I knew, *then*, what he was going to do.

His voice was husky as he said, 'Let's test its magic, shall we, *mam'selle?*' And he pressed his lips to each of my breasts in turn.

I gasped. 'Please, Nathan. Please.'

He looked so beautiful, with his brown curls falling over his forehead, and his lashes so dark and thick. Although his shirt hung loose, he was otherwise fully clad; but I could see the bulk of his arousal, where his gamekeeper's breeches hugged his loins, and my mouth was dry with longing again.

He was fondling my stocking tops, and the bare inner flesh of my thighs. My secret parts lay open and hungry for him still, yearning for his tongue again, and for him. Lifting the talisman in his hand, he brushed it, oh so lightly, along my flesh, *there* – I was so warm and so wet that I groaned aloud. He took the talisman away from me but still held it as he moved further up my body, trailing it over my navel and breasts to my face. Gently he eased it into my mouth.

'Take it, Madeline,' he urged. 'Take it into your mouth and suck it.'

I did, almost desperately. The wood was warm and smooth, and somehow the fact that he was sliding it into my mouth was so arousing that I tongued it hungrily, again and again. Then he pulled it out.

I should have been afraid. But instead I waited breathlessly as he moved lazily down my body again, and I wondered, how did he exert such extreme control over his own body, when my whole being was clenched with wanting him, when every one of my nerve endings was craving the release only he could offer? He held the talisman up, so that in the light of the fire I could see how it was black and shining with the moisture from my mouth. And then, very carefully, he reached between my legs with his free hand and parted the slick folds of my flesh there, and I gasped as he eased the talisman into me, inch by sweet inch.

I was panting. I was lifting my hips, I was clutching at its thickness with my inner muscles, turning my head from side to side in desperation. 'More. Please – more.'

He twisted it slightly – *oh, the pleasure he was bestowing* – and that dark, haunted look was in his eyes again. 'Are you begging me, Madeline?'

'Yes. *Yes*. Nathan, I'm begging you. *Please* . . .'

He let out a soft sigh, and inserted the talisman further. Then – oh God, then his tongue was trailing luxuriously downwards, to – to *there*, just above where the last inch of polished wood protruded.

I was clawing at the sheets and my hips were writhing. He was crouched between my legs, so that I could see his dark tousled head and his powerful arms and shoulders; I could feel his tongue licking and stroking, while at the same time he continued to use the talisman to probe and thrust, probe and thrust deep inside me. He looked up at me, his gaze burning. 'Give yourself up to the pleasure, *mam'selle*,' he murmured. 'Give yourself up to me.'

Moaning aloud, I felt my inner muscles squeezing on the polished wood inside me, while his tongue rasped wickedly over the tiny nub that was the centre of all my pleasure. I threw my head back and I think I screamed out his name as my crisis coursed through me. It was like climbing up a cliff face then falling over the edge – not into darkness, but into bright, splintering waves of pleasure that rolled over me, then lapped lingeringly at all my nerve endings.

At last – at long last – I lay back, sated and spent, on his bed. I had never known that such intensity of pleasure could exist. He eased the talisman out and I sat up, feigning calmness but inwardly quite distraught.

'Did you enjoy that, Madeline?' he asked. 'Do they do it like that in Paris?'

I shrugged, pushing back my hair. 'Sometimes.'

He got up and walked over to a shelf by the door where I'd noticed some books, but it wasn't a book that he was after. As he came back, I saw that he was threading a slender black leather thong through the hole at the end of my talisman, and that the thong was in turn attached to another, longer strip of leather.

I'd pulled myself up to sit on the bed, with my blouse loosely round my shoulders and my arms hugging my knees. He sat next to me, and I managed to keep my voice cool as I nodded towards the talisman. 'More gamekeeper's tricks?'

He grinned down at me. 'Wait and see, *mam'selle.*' Carefully he wound the longer piece of leather around my naked waist, stroking me all the time. 'Your waist is so slender,' he murmured. 'And your skin is like silk, Madeline.' He tied the thong and slid it around, so that the talisman, on its dangling loop of leather, hung – *there*. Down below my belly. Just long enough to fall between the tops of my thighs . . .

I had to grab the bedhead, to keep myself steady. I had to clamp my lower lip between my teeth to stop myself from groaning aloud, as he moved the talisman thoughtfully to and fro, rolling it against my still-aroused flesh. 'You are going to keep it on, Madeline,' he said.

'You're going to wear it, always, for me. And –' he gave his wicked smile '– haven't you forgotten something?'

I didn't know what he meant. I was confused, I was afraid – even more so when he took my hand in his and started fingering my sensitive palm. 'I assume,' he said, never taking his eyes from me, 'they taught you in Paris that if you let a man do the sorts of things to you that I've just done, then you don't leave him unsatisfied?'

He placed my hand over his breeches so that I could feel the pulsing hardness there, and dark excitement shivered through me, but at the same time a dart of searing shame. *Whore. Whore.* His eyes never left mine, but already he was unfastening his breeches and was guiding my trembling fingers to his rearing erection. He kissed my cheek, then my lips and murmured, 'I'm quite sure you know what to do.'

I felt a moment of quick, sharp fear, because his masculinity was intimidating, and the sexual tension quivering in his powerful body made his voice raw. My fingers could scarcely encompass his veined thickness, but his hand fastened again over mine, soothing me, encouraging me in my stroking movements. Oh God – the thought of *that* inside me – all that power, that strength . . .

I could see his chest muscles tensing beneath his open shirt, and could hear that his breathing was ragged. Excitement quivered at my belly as his semen began to spurt over my loins and thighs, and his penis seemed to give great leaps in my hand. He had a cloth ready, and almost caressingly he wiped me clean; then he leaned over me at last, put his hand beneath my chin and tilted my face very gently up to his. 'Madeline? Listen to me. I shall say nothing of this, and you needn't, either. Believe me, there's no harm done.'

Again, the spark of sheer, terrifying need was shooting down to the base of my belly to *there*, that secret place between my thighs. *I'd begged him. I'd begged him.* But I tried to echo his words lightly. 'No harm done,' I said, though inside I was shaking.

He waited a moment, stroking my hair, then said, 'Try not to frown at everything I say, Madeline. Just one more question. When I *do* sell your bracelet for you, you're not going to use the money to go running back to Paris, are you?'

Oh, God. That was the last place I would go. I shook my head.

'Good,' he murmured.

And – he smiled. That was all. We rose, and dressed. He didn't kiss me, he didn't even touch me, but I heard him whistling some tune softly under his breath as he walked with me down to the edge of the woods, and I imagined that his eyes were still burning into me as I hurried through the darkness of the gardens and into the house. I ran up the narrow servants' staircase to my bedroom, where I changed into my nightdress and tried to sleep; but I soon realised that however I lay, whichever way I turned, the gamekeeper's talisman still fell between my thighs and caressed me wickedly, reminding me of his kisses, of his power.

Never. Never had I imagined I could feel like that.

Chapter Five

The next day, and the day after that, I went over every minute of the time I'd spent at the gamekeeper's cottage. During the long February nights I would gaze out of my window to the woods, thinking that I saw the light of his lantern, or smoke curling from the chimney of his cottage. When I was in my bed and the house was silent and I missed my bracelet to twist against my wrist, I used the talisman instead, pressing it almost harshly against my secret place and clasping my breasts with my free hand as I reached my crisis, thinking of him, always. Each time I resolved afterwards, *I will not see him again. I must not see him again.*

He rang me two weeks later, at the beginning of March.

This time Mr Peters came up to my sitting room. It was past five in the afternoon, and almost dark outside. Miss Kenning was with me, reading a book about English architecture, and I was seated at the table by the window writing a letter to my guardian, but I'd parted the curtains to gaze out at the woods where the gamekeeper's cottage was. Mr Peters cleared his throat and said, 'There is a telephone call for you, ma'am.'

Miss Kenning put down her book, her eyes darting

curiously from Mr Peters to me; she knew that he would have told me immediately if it was my guardian. I said, 'Who is it, please?'

'He wouldn't give his name, ma'am.'

Striving to appear calm, I followed Mr Peters downstairs to the telephone in his office, aware that he would be outside listening to every word I said. I picked up the phone. 'Hello?'

There was a pause, then I heard his voice. 'I've sold your bracelet. And I was hoping that you might meet me again, *mam'selle.*'

The talisman nudged slickly at the top of my thighs and suddenly my blouse seemed too tight, too confining against my breasts. I said, 'Thank you so much. I'll have to arrange something else, I can see. But it's kind of you to let me know about the dress.'

Nathan paused again, no doubt realising that I wasn't able to speak freely. 'Come up to the clearing, tonight,' he said. 'Can you?'

'Yes. Yes, I can . . .'

'I'll meet you there. At eight. You'll be on time, won't you, *mam'selle?*'

'Very well,' I said, 'and thank you again. Goodbye.'

I put the phone down and left the office, but Mr Peters was still there, pretending to examine a piece of china on the table just outside the doorway. 'Oh, Mr Peters,' I said to him. 'That was a call about an item I ordered from a London catalogue. The manager rang to say that unfortunately it's not in stock.'

Once I was out of Mr Peters' sight, I almost ran up to my room. Miss Kenning had gone, thank goodness, so I closed my door and leaned against it, then I put my hands to my cheeks and hurried across to the window. *Eight o'clock. I had to wait, till eight o'clock.*

Harriet came at six to run my bath and to lay out my clothes, but I wouldn't allow her to either dress or undress me – I never did. In fact I'd taken to wearing a heavily pleated cotton petticoat; its bulk concealed any hint of the outline of the talisman beneath. Harriet often lamented my clothes.

'His Grace the Duke surely wouldn't mind if you ordered new gowns from London, ma'am, would he?' she would say. 'Lady Beatrice, now, when *she* stayed here, she had trunks of fine clothes delivered from London and Paris nearly every week . . .'

I knew already that Lady Beatrice had been married to the old Duke's son, who had died in the war; but Beatrice lived in London now, although my guardian had never introduced her to me there, or even mentioned her. Once Miss Kenning had shown me some photographs of her wedding day, which she'd found in a drawer in the library, and Lady Beatrice looked so beautiful, but something in her eyes also made her look cold and proud.

I took my bath in privacy as usual, while Harriet tidied my rooms. I never took off the talisman, not even when bathing; she never guessed that, whether I was naked or fully clad, the gamekeeper's leather cord clung tightly around my waist, with the polished wood of the talisman dangling heavily below the base of my belly.

At half past six the gong sounded as usual for dinner, and I went down to join Miss Kenning. Lottie Towndrow was there as well, and my heart sank, but she was too busy lecturing Miss Kenning about historic architecture to acknowledge my arrival. She turned to me, however, when the servants started laying out our plates, asking, 'What have you been doing today, Madeline?'

'Oh, the usual,' I answered. 'Reading a little. Walking in the garden.' I knew that she despised me. *Nathan*, I was thinking. *Nathan*.

I saw from her expression what she thought of my reply. 'You really should find something useful to do with your life, you know.' She was helping herself to the vegetables the servants were proffering – she refused to eat meat – and turned on me again. 'Most women of your station at least help from time to time with a charity of one sort or another. I'm involved, as it happens, with an educational foundation in Oxford – it was set up to help women from poor families learn to read, and to widen their limited horizons.'

I thought, with sudden burning intensity, *What business did she have, to be here at Belfield Hall?* Whether she had the Duke's permission or not, how dare she make herself free with his hospitality? How dare she explore the Hall's private records?

'The work you do for these women sounds admirable, I'm sure,' I said, reaching for a glass of water. 'Would you feel that you were widening their horizons, I wonder, if you showed them the kind of documents you showed to me a few weeks ago, Miss Towndrow?'

Lottie's fork rattled against her plate. Miss Kenning was intrigued. 'Oh, what documents, Madeline dear? You never mentioned them to me. Were they something I would be interested in?'

Oh, my love, I dream of your tongue pleasuring my secret parts . . . 'Miss Towndrow found some old letters in the basement,' I told Miss Kenning calmly. 'But any interest they might hold would be of limited appeal, I'm sure.'

Lottie was looking furious with me. I pretended to carry on enjoying my food, but really I was eating very little. I was thinking of Nathan. *Nathan.*

I was nervous again by the time I'd walked up to the clearing. I'd remembered to bring a torch and he must have seen its flickering light, for he came forward to meet me, and something in me turned over when I saw him.

'Madeline.' He took my hand and kissed the inside of my wrist, but then he let go of it and I realised he was saying slowly, 'You know, *mam'selle*, I've been thinking that perhaps this wasn't such a good idea after all.'

What? My heart plummeted.

'If we'd been able to talk properly on the telephone,' he went on, 'I would maybe have suggested getting the money to you some other way.'

I felt so cold, because I guessed from his words that he hadn't really wanted to see me at all. I stammered, 'Of course. I shouldn't have asked you to sell it for me like that. You'll think me a fool—'

'Oh, *mam'selle*,' he broke in. And he put his hands steadily on my shoulders. 'I think nothing of the sort. How very determined you are, to hide your beauty. How very determined you are to hate yourself. The money for your bracelet is in my cottage. Will you come inside?'

'I – I cannot stay for long. I promised my companion Miss Kenning that I would be back in an hour—'

He pulled me closer. He said, 'Miss Kenning be damned.'

My heart was thundering. His face was so beautiful, all lean jaw and hard cheekbones, and he hadn't shaved for a while, and . . . *oh*. The thought of running my hands against his skin, of pressing my lips to his lovely mouth, made my insides curl up with longing.

He gave that wicked grin again, and he led me into his cottage.

A fire glowed in there, and a lantern was casting warm shadows around the room. I was trembling again, but with delight now, because he was skimming his finger-tips along the tender skin beneath my ear, making me shiver and burn at the same time.

'You need to value yourself,' he said. 'You need to stop judging yourself so harshly.'

I tried to laugh. 'Believe me, if you'd heard what the nuns at the convent used to say about me, you would understand my low opinion of myself.'

He made me sit on an old wooden chair by the fire-place, then he swiftly knelt to put more logs on the fire. 'I imagine nuns aren't very charitable where young girls are concerned. So you went to a convent? Was it in Paris?'

'It was in Nantes. I was sent there when I was ten.'

He drew up a stool and came to sit next to me. 'Didn't you miss your home?'

I made myself meet his gaze calmly. 'I grew used to life at the convent,' I said. 'But the nuns didn't grow used to me. My mother had arranged for me to board there until I was seventeen – but I was expelled a year early.'

'Why?'

I wanted to say, *Stop. I don't want you to know. I don't want to remember anything* . . . Instead I said, very quietly, 'A friend of mine was being punished – caned in fact – by the Mother Superior, for meeting a gardener's boy at night. I took the Mother Superior's cane and broke it.'

His eyes never left me. 'This girl must have been a good friend.'

'She was. I was very unhappy when I first arrived at the convent, and she took care of me. Her name was Dervla, and she was from Ireland.'

He was raising my wrist to his lips, kissing the scars like a caress. 'Did your time at the convent make you to do *this* to yourself, as you grew older? Or was your mother's death the cause of it?'

I shrugged, feeling cold again in spite of his warm touch. 'It became a habit of mine,' I said, 'something I couldn't help doing—'

Then I broke off, because he had stood, and was drawing me closer; he was pressing his lips to my face and throat, and his hands were skimming my hips and my waist. Beneath my dress and my thick petticoat, he'd found the leather thong of my talisman – I could feel its heavy weight moving against my belly, against my sex – and he was murmuring, 'I want to make love to you *now*, Madeline. I need to make love to you.'

Then, oh God, he was kissing me again, and my lips parted for him almost the instant he touched his lips to mine. I felt a molten tide of longing as his expert silken tongue explored my mouth, and even while he was still kissing me, he was swinging me up in his powerful arms and effortlessly carrying me to that little bed low in the corner. By the time he had laid me down upon it, had swiftly tugged off his boots and breeches and peeled back his shirt, my body was on fire with longing for him.

Nathan. I drank in the strong lines of his hard-muscled shoulders, his slim but lean hips and powerful silken-haired thighs, the strength of his desire for me – he was completely unashamed of his potency. Lowering himself to the bed, he unbuttoned my old gown and pulled it over my head; he arched his eyebrows at my petticoat, and removed that also. '*Not* from Paris,' he observed as he held it up, his eyes dancing.

Suddenly my eyes danced too. 'It's guaranteed,' I told him, 'to provide warmth in the coldest of English winters.'

'*Mam'selle*,' he whispered, 'I will keep you warm.'

Oh. And he gathered me in his arms, pulling down my brassiere and my panties, while my heart thumped, so hard. He lowered his head to my breast, taking the nipple in his mouth and stroking it with his dextrous tongue; then he drew back a little, and said, in a low voice that made my nerve endings tingle, 'I want you to kneel before me, Madeline. I want you to beg me for what you want.'

Dismay chilled me. *This was like before.* 'You know,' I stammered, 'you know what I want, Nathan, more than anything . . .'

'I need to hear it.' His voice was harder, and I felt a tremor of fear. *Why, oh why did he make me do this?*

Then he smiled, and stroked my hair, and I melted because I wanted him so badly. I knelt before him almost naked on the bed, sitting back on my feet with my thighs slightly parted, while he reached to stroke his hand over my belly, then down through the whorls of my maidenhair to slide his fingers to and fro between the folds of flesh at my core, tapping his thumb against the tiny nub of sensation there; feeling my hotness, my wetness, my readiness. 'Say it,' he murmured. 'Say it.'

I remembered Babette telling me, *One day, you too might meet a man for whom you'll do anything.* I cannot recall my exact words, but if I had begged him before, this was so much more. I told him that I was his; that I adored his kisses, and that I thought I would die if he didn't take me now. I caressed his thrusting erection with my mouth and lips, until he began to lower me to the mattress, on my hands and knees, and he was behind me, kissing my buttocks, rubbing something intensely cool on them and between them – oil? – then pulling the leather thong round and inserting the wooden talisman into—

Where? Oh, no. He wasn't, he couldn't . . .

I could feel it going slickly between my bottom cheeks. I tried to protest, but he was moving it in and out, in and out, and already dark, shameful waves of desire engulfed me. Still pressing kisses to my ribs, he removed it at last, pushed it aside and rolled me onto my back, using his strong thighs to part my legs. He was arched over me, gazing down at me, his expression unreadable – then his powerfully erect phallus was nudging and thrusting, and I flung my arms around him as he drove himself deeply, urgently into me.

And I felt the breath leaving my body. My legs were wrapped around his hips, clutching him tight, and I heard myself uttering soft, guttural cries as he possessed me – so deep, so strong. He stilled for a long moment, while I moaned again with yearning, and he rested his weight on his powerful forearms. 'Tell me what this feels like, Madeline. Tell me.'

My heart was thudding. 'It feels as if – I am yours.' I was breathless with need. 'As if I were a part of you . . . *oh*.'

He moved himself slightly so I could feel his thickness pulsing even deeper at the heart of me. 'Do you like me possessing you, Madeline?' he said huskily. 'Do you like me inside you? Would you let me do – *anything*?'

Oh God, I could scarcely breathe, such was my desire. 'Yes. Yes. Anything, Nathan, I would let you do anything. Please. Oh, *please* . . .'

He lowered his mouth to my breast to draw out one nipple, elongating it, half-biting it, then he began to drive himself into me again almost harshly, rotating his lean hips; the feeling was exquisite. Suddenly he clasped my wrists and spread them either side of me, pinning me down; then, his eyes never leaving me, he increased his pace. Helplessly pinioned, I felt my insides ignite as with his teeth he pulled again at my nipple, and I cried out as waves and waves of pleasure began to flood me. *Nathan*.

He rained kisses on my skin, my throat, my breasts; my hands flailed on the bed, then were free, searching for something – anything – and in the end I found him, of course, my fingers raking his back and shoulders. I clung to him as if he were my only safety. He was still so strong within me, moving fast and hard until there was no place higher for me to climb, and I entered the scalding storm of sensation that marked his possession of me, his complete possession. My world exploded in splintering shards around me.

When at last I lay still, he bent to brush his lips across my cheek and my throat, then he pulled out of me and, as I slowly opened my eyes, I realised he was bringing himself to his own harsh release. For a moment he bent to kiss me again, his mouth hard and hungry, then he was pumping out his seed in milky streams over my belly, and groaning out my name.

Afterwards he cleaned me and held me very close, cradling my head against his powerful chest so that I could hear his heart beating while I pressed soft kisses to his skin and nestled into his arms. But – the things I'd let him do to me. The way he'd pinioned me. Punished me, almost. *The talisman.* He'd known exactly how much I could bear, exactly what he had to do, to bring me to my release.

He raised himself on one arm and gazed down at me. 'Pleasure and pain, *mam'selle*,' he said softly. 'They are two sides of the same coin. Has no one told you that?'

I shuddered, but he didn't see it because he was rising from the bed, unfastening the thong of the talisman at the same time. 'Wait there,' he ordered. 'Stay as you are.' He carried my talisman over to the stone sink in the far corner, but came back with it only moments later and began to prise my legs apart again, running his fingers along the inside of my thigh.

And he was pressing – *rolling* – the talisman against my skin there. It felt wet and cold. 'Nathan. What . . .?'

'Stay still.' His instruction was almost harsh. A few moments later he lifted it away, and as I looked down I felt my blood chilling, for on my upper thigh was the imprint of the falcon, scarcely longer than my little finger, but black and almost sinister against my skin. Nathan must have seen my expression. 'It's ink mixed with pine resin,' he said. 'It's a mark of ownership – to show, Madeline, that you're mine.'

The falcon's eyes slanted knowingly up at me. My throat was dry. 'Will it come off?'

'Eventually, of course.' He fingered the skin around the hook-beaked falcon and blew gently on it; then his eyes burned into my face. 'Do you mind, *mam'selle*? Do you object to being mine?'

What could I do? He was holding me, he was kissing my throat and my breasts so tenderly, and that surge of wanting him enveloped me again. 'Yours,' I breathed. 'I'm yours.'

Looking back, it was as if a kind of madness had over-taken me with his first touch, his first kiss; a kind of fever in my blood. For the next hour, he steadily made love to me; he made me his. I knew that I was behaving like a whore, even as I called out his name and pulled him close; I knew I was shameless, to give myself so utterly, so completely. But I was also thinking, *Now the Duke can marry his Sophie*. Because I was ruined, for sure.

I had no idea how long this man would want me – but I wanted him, so very much.

★　★　★

He asked me more about my past, so I explained to him that I'd returned to my home in Paris when I was expelled from the convent.

'For disarming the Mother Superior when your friend Dervla was being punished.' There was a gleam in his eye. 'And in Paris, did your parents keep you under lock and key?'

'My father died when I was two,' I told him. 'And my mother found me a chaperone from England – Miss Kenning.'

'Ah. That explains why you speak English so well.'

He was caressing my cheek; I took his hand and kissed it. 'Indeed. Dervla taught me English, but with an Irish accent.' I smiled a little at the memory. 'Miss Kenning went to great pains to remedy *that*. But poor Miss Kenning has never been a terribly effective chaperone. She used to forget my very existence sometimes, I think, so engrossed was she in exploring Paris's churches and museums for hours on end.'

'So did you escape, Madeline?' He looked amused. 'Did you search for mischief with some new friends? Did you break the young men's hearts?'

'Of course.' My voice was light. 'But what about you? How long have you been a gamekeeper, Nathan?'

He caught my fingertip with his mouth and nipped it gently. 'Since the war ended.'

Oh. My breath caught in my throat. 'Were you in the war?'

'I was in France, yes.' His voice had changed. 'And I saw things there that I never want to see again. But as

73

for you, *mam'selle* –' and his brown eyes were dancing once more '– I want to see you again, and again, and . . .'

He gave me the money for my bracelet – I can't remember even noticing how much – and at last, when it was almost ten, he walked with me back down to the edge of the woods. I saw him gazing at the Hall in the distance and noticed how his eyes were shadowed again, but the shadows had gone when he looked down at me. 'Won't anyone there have missed you?' he asked.

I shook my head. 'I've told you – Miss Kenning won't even have noticed I've gone. She's halfway through a four-volume history of English architecture that she found in the Duke's library, and she's lost in descriptions of cornices and architraves.'

He laughed. 'How fortunate for your admirers in Paris that you had such a careless chaperone. And fortunate for me,' he added. 'I'm so glad you came to Belfield Hall.'

I entered the Hall by a side door and hurried up to my room, where I lay on my bed in the darkness. I turned restlessly under my heavy counterpane, hearing all the clocks striking midnight, then one, then two; but I found myself unable to sleep. Even when the servants rose and started their tasks at six, I was wide awake still, my mind churning at my own recklessness, my own duplicity – because what I'd told him had nearly all been lies.

Chapter Six

After that, I met Nathan whenever I could. We would either prearrange our meetings up at his cottage, or he would ring me at the Hall. 'I'll call myself Mr Villiers on the telephone,' he said. 'You can tell the staff that I'm dealing with your legal affairs in London.'

'Mr Villiers,' I teased him. 'Mr Villiers, my lawyer.'

I simply could not stop thinking about him. My skin was glowing and my eyes were bright. *How could no one see it? How could no one guess, about the gamekeeper and me?* Calmly I would tell Miss Kenning that I intended to take the air in the gardens, or to sketch the orchids in the hothouse – she hated the scent of exotic flowers, so I knew that she would never offer to come with me. And then I would steal out of the back of the house in the afternoon or in the darkness of the evening and climb to the clearing, where Nathan's cottage was.

I saw how, under his tender care, the baby hare grew strong again. One blustery March day Nathan set the beautiful little creature free, and as he held his dogs back we watched the hare move away into the bracken, his long velvety ears laid back and his nose eagerly twitching.

I was anxious for him. 'Will he be able to find his family, Nathan?'

'Possibly not. Unlike rabbits, hares are solitary creatures.' He gave me his lovely grave smile. 'But he'll be happy enough.'

'He'll perhaps dance under the moon,' I said.

I couldn't help but realise that there was something dark and damaged about Nathan. I was frightened by the way his eyes suddenly went so cold when he told me to beg – I still didn't understand why he made me do that – but I guessed that it was perhaps due to his experiences in the war, and I knew better than to question him. Besides, the moment he touched me – the moment he *looked* at me – I couldn't refuse him.

I'd had no idea that I could be aroused again and again to such extremes of physical pleasure, yet he was always so careful to protect me from pregnancy, despite the strength of his passion – either withdrawing before his emission, or using a sheath. But whatever he did, however he made love, he always made it plain that I was his. The gamekeeper's talisman that hung from the thong around my waist reminded me of it always, nudging my belly and my sex every time I moved. Every time I breathed.

I asked Harriet one afternoon how many gamekeepers the Duke employed, but she didn't know. 'They tend to live in the village, ma'am,' she said. 'We don't see them often.'

'I heard,' I tried to say casually, 'that some of them have cottages up in the woods.'

'That may be so, I really don't know. Ma'am –' she turned to me impulsively '– aren't you terribly lonely here? I know His Grace has to stay in Ireland on business, but he surely wouldn't mind you living for a while in his London house? You could maybe ask him, next time he rings.'

In his last letter my guardian had told me, with regret, that yet more difficulties with the Irish settlement meant that he was forced to postpone his return once more. I'd written back to say that he must not worry about me. And I told Harriet, 'I would rather be here than in London.' *I would rather be here than anywhere in the world.*

She said no more, but she must have been talking to the other staff about me, because less than an hour later Robert the footman knocked on my door and came in carrying a portable gramophone. 'Nobody else uses it, ma'am,' he explained as he set it up. 'Lady Beatrice used to keep it in her room for when she came here from London – she was a lively one.' He grinned. 'But those days are over. Here are some records too.' He put them on the table beside the gramophone, and I was touched.

'You're very kind,' I said.

'That's all right, ma'am. We know it's a bit quiet for you here.'

He'd left me six records, and the first one I put on was 'All I Want is You' – sung by the Duke's Sophie.

> *My man with the blue sad eyes,*
> *I want to make you smile.*
> *But what does it take for you to realise*
> *I've given you my heart, for such a long while?*
> *Oh, yes, it's true. All I want is you . . .*

I danced slowly around the room, imagining I was in Nathan's arms.

I played that record often. Sometimes, if the rain poured down, days could pass before I saw Nathan, and I missed him so much; but as the wet afternoons became fewer and the evenings lighter, we saw each other almost every day. Nathan would guide me around the woods and the fields beyond, his faithful dogs at his heels, and I experienced spring in the English countryside, seeing the unfolding of April foliage in the secret glades where the bluebells formed a misty carpet the colour of the sky.

Then we would go back to his cottage and he would calmly undress me. He would make me kneel before him while I told him in a clear voice how much I craved his love. He would use the leather thong around my waist to draw my naked body towards him, then make me take the talisman in my mouth till it was moist, and use it to intimately pleasure me until I was wild for him to possess me.

'I like to think of you wearing it always.' He would stroke the talisman and kiss the brand on my thigh as well. 'I like to think of you as mine.'

He continued to surprise me, in so many ways. One afternoon, for instance, I looked at the books that he kept on a shelf in his cottage. '*Land Management Methods*,' I read aloud in wonder, lifting the heavy book down and turning its densely printed pages. I picked out another. '*The Wheat Crop in English History* . . . what's this, Nathan?' I turned to him, teasing him. 'I didn't know you were a scholar.'

'Oh, I like to keep a little light reading for the winter months,' he grinned, and proceeded to distract me – which was easy enough. And still no one knew about the gamekeeper and me. Miss Kenning would potter around Belfield Hall marvelling at the treasures to be found there. Lottie still visited, making free with the Duke's library or records room, but I guessed that she was avoiding me, and I was glad of it.

No one realised that almost every afternoon I would hurry through the park and up the woodland paths – now bordered with great clumps of yellow primroses – to meet my gamekeeper at his cottage. Sometimes he would make love to me almost roughly before either of us had properly removed our clothes. He would lift me to sit on his table, perhaps, rucking up my skirts and fondling my thighs above my stockings, bending to rasp his tongue up and down my sex before opening his breeches and penetrating me slowly, so I could look down past his taut abdomen to the powerful shaft of his phallus driving deep between my parted thighs. 'Please, Nathan,' I would beg, breathless with hunger for him. 'Please.'

I wore pretty underwear now, having retrieved the silk lingerie from London that I'd packed away, and Nathan loved it all. Of course, I still wore my drab skirts and gowns, and the thick petticoat so no one would glimpse the outline of my secret talisman. I suppose I knew, deep down, that my happiness was transient; certainly I had not forgotten my past, and I never could. I knew nothing was finished, nothing was over – that letter had reminded me that somebody knew who I was, and where I was.

I knew I ought to trust no one, other than myself. But God help me, I was starting to trust Nathan.

One bright spring afternoon in his cottage, as I lay in his arms after we'd made love, I drew my fingertip along the sensual curve of his mouth and whispered, 'Nathan?'

His eyes, which had been closed, opened steadily. His beautiful brown gaze met mine. 'What now, *mam'selle*? More?'

I nestled my naked breasts against the delicious hard-ness of his chest. 'More of you?' I teased. 'Yes, please. But first – Nathan, I have something to ask you. Do you remember when we first met, and how I was trying to work out how to use that pistol?'

'Oh, God. The Ruby. You were lethal. It almost went off in my face.'

'I know. I'm sorry.' I nuzzled my lips against his throat. 'But – Nathan, will you teach me how to use it *properly*?'

I had his full attention now, I could see. He hauled himself up on one elbow to face me and said, 'Why?'

I laughed. 'In France,' I said airily, 'we used to go on shooting parties, in the countryside. To be able to shoot was considered a great accomplishment amongst the ladies. I was no good, because I'd never had lessons.'

He drew his finger down my cheek. 'You do realise, don't you, that I was afraid you meant to harm yourself on the night we met?'

For a moment I froze; then I clasped his hand. 'Absurd,' I retorted. 'I only wished to learn how to use my pistol. Will you teach me, Nathan? *Please*?'

'So that you can astonish all your old friends with

your prowess when you return to France some day?' He smiled. 'Of course, you must miss Paris.'

'A little.' I peeped up at him, fluttering my eyelashes. 'But I've found other diversions – for the time being.'

'Is that what I am? A diversion?' He caught my hand, pressing wicked kisses to it. Then he looked at my wrist, where the old scars were pale on my skin, and he said more softly, 'At least you've stopped hurting yourself now, Madeline. I'm so glad.'

And so he taught me to shoot. He nailed a straw target to a tree at the edge of the clearing, and I remember that I skipped for joy when I hit the centre three times in succession.

'Well done,' he smiled. 'Well done, *mam'selle.*'

I'd been worried that the sound of gunfire might attract attention, since it was no longer the shooting season. But he told me that certain creatures ranked as vermin, so crows and magpies, rats and rabbits that damaged the farmer's crops could be shot at any time of the year. He was a patient teacher, and a skilled marksman himself – in fact he excelled at everything I'd seen him do.

Once, after we'd climbed to a glade high in the woods where rabbits large and small bobbed between their warrens, he unslung his shotgun from his back and told me it was time for me to shoot live prey instead of targets on tree trunks. But when he handed me his gun, I couldn't do it.

'The rabbits are so pretty,' I pleaded. 'And I can see some babies there – please, Nathan, don't let's shoot them!'

'They're vermin,' he said flatly. Once again I saw the

hard side of his character, the part of him that was an experienced gamekeeper and had fought in the war. 'If you allow the rabbits to run riot on the estate, you might as well abandon it. They destroy the crops and the hedgerows, and even the trees die off once the rabbit warrens have undermined their roots.'

'I understand.' I took his hand and kissed it. 'But please, it's such a lovely afternoon. Can't we leave them, just for today?'

He laughed and pushed a strand of my hair back behind my ear. 'Playing your games with me again?' he teased. 'You would never be able to run an estate. But – beg me, *mam'selle*, and I'll spare the rabbits for today.'

'Beg you?' I hesitated. 'Here?'

'Yes,' he said softly. 'Here.'

His eyes always went dark when he spoke to me like this. I would see his expression grow tight, almost dangerous, and at that moment something would curl deep in my belly – acute desire for him, and also some inner warning. But I could no more resist him than I could do what I should have done in the first place – pack my few things, take the money Nathan had given me for my bracelet, and leave Belfield Hall.

I sank to my knees, the colour already flooding my cheeks, and with the sweet scent of the bluebells all around us, I unfastened his breeches and cupped the familiar bulk of his manhood in my hands. He was already half-aroused, and slowly I tasted him with my tongue before drawing his rapidly hardening erection deep within my mouth, while he grasped my shoulders and let out a harsh breath and thrust steadily, strongly.

Afterwards, when he had pleasured me also, he gathered me to him. 'The rabbits are spared target practice today, *mam'selle*,' he breathed.

One day soon after that, Nathan asked me what I thought of the Duke, my guardian. 'I don't know him well,' I said. 'Although he was my mother's cousin, I didn't even know of his existence until early last year, when my mother died.'

'Strange,' he said, 'that your mother didn't mention him.'

I looked down at my hands. 'There was some – estrangement. But I shall never forget how kind the Duke was, to take responsibility for me so quickly when he learned that I was his ward.'

'It must have been a dreadful burden for him,' Nathan teased gently, 'to be given an enchanting French girl to care for. Why did he banish you to Belfield Hall?'

'I've told you, he didn't,' I corrected him quickly. 'He encouraged me to stay in London for as long as I wished.'

'But he didn't want you staying at *his* house?'

I caught my breath. What had he heard? I answered steadily, 'He thought I might enjoy London society more if I stayed at the house of a neighbour of his, Lady Tolcaster, who has two daughters about my age. The intention was that Lady Tolcaster should take her daughters and me to parties and balls. But – it didn't work out.'

'Could I hazard a guess that these daughters of hers were madly jealous of you?'

I shrugged. 'Maybe. And it didn't matter anyway, because I hated London.'

'So do I. I'm glad you share my tastes.' He drew me closer, running his fingers gently through my hair. 'Most of all – I'm glad that you came to Belfield Hall, *mam'selle*.'

I feared that my inner joy must be dangerously apparent to all at Belfield Hall; but that evening my happiness was quelled, because as I was scanning the newspapers in the Duke's library, looking for news of Ireland as usual, a stark headline blazed out at me. IRISH KILLINGS. I read on. *Thirteen Protestant men, suspected of being spies for the British army, have been shot in a gun battle in Dunmanway, County Cork . . .*

The print blurred in front of my eyes. Shootings. A battle.

The door opened and Mr Fitzpatrick came in. 'I'm so glad to find you here,' he said in his cheerful way. 'I was speaking on the phone to His Grace last night – and I'm afraid I'm going to have to go to Ireland to see to the estate's accounts there a little earlier than I thought, so I'll be away for a while, I fear . . . Miss Dumouriez. You look pale. Are you quite all right?'

'I was reading this.' I pushed the newspaper towards him.

Quickly he glanced at it, then he looked up at me. 'I see there's trouble in County Cork; but there's often trouble in County Cork, unfortunately. Believe me, Dunmanway is a *very* long way from the Duke's estate in County Wicklow and even further from Dublin.'

'But—'

'You need have no fears on his account,' he told me gently. 'The Duke himself would tell you that. Yes, there *are* problems in Ireland – some Republicans are still reluctant to accept the Treaty – but there are to be elections soon, and that should settle everything. Your guardian's duties consist chiefly of sitting in big meeting rooms in Dublin, going through paperwork and legal minutiae. He never expected to be away for so long, but he feels that he must stay until the elections are over. Ring him, if you need reassurance, won't you? And last night on the telephone, he asked me to remind you that you're most welcome to stay at his London home with Miss Kenning, any time—'

'No,' I interrupted. 'I'm all right here, really I am.'

'Very well. But you will ask me, won't you, if there's anything that you need to know before I go? Oh, and His Grace told me, in confidence, that he hopes to be returning to England in a matter of weeks.'

I wished Mr Fitzpatrick a safe journey to Ireland. Then I sat on in the library, staring into nothingness until at last Robert came in and asked me if I wished him to light a fire. 'It's past ten, ma'am,' he added helpfully.

Only then did I realise how cold I was. Quickly I rose and made my way to my room, but once in bed I lay wretchedly awake. How would I tell my kind guardian about Nathan? How could I have blinded myself to my future and pretended to myself that my past was of no relevance any more? The answer was obvious. When I was with Nathan, nothing mattered. Nothing at all.

Chapter Seven

I'd already realised, to my surprise, that Nathan had an old motorcar, an open-topped Morris, that he kept parked beside his cottage. Sometimes when I arrived he would have the bonnet lifted and his sleeves rolled above his elbows, and he would be doing something or other to the engine that he would try to explain – using mysterious words like *crankshaft* and *throttle-lever*. I would laughingly shake my head and say, 'It's no good, *mon garde-chasse*.' I had started calling him that in French – my gamekeeper – whenever he confused me with obscure English words. 'I wouldn't understand you in French, let alone in English!'

The first time he suggested taking me for a ride in his car, I was thrilled then dismayed. 'Your car? But we can't. I would be seen.'

'Not if I put the roof up. And you could wear a hat with a veil – many ladies do.'

So the next time I walked up to his cottage, I carried a simple straw hat, to which I'd attached a long piece of chiffon cut from an old stole of mine. Nodding approval, he put up the canvas roof on his car and helped me into the passenger seat.

'It's a far cry from the Duke's Daimler, I'm afraid,' he apologised.

'I love your car,' I declared, and I really did. I was exhilarated to be sitting beside him on the bench seat as we rattled down the track. I clung to my straw hat as we swung round one sharp corner after another. I was fascinated by the way he knew exactly what to do with all the pedals and levers and buttons.

After that, he often took me out along the quiet country lanes, sometimes with his dogs sitting in the back. One warm day, when he'd left them dozing in the sun in front of his cottage and we'd driven for a mile or so, he caught me gazing intently at what he was doing, and he said, with his quick smile, 'This car fascinates you even more than I do, I think, *mam'selle*. You cannot believe that something so old and battered can still function, can you?'

I plucked up my courage. 'Nathan,' I said. 'Please, please will you teach me to drive?'

He was slowing down, and I held my breath. He stopped, pulled on the handbrake firmly with his right hand and turned to me. 'It depends what sort of payment you're offering,' he said in his husky voice.

My heart lurched. 'Anything,' I breathed. 'You know that. Anything.'

'Very well. I'll teach you to drive.' He gave a slight nod. 'And we'll go somewhere different today.'

'Oh, *where*?'

'It's a surprise.' He grinned. 'I'm going to give you some instructions that I want you – strictly – to follow. Do you agree?'

More of his games? That pulse of excitement flickered low in my belly again. 'I promise,' I said lightly.

With that he climbed out, I slid across to the driver's seat, pushed aside my veil and eagerly awaited his instructions. He explained everything so carefully and patiently before we started off, but I was confused by what those three different pedals were for – I couldn't remember which was which, and when I eventually got the car moving, the engine juddered to a halt moments later.

'Oh,' I muttered. '*Merde.*'

'You put your foot on the reverse pedal by mistake,' he said calmly. 'It's set a little further back than the two other pedals – you see?'

I was mortified – I'd wanted to do this well. But he described exactly what I had to do all over again; he was a wonderful teacher, and most of all, instead of mocking me whenever I did something wrong, he was full of calm praise for the smallest thing I did right.

I managed to get the car moving at last, though I was still nervous of its power. And also, if I was honest, I was completely distracted by the sight of his bare forearms – he'd rolled up his shirtsleeves, and as he reached across to show me how to use the handbrake to my right, my breath caught in my throat and I simply wanted to kiss him. But I tried to concentrate; I tried really, really hard.

We went further than we'd been before, avoiding Belfield village but heading out along the rolling Oxfordshire lanes – to give me more practice, he said. He explained again about the gears and told me to relax my grip on the wheel, so that I wasn't fighting the steering every time the car went over lumps and bumps in the road. At last I found that I was actually able to enjoy the ever-changing vista of fields and wooded hills, but then I had to concentrate again when he told me to turn left and I found myself negotiating a narrow lane lined by hedges thick with scented honeysuckle.

'Slow down,' he said. His voice was different. 'And get ready to stop. I'm going to drive now, Madeline.'

For some reason a shiver tingled down my spine, but I obediently pulled the handbrake on while he climbed out.

'Move across to the passenger side,' he instructed softly. 'And take off your hat and veil.'

'But—'

'No one's going to see you here.'

So I did. And he stood by the open door beside me and pulled out of his pocket – a black silk scarf. A blindfold. As he tied it carefully over my eyes, I was frightened. Didn't he remember how afraid I was of not being able to see? 'Nathan,' I began. 'What—?'

'It's all right,' he soothed. 'It's all right.'

But blackness enfolded me and my breathing was tight. I couldn't help but be reminded of my fear on the first night that I'd met him, up on the hillside. I said, 'You didn't tell me that this would be part of your bargain.'

'I'm going to take care of you, *mam'selle*,' he assured me. 'I swear it.'

But my heart was thudding with disquiet as he got behind the wheel and set off again, following the lane as it twisted and turned. Although the sun was still warm,

I'd gone cold, and I clasped my hands together tensely. *Why*? Why did he do these things to me? Just when everything seemed so perfect, why did he do something like this, which made it quite simply impossible for me to trust him?

At last he pulled to a halt, but by the time he came to open the door and help me out, I was shaking.

'Madeline,' I heard him say. 'Madeline?' He was untying the black scarf, tugging it off. 'What's wrong?'

I'd lurched away from him, dazed by the sudden light. '*Everything*. Just when I think we're becoming close, you do something like this to me, and I *hate* you for it—'

'Stop.' He'd taken two strides forward and was holding me tight. 'You're overreacting.'

I pushed at him with all my strength. 'I'm not . . . overreacting.' I stumbled over the word and was furious with myself. 'Don't be *condescending*, Nathan – sometimes you frighten me, and I simply don't understand you . . .'

My voice broke. He held me close again and two silent tears squeezed from under my lids as he enfolded me in his arms and pressed kisses on the top of my head.

'Please, Madeline,' he murmured. 'Please forgive me. And smile – you look so sweet when you smile. Turn round. Turn round, and look.'

I looked. He had stopped the car in a broad gravelled courtyard and beyond the courtyard was a house – a big mansion of honey-coloured stone that glowed seductively in the afternoon sunshine.

I caught my breath, because once it must have been

so beautiful. It was *still* so beautiful. I found myself walking slowly towards it.

'Whose house is—' I broke off and corrected myself. 'Whose house *was* this?' My voice was little more than a whisper, because I felt that we were intruding somehow.

'It belonged to someone I knew.' He'd followed me and stood at my side. 'But as you can see, it's not been lived in for years.'

Though nothing like as big as Belfield Hall, the house was exquisite, with its mullioned windows and many-gabled roofs, and festoons of wisteria rampantly climbing its ancient walls. But some of the windows were broken, many roof tiles were missing and weeds grew thickly in the courtyard. 'What happened to this place?' I breathed. 'What happened to the people who lived here?'

He was guiding me towards the front door. 'It's a long story.' He paused to pull a tangle of ivy from an old stone urn that stood beside the entrance. 'Certainly the last owner didn't intend to leave the house in this condition, but certain people conspired to ruin his lands. And it was done so easily – the river that flowed through the grazing lands of the estate became contaminated. It was quite likely a deliberate act and it meant, to put it briefly, that all the cattle became sick and died, and the tenant farmers and their families were no longer able to make a living.'

I had never heard him sound so bitter. 'If this contamination was deliberate, Nathan, couldn't the person who did it be prosecuted?'

'The person who did it was clever. You see, there are some very old mine workings in the area, and it's likely that one or more of the underground drainage channels collapsed, letting the poisoned contents leak out. Difficult to locate them and difficult to prove it was deliberate. But now that we're here, let me show you around.' He pulled a big key from his pocket and began to unlock the studded oak door.

I said, slowly, 'You have a key.'

'The last owner asked me to keep an eye on it.'

'Where does he live now?'

'He's dead. He died during the war.'

I waited for him to tell me more, but he didn't and besides, by then he was leading me into the main hall, which had a beauty of light and spaciousness that I found quite heart-rending. The place had clearly been abandoned for years, and the few pieces of furniture that remained were relics of a past age. Nathan bent to pick up some pieces of broken stained glass that had fallen from a high window and lay amongst dried leaves that must have blown in during a gale. 'Back to nature,' he said. 'Nature is a powerful thing.'

He looked so lonely standing there; I caught my breath at the yearning that suddenly flooded me. Reaching up, I lifted my hands to cup his beautiful face; I stood on tiptoe and I kissed him on his mouth, so tenderly.

'Madeline?' he said. 'Madeline. What was that for?'

I answered simply, 'For teaching me to drive. For bringing me here. For – everything.'

He caught my hand and pressed his mouth to my

scarred wrist with a hint almost of desperation in his eyes. 'Don't make of me what I'm not, Madeline, for God's sake—'

'Hush,' I whispered, putting my finger to his lips. He looked so desolate, this strong proud man, and I could think of only one way to make him feel better about himself. I pulled the black silk scarf from his pocket while he watched me wonderingly; then, moistening my lips provocatively with the tip of my tongue, I reached up. And began, carefully, to fasten the black scarf around his eyes.

'Madeline,' he said. He reached swiftly to touch my arms. 'Madeline – I don't—'

I kissed his lean jaw swiftly, and then his wide, sensual mouth again, to silence him; I knotted the scarf at the back of his head and I heard the indrawn hiss of his breath.

I wanted him. I wanted him there and then. And I thought – why should *he* always be the one to take the initiative? Why shouldn't I? I sank down before him, letting my hands run down his chest to skim his hips. His soft groan delighted me. I was on my knees, I was reaching to caress him *there*, through his clothing; I realised with a thrill of excitement that he was already aroused – *oh*. I licked my lips and began to unfasten his breeches.

He caught his breath, sightless behind the black blindfold. He said huskily, 'Are you playing games with me, *mam'selle*?'

'Games you'll like,' I murmured. 'Games you'll take to, *mon garde-chasse*, like – like a duck to a lake.'

He let out a shout of laughter. 'You mean like a duck to water. But I love your English. And I *love* games—'

He broke off, because I'd freed his stiffened phallus. Enthralled at the sight, I ran my fingers lightly up and down the silky-smooth skin ridged with veins, then I backed away and heard the rasp of his indrawn gasp of frustration. 'One moment,' I whispered.

I smiled to myself as I unbuttoned my frock and let the bodice slide down to my waist so that my flimsy lace-edged brassiere was bared; then I knelt again, reached for his hands and pulled his palms down against my breasts, so he could caress their tips through the satin that cupped them. He let out a soft groan and his erection reared anew, at which I extended my tongue to flick slowly up and down its thickness, then circled the sensitive skin at its engorged crown until I heard his breath hissing through his teeth. His hands were clutching fiercely at my breasts now, tearing down my brassiere and pulling, squeezing my taut nipples until indeed I was the one groaning aloud for my blindfolded gamekeeper.

Feverishly I unfastened the buttons of his shirt and ran my palms over his gloriously muscled abdomen, then I cupped him, down there, feeling the heavy bulk of his masculine parts. At last I took him in my mouth, caressing the whole hot, thick velvet length of him, hearing the harsh rasp of his breathing as I used my lips and tongue until he was clutching my shoulders almost desperately.

'Madeline. *Madeline.*' His voice raw, he lifted me to my feet and tore his blindfold off, his eyes fiery slits of desire. 'I want you. I want you *now*.'

He dragged me close so that the heat of his erection pulsed against my belly, and as his hungry mouth caught mine in a deep kiss, a shudder of longing all but engulfed me. He wrenched down my already-loose gown and brassiere so they pooled to the floor, and his eyes widened then darkened as he saw that beneath them I wore only my stockings and lace-edged panties and the dark leather cord of the talisman. Grasping the talisman itself, he tugged my panties aside and stroked the wooden peg strongly between my thighs until I was slick with desire, then he pinioned my wrists and pressed them back against the wall as I gasped out his name.

'Tell me,' he said almost harshly. 'Tell me what you feel. Tell me what you want.'

I was on fire. Every single part of me was on fire for this incredible man. 'I am yours, Nathan,' I gasped. 'I am yours.'

'Did you use the talisman last night, Madeline?' His voice was hoarse; he was rolling the wooden peg between his fingers then pressing it once more against my sex.

'Yes. *Yes.*' I could hardly breathe for the pleasure igniting at the base of my belly.

'What did you do?' he grated. 'Tell me exactly.' He'd torn off my panties completely, ripping them so he could thrust the talisman into my hotness, my wetness, and at the same time was sliding his fingertips wickedly to and fro across the heated nub of my desire.

'I was in my bath,' I whispered. 'The warm water was lapping against my breasts, and I was thinking of you. I was wearing the talisman, I always do—'

'No one else knows that you wear it?' he interrupted. 'No one has any idea that you meet me?'

I almost laughed aloud at the thought of telling Miss Kenning or Harriet, *Oh, I go out to meet my gamekeeper most days. He does things to me that I cannot begin to describe* . . . 'I bathe in private, always. And last night, I used your talisman to pleasure myself. I – oh!'

He'd started twisting it, making me gasp. 'Did you slide it deep inside you, *mam'selle*?' he prompted.

I groaned aloud. 'Yes. Yes, I did . . .'

'Did you imagine it was me? Did you touch your breasts and imagine my mouth – all over you?'

My hips were squirming with liquid desire. 'Yes. Please, Nathan, oh, God, oh please . . .'

Without another word, he tugged out the talisman and slid it round so that it hung behind me; then he hoisted me up so we were face-to-face and he was supporting my weight. He made me clasp my thighs around his waist, and I threw my arms around his shoulders, my mouth hungrily seeking his as he thrust himself up and inside me. He was rough, he was harsh, but I begged for more, and with each deep and thrilling stroke he was bringing me closer and closer to my crisis, pinning me against the wall with the force of his ardour until I felt heat spread through me like fire. My climax hit me with quite shattering impact as I cried out his name, clamped my legs around him and dug my nails fiercely into the taut muscles of his back.

He was still inside me, pounding steadily to drive me to the extremity of pleasure and beyond as my crisis continued to pour through me in engulfing waves. I was shaking as he lifted me from him and pushed me to my knees before him. He made a sound deep in his chest as I eagerly took him once more in my mouth, then he tangled his fingers in my hair and groaned out my name as he thrust again and again until I felt his hot seed spilling into my throat. I swallowed and licked as his powerful body jerked repeatedly, then, finally, was still.

There was an old couch nearby, covered with faded velvet. He drew me to it, making me sit next to him, then he gathered me in his arms and kissed the top of my head. 'Tell me I wasn't too rough?' he breathed.

Feeling almost too weak to speak, I leaned my head gratefully against his warm chest. 'Oh, *Nathan*.'

He frowned a little and pushed my hair away from my cheek with a tenderness that tore at me. 'I *was* too rough? Madeline? Madeline?'

I eased myself away from his grasp, just far enough to be able to lift my gaze to meet his. 'The word is – *parfait*,' I breathed at last, smiling sleepily. 'Perfect, *mon garde-chasse*.' He pulled me very close again.

'*You* were simply perfect,' he said huskily. '*Mam'selle*, you *are* perfect.'

But when I straightened my clothes, as I looked around one last time, I saw something that made me cold again, unsteady again – a telephone, on a shelf in the corner. Was that the telephone he used to ring me? *Why hadn't he told me*?

I prepared myself to ask him – but when we went outside into the sunshine, I grew even colder, because he was drawing out that black silk scarf once more.

Chapter Eight

'Some of your games I like, but this one I don't,' I said. 'Nathan, is the blindfold really necessary?'

His face remained impassive. 'You made me a promise.'

'Very well.' I lifted my chin defiantly. 'As long as you keep *your* promise, and let me drive again – the moment you consider, in your infinite wisdom, that it's safe to take the blindfold off me.'

He began carefully. 'I'm not sure that I did promise, Madeline. And though you drove my car very well earlier, perhaps you've had enough for today—'

I pushed at his hand that held the scarf. 'No driving, no blindfold. It's as simple as that.'

He pressed his beautiful lips together, then he nodded, but I was upset again. I wouldn't let him help me into the car, and I sat rigid as he fastened the blindfold over my eyes. Why do this? So that I wouldn't be able to tell anyone about the location of the half-ruined house? But who was I likely to tell about it, for heaven's sake? About as many people as I was likely to talk to about *him*. Nobody, in other words.

He started up the engine and drove us away from there without speaking. But after a quarter of an hour or

so, he stopped the car and pulled on the handbrake –
and I realised he was reaching to push aside my veil and
remove my blindfold. 'Your turn to drive, then,
mam'selle.' He got out and began to take the canvas roof
down. 'And we'll have some fresh air – no one's likely to
see us on these country lanes.'

I didn't smile back. I didn't say anything as I moved
across and took the wheel in my hands. As for what
happened next – I reacted stupidly, I can see that now. I
was upset about the blindfold, and I was reckless. I
drove too fast.

At first Nathan was patient. 'Please go a little slower,'
he said. 'There are some potholes ahead, and unless you
take more care, you might damage my tyres.'

So I slowed for a mile or so, but soon I let the car
gather speed again, and though Nathan was very quiet,
I saw from the corner of my eye that his jaw was set
tensely. *It serves you right,* I thought. *It serves you right,
for not trusting me to drive from the house. Surely you can
see very well that I'm capable. That I know exactly what
I'm—*

'There's a sharp turn ahead,' Nathan said through
gritted teeth. 'You must brake, Madeline – brake *now,*
and shift into a lower gear, and – *Madeline!*' Suddenly
he was hauling at the steering wheel. 'Sweet Jesus,
Madeline! Get your foot on the damned brake pedal!'
He'd wrenched the wheel round, and no wonder – I'd
been heading straight towards a sturdy oak. 'Stop the
engine,' he ordered, 'and get out. I'm driving the rest of
the way, do you understand? Jesus. Jesus . . .'

Somehow he'd flung himself across my lap to pull at

the handbrake and his old car tilted crazily before right-ing itself and grinding to a halt on the rough grass verge. I collapsed over the steering wheel in a trembling heap. I'd thought – I'd really thought – that we were both going to die.

Swiftly he pulled me close to him. 'Oh God, Madeline. You're shaking. I didn't mean to shout at you like that, but it looked as though you were going to drive straight into that bloody tree.'

'I – I'm sorry, Nathan.' I could barely speak. 'Your car – do you think I've damaged it? If I have, I'll pay—'

He broke in, 'It's not my car I'm worried about. Not my bloody car. It's *you*.' He'd flung his arms around me and was holding me close; then he was cupping my face with his hands, and he was gazing down at me with something fierce and primitive blazing in his eyes. My heart was beating wildly. Before I knew it, our mouths were colliding – oh, yes, my lips were as eager as his – and I heard the low growl of appreciation that he made in his throat as I opened to him; his mouth was cool and sensual as it slid over mine, his tongue was insinuating, stroking, thrusting, and I welcomed him eagerly.

Dear God, I was going to hell. My mother, the nuns – everyone had told me I was going to hell. But as his kiss intensified, I didn't care; I simply revelled in the delicious certainty of once more being wrapped in his strong arms. I revelled in being able to tangle my fingers in his over-long hair, in allowing his musky man-scent to invade my senses, while raw desire tingled in all my nerve endings.

'Nathan,' I breathed. 'You want this – you want *me* – again?'

'Again,' he said. 'Oh, Madeline. Again, and again, and again.'

He was laughing, I was laughing. Suddenly he pulled me towards him and lifted me so that I was astride his thighs, facing him; we were still hungrily kissing – my arms were wrapped tightly around his lovely shoulders – but at the same time he was reaching between my splayed legs. My skirt was up around my waist, and my panties were – ripped to shreds, I suddenly remembered, and in his pocket. I giggled. He'd thrust the talisman aside and was raising me again by my hips, then letting me down with great care, so that his iron-hard phallus was nudging at my core.

I still gasp aloud when I remember the scene now. We were in that open-topped car on a public road, where anyone might pass, yet we were shameless. With a harsh sigh he began to enter me, inch by powerful inch, and it was wonderful – I matched him stroke for stroke, riding him as waves of sheer pleasure washed over me; I clawed at his back as my need devoured me, and at last I shattered around him, sinking into his embrace, whimpering with delight against his warm chest.

It's not my car I'm worried about, he'd said. *Not my bloody car. It's you.*

He eased me off him. I caressed him until he pumped out his seed, and afterwards he held me tenderly, pressing his lips to my hair. 'Time to tidy up,' he said, reluctantly. He kissed my hand and began to button up my dress, but I still saw mischief in his eyes, laughter even; after all, we were still tangled up together in his car, and my clothes . . . *oh, my.*

I crawled along the seat to the passenger side, where I sat and tried to smooth my hair with my fingers. 'Now your car's even more of a mess than it usually is.' I could hear the happiness in my voice.

'For the most delightful of reasons.' He leaned across to press a kiss to my forehead. 'We'd best be on our way, *mam'selle*. And this time, I'll drive.'

I put my head to one side and gave him a mischievous smile. 'But I did well, didn't I, Nathan? Driving your car, I mean?' I caught his look of astonishment. 'Well,' I went on, 'apart from the very last bit, I suppose . . .' My voice trailed away.

He lifted my hand to his lips and said, with mock solemnity, 'Apart from almost crashing into a tree, *mam'selle*, you were – spectacular.' I didn't know if he was referring to the car or the sex or both, and I didn't mind. *My gamekeeper.* I was recklessly, stupidly exhilarated because he'd said he cared. Sheer joy pulsed sweetly through my veins for the remainder of our drive.

But when we reached his cottage, my happiness evaporated – because Lottie Towndrow, the clever researcher from Oxford, was there.

She'd left her bicycle leaning against the wall, and was sitting on the bench by the front door looking perfectly at home reading a book while Nathan's two dogs dozed at her feet, although they jumped up and bounded towards the car as soon as they heard it drawing near. She rose and strolled towards us also, dressed in jodhpurs and a checked shirt, looking sleek and cool with her long red hair flying free.

She reached Nathan's side just as he was opening the car door for me. After giving me a dismissive glance, she put her hand on Nathan's muscular arm.

'Oh, Nathan, darling,' she said, 'I came over to borrow some of your books. I do hope you don't mind?'

Darling, I registered. *Nathan, darling.*

'Not at all,' he said evenly. 'Lottie, have you met Madeline, the Duke's ward?'

'We've met.' She gave me another cool stare. 'At Belfield Hall, in fact, though it's such a vast place that our paths don't often cross.'

'Oh, they have at times,' I said pointedly, thinking of the letters she'd asked me to translate. But she clearly wasn't going to give me a chance to bring the matter up.

'I've almost finished my work at the Hall,' Lottie said. She still scarcely looked at me – her eyes were devouring Nathan. 'But I wondered if you'd let me take these for a while, Nathan.' She was pointing to two thick volumes she'd left on the bench by his door. 'I was half-expecting you to call at my house some day – but presumably you've found other matters to divert you.' *This* time she looked at me.

I was feeling unsteady again. So Nathan knew Lottie – rather well, it seemed. And those books. How could I have forgotten them? Would a gamekeeper really have books titled *Land Management Methods*, and *The Wheat Crop in English History*? Would he really speak to someone like Lottie – and she to him – as if they were social equals?

Nathan offered to make tea and we sat outside in the spring sunshine while Lottie chattered away to him about Oxford, and history, and literature, and I might as well have not been there. Nathan spoke now and then, but was restrained. And I sat feeling stupid, and so terribly jealous.

After a while, he turned to me. 'Lottie's probably told you she's writing a thesis on the history of the Oxfordshire nobility,' he said. 'No doubt somebody, somewhere, will want to read it.'

Oh – a gentle piece of mockery. His brown eyes danced and he gave that secret grin, just for me. Immediately I felt happier – but not for long. Lottie put down her cup rather abruptly.

'I'm already engaged to give lectures on the topic,' she announced breezily, 'all around England. Well, Nathan darling, I really should be on my way – I'll get your books back to you in the next week or so, I promise.' She stood up, putting the books in a leather satchel.

That's it, I thought. She's going now. Nathan stood up too, to see her off, and I began to breathe more easily.

But then – right in front of me – Lottie pulled him to her by his shirt front, she stood on tiptoe and she kissed him on the lips. *On the lips.* Only then did she finally get on her bicycle and set off down the grassy track. For a moment or two I could hardly breathe.

What is she to you, Nathan?

He came back and put his arm around me. 'Don't worry about her,' he said. 'She's jealous of you, that's all. I didn't realise that you'd already met her.'

I pulled away from him. 'I've met her a few times, at the Hall. She's been rooting amongst the old books and papers there.'

'Has she?' He looked startled. 'Does the Duke know?'

'I – I don't know.' My eyes flew up to his. 'I just assumed she had his permission.'

'I doubt it,' he said flatly. 'I very much doubt it. I suppose that you and she haven't exactly become friends?'

'No. I feel—'

'You feel what, Madeline?'

I shrugged. 'She despises me. I know it.'

He drew me down to the bench, keeping his arm around me. 'She's wild with envy,' he said softly, 'because you're so beautiful and sweet. That's all.' He gave me his gentle smile. 'But if I were you, I wouldn't talk to her. Or listen to anything she says.'

Tentacles of miserable suspicion were still prickling at my skin. *The way she'd kissed him.* The way she'd looked at me, when we arrived at the cottage in Nathan's car. With amusement, and disdain, and – pity.

'Nathan,' I said, pleating the fabric of my dress between my fingers, 'were you and she once lovers?'

He was silent for a while, during which time my heart sank to its lowest ebb since I'd met him. He said at last, 'Lottie and I were – *lovers,* yes, as you put it. Without any sort of commitment. That's what she likes.'

I was stupefied. Of course I knew he'd have had many lovers, I'd be a fool to think otherwise – but Nathan and *Lottie.* I could barely breathe.

He was holding my hand and stroking my palm in that way of his. 'I didn't tell you,' he went on, 'because it didn't seem important. Because *she* wasn't important. How could I look at anyone else, when I have you?'

I was silent.

'You are mine, Madeline,' he said. 'Mine. She's not said anything about me, has she?'

'No. No.' I'd found my voice at last. 'If she had, don't you think I'd have asked you about her? I don't see how you can be so calm . . .'

He was still holding my hand. 'I told you – our affair meant nothing. Lottie isn't the kind of person who invites affection. She has unusual tastes.'

'So I'd guessed,' I muttered, remembering the way she'd made me translate those hideously salacious letters. 'In her reading, at any rate.'

'Not just in her reading.' And I saw him hesitate. *Oh, no.* What was coming next? 'Madeline,' he went on, 'I know that you've had a certain amount of sexual experience. But I wonder if you've heard of domination?'

I coloured and my breathing became tighter. 'I've heard of it, yes.'

'Well, Lottie is fond of being dominated,' Nathan said calmly. 'She likes to be in the power of a strong and virile man – she enjoys being bound and gagged, maybe blindfolded too, during a sexual encounter.'

I was still endeavouring to be calm. 'So you did that to her? You blindfolded her, and tied her up?'

His fingers were toying idly with mine, then he looked at me directly. 'I'm glad you used the past tense. Yes, she liked me to dominate her. But we've not been together in that way for some time, and she's very jealous of you. She's told me so—'

He broke off as I stood up, and I was afraid he might see how I was trembling with anger. With distress. *They talked about me?* This was too much. I said in a low voice, 'I think I'd like to go back to the Hall now, if you don't mind.'

He stood up too, his face grave. 'I'll walk down through the woods with you. But – you're not seriously worried about Lottie, are you?'

I shivered. *Yes. Yes, I am. I hate her. I hate having to know what you've done with her . . .* He gazed at me a moment longer, then he whistled up his dogs and we set off down the path.

He put his arm around me as we walked, pulling me closer to him and adjusting his long stride to match mine as the dogs bounded gleefully ahead. But I was still cold. I'd protected myself from emotion ever since I was a child, and with good reason. I'd walled up my heart and I'd let no one in. But with this man's caresses, and his tender words, I'd felt something stir into life inside me that was far more than simple sexual desire, and far more dangerous.

And now – since our conversation about Lottie – I'd realised he was probably fearing that I'd make emotional demands on him, ask him for commitment even. Perhaps he was already wishing that what had taken place between us had never happened.

He halted when we got to the boundary of the Hall's gardens and whistled his dogs close, while I prepared to set off across the shrubbery by my usual route. But he stopped me by putting his hands on my shoulders and turning me to face him.

He said steadily, 'Are you regretting what's happened between us, Madeline?'

I shrugged. 'No more than you, I imagine.'

He lifted my scarred wrist and kissed it. 'I'm not regretting it. Don't do this to yourself, Madeline. You must stop thinking of yourself all the time as if you were unworthy of any happiness.'

'But what if that's correct?' I pulled my hand away from him. 'What if *you're* the one who's wrong, for thinking I'm – what I'm *not*, Nathan?'

His eyes were unreadable. 'I know you well enough,' he said. 'You'll meet me again, *mam'selle*?'

My breath caught in my throat. Then – 'Yes,' I whispered, 'yes,' and I was in his arms, and he was holding me close and pressing his forehead to mine.

'Tomorrow,' he said almost tenderly. 'At my cottage, around eight in the evening. Yes?'

A huge lump suddenly came to my throat, so I couldn't speak. I nodded instead.

'You'll be on time?'

'Aren't I *always*?'

'Of course. Forgive me. And please smile, Madeline,' he whispered. 'You look so sweet when you smile.'

He kissed my hand, then I walked quickly through the leafy park and the gardens towards the house. This could not go on, I thought rather desperately. I would be a fool not to realise it. But I knew, all the same, that I would continue to wear his talisman, I would continue to be his – since I certainly could not bear to be the one to end it.

The very next day, a new blow came from an unexpected quarter, because the old Duchess arrived at Belfield Hall.

Chapter Nine

Harriet had told me once that the Duchess had never stopped grieving the death of her only son. 'He died in the war, in the very last year of the fighting,' she explained. 'Tragic, it was.'

'So that was when my guardian became the next heir?'

'Oh, bless you, no, ma'am. There was another heir, some cousin called Lord Edwin, but he was only a sickly boy, and *he* died too. Then the old Duke died – that was two years after the end of the war – and the new Duke, your guardian, appeared from nowhere, so to speak, to inherit Belfield Hall and all that went with it. The Duchess moved into the Dower House, and that was that.'

Apart from this, I knew very little about the Duchess. The servants had hardly mentioned her, except for Betsey hinting at the general relief that she'd taken all her cats with her; although before I set off for Belfield Hall last November, I'd tentatively suggested to my guardian that perhaps I ought to make the Duchess's acquaintance.

'You could call on her as a matter of courtesy, I suppose,' he'd replied. 'You might have better luck than me. She's usually on her deathbed whenever I attempt to visit.'

I'd kept making excuses in my mind not to pay that call – I thought that perhaps ill-health had made her a virtual recluse – and since my guardian never mentioned her again, I'd assumed that she had no desire at all to meet me. But the morning after I'd met Lottie at Nathan's cottage, Harriet was in my room, tidying my clothes and no doubt secretly lamenting their drabness as usual, when she happened to glance out of the window. And I heard her mutter, 'Oh, my goodness me.'

I turned swiftly. 'What is it, Harriet?'

'Not wishing to sound disrespectful, ma'am,' she said flatly. 'But it's the old – I mean, it's Her Grace the Duchess. Seems like she's decided to pay a visit.'

Hurrying to the window myself, I saw that an open-topped Rolls-Royce had pulled to a halt in the front courtyard and Mr Peters was already opening the car door, bowing low as an elderly lady climbed out. *The Duchess*. She was very straight-backed and dressed all in black, and as she gazed up at the house, I felt as though she was looking directly at me.

My heart sank. I went to find Miss Kenning, who was sketching happily in the portrait gallery, though when I gave her the news she jumped to her feet, scattering her paper and pencils. 'Oh, my goodness. I'd better get changed, Madeline – whatever shall I wear?'

I tried to soothe her. 'I don't imagine you need to change. I just thought that perhaps she might wish to meet you, as well as me.'

'Since I'm your companion. Dear me, yes indeed . . .'

Poor Miss Kenning continued to be in such a nervous state that I rather wished I'd left her in peace, and it turned out that I could have done so, for within a quarter of an hour, I received a summons to visit the Duchess on my own, in her former set of rooms – apparently the old lady had telephoned Mr Peters last night to ask for them to be prepared for her visit.

I wished I'd known of this. I wished I'd been forewarned. With a sense of great apprehension I followed Mr Peters to the Duchess's suite on the second floor; I had never been in there, of course, and as I entered her private parlour I stopped involuntarily, for all the blinds had been fully drawn against the daylight, and at least three cats wandered around. She must have brought them with her in their baskets; I tripped over one, and no wonder – apart from the glow of the coal fire, the room was lit only by two oil lamps. I remembered Harriet telling me that when the new Duke installed electricity in the Hall, the Duchess had sent orders that it was on no account to be put in her rooms.

I stuttered an apology for falling over her cat. 'It is a little dark in here,' I said. And the heat from the fire was stifling.

She was gazing at me from a high-backed chair, with one hand on an ivory-tipped stick and the other stroking yet another cat, a ginger one, on her lap. She wore a black shawl round her thin shoulders and a black cap on her head. 'I know what you're thinking,' she pronounced. 'Why don't I use electricity? Because it's expensive. Because it's new-fangled nonsense. Besides, why trust these gadgets when oil lamps have served us for years?'

I wasn't sure whether or not she was expecting an answer, so I remained silent while she looked me up and down.

'So you're Lord Ashley's ward,' she said at last.

Lord Ashley? Now I was completely confused. Why on earth did she still call the Duke by his former title?

'You're a quiet one, aren't you?' The Duchess's sharp eyes never left me. 'Come nearer, child.'

I took one reluctant step and she leaned forward in her chair to inspect me. 'Hmm,' she pronounced at last. 'You're eighteen, aren't you? And a pretty chit – in a French sort of way. They say that your mother was Lord Ashley's cousin. But what's the true story?'

I stiffened. 'What you've just said is quite correct, Your Grace. My mother's father – my grandfather, that is – was brother to the Duke's mother, who was French herself—'

She waved her hand to silence me. 'Then why did no one in England know of your side of the family? Why did no one know of your existence until recently?'

'There was a family rift long ago, I believe, Your Grace—'

'Stuff and nonsense,' she interrupted. 'Who was your father?'

How often had I told this story? I told it again. 'My father was a baron, with lands in Normandy and a mansion in Paris. But he died long ago, and now my mother is dead also.'

'And the Duke believed all this? He believed everything you told him?'

What? Panic made my senses swim, but somehow I

stayed outwardly calm. 'My guardian knew that I was an orphan, and he was most generous to me in my need.' I lifted my gaze steadily to meet hers. 'I understand that you too, Your Grace, have suffered grievous losses—'

I broke off, because suddenly the old lady let out a sob. 'My son,' she whispered. 'My darling Maurice, my son . . .'

She was weeping quietly. I was horrified at the effect of my words. The ginger cat leapt from her lap to stalk imperiously towards the fire. 'I'm so very sorry,' I said, looking around for the bell-pull. 'Should I fetch someone, Your Grace? Mr Peters, or Mrs Burdett, perhaps?'

'No. No.' She dabbed at her eyes with her lace-edged handkerchief, then drew a deep breath before beckoning me closer and pointing to a table on which sat a leather-bound album. 'Bring me that,' she ordered. 'And come and sit by me.'

So I picked up the heavy album and put it on a smaller table beside her, then I sat on a stool while she leaned across and started turning the pages. The album was filled, I realised, with photographs of her son – Maurice as a child in a sailor suit, Maurice in his Eton uniform, Maurice's wedding day, Maurice as an officer in the army.

'He was so handsome,' the Duchess lamented. 'As handsome as his father, Marianne.'

'My name is Madeline, Your Grace,' I said. And I didn't think he was handsome, with his sharp dark eyes and black moustache and fleshy face. I was relieved when Robert arrived with a tray of tea, because then she put the album aside, told me to pour, and when I'd done so she asked me what I thought of Belfield Hall.

I said that I thought it very imposing, and considered it an honour to live here.

'Do you, now?' she mused. Her sharp eyes were completely focused on me. 'I would have thought,' she went on, 'that a pretty thing like you would prefer by far to be in London or Paris, dancing away to that jazz music, or going to parties and eating at fancy restaurants with your friends. What do you think of Lord Ashley, hmm?'

Lord Ashley again. Why did she persist in calling him that? She made me anxious, she made me nervous, though I answered her steadily enough. 'As I've said – my guardian the Duke could not have been any more kind to me, Your Grace.'

She snorted. 'Kind, eh? And is that what you want from him? Kindness?'

I sat very still, my heart thumping, until at last the old Duchess leaned forward on her stick and spoke again. 'You must be lonely here,' she pronounced. 'It's not good for a girl of your age to be on your own.'

'I've a companion,' I began. 'Miss Kenn—'

She brushed my words aside. 'From what Peters tells me, you could be roaming around the countryside at all hours of the day and night, and that ninny of a companion of yours would have no idea.'

I'd gone rather cold. *Did Mr Peters suspect?* Did the rest of them suspect?

The Duchess hauled another cat onto her lap, a tortoiseshell this time, and petted it fussily. 'Now, I've got an idea,' she announced importantly. 'I'm going to move back here, to the Hall. What do you think of that?'

What? 'I beg your pardon, Your Grace?'

'I'll move in with you, child. Why not? We'll be company for one another.'

Her clothes smelled of camphor, the room smelled of cats and I thought I'd glimpsed malice in her eyes. I was utterly dismayed. 'Your Grace,' I said, 'perhaps the Duke should be consulted first, since his concern must always be for your comfort and well-being. And I understand that he might be home soon—'

'Do you?' she broke in crisply. 'Then again, he might *not*. And I appreciate your interest in my well-being, but I'll be perfectly comfortable here, thank you – after all, Belfield Hall was my home long before it was Lord Ashley's, and half my possessions are still here anyway. I'll tell my maid Stanforth to begin sorting out what I'll need to bring as soon as I get back to the Dower House.' She leaned forward, causing the cat on her lap to protest loudly. 'Come closer, child. Yes – *you're* a pretty one. A little minx, I should think, with those mischievous blue eyes of yours. And once I'm here, no doubt Beatrice will visit often.' Her sharp chin jerked up. 'Have you met her yet?'

Her dead son's widow. I was still reeling. 'No, Your Grace. I haven't had that honour.'

'Well, you'll meet her soon enough,' she pronounced, 'because Beatrice is arriving here this afternoon, from London. I spoke to her on the telephone yesterday – she promised to meet me here at three, and she'll return with me to the Dower House to stay for a night or two. So off you go, child, I need to get ready for her. But I shall look forward to moving in. And I rather think that we'll be good friends, you and I.'

I walked slowly back to my own rooms, completely dismayed.

The Duke would be pleased, I told myself rather desperately. The Duke would be pleased that I'd been so courteous to her . . .

But she was going to live here. She would be tracking my every move. *From what Peters tells me, you could be roaming around the countryside at all hours of the day or night* . . . My heart was still sore over Nathan's revelations about Lottie, and I struggled to readjust to this new blow. Back in my room I sat down and looked at the letter I was writing to my guardian, and wondered how to broach this latest news. *You will be glad to hear that the Duchess paid me a visit today. She talks of moving back in* . . .

Perhaps she wouldn't. Perhaps her visit was a whim, and she would forget about it as soon as she returned to the Dower House. Perhaps . . . I was gazing out of the window, my thoughts in such turbulence that it took me longer than it should have to realise that another car had arrived.

In the courtyard stood the Duchess's gleaming Rolls-Royce and, next to it, the Ford that Eddie used for errands, but there was another car there too, parked a little way from the others, and I recognised it instantly: it was Nathan's. I got slowly to my feet. Why was he here? Surely, surely he wouldn't have come here for me?

Over by the stable block, on the far side of the courtyard, some of the Duke's grooms were gathered around a beautiful chestnut horse with a pale gold mane. The

Duke still kept horses because his visitors often enjoyed the opportunity to ride, he'd told me; besides, I guessed that he would be most reluctant to dismiss the many grooms and stable-boys whose families had worked at the Hall for generations.

Grooms and stable-boys, yes – and standing in their midst was Nathan. He had his back to me, but his figure was unmistakeable, with his over-long curling brown hair and his strong shoulders. I laced on my outdoor shoes, pulled a cardigan over my dress and hurried downstairs through the main hall into the courtyard. *To see what was going on*, I told myself. To find out what he was doing here. Wearing his usual gamekeeper's breeches and sleeveless leather waistcoat over his shirt, he was chatting familiarly with the grooms, admiring the chestnut and running his hand down its powerful neck. Beside him was a woman with cropped dark hair, elegantly clad in a crimson cardigan coat and high-heeled shoes.

As she talked to him, her eyes were dancing with flirtation and her body gestures were saying, *Look at me. Aren't I sophisticated? Aren't I beautiful?* Just for a moment she reminded me of Lottie, with her air of complete confidence and her pale clear skin. Then I saw that she had a box camera in her hand, and she was evidently persuading Nathan to pose for her; he must have agreed at last, because she started to move back to take his picture.

He folded his arms across his chest and aimed his mocking smile at the camera as he stood with his booted legs slightly astride. 'Like this?' he was querying.

'Perfect, Nathan,' she drawled. 'Simply perfect.'

There was a world of meaning in her words. My breath caught. *Another* clever woman after Nathan Mallory – and he was clearly an expert on horses as well as women, because once his photograph had been taken, he turned back to inspect that animal as if he were about to buy it, examining its forequarters and gently stroking its nose. I shivered. Why was he here? Who was the woman?

He turned just then, and on seeing me he started slowly to smile, baring just a hint of his gleaming white teeth. '*Mam'selle*,' he said. He touched his forelock, with laughter dancing in his brown eyes, and oh, God, in spite of everything I longed to run into his arms then and there, but I couldn't, of course. And I'd realised that something was very wrong.

Those grooms had been talking to Nathan, not as if he were their equal, but with respect – with deference, even. And the beautiful woman treated him as she would a friend. Someone of her own rank.

A gamekeeper? A humble gamekeeper? The suspicions I'd tried for so long to suppress were clamouring in my brain, but before I could say or do anything, the elegant woman with short dark hair was resting her hand on Nathan's muscular forearm, and at the same time she'd turned to let her eyes flicker over me. *He's mine*, I was muttering under my breath. *He's mine*.

'Who's this, Nathan?' She was glancing sideways at him merrily, as if I was some new amusement on offer.

'This, Beatrice,' he said smoothly, 'is the Duke's ward, *Mademoiselle* Madeline Dumouriez.'

'Oh, of course!' she exclaimed. She walked towards me in her high-heeled shoes and held out her hand, so I was forced to let my fingers rest briefly in hers. 'How do you do, Mademoiselle Dumouriez?' Her French accent as she pronounced my name was flawless. 'I am Lady Beatrice.'

I felt my heart sink; I should have recognised her from the photograph album. I should have been prepared. 'Lady Beatrice,' I said.

Her dark eyes ran over me, then over Nathan again; I'd seen the way she rapidly assessed my plain shoes, my old-fashioned dress and cardigan, and she looked as if something – me, most likely – amused her hugely. 'I've come here,' she said, 'because I believe the Duchess is visiting the Hall, and I intend to accompany her back to the Dower House, where I shall be staying for a few days.'

She turned to Nathan. 'Thank you so much for giving me that lift from the station – your company, as ever, was far more entertaining than having to endure a tedious taxi ride. And it really is too bad that the old house has fallen into such decline. We must meet again soon, and perhaps we can talk it over. You know how very interested I am in worthy projects.'

She touched Nathan's cheek in an almost intimate gesture of farewell – oh, my stomach knotted with jealousy at that – and, with her camera slung on a long leather strap over her shoulder, she turned to stroll towards the front door, where Robert the footman already stood stiffly to attention.

I stared after her until she'd disappeared inside.

Nathan beside me said, 'She is the Duchess's daughter-in-law – they're old friends.'

'But – but she said she came here from Oxford with *you . . .*'

'I drove to Oxford on some errands this afternoon, and happened to see Lady Beatrice waiting for a taxi by the station. She'd just arrived on the train from London and I offered her a lift.'

'So you know her.' What a stupid thing to say, I chided myself – quite clearly he did. And a thousand other confused thoughts were busy whirling through my brain. Lady Beatrice was one of the aristocracy. If her husband hadn't died in the war, he would have been the Duke, and she would be the Duchess of Belfield. Yet she'd spoken to Nathan – my gamekeeper, who lived in a cottage in the woods – as if he were her equal. And – *the old house?*

Nathan was smiling at me softly, his lips curving in that sensual way – *oh, the things I had let those lips do to me.* 'You look puzzled, *mam'selle*,' he said.

'I don't understand.' I made myself meet his steady gaze. 'I thought – I wouldn't expect her to be so familiar with . . .' My heart suddenly started beating rather unevenly. 'She was talking about a house. She meant the one you took me to visit yesterday. It's yours, Nathan. Isn't it?'

He said nothing. His silence spoke for itself.

'Why did you lie to me?' I breathed. 'Why did you let me think you were a gamekeeper?'

He spoke at last. 'I'm not rich,' he said quietly. 'You've seen for yourself what kind of condition my estate is in.'

'You told me that the last owner of that house died in the war—'

'Its last owner was my father, and he died almost bankrupt. So I didn't really think it mattered what – or who – you thought I was.'

I was shaking my head slowly. 'You didn't think it *mattered*, telling the truth to me?' I looked around quickly, but the chestnut horse had been led back to its stable, the grooms had all gone and we were alone. '*Nathan.*' I struggled to keep my voice calm. 'All your talk of socialism, and equality. The way you implied that you were one of the people, happy with your cottage, your old clothes, your way of life . . .'

His eyes were inscrutable again, which always frightened me. 'I own several hundred acres,' he said. 'But you were correct in assuming I'm poor. My estate is profitless, and my ancestral pile is a ruin. I told you why.'

'The contaminated water supply.'

'Exactly. The farmlands are no longer viable.'

I understood that much. 'But I met you, that first night, on the Duke's estate! Your cottage is on the Duke's estate!'

'No it isn't.' His voice was tense. 'You were on my land, not the Duke's. I live at that cottage because, as you've seen, my real home – the house that has belonged to the Mallory family for generations – has become uninhabitable. And I cannot afford to repair or maintain it.'

I whispered, 'You should have told me all this, from the beginning. Just as you should have told me about Lottie—'

'I know,' he agreed.

'*What*?' I was speechless with indignation.

'I know.' He was still calm. 'It was rather wrong of me. But, you see –' and suddenly, his lovely brown eyes began to gleam again '– you and I were having so much fun.'

Fun. His aroused body in my hands, his delicious mouth and tongue simply everywhere, the things he did with my gamekeeper's talisman – *oh.* My cheeks felt drained of colour, my chest was tight.

'I'm glad I amused you,' I said bitterly.

He sighed, and ran his hand through his thick hair. 'Madeline,' he said, 'I'm sorry. At first, I thought you were hoping for the Duke, one way or another, but I quickly realised that I was wrong. And then, I didn't want to spoil the times we had together. Since we were enjoying ourselves –' his voice became husky '– so very much.'

All of a sudden, everything about this man – his shirt open at the neck, his smile so white in his sun-browned face, his curly hair enticingly brushing his temples – made me feel so unsteady that I was almost gasping for air. *I'd like you to beg,* mam'selle.

I wanted my gamekeeper back. Yes, I would go down on my knees for Nathan Mallory, here in this open courtyard. But . . . . *There is no hope for us,* I wanted to cry out to him. *If you could deceive me over something as vital as your true identity, there is no hope for us.*

And perhaps there never was.

He was watching me gravely. 'I'm sorry that you've found out this way. I should have told you.'

'Yes, you should have, Nathan.' I drew in a sharp breath. 'But it doesn't really matter now, does it? Since neither of us trusts the other in the slightest.'

'Madeline—' He was reaching after me to stop me from leaving him, but by then we were no longer alone – some groundsmen were coming round from one of the outbuildings, carrying big wooden rakes to do their daily job of smoothing out the gravel on that vast forecourt. So I took advantage of the distraction to hurry back into the house and up to my room, where I sat and pressed my hands to my hot cheeks.

And that night, my old, bad dreams came back.

I am locked in the bedroom again. It is dark, and I am crouching in the corner, and the Marquis is standing by the door. I can hear my own rapid breathing as if it were some-one else's. 'No,' I whisper as he comes steadily towards me. 'No, monsieur, please.' I am ten years old. I can smell the musky scent of the cologne he wears. The Marquis's voice is sharp as he says, 'It's your fault. You are a wicked child, Madeline, and you deserve this.'

Please. I'll be good, I promise I'll be good. I crouch in the corner while he takes off his evening coat, and my senses are overcome with terror, because I know what comes next. Nowhere to hide now, Madeline. 'Say it,' he commands. 'Say it.'

I scramble to my feet and make a low curtsey. I stam-mer, 'My name is Madeline, and what can I do to please you? What can I—'

He pushes me onto the bed; he is so strong, and his breath is hot on my cheek. 'You offer too great a temptation. Do you understand? My God, Madeline, do you?'

Afterwards, when he has gone, I am sick over and over again, but I know he will be back. I know he will lock me in my room again and—

My dream ended abruptly, and I woke, cold with terror. In the distance, I could hear all the clocks in Belfield Hall's great reception rooms striking two. The Marquis was dead, he had died years ago, but I lay shaking, aware that if Nathan knew everything, he would despise me utterly.

No one, least of all my mother, knew who my father was. Yes, my mother had been married briefly to a baron at the time I was born, but whether I was actually his daughter was very much open to question, since my mother was nothing but a high-class whore. It was true that the Duke of Belfield was my mother's cousin and legally my next of kin, but if he'd been told what he should have been told, he would have kept me as far from his own life as possible.

I remembered the letter that I'd burned, from some unknown enemy. *I knew your mother in Paris. Her name was Celine Dumouriez. Like you, she was beautiful. Like you, she was a whore.* I rocked myself on my bed alone in the darkness, simply hurting, because although Nathan had deceived me, I'd known all along that I deserved no better.

Chapter Ten

My hopes that the Duchess might reconsider her decision to move back to Belfield Hall were swiftly dashed. She moved in four days later, and during that brief interval of time Belfield Hall was turned upside down. *Her Grace will want this, Her Grace won't want that,* Mr Peters could be heard pronouncing as he consulted his lists and sent the servants rushing around the house with so many tasks to perform that the footmen were reduced to a state of near-panic and the housemaids to tears.

It took me longer than usual to complete my next letter to my guardian. Time and time again, I wondered how to broach the subject. *By the way, you will be pleased to hear that the Duchess has decided to stay here for a while.* Or: *we are all very glad the Duchess is honouring us with her presence* . . .

That would have to do – for all I knew, the Duke might have told her she was welcome here at any time, and it was not my place to say otherwise. I finished my letter at last, and after giving it as usual to Mr Peters for posting with the rest of the Hall's mail, I waited anxiously for the Duke's reply.

'Are you all right, ma'am?' Harriet asked me a few days after the Duchess took up residence. 'It's not my place to say it, what with you being His Grace's ward and everything – but I know you must be upset that the Duchess has come back. Nearly all of us are. But you mustn't let the thought of her make you ill, ma'am, you really mustn't.'

Nearly all of us are. Harriet meant well, but I'd been freshly dismayed by the realisation that most of the staff at Belfield Hall, except for Mr Peters, absolutely loathed the Duchess. Hour by hour I heard about the chaos that was following in the old lady's wake as she established herself in her rooms and proceeded to roam the house, followed by her lady's maid, the prim-faced Miss Stanforth, demanding this, criticising that; summoning Mrs Burdett to her at barely a moment's notice to completely revise the household routines, and undoing the many changes that the new Duke had introduced to make the servants' lives easier.

Within two days of her arrival, the Duchess demanded that oil lamps be put back in the drawing and dining rooms, saying that the new electric lights were never to be turned on in her presence. The Duke had permitted Mrs Burdett to buy vacuum cleaners for each floor, but the Duchess banished them – she could not abide the noise, she said, and besides, the old-fashioned ways were the most thorough. 'After all, what are servants for?' she demanded. No one dared to reply. And so the housemaids had to once more go down on their knees to sweep the carpets with brushes and dustpans, while the footmen had to trim and refill the oil lamps twice each day – a laborious task they'd hoped was over for good.

Then there was the matter of the portrait gallery, up in the east wing. The Duchess, on only her second day in residence, told Mr Peters that there were several portraits of her son – great, heavy oil paintings – which she wanted hung on the main wall of the gallery, where up till now several Stubbs paintings had held pride of place.

These portraits of the dead heir, Lord Charlwood, had been stored in a lumber room, because, I gathered, no one considered them to be very good. But the Duchess insisted, although Mrs Burdett argued strongly against them with Mr Peters. 'They're too heavy,' I heard the housekeeper say to him. 'Far too heavy.'

But Mr Peters ordered Robert and Richard the footmen to put them up, and within days Mrs Burdett was proved right – those paintings fell off in the middle of the night, with a crash that shook the entire east wing. A quantity of plaster came down too, and one of the great chandeliers as well. The whole room had to be closed off, and the remaining furniture and paintings were covered with dust sheets to await the workmen.

'What can have made her even *think* of moving back here?' Harriet sighed aloud to me one day as she tidied my sitting room. 'And Cook is really, really upset, because the old witch – beg pardon, ma'am, the Duchess – is finding fault with her cooking, just like she used to, and poor Cook is in such a fluster that she's talking of handing in her notice. And oh, ma'am, I've asked Robert to bring you up a pot of tea, and some cucumber sandwiches – you like those, don't you? – because everyone's saying how you're really not eating enough to keep a sparrow alive!'

Thus Harriet continued with her friendly chatter, but I could not wait for her to leave. When she had, I paced my room again and gazed out of the window at the wooded hillside in the distance.

I'd foolishly hoped Nathan would ring me, but he didn't, and as each day went by I missed him so badly. I wished I still had my bracelet, to take the pain away. Did it matter so very much that he'd not told me who he was? After all, I'd lied too, and I'd made mistakes; I'd assumed from the beginning that he was a lowly gamekeeper, and that must surely have hurt his pride. That was perhaps why he'd made me beg for his lovemaking – which I missed, so much. The talisman hanging next to my sensitive skin was such a torment to me, reminding me of him every time I moved, that I took it off and locked it away. But even without it, I couldn't forget him. Not for one minute.

I started to punish myself by eating as little as possible, as I had when I was a child. In the vast dining room, in the gloomy light of the oil lamps, I would toy with the food on my plate while the Duchess talked to Miss Kenning about the days when her husband was alive. 'The parties that we used to have here at Belfield Hall were quite magnificent,' she loved to exclaim in her loud voice. 'And the guests! The very cream of society would be here. The Earl of Warwick – he was a dear friend – used to say to me, "No one in the entire country can match the parties you hold at Belfield."'

Then the Duchess would sigh loudly, look at her dinner plate and turn to whichever of the footmen was

unfortunate enough to be standing nearby. 'These vegetables,' she would declare, 'are quite inedible. I cannot
imagine what Cook was thinking of. Take them away –
immediately – and tell her that I said so.'

I would sit silently over my untouched food, although
sometimes one of the footmen I knew, like Robert or
Will, would try to offer me a little more. 'This lamb is
very tender, ma'am,' they would whisper when the
Duchess had turned away from me to lecture Miss
Kenning on the evils of undercooked cauliflower. 'Cook
hoped you might like it.'

'Thank you,' I would reply with a grateful smile,
but as soon as I could, I would push my food aside
and hurry up to my room before the Duchess insisted
that I join her for a game of cards, or to read aloud
to her.

'I really do not know what to make of that girl,' I heard
the Duchess say loudly to Miss Stanforth at the end of
the first week of her stay. 'She has no conversation and
no manners. Well, I believe that dear Beatrice will be
visiting very soon – she might be able to educate her in
polite behaviour. And I suppose we have to make allow-
ances – the unfortunate girl is French, after all . . .'

My life changed completely with her arrival. Even if
I'd decided to swallow my pride and go to Nathan, I no
longer had the freedom to do so, because the Duchess
either wanted me dancing attendance on her in the Hall
or insisted on my company if she chose to go out for an
afternoon drive. One day Eddie drove us to a tea party
at a mansion just outside Oxford, and there the Duchess
and her friends sipped tea and ate tiny cakes while the

hostess quizzed me about Paris, at the same time eyeing my appearance with ill-concealed disdain.

'Oh, Paris,' I heard the younger women exclaim to one another, 'there is nowhere like it for clothes! I was there only last month, and both Worth and Jeanne Paquin have the most marvellous collections this season. I ordered so much, I swear my husband went quite pale when the bill arrived . . .'

They looked at me, in my usual plain dark skirt and blouse with long sleeves to hide the old, pale scars on my wrist, and I saw their lips curl. 'Really,' I heard one of them whisper loudly, 'one would never know that she was the Duke's ward. Such a drab little thing. And at Lady Tolcaster's, you know, where she stayed last summer, there was talk, yes. Something happened there, something quite *unfitting* . . .' After that they moved away, leaving me on my own with my face burning.

I quickly discovered that the Duchess loved card games, and one of the first things she did was to invite the favoured few to the Hall to play bridge. But I only knew bezique, at which I wasn't at all good, and when I suggested dominoes, they all shrieked with laughter.

Most of all, I hated mealtimes, with just the Duchess and me and Miss Kenning in that vast dining room while the footmen stood by – luncheon at noon, and dinner at half past six, always. The Duchess found my companion an oddity, and would simply stare at her as poor Miss Kenning enthused in her nervous way about the Hall.

'I feel extremely privileged,' fluttered Miss Kenning, 'to be living in such a wonderful place.'

'So you are, my dear woman,' the Duchess proclaimed. 'So you are.'

After the meal the Duchess would get rid of Miss Kenning – *lucky her,* I would think – and her gaze would often descend on me. 'To my sitting room, Marianne,' she would pronounce – she *still* couldn't get my name right, I'd begun to think she did it on purpose – and so I would follow her, to sit surrounded by her cats, stitching away at some stupid piece of embroidery and to be honest making a complete pig's ear of it. She loved to talk on and on about all the grand court occasions she'd regularly attended. 'My late husband was a great friend of the King's, you know. We will never see anything as magnificent as his coronation – and everyone told me that my gown was the most exquisite thing *on this earth . . .*'

I learned all this within the first week of her stay. The Duchess also told me again and again about the death of her beloved son Maurice, Lord Charlwood. 'He died leading his men against the enemy,' she lamented. 'So brave. So very brave. My darling son would have made such a fine Duke, with Beatrice at his side—'

Just then one of the Duchess's cats sprang onto my lap, making me accidentally stab my finger with the needle so that a drop of blood fell on my embroidery. 'So clumsy,' scolded the Duchess as I tried to dab at it with a handkerchief. 'You really are so clumsy, Marianne.'

Anxiously I waited to hear from my guardian. Mr Peters brought the mail to the breakfast room every morning at ten, on a silver salver, and I always looked to see if there was anything for me.

'Are you expecting a letter?' the Duchess asked one day as she buttered her toast with her usual crisp precision. 'Your face falls as low as can be whenever Peters brings in the mail and there's nothing for you.'

'My guardian usually writes regularly to me, Your Grace—' I began.

She put down her toast and stared at me. 'Do you realise how *extremely* busy he is, on important government business? Besides, he knows that he can rely on *me* to take care of matters at Belfield Hall.'

I caught my breath. Did she mean that – he knew? I stammered, 'Of course, Your Grace. But I wasn't sure if—'

'Really,' she cut in, 'you should stop concerning yourself with matters that are the responsibility of your elders and betters.'

She busied herself adding sugar to her tea, and I sat there in a daze while Nell and Betsey attended to the various hot dishes that sat on little spirit stoves – bacon, sausages, kedgeree, eggs. Had I got everything so wrong? If so – what a fool I'd made of myself, by writing to tell my guardian that the Duchess was here, if he already knew, and approved! Even so, he would surely write or ring me, especially as, according to Mr Fitzpatrick, he might soon be planning his return.

But I heard nothing from my guardian – and I heard nothing from Nathan either. Even though I'd locked his talisman away in an attempt not to think about him, to my distress I still dreamed of him.

My dreams were so real that in my sleep I thought he was there in my room, standing beside my bed with a calm smile on his beautiful face. In my dreams I was naked, because he'd ordered me to bare myself for him; I would sink to my knees, my head bowed, simply begging for his love, and at last he would come to me and lift me in his strong arms to lay me on the bed and make love to me, thrusting steadily until he spilled his seed deep within me.

You are all mine, he would say in his husky voice. *Mine,* mam'selle.

I would wake from those sweet dreams of longing to find my hand clamped against my sex as my climax pumped through me, and I would be crying out his name.

Chapter Eleven

About three weeks after the Duchess's arrival, she insisted that I accompany her to a garden party at the home of some friends of hers, the Carstairs family, who lived near Oxford. It was a warm afternoon, and I'd realised as soon as we arrived that although the older guests were sitting outside on the terrace under sunshades, most of the young ones were dressed for tennis. The men wore white trousers and shirts; the girls were elegant in long white skirts and lawn blouses.

I was in my usual dark skirt, with a long-sleeved and high-necked blouse that was far too warm for such a pleasant day. My heart sank as the girls surrounded me, clamouring in their high-pitched voices, 'Oh, Madeline – you really *must* play tennis with us!'

Cissie, one of the Carstairs daughters, was even more insistent. 'There's absolutely no getting out of tennis here, my goodness no,' she announced. 'We're all up for it, aren't we, girls? You can borrow an outfit from me, Madeline, and get changed in my room.'

They were all awaiting my reply. 'You'll excuse me, please,' I said. 'You see, I can't play tennis.'

'Oh,' they exclaimed. 'What a beastly shame.' They were openly laughing at me now. 'Come on, girls,' said

Cissie, 'let's see if we can thrash the men at doubles, shall we?'

I was left alone, but the last thing I wanted to do was go and sit on the terrace with the old Duchess and her friends to be quizzed as to why I wasn't on the tennis court with the others. Why I wasn't enjoying myself.

There was a walled rose garden nearby and I went to it seeking shade, for the sun was too bright and the scent of the nearby lavender beds was almost overwhelming. Soon I was out of sight of the house and I thought I'd found solitude, but suddenly I heard footsteps behind me, and I whirled round to see Cissie's older brother, Archie. He wore a striped blazer and white trousers, and as he casually lit a cigarette he was surveying me in a way that instantly set my nerves jangling with alarm.

'So you're not up for tennis then, Miss Dumouriez?' His face was slightly pink from the heat.

'No,' I said hurriedly. 'No, I can't play it very well.'

'Me neither. It's a bore anyway, tennis, if you ask me.' He came a little closer. 'It's pretty dull for you here, isn't it? Do you fancy a drive in my motor?'

'Thank you, but no.' I was already moving away. 'And I really ought to return to the Duchess—'

'I bet you miss Paris,' he said. 'I bet you miss dancing and nightclubs and all the rest. Gay Paree, eh?'

There was a high stone wall behind me separating the rose garden from a shrubbery, and I'd backed up to it. But after tossing his cigarette aside, Archie followed me and put his hands on the wall on either side of me, effectively trapping me.

'You'll have learned a few tricks to please the men in

Paris,' he went on softly. 'I'd rather like you to show me them, *mam'selle*. Word has it that you've – you know, been around a bit, and that's why you were banished from London. But you're having the last laugh, aren't you – because far from having a dull time here, you've taken up with the Mallory fellow. You've just turned my offer down, but you enjoy driving around the country-side in *his* motorcar, don't you?'

I froze. Archie laughed. 'Everyone knows what *he's* out to get. And most of you girls seem eager enough to give it to him.'

Lottie. Lottie must have talked. Or we'd been seen . . . I tried to get away, but he grasped my wrists and pinned them against the wall, hurting me. 'Get off me,' I said. 'Get *off* me.'

If anything his grip tightened. 'Mallory's poor as a church mouse,' he went on. 'But I've heard he's got *some* assets that have you ladies clamouring. I've heard also that you and Mallory have had a bit of a disagreement; a parting of the ways, so to speak. And you must be missing what he provides.' He winked lewdly. 'As it happens, I've got a nice little flat in Oxford. We could drive over there any time, and be private and comfort-able, you know?'

He put his hands on my breasts, grinning.

I tried desperately to push him away, but he was strong; he smelled of cigarettes and stale cologne, and panic was flooding my veins as I struggled and kicked.

But suddenly, someone was wrenching him away from me, making him stagger; it was Nathan. *Nathan was here.*

'You bastard, Carstairs,' he said.

I reeled back against the wall. Archie was pulling himself together, flexing his fists. 'Mallory,' he sneered. 'You dare to touch *me*?'

Nathan did more than that – he punched him on the jaw. Archie stumbled to the ground but somehow struggled up, blood spilling from his lip, and launched himself at Nathan, only for Nathan to hit him again. The two men fought with a ferocity that frightened me – Nathan was so much the stronger and fitter that I really feared he might kill Archie. I ran towards Nathan, trying to pull him back. 'Nathan. Stop—'

'Stay out of this.' I scarcely recognised Nathan's hard voice as he shrugged me off. A few moments later Archie was on the ground, gasping for breath, and Nathan stood back from him, his eyes blazing. 'I'll let you go for now, Carstairs,' he said. 'But if you touch Miss Dumouriez again, I'll make sure everyone knows about your taste for middle-aged whores in Oxford.'

Archie slowly stood up and straightened his jacket, his expression dark with hatred. He took one last look at me and limped away. I was shaking. 'Nathan. What are you *doing* here? And Archie, he'll—'

But then I broke off, because Nathan was reaching for me. 'Archie will keep quiet,' he said. 'He's a rat. And I'm a guest here – Cissie invited me. She seems to have a *tendre* for me, although normally I wouldn't have dreamed of attending. But then I heard – that *you* might be coming.' He was slowly drew me into his arms. 'I've missed you, *mam'selle*.'

He was tracing one finger down my face, and my breasts were already aching for his touch. 'You've lost weight,' he went on gravely. 'You've not been ill, have you?'

'No. No, I'm fine. But—' *I've missed you. I've missed you so.* I nestled into him and he held me very tight.

'Thank God I came,' he said. 'I could have punched Archie Carstairs to kingdom come.'

I was gazing up at him, hungrily drinking in his lovely lean jaw, his hard cheekbones, his tantalising, sensual mouth – *and remembering the things his mouth had done to me . . .* 'Nathan,' I said, 'he knows about us. I don't know how. But he might talk.'

'He'll keep quiet, if he's any idea of what's good for him.'

I shivered slightly, remembering Nathan's speed and strength in that fight. 'That thing you said, about him and middle-aged whores – was it true?'

He laughed. 'He keeps a mistress in Oxford who's *at least* thirty.'

'So old!' I smiled.

'There's more. She pretends to be his nursemaid, apparently, and spoon-feeds him baby food . . .'

I pulled a face and put my hands over my ears. 'I don't want to hear another thing.'

'I'm not surprised.' He grinned, but then he looked serious again. 'I had to come here, Madeline. I had to see you. I couldn't stop thinking about you. I couldn't stop hoping that you would forgive me. I've missed you.'

Oh, Nathan.

'And,' he said, 'there's something else.' He reached into his jacket pocket and pulled out a small velvet box. 'I've got your bracelet.'

My mouth was dry. 'You told me that you sold it. You gave me the money—'

'That was my money.' He was looking at me intently. 'And I asked the jeweller in Oxford – the one who'd valued it for me – to find out more about it if he could, when he next went to London. He's just paid a visit there, and he couldn't wait to tell me the news. Did you know, Madeline, to whom your bracelet once belonged?'

'I asked you to sell it.' I'd gone cold. 'I *told* you to sell it . . .'

He ignored me. 'It was made over a hundred years ago,' he said flatly, 'and its most recent owner – apart from *you* – was the Marquis de Valery. Now, I've heard of him. He was one of the most notorious high-livers and lechers in Paris before the war. What were you doing with that man's bracelet? Why were you using it to harm yourself?'

Then he saw my face. Quickly he drew me to a nearby stone seat and held me. 'Oh, Madeline, it doesn't matter. Nothing matters, except that I've missed you. Oh, God, I've missed you, *mam'selle*, so much.' He tilted my face up to his, and with his clean handkerchief he wiped away the tears that I'd tried so hard not to let him see. 'Some day,' he went on, 'you must tell me – *everything*.'

He rocked me in his arms until at last I was able to look up at him. 'Will you keep the bracelet for me, Nathan?'

'Of course,' he said, putting the box in his pocket again. 'Of course.'

'And I'll pay you back the money you gave me for it. You *must* let me pay you—'

'Some day,' he interrupted. 'But now, I want to drive you straight to my cottage. I want to kiss you, and make love to you, and do all sorts of deliciously unspeakable things to you . . .'

He was pressing kisses to my wrist and all my longings for him flooded me, making resistance impossible. 'Nathan. *Nathan*,' I said, trying to pull away, 'I came with the Duchess. I have to go back to her.'

He let go of me. 'I heard that she'd moved in. Are you coping?'

I shrugged. 'I'll survive.'

'As bad as that? And she's here *now*? In that case, I'll come and say hello to the old witch. That's what they call her, you know.'

I almost laughed. 'I do know. But is it wise to go and join them all, when you've just knocked Archie Carstairs almost senseless?'

He grinned. 'I'll do it again, if he so much as looks at you.' Then he became more serious. 'Look. You've already said that there's gossip about us, so it's stupid to pretend that we don't know each other. Let's try to act as if we're just friends.' His eyes danced wickedly. 'Let's try to forget that all I really want to do is drag you off to the bushes, and kiss you all over until you can hardly move, and—'

'Nathan.' I was still smiling, but his expression was completely serious as he cupped my face in his hands.

'Madeline,' he said. 'You're so good for me, *mam'selle*,

that I can't do without you – it's as simple as that. Do you promise to come to my cottage again?'

I curled myself in his arms. 'Yes. Oh, yes.'

'And some day,' he went on gravely, 'you'll tell me *everything*?'

I hesitated. 'Some day.' But I hoped that day would never come.

We walked together to where the older guests were gathered on the terrace, drinking champagne and eating bowls of hothouse strawberries. Already he was moving away from me, to greet some people he knew. But he nodded to me and mouthed, 'Some day, Madeline.'

Nathan stayed on for a while at the Carstairs' tennis party, and I realised how much speculative gossip his appearance had caused. 'So rare,' I heard the older ones whispering, 'for Mr Mallory to accept an invitation nowadays.'

'It's Cissie's doing,' someone else pronounced. 'Dear Cissie is sweet on him. Foolish of her, of course; but he *is* a remarkably handsome fellow, there's no denying.'

The Duchess joined in at this point. 'He's virtually destitute, and he's a socialist, like his father. Good heavens, I never expected to see someone of his sort invited here. It's thanks to men like him that we're seeing such a decline in standards everywhere.'

I had just brought the Duchess her tea and her parasol, and I sat silently beside her. *Nathan came here because of me,* I kept reminding myself. *Because of me.* And he'd hit Archie Carstairs for me. It was impetuous of him, it was foolishly reckless, but I was dancing inside. *I'll do it again,* he'd vowed, *if he so much as looks at you.*

Once the strawberries had all been eaten, someone suggested a croquet game and Nathan came over to ask me if I would join in. 'You have played croquet, haven't you, *mam'selle?*'

'Never,' I said honestly.

'Never? Then let me show you how.'

I was all too aware of many pairs of eyes focusing narrowly on us while he demonstrated the rudiments, standing behind me and putting his hands over mine as he showed me how to use the mallet. I heard him murmur, 'I want you, *mam'selle*. Now.' My own desire churned deep in my belly, and I thought, *People must see. They must surely know, what we are to one another.*

Cissie Carstairs came back from the tennis courts just then, looking hot and cross – I heard someone say that she and her doubles partner had been soundly trounced. She wandered over to watch the croquet and I heard her mutter to a friend, as Nathan gave me yet more guidance, 'No wonder the French girl told us she couldn't play tennis. She's found herself a far more entertaining proposition. But her *clothes*! So unspeakably drab . . .'

I think Nathan heard her too. 'Your turn now, Madeline,' he said calmly. 'And please smile. You look so sweet when you smile.' The wicked twinkle in his eyes sent sparks of sensual delight flying through me, because that look said, *Take no notice of any of them. You are mine.*

For the next week, we met every day. The Duchess developed a cold immediately after the tennis party and took to her bed, causing a great commotion as the servants hurried up and down to her room with hot lemon potions and broths. The doctor called every morning and afternoon, and Mr Peters commented gravely to all and sundry on Her Grace's progress. This, for me, was heaven-sent. This meant that I could be with Nathan almost whenever I pleased. Miss Kenning retreated, with a sigh of relief, to her books and her room, while I was able to slip out of a side door and up to Nathan's cottage. We walked, we talked, but most of all we made love.

The first time we met after the tennis party, I came to his cottage wearing the talisman. He'd already started to undress me, but when he saw it hanging from its thong around my waist his face darkened.

'Madeline,' he said in a low voice. 'You don't have to wear that any more.'

I froze. 'Why?'

He hesitated. 'Nearly losing you – *missing* you . . .' He spread out his hands and shook his head. 'I've made mistakes. I've done things I regretted, and I want to make amends.'

'You regret the talisman?' I whispered.

He drew his hand across his forehead. 'I'm not sure how to explain. I suppose I was testing myself. Testing *you,* even.'

I grasped his hands and kissed them urgently, then I sank to my knees. I wore my stockings and garters; otherwise I was naked before him. I tried to say light-heartedly, 'And did I pass the test?'

He was silent, his jaw clenched, and my heart was thudding with apprehension. With fear, almost. *No. No, please, I cannot lose him now . . .* Swiftly I pointed to where the talisman lay between my thighs. 'Please, Nathan.' I could hear an urgency in my voice that almost frightened me. 'Make me yours with it. I *want* to be yours.'

He must have heard that urgency too. 'Very well,' he said slowly. 'It's your choice.' But that darkness was in his eyes again, and his teeth were clenched as he carried me to his bed, laid me there and eased the talisman slowly into me, in and out until I was groaning with need. Then he unfastened the leather thong and flung it, with the talisman across the room and made love to me almost savagely, thrusting into me again and again until I rose to meet him and both our bodies were sweat-sheened. I almost felt that I needed to shield myself from the look of burning possession in his eyes.

The rest of our week was happier. One hot afternoon, we collected some wild strawberries in the woods, and back at his cottage he stripped me bare, arranged the fruits on my breasts and belly and nibbled them from me one by one, his tongue licking and savouring. I did the same to him until we were messy and laughing and so aroused, and after we'd made love we both went to wash ourselves under the pump in his yard, shivering with delight under the stream of cold water.

Afterwards he helped me to dry myself.

'You still smell of strawberries,' he murmured, nuzzling his lips against my breasts. 'Delicious.' Then he gazed down at me, his expression suddenly more serious. 'Madeline. I realise you have secrets from your past that you don't want to share. But some day soon I hope you'll trust me enough to tell me whatever needs to be told. Do you promise?'

I'd gone very still. Then I said, with an effort at lightness, 'I think I've already told you quite enough.'

'I don't think so,' he said.

I tried to keep my tone casual. 'Believe me, Nathan. You really, really don't want to know any more.'

'I do,' he said gravely. 'For *your* sake.'

I wiggled my finger in his face, I pulled him to me again and I delicately licked a stray piece of strawberry from his beautiful bronzed chest. 'Ah, but I like to keep my air of mystery, *monsieur le garde-chasse,*' I said.

I think that Harriet suspected something, but all that she said, as she laid out my clothes one morning, was: 'We're all pleased to see you looking so much better, ma'am.'

I visited the Duchess in her stiflingly hot bedroom one morning after the doctor had been. She lay propped up against her pillows, swathed in a bedjacket and night-cap, with two cats curled on the counterpane. I offered my condolences, and muttered some vague reply when she asked me what I had been doing; at which she shook her head impatiently.

'Well, I must say, Marianne,' she declared, 'there's little point in you coming to visit me, since you're as quiet as a church mouse!'

I hurried away as soon as I could, because I was due to meet Nathan.

I realised around that time that he'd begun to work on his old house, as he'd often talked of doing, and one afternoon, while the Duchess was still bed-bound, he drove me up there. 'I can at least try to keep the rain out,' he explained as we stood in the courtyard gazing up at the roof tiles he told me he'd repaired. 'But there's still so much to do.'

'Nathan, let me help you.' I grasped his arm.

'You? Madeline, that's sweet, but—'

'I can! This afternoon! I can sweep up the leaves that have blown inside, and I can get rid of the spiders' webs, and all sorts of things. After all, they say many hands make easy work.'

'You mean many hands make *light*—'

'Oh, it's the same thing,' I interrupted crossly. 'Please let me! Please! With the Duchess in bed, I needn't be back at the Hall – oh, for hours!'

Laughingly he agreed, so I set to work, though every so often he would stop to kiss me, exclaiming aloud when he saw the cobwebs in my hair. 'I've made a skivvy of you, *mam'selle*.'

'A – skivvy.' I pronounced it carefully, then peeped up at him from under my lashes. 'Whatever it means, I like being your skivvy, Nathan.'

He laughed and swung me around in his arms.

He'd brought a hamper of bread and cheese and lemonade, and after a while we went and sat in the garden to eat, while the dogs chased rabbits from an overgrown vegetable patch and Nathan flicked through a newspaper. I leaned against his shoulder and saw that he was reading about the general election that might have to be called later that year. Nathan had already told me that the Labour Party stood a chance of vastly increasing the number of seats it held in Parliament.

'The Labour Party. It's led by – Mr Ramsay MacDonald,' I said, proud of myself for remembering the name. 'He believes in socialism, and he was always opposed to the war.'

He was surprised. 'How do you know?'

When I explained to him that I'd been regularly studying the newspapers in the Duke's library, he was pleased. 'Just remember never to mention Mr MacDonald's name in the Duchess's hearing,' he reminded me. He enthused about the Labour Party's beliefs that everyone should be entitled to a job with a living wage, and I loved the way he talked to me as if I were his equal, and not a foolish girl from Paris whose mother was a whore and whose past was – unspeakable. I adored those precious few days with him while the Duchess was ill: talking with him, being with him and making love deliciously whenever and wherever our desire overcame us. I was more than foolish; I pretended to myself that my happiness would never end.

On the sixth day of the Duchess's illness, as I hurried up to my room at about half past five to get ready for dinner, Harriet was waiting – to tell me that the Duchess was demanding to see me.

I'd been with Nathan, of course; I was still glowing from his lovemaking, but suddenly I was cold.

'She's in a bit of a temper, ma'am,' Harriet warned me. 'Her Grace is a mite feverish, Mrs Burdett thinks. And she's been looking through her blessed photographs again . . .'

I hurried to her rooms, thinking, *Nathan. Someone has told her about Nathan and me.* But no; as Harriet had said, she had all those photograph albums around her, she was sitting up in her bed, and as soon as she saw me she began shaking her head and dabbing her handkerchief to her eyes. 'My son. He should have been the Duke. And instead, we have that – *upstart.* That terrible, terrible upstart, your guardian, Lord Ashley . . .'

I reeled back, but she'd only just begun. I don't know why she'd chosen that particular day to unleash her venom, but the photographs had clearly helped to trigger it, and I think she was hardly aware of my presence, as she went on in her high-pitched voice about how the Duke – Lord Ashley – wasn't really the heir, but a changeling.

'He was a coward in the war,' she said, 'he fled England to avoid conscription. And as to his tastes in women . . . He took up with someone called Sophie Davis, who once worked below stairs *here*, and became a dancer and a common singer. If he married her and she bore him an heir, it would mean that the son of a scullery maid would become the next Duke. Unthinkable. *Unthinkable!*'

At last she stopped and waved me away, and I left her room still reeling. How could she say the Duke had been a coward in the war when he'd flown aircraft behind enemy lines and had been badly burnt? She hated the Duke, hated him. And yet she had implied that he was quite happy for her to stay here!

I stopped in the corridor, my heart beating fast. It was five long weeks since I'd written to my guardian – and yet *still* I'd received no reply from him. I thought, *I must ring him*. After hurrying to fetch his telephone number from my room, I pulled up on my way back downstairs, remembering that Mr Peters had an almost miraculous habit of knowing whenever anyone drew near the telephone in his office. But there was another telephone in the library; I set off there instead, but just as I was approaching the door I saw Mr Peters, coming along the corridor towards me.

'I believe dinner is about to be served, ma'am,' he said.

I turned from him without speaking. I thought again of my letter, which I'd been forced to entrust to Mr Peters, and wondered – *Had the Duke ever received it? Had it even been posted?* Did he have any idea at all that the Duchess was here?

Chapter Twelve

'Lady Beatrice is coming here?' I repeated the next evening to Harriet. 'Do you mean it? That she's actually going to stay here at Belfield Hall?'

Harriet had arrived to lay out my clothes for dinner as usual, but she was flustered and upset. In the servants' hall they'd only just heard the news, she told me. 'Her Ladyship stayed here before, ma'am. Before the new Duke arrived. And she and the Duchess together . . .' She shuddered.

I was still shaken by my suspicions about the Duchess after her outburst of vitriol last night. To make matters worse, Nathan had told me only this afternoon that he had to go to London to try to raise some money to save his estate: 'Otherwise it will all have to go,' he said flatly.

'The house too? But you've been working so hard on it,' I'd exclaimed. 'You can't even *think* of selling it!'

His expression was grave. 'I might have to, if I can't raise the money. But I've made all the appropriate appointments in the city, over the next two weeks.'

'You mean it might take two weeks, to simply *talk* about saving your estate? But—' I cut myself short and tried to calm myself. 'I don't believe you,' I teased. 'I think you're going to London for wild women and parties, Nathan Mallory.'

He laughed and held me close. 'My days of wild women and parties are over for good.' He took my hand and kissed it. 'I hope you know that you're the only wild woman I'll ever want.'

We were at his cottage, and I was naked, in his arms – my favourite place to be. 'I shall wear your talisman,' I promised. I still wore it, despite what he'd said earlier, and now I drew the wooden peg softly down my belly and over the brand he'd imprinted on my skin. It was fainter now, but the falcon's head was still identifiable. 'It will remind me all the time that I'm yours, Nathan.'

But a shaft of anxiety pierced me, because his eyes had gone very dark, and for a moment I was afraid of him, as I used to be. 'You don't have to wear it, or use it,' he said quietly at last. 'I've tried to tell you that. I'd rather you waited – for me.'

'Untie it, then,' I breathed. 'Untie it and I'll lock it away – but don't make me wait too long.' He did so and I put the wooden peg carefully down beside my clothes; then I straddled his hips and caressed the tip of his engorged phallus with my fingers, murmuring his name as I began to guide him deep, deep inside me. 'I want to give you some moments to remember me by,' I whispered.

He laughed, and pulled my head down so he could kiss my lips. 'My wild woman,' he breathed.

But Nathan had left, as he'd said he would; I'd locked my talisman away in my chest of drawers, and Lady Beatrice moved into Belfield Hall, filling the best set of guest rooms with her seemingly endless luggage from London. Of course, the Duchess was delighted at her arrival, and rose from her sickbed quite swiftly. Later that day, I was summoned to the Duchess's sitting room to take afternoon tea with them both.

'Dear Madeline!' Lady Beatrice exclaimed as I entered the room. 'Ash's charming little French ward!'

She proceeded to talk to me pleasantly about Paris, displaying her knowledge of its theatres and its exclusive *modistes* – she clearly went there regularly. But then she drew me aside from the Duchess, who was fussing over one of her favourite cats, and she said, with that smile of hers, 'If you go up to your room, Madeline, you'll find that I've got a surprise for you.'

The scent she wore, of musk roses and patchouli, temporarily overwhelmed me. I was terribly afraid that we now had two interlopers at Belfield Hall, and that my guardian had no knowledge of Beatrice's presence either, even though she called him by the name his friends used – *Ash*. 'What kind of surprise?' I asked her slowly.

'Go and see,' she encouraged, nodding towards the door.

So I hurried up to my room.

And Dervla was there. Dervla, my friend from the convent, whose mischief – and my part in trying to defend her from the consequences – had got me expelled. 'Oh, Maddie,' she cried, running to me with sparkling eyes. 'How absolutely wonderful to see you again. I'm Lady Beatrice's new maid!'

A word, now, about my friend Dervla. Barely a year older than I was, she had shown me great kindness at the convent at a time when I'd been terribly unhappy.

Her parents were Irish but lived in Paris, and as devout Catholics they'd sent her to the convent in Nantes because they'd wanted her to become a nun.

A nun? *Dervla?* 'Darling Maddie,' I remembered her laughing to me once. 'I'd rather be on my knees sweeping the floors of this hateful convent than praying like those shrivelled-up holy sisters, and that's a fact.' Between us, we'd driven the nuns to distraction with our mischief. Now here she was, at Belfield Hall, and we began to laugh and chatter as we used to in the old days, though after a few minutes of this I glanced at the clock on the mantel. 'Won't Lady Beatrice mind you spending so long with me, Dervla?'

'Oh, no. Bless you, Maddie, Her Ladyship knows that you and I are old friends.' And she explained, in her easy Irish way, how after I'd left the convent to return to my mother's house in Paris, she ran away, just a few months later. 'I couldn't bear to live there any longer, and that's a fact!' she declared. 'And I wasn't going back to my mother and father in Paris, who'd wanted me to be a nun – oh, no, I'd had enough of all that, so I thought – I'll go to London! I worked in a smart hotel for a while. But then I took it into my head that I would like to be a lady's maid, so I went to an employment agency – they are all the thing in London now – and I was hired by Lady Beatrice almost immediately. Don't you think she's beautiful?'

I said that I thought she was very elegant.

'Yes, indeed! I was just an under-maid at first, but I've learned so much – Lady Beatrice is very kind. When she told me she was planning to come and stay at Belfield Hall, and she mentioned the Duke of Belfield's ward

– well, I could hardly breathe for excitement, because I realised it was *you*! Oh, I was so excited at the thought of seeing you again, and Lady Beatrice was pleased too. "A happy reunion of old friends," she said. Now, tell me everything you've been doing, will you, darling? Lady Beatrice has said I can have a *whole hour* with you before I need to go and dress her, though dressing her, I tell you, is a treat – her clothes are so lovely, she gets them all from Paris . . .'

And so she chattered on.

The other servants took to Dervla quickly. 'She's a sight better than the maid Lady Beatrice brought with her when she last stayed,' Harriet told me. 'Margaret, she was called. Thank goodness she's not here – she gave us all the shivers.'

Dervla I recognised as an ally, but Lady Beatrice was another matter – I did not trust her at all. I worried over whether I ought to write to my guardian again, since I was sure that any phone calls I made would be overheard; but the thought of having to give my letter to Mr Peters to post stopped me in my tracks. I was starting to feel afraid, and very alone. At least we were no longer visited by Lottie Towndrow. I asked Mrs Burdett if Lottie was likely to be here again, and she answered, 'Oh, the Oxford miss? She's gone off round England giving lectures. She's a bit too clever for her own good, that one.' That was a rare hint of indiscretion from the ever-correct Mrs Burdett.

One of the worst things about Beatrice's presence was that I was forced into local society again. She had pronounced to the Duchess during dinner that the Duke would most likely want to present me in London next spring. 'But Madeline will be totally unprepared!' Beatrice continued, as if I were not there. 'She really should grasp any opportunities to socialise – she leads far too quiet an existence.'

'I don't mind being quiet,' I said. 'Really.'

But Lady Beatrice would have none of it, and immediately made arrangements for Eddie to drive the Duchess and me to a summer tea party the next day, and the day after that to a charity event in Oxford. More invitations rolled in, and at first Lady Beatrice accompanied us; but after a week of this, she was more than likely to make some last-minute excuse and go off by herself in her lovely blue sports car.

She had acquaintances of her own, I gathered, in the neighbourhood, and one particular friend – I knew he was an aristocrat, nothing more – had a country mansion in Newbridge, only a few miles away. A week after Beatrice's arrival at Belfield Hall, this friend drove over to dine with us – and the minute I saw him, I felt cold with dismay.

His name was Lord Sydhurst, and I'd met him last summer in London. 'Miss Dumouriez,' he said, making his bow first to the Duchess, then coming towards me. 'How delightful to meet you again.'

There were, I think, about twelve of us at that dinner, since both the Duchess and Lady Beatrice had invited other guests. But all that I remember was Lord Sydhurst, watching me from further down the vast dining table with his pale, hooded eyes, and as soon as the final course came to an end I was on my feet.

'You'll join us, of course, for cards?' the Duchess said to me pointedly.

'No, Your Grace.' I couldn't wait to get away. 'If you'll all excuse me, I feel a little tired.'

Lord Sydhurst's mouth curled in a slight smile. 'You probably find cards a tedious pastime after Paris and London,' he remarked.

My cheeks burning, I tried to respond but couldn't, and I fled up to my room, hating myself for my cowardice and hating *him*. For Lord Sydhurst was the reason why I'd exiled myself to Belfield Hall, and now my room no longer seemed my sanctuary.

After my arrival in London in the spring of last year, my guardian had pressed me to stay with him in his Hertford Street mansion, but I'd refused – I had already realised that my presence there would be a burden to him and his Sophie. So I had pretended that I was keen to socialise with young people and to have fun. 'I've heard so much about London,' I told him, feigning eagerness. 'The entertainments, and the parties.'

'Of course,' my guardian had said. 'Though I'm hardly the person to chaperone you, since I know so little of London society. But I do have an acquaintance, Lady Tolcaster, whose daughters are about your age. And I think she would be delighted to let you join her family for this summer's social events.'

More than that, Lady Tolcaster insisted that I and Miss Kenning should immediately move in with her, offering us accommodation in her Mayfair house that was almost as large and splendid as the Duke's, but soon I discovered – as I'd told Nathan – that her two daughters hated me. I'd also realised why Lady Tolcaster was so eager to have me as her guest – she was hoping to ensnare the Duke as her son-in-law.

The unpleasantness of the two daughters and the machinations of the mother made my time there unhappy. The Duke sensed my disquiet, I think, since he reminded me regularly that I was welcome to return to nearby Hertford Street any time I wished, although I always declared, with a smile, 'Oh, no, Your Grace. I'm really quite happy here.'

But I wasn't. I attended parties and dances, and the Duke had bestowed on me a more than generous allowance, so I felt obliged, as I've said, to buy myself new clothes and lingerie. But in reality I was simply determined to endure my time there as best as I could.

One night at a reception the Tolcaster girls were particularly unpleasant to me, whispering to all their friends that the Duke had banished me from his house because he wanted to be alone there with Sophie – his scullery maid, they openly called her. I'd been so angry that I'd burst in on their little group, saying heatedly, 'You are telling lies. My guardian is good and kind, and his Sophie is far more beautiful and far more of a lady than any of you will ever be.'

A crowd had gathered by then, and amongst them was Lord Sydhurst. He'd stepped forward and said, 'Miss Dumouriez.' I'd whirled round on him, my colour high. 'Just a word, my dear,' he went on. 'I don't really think it's wise, to defend the Duke's whore in polite society—'

He had broken off then, because I'd flown at him. In full view of everyone at that gathering, I knocked his glass of wine from his hand, and it spilled all down his silk waistcoat. He walked off abruptly, to tell Lady

Tolcaster that earlier in the evening I'd made a shame-less attempt to seduce him, and the result was inevitable: Her Ladyship summoned me to her parlour and told me, with her phial of *sal volatile* close to hand, that she wouldn't have me in her household for a moment longer. 'Not even if the Duke of Belfield himself were to make it a condition of offering for my dearest Eleanor, or my sweet Margery – never!' she declared.

When my guardian heard of my banishment from the Tolcaster household, he'd given me every chance to put to him my side of the story, but since that would have meant telling him what the gossips were saying about Sophie I made no attempt to defend myself, and instead said that I'd had quite enough of London.

'I would like to go to Belfield Hall,' I told him earnestly. 'I really, really would.' And so I travelled to Oxfordshire with Miss Kenning, but now the unwelcome reappear-ance of Lord Sydhurst filled me with new trepidation. To my dismay, the fair-haired aristocrat became a regular visitor to Belfield Hall, and one afternoon when he'd contrived to get me alone, he said, 'It's so interesting that our paths should cross again, Miss Dumouriez. I've often thought it was a little drastic of the Duke to banish you here. Presumably he had no idea that at Lady Tolcaster's, you tried so spiritedly to defend his whore, Sophie—'

My fists were clenched. 'Don't call her that. Don't.'

'Very well,' he said. 'After all, you should know all about whores. Since your mother was one.'

I think I stopped breathing. I simply stared at him, my heart pounding against my ribs, as he strolled from the room. *I met your mother in Paris. Her name was*

Celine Dumouriez. Like you, she was beautiful. Like you, she was a whore. Did he send that letter? If he'd been to Paris before the war – if he'd known my mother – what else did he know?

Soon after that, Lord Sydhurst returned to his nearby home. But that night, alone in my bedroom, I got my pistol out again.

The very next day my guardian rang me. It was Mrs Burdett who hurried up to fetch me to the telephone; I think that she had deliberately bustled Mr Peters away on some pretext or other, so that I should have some privacy. I hoped she didn't guess how hard my heart was beating as I picked up the phone.

'I thought I'd better ring,' the Duke said, 'since I've not heard from you for a little while.'

His voice was as kind as ever, and my breath caught in my throat. 'You didn't get my letter?'

There was a brief silence. 'No, Madeline. No. I've not had anything from you for several weeks.'

I looked quickly round: no Peters, no Lady Beatrice, no Miss Stanforth. 'I wrote to tell you,' I said, 'about the Duchess being here, and Lady Beatrice—'

'Stop,' he ordered. 'Repeat what you've just said, will you?'

So I did. He was calm. He appeared unperturbed. But he *didn't know*. He'd not received my letter, and he didn't know. He talked to me carefully and explained that I wasn't to worry. His responsibilities in Ireland were almost concluded, he said, and he was already preparing to return home – then he would be able to deal with everything. 'As long as you're all right, Madeline,' he said. 'As long as you are keeping well.'

'Yes,' I breathed. 'Yes, I'm well, thank you. And – take care, Your Grace.'

I put the phone down, my hand trembling. He hadn't known. *He hadn't known.*

Dervla visited my rooms later that day. She was quite besotted with Lady Beatrice – indeed, her eyes sparkled when she talked about Beatrice's latest clothes, and her knowledge of the fashionable world. I asked Dervla again if Lady Beatrice minded her spending time with me. 'Oh, goodness, no,' she exclaimed. 'She realises how lonely you've been, Maddie, and she's glad that we're friends. She's so kind like that. So generous.'

Later I escaped from the house to walk around the garden, missing Nathan, worrying about my guardian and the interlopers in his house. Nathan should be back from London within the next few days, and after that, the Duke would arrive from Ireland – but then what would happen? I couldn't deceive my guardian about Nathan, but I couldn't bear to give Nathan up either. I returned to my room, and fresh shock rippled through me, because Dervla was there again.

Normally, of course, as a lady's maid she wore a plain print dress; but now she was pirouetting in front of my full-length mirror in an emerald-green gown with a beaded bodice and slim shoulder straps. Her rather unruly blonde hair had been skilfully cropped – it must have been done in the short time since I'd last seen her – and her face was painted with make-up.

I didn't understand. As I came in she spun round. 'Maddie – I thought you might like to see me, in this simply perfect dress!'

'Where did you get it?' I felt rather cold.

She didn't notice my coolness; she was still preening herself. 'Oh, Lady Beatrice was amusing herself by dressing me up. And she brought in her own hairstylist and told her exactly how to cut my hair – isn't it lovely?'

I could hardly answer. *Lady Beatrice – again.*

'And look, just look what Her Ladyship has given me!' Dervla was slipping down a shoulder strap to show me an expensive brassiere in pale cream satin with lace edging; then she lifted her skirt high to display matching panties and silk stockings. 'Lady Beatrice knows how I love pretty things, and she enjoys watching me dressing up. Well, you've seen me in all my glory. Now I'll go and take the dress off again – but oh, I do love it so!' She almost danced from my room.

I stared after her. *Dervla. Oh, Dervla, what are you doing?*

Later that day, Lady Beatrice sent *me* some of her evening gowns. Dervla, wearing her old print dress again, brought them to me. 'She doesn't want them any more, Maddie,' Dervla explained. 'She says it's not done in London, to wear the same thing more than once, so she thought that you might like them.'

I put all the gowns that Lady Beatrice had offered me to the back of my wardrobe. But Dervla was irrepressible – for example, the next morning she burst into my sitting room with a magazine that they'd all been reading in the servants' hall. 'There's an article about Sophie, who used to be the Duke's mistress!' she told me excitedly. 'You'll have met her, won't you, before she left London last autumn? She's famous, Maddie, she's a huge success in New York – and look, Robert's lent me her latest record. He bought it in Oxford, on his afternoon off . . .' Quickly she put it on my gramophone and sang along to it, moving to it as if she were on stage.

> *Now listen to me, sweetheart, 'cause since I met you*
> *My friends all say I'm crazy, don't know what to do.*
> *Can't sleep at night, can't think, can't dance,*
> *Just wander around with my mind in a trance.*
> *All I'm thinking is, Where are you?*
> *'Cause I'm breathless – just breathless for you.*

'Thank goodness she sings better than you do,' I said wryly when she'd finished. She giggled and put it on again so we could dance together. But something about the song brought a lump to my throat and Dervla must have seen it, because she took one look at my face and hurried to turn it off.

'Oh, Maddie,' she exclaimed. 'Maddie, darling, what's wrong?'

'Nothing at all,' I said quickly. 'Put it on again.' And we danced, and sang the chorus together, giggling when we forgot the words.

But I couldn't stop thinking about my letter to my guardian that had gone astray; about Beatrice and the Duchess taking over the Hall, and Lord Sydhurst. I missed Nathan more each day – and I was still trying to pretend that I wasn't desperately afraid.

Chapter Thirteen

That evening, the Duchess and Lady Beatrice drove over to a dinner party at Lord Sydhurst's house, where they were planning to stay overnight. I had been invited too, but I'd quickly made some excuse and had told the staff that I would take my evening meal in my sitting room, where Harriet brought it to me half an hour later.

'I'm sorry for the delay, ma'am. But Mrs Burdett's taken the night off to stay with a friend in Oxford, seeing as Her Grace and Lady Beatrice are away – so everything's at sixes and sevens, so to speak.' She drew my curtains shut, piled more logs on the fire despite the June warmth, then left; but my meal of overcooked lamb cutlets sat untouched, for I'd started to feel the old darkness, the old fear overwhelming me.

You are a wicked child, Madeline, and you deserve this. You offer too great a temptation.

I tried to read for a while, but at around ten o'clock I suddenly got to my feet again, because I could hear music. Where was it coming from? The ground floor? The basement? But who . . . ? I opened my window and listened. The faint melody of 'Breathless For You' was floating up to me. Someone was singing the words, shrilly and out of tune – and I thought I knew who it was.

I hurried downstairs and, as I drew nearer to the servants' hall, the music grew louder. The door was half open, the big table had been pushed into a corner, and Sophie's lovely song was being played on a gramophone in the corner while Dervla sang raucously over it, almost shouting the words – and she was wearing that emerald-green dress. My breath hitched in my throat.

The lights were turned down low. Some bottles of wine and half-empty glasses stood on the table, and from the way that Dervla was singing I guessed she was drunk. Robert, Richard and Eddie had pulled chairs up and were watching her avidly, because she was wriggling seductively out of that dress, pulling down the shoulder straps to show her flimsy brassiere, then lifting up the beaded skirt to show her stocking tops, before shrugging the dress off completely and letting it slide to the floor.

Apart from her stockings and high-heeled shoes, she was only in her underwear now – that brassiere and her lace-edged panties. The male servants were cheering. 'A shilling, Dervla,' Richard called. 'A shilling to take your stockings off.' He threw a coin into Eddie's peaked cap, which lay upside down on the floor in front of her and already glinted with silver.

Dervla gave him a flirtatious glance and did a few steps to the music. 'One stocking,' she said, wagging her finger at him. 'Only one.' She undid her suspenders and rolled one silk stocking carefully down her leg, with that teasing smile always on her face. Most of the housemaids were watching her too by now; some of them, like Betsey and Harriet, were laughing, but others, like Nell, looked upset. While Dervla waved her stocking in the air, Richard drank back his glass of wine and stood unsteadily to hold up another coin. 'Here's another shilling, lass, if you sing us that tune you sang before.'

Dervla gave a mocking curtsey and began. It was a version of a song that I'd heard once before, being roared out in the billiards room at an unusually lively London party to which Lady Tolcaster had briefly taken her daughters and me, only to haul us away again very quickly. Dervla sang it while she walked to and fro in her underwear, her hands on her hips, twirling now and then to show her almost-naked figure, while the footmen clapped and cheered.

> *Good evening, my name's Sophie, and I am Belfield's tart.*
> *I might be just a servant, but I'm the Duke's sweetheart.*
> *The moment that I saw him, my heart began to knock,*
> *Because, you see, it's known to all, he's got a massive—*

Suddenly a door crashed open at the far end of the servants' hall and Will charged in, his fists clenched, his face dark. 'How dare you!' he was shouting. 'How bloody dare you. None of you lot are fit to clean Sophie's shoes.'

Nell ran to try and stop him. 'Will. Oh, Will, dearest—'

Will pushed poor Nell aside. Someone – I think it was Eddie – made jeering noises and Richard called, 'Give it a rest, Will. Still dreaming of screwing the Duke's whore yourself?'

Will hauled Richard from his chair and hit him. Richard tried to hit him back and within moments pandemonium reigned in the servants' hall. Will, stronger than any of them and sober too, was attempting to get at Richard again, but the others were holding him back. Nell was still crying out, 'Oh, Will. Oh, Will,' and was reaching for him, but Will was pushing her away. 'Leave me alone,' he growled, 'damn you, you silly girl, leave me alone,' and Nell ran away in floods of tears.

I did the only thing I could think of doing. I ran up into the main hall and rang the fire alarm, which was a huge metal bell hanging in a recess at the foot of the staircase. I swung the cord again and again until my own ears were ringing with the din, then I hurried up to my room, from where I could hear everyone running in panic around the house, shouting, 'Where's the fire? Where is it? Who sounded the alarm?' Then came the stern tones of Mr Peters, roused from his private rooms. 'Who rang that bell? If there is no fire, then I demand to know the culprit!'

At last silence descended. But in my room I sat a long time in the dark, feeling sick with anxiety. *Dervla. What in God's name are you doing?* Eventually I changed into my nightgown and went to bed at last, although in the middle of the night I woke in the darkness, and I was afraid all over again of the silence of Belfield Hall, and the stillness of the countryside that lay around it. I thought I heard something moving outside my window – *impossible*, I told myself – but my skin was cold. *Nowhere to hide now, Madeline. Nowhere to hide.*

And did I hear foxes, crying out their desire in the woods above Belfield Hall? Scrambling out of my bed, I pushed the heavy curtains aside and looked out at the distant moonlit hillside, half-expecting to see Nathan, my beautiful gamekeeper, striding along the paths he knew so well, gazing down at the Hall. But he was in London, and I missed him so. Needed him so.

Desperate with yearning, I went to unlock the drawer where I'd hidden my talisman. And although he'd asked me not to, I used its firm length to pleasure myself that night – but it was Nathan's hand I imagined on my breast, Nathan's strength I imagined inside me, Nathan's mouth covering mine and soothing my moans of need as I reached my crisis.

I slept at last, but my old dreams came to me, my bad dreams, which whispered of despair and helplessness and black, black places.

The next morning, Dervla came bursting into my room as if she hadn't a care in the world. I'd been brushing my hair and scraping it into a plain navy ribbon. 'Is Mrs Burdett back?' I asked her.

'Yes, indeed.' Her eyes were shining. 'But last night, without her, we had such a grand time. Robert, he's a one – he said, while Mrs Burdett's away, why don't we have a party? So we did, we had wine, and everything—'

'I heard you singing,' I said.

She turned a little pale. 'Oh, Maddie. It was just a bit of fun.'

'Fun? To mock the Duke's Sophie?'

'I was drunk. We were all drunk, it meant nothing—'

I asked quietly, 'Where did the wine come from, Dervla?'

'From Lady Beatrice,' she whispered. 'Maddie, Her Ladyship told me to give it to everyone, as a present, and then . . . She told me to do it. She told me to dance and sing, and the rest . . .' She lowered her voice and clenched her hands together. 'I think that she was watching.'

My throat had gone quite dry.

'She was watching,' she went on, 'she and her friend, Lord Sydhurst. They were supposed to be staying at his house for the night, but they arrived back here at around ten, and Lady Beatrice had already given me the wine. She told me to get everyone to enjoy themselves, and—' She lowered her voice even more. 'She's done that sort of thing before, she and Lord Sydhurst. Sometimes, Lady Beatrice frightens me. She and her friends meet at different places – often each other's homes – and they like to take photographs, of – of people doing things. In London, she has a lady's maid called Margaret, who's been with her for ever such a long time, and Margaret tells me all this.'

Harriet had mentioned Margaret. *Thank goodness she's not here – she gave us all the shivers*. 'So Margaret is still with her?'

'Yes. Do you know her?'

I shook my head. 'No. No, I'd heard her name, that was all.' And I was worried all over again about Lady Beatrice and Lord Sydhurst, my enemy from London, watching Dervla last night. *Telling* Dervla to do what she did last night. I tried to remain calm. I said, 'If Lady Beatrice frightens you so, why do you work for her?'

She bridled at that. 'Because she's generous, and most of the time she's fun! And you ought to have some fun too . . . Oh, Maddie, forgive me for last night, will you? Please?'

She ran to put a record on my gramophone – a tango – and did a few smart steps, then held out her arms to me. Reluctantly I got up to join her. I was still mystified, I was still anxious – *what would my guardian say? How would he deal with all this?* – but we danced, and Dervla relaxed again. 'Lord knows,' she said, 'you were full of mischief at the convent. And you could have stayed in London, couldn't you? – Lady Beatrice told me so – but instead you chose to come *here* of all places. You just hide away. You're wasting your life—'

The record had stuck, and was playing the same notes over and over again. I must have looked stricken, because Dervla ran to turn it off and then pulled me tightly into her arms. 'Oh, I'm sorry. We're still friends, aren't we, Maddie? Please?'

She hugged me one last time, then left me to go to her precious Lady Beatrice.

Dervla was quite right about the convent in Nantes – she and I had been the bane of the nuns' lives. Initially we delighted in petty mischief, but as we grew older we bribed one of the convent maids to bring us some cheap cotton dresses and lipstick, and when the weather was fine we would get out by the back stairs to walk the quarter-mile into Nantes, where there was a lively square lined with cafés and bars. We looked older than we were with our make-up on, especially Dervla, and we quickly had groups of young men gathering admiringly round us.

But Dervla was more adventurous than me, always. One summer night, after Dervla had got us both into a bar where there was dancing, two young men bought us drinks and invited us to sit with them at a table in a dark corner. But while Dervla giggled and flirted, I sat in absolute silence.

'You're a quiet one,' my man teased me. 'Cat got your tongue?'

I truly was unable to speak by then, because I'd seen that Dervla was stroking her man's thigh under the table in the darkness. She looked at me and winked, and a moment later her companion gave a sort of strangled cough, because she'd undone his trousers, and from where I sat I could see she'd taken his erection in her hand and was rubbing it, hard. His flesh was rigid in her fingers; she was smiling slyly at him. He half-covered his face at the moment of his climax and his whole body shook. 'Oh,' he said, as Dervla continued to caress him under the table and skilfully caught his emission in her handkerchief. 'Oh, my God.'

My companion's hopes were clearly raised, because he'd already put his hand on my leg. 'My turn,' he was whispering thickly.

But I knocked him aside, and stumbled to my feet.

'Maddie,' Dervla was laughing – she was quite drunk. 'My God, what's wrong with you . . . ?'

I didn't hear the rest, for I'd fled outside to hurry through the streets of Nantes and back to the convent, where I crept up to my narrow iron bed and lay awake and shaking. That was the kind of thing the Marquis had made me do to him, when I was so young. And though the Marquis had died years ago, my stomach was heaving with fear, and I'd been sick that night, over and over again.

I'd stopped going out with Dervla after that, although she continued her adventures regardless, and being caught with the gardener's boy in an outhouse was the incident that led to her being caned and to my expulsion. I was still fiercely loyal to her, you see, and I hadn't been able to bear hearing the sound of that vicious cane being brought down on my friend again and again. I'd returned in disgrace to Paris, where my mother, still living in the large house that had been bequeathed to her by the Marquis and still enjoying her parties with whoever happened to be her lover at the time, quickly hired Miss Kenning and virtually forgot my existence.

It was around then that I'd started wearing the emerald bracelet, which had lain locked in a drawer for years. I put it on, and I began to twist it, scouring my skin, using it for the punishment that I knew I deserved. Dervla and I exchanged letters for a while, but then we lost touch. And now, here at Belfield Hall, I felt freshly estranged from Dervla; I was growing more and more perturbed by the power that Lady Beatrice seemed to have over *everyone*.

And then – the Duchess announced that she was going to hold a summer party.

As soon as Mrs Burdett heard about it, she came to seek me out. 'Can't you persuade the Duchess against this idea of hers, ma'am? Is it really fitting, to arrange an entertainment of this scale without His Grace the Duke's permission?'

I tried to pass it off lightly, though secretly I was horrified. 'Oh, Mrs Burdett,' I said, 'you must know that once the Duchess has her mind set on something she simply will not let it be altered. And presumably her party will only be a very small affair—'

'Her Grace is talking of inviting over one hundred people,' Mrs Burdett interrupted grimly. 'I don't consider that a small affair, and how Her Grace thinks we can arrange it, in such a short time, is beyond my understanding.'

I could almost hear her thinking, *And if you hadn't come to stay, the Duchess would never have taken it into her head to move back here, and we wouldn't be in this pickle.* 'Well,' Mrs Burdett said at last when I didn't reply, 'I suppose we'll all just have to make the best of it.'

That evening I resolved to ring my guardian, but Mr Peters was working in his office, and when I set off towards the other telephone in the library I almost collided with Lady Beatrice. 'Madeline,' she said. 'I've had some new gowns delivered from Paris – you must come and look at them with me!'

I felt I was being watched. I felt I was being guarded. The next day I tried to suggest to the Duchess that it might be rather exhausting for her to take on the planning of such a large affair, but she waved my concerns aside and said airily, 'No need to worry *at all*, Marianne.' She still couldn't get my name right. 'We are very fortunate,' she went on, 'because dear Beatrice is going to see to everything.'

Indeed, Lady Beatrice took over the entire household in the process of organising this party, and Lord Sydhurst visited almost every day, wandering around the Hall with her, giving his advice about décor and refreshments. 'As if he owned the place,' said Harriet with a shudder. I always stayed in my room until he'd gone.

Then Lady Beatrice took me completely aback by telling me that she'd arranged the party for *me*. I'd been summoned to the Duchess's sitting room to take afternoon tea with them both, but the Duchess had bustled off a few moments earlier saying that she had distinctly heard the sound of a vacuum cleaner somewhere in the distance.

'You arranged the party for me?' I repeated in disbelief. As far as I could tell, I appeared to be the last person on Beatrice's mind, and my distrust of her had only grown since Dervla had told me that she had secretly encouraged that servants' party and had most likely watched it all with her friend Lord Sydhurst at her side.

'Oh, yes, Madeline,' Lady Beatrice was saying. 'For you.' She tried to take my hand, though I snatched it back – I didn't want her to see the scars on my wrist, which were hidden as usual by my long-sleeved blouse.

'I thought,' she went on, her dark eyes gleaming, 'that it was time you had a little excitement in your life, my dear. And I've been thinking that in your honour, we should have a French theme – although given the Duchess's views on foreigners, I shall broach the subject extremely tactfully . . .'

I remember noting as she talked that she was wearing an exquisite dress – even I could not help but admire it – of cream silk striped with pink, while over her shoulders she'd slung a pink cashmere cardigan. 'Yes,' she went on, 'we could have *tricolors* hung everywhere. Naturally, all the wine will be French, and we simply must have some French dishes on the menu . . .'

The Duchess stormed back in at that point. 'Vacuum cleaners!' she announced. 'I simply will not stand for this American nonsense. Servants are employed to do the cleaning thoroughly and by hand – that's how it always has been, and always will be.' She sat down and, after pulling a protesting cat onto her lap, began to discuss the floral arrangements with Lady Beatrice. I left the room.

Over the next few days I kept as far away from Lady Beatrice as I could, and from Lord Sydhurst, with his pale hair and his pale eyes. The servants detested him. 'He's got his nose so high in the air it's a wonder he sees where he's going,' I heard Harriet muttering scornfully. Between them Beatrice and the Duchess concocted their party plans, and when Mrs Burdett warned Lady Beatrice that the servants were quite likely to revolt over all the extra work involved, Lady Beatrice told her that she would arrange for some temporary staff – as many as a dozen maids and footmen – to be brought over from Oxford for the evening of the party.

'As if they'll know,' said Nell to me, 'how we do things here, and where everything is!'

One afternoon, when I'd returned from a walk by myself, Beatrice knocked at my door and swept in.

'Madeline, I have the final guest list here,' she announced, thrusting a sheet of paper into my hands and settling herself in a chair. 'You must tell me, my dear, if I've missed anyone off.'

I sat on my settee and scanned the list quickly, running my finger down the page and recognising familiar names from the Duchess's usual circle. But suddenly, towards the end, one name jumped out at me. *Nathan Mallory.*

Beatrice must have seen the expression on my face, because she glided quickly over to sit next to me, to see where my finger had stopped. 'Oh, dear Nathan,' she said. 'I really had to invite him.'

I was clutching the list in my hands. *Of course Beatrice knows him, you fool.* Hadn't I seen her with him in the courtyard, after he'd given her a lift from Oxford station? That was how I'd learned that he was a land-owner, not a gamekeeper . . .

'I thought Mr Mallory was in London,' I said slowly. 'And I didn't think that he and the Duchess were on particularly good terms.' I remembered the Duchess sneering about Nathan at the Carstairs' party. *He's virtually destitute, and he's a socialist, like his father. Good heavens, I never expected to see someone of his sort invited here.*

'Oh, he'll come in spite of the Duchess,' Beatrice said. Something cold was trickling down my spine as she gave me her sudden dazzling smile. 'I do know, of course,' she went on, 'that you've recently been seeing rather a lot of Nathan. But did you realise that Lottie and I have known him for considerably longer than you? You have met my friend Lottie Towndrow, haven't you?'

Lottie and Beatrice were friends? I gazed at her, stunned.

'Dear Nathan,' Beatrice was musing. 'He went through a very wicked patch, you know, a few years ago. He was angry, furiously angry, over the financial collapse of his father's estate, and so he spent what little money he had on the high life in London. Or the low life, depending on which way you look at it.'

She suddenly leaned forward to touch my arm. 'What do you like best about Nathan Mallory, I wonder? His rather wicked good looks? His skill? His stamina? And of course, there's no denying it – he's so very – *well-endowed*, as we ladies like to put it.'

Beatrice leaned back to light a cigarette in her long ivory holder, smiling that languid smile of hers. 'All in all, in London after the war, dear Nathan was in great demand, though Lottie and I always had a prior claim on him. For a while, the three of us were all but insep-arable. The clubs, the fancy-dress parties, the midnight excursions – oh, my dear, we were quite wicked. For old times' sake I'm really hoping he will come to this party of ours.'

Nathan had been Beatrice's lover, as well as Lottie's? I wanted so badly to believe she was lying – but somehow I knew that it had to be true. I stood up and held open my door. 'If you don't mind,' I said, 'I don't like people smok-ing in my room. The smell makes me feel a little sick.'

She came towards me, and with the hand that wasn't holding her cigarette she trailed her finger down my cheek, lifted my chin – and kissed me. Her mouth caressed mine, her tongue was trying to part my lips with light tantalising touches, and I jumped backwards – I think I was shaking with shock.

She tilted her head slightly. 'Perhaps Nathan got bored with you,' she murmured. 'A pity. Between us, we could have explored some new ways to enjoy ourselves . . . Never mind. I'm so very glad that you approve of my guest list.'

And she glided calmly from my room, although she must have heard me slam the door after her when she'd gone. *His skill. His stamina. And of course, there's no denying it, he's so very well-endowed . . .*

Why hadn't Nathan told me about Beatrice? I'd coped, just, with the idea of Lottie – but how could he not have told me about Beatrice? Did she share the same tastes as Lottie? *Lottie is fond of being dominated . . .* Oh, God, my mind was whirling with hateful images, of Nathan and Lottie and Beatrice – together.

Chapter Fourteen

On the day of the party, Belfield Hall was in turmoil. There had been no last-minute reprieve, no message from my guardian; in fact I was beginning to wonder if I'd misunderstood the phone call when he'd told me he was preparing to return home. Meanwhile, all the servants were rushing around under Mr Peters' stern orders, and the footmen were climbing ladders both outside and inside the house to put up the red, white and blue bunting that Beatrice had ordered from London. A string quartet arrived during the afternoon and the noise they made tuning up in the gallery meant that Harriet, when she came to me at around six, had her hands over her ears.

'They sound like the Duchess's blessed cats having a set-to,' she muttered. Then she broke off. 'Ma'am! *Ma'am*? You look – beautiful!'

I gave her a delicate twirl. 'So you like my dress, Harriet?'

'Indeed I do,' she breathed. 'It's lovely. But wherever did you get it from? You've not been shopping. There have been no deliveries . . .'

'It was lent to me,' I said. 'By Lady Beatrice.'

'By Lady . . . Oh, it fits you perfectly, ma'am! Isn't Her Ladyship generous?'

Generous with her favours. Generous with her body. Beatrice and Nathan. Beatrice and Lottie and Nathan. I closed my eyes briefly to shut out the hateful images and smoothed down the long designer frock of midnight blue satin that had been at the back of my wardrobe ever since Dervla brought it to me, along with the other garments Lady Beatrice had seen fit to bestow on me. This afternoon, after locking my bedroom door, I'd tried them all on and decided on this one. It was cut on the bias, to hug my figure. It had short cap sleeves, a low neckline, and an even lower back. I wanted to see Beatrice's face, when she saw me in this gown. I wanted to see Nathan's face, when he saw me in this gown.

I wore no brassiere, I wore no panties, because their outlines would have shown under the close-fitting garment. I wore only a garter belt to hold up my silk stockings, and a pair of high-heeled silver shoes. I'd decided, as soon as Beatrice had shown me her guest list, that I had two options – either to avoid the party altogether, or to make sure that I stunned them all. I'd chosen the latter. 'Oh, my,' Harriet kept saying as she admired me. 'Oh, my.'

Poor Harriet, she'd had so little joy in being my maid, and now she looked crestfallen, because she'd not been allowed to help me get dressed in my finery. But I didn't want her to know I wore so very little beneath it. I didn't want her to know that smoothing on the sleek blue satin dress had brought the colour to my cheeks, because I'd imagined Nathan's hands and lips sliding down my freshly bathed skin just as the satin did.

To pacify Harriet, I sat before my dressing table and

let her brush my hair, arranging my dark curls so they fell in artful disarray over an elegant blue satin bandeau.

'You will wear some make-up, won't you, ma'am?' Harriet was still looking awed. 'You *must*, with that beautiful dress.'

So I put on some face powder and red lipstick, and painted my eyes with kohl, until Harriet gave a little sigh of satisfaction before leaving with the remark: 'You'll be the belle of the ball, ma'am.'

I hoped so. I gazed at myself in the mirror and I could still see the hurt in my eyes, the sheer hurt that Beatrice's news had brought me. After Harriet had gone I paraded in my sleek gown, picturing myself meeting Nathan's shocked gaze when he caught sight of me tonight. 'I thought this was the kind of thing you liked,' I would say to him. I couldn't forget what Beatrice had said. *Perhaps Nathan got a little bored with you.*

Nathan was definitely back from London. I knew because 'Mr Villiers from London' had telephoned the Hall that afternoon, asking for me. I'd told Robert to inform Mr Villiers that I was too busy to take his call – but what would I say to him tonight? *Nathan, with Beatrice and Lottie.* My chest pounded with betrayal.

Suddenly I heard a tap at my door. I went to open it and Dervla came in.

'Maddie, I just wanted to see if you were ready for the party—' She broke off. 'Oh, my! It's one of the dresses that Lady Beatrice gave to you!'

'Indeed.' I did a pirouette in front of her, just as I had for Harriet, and she clapped in delight. 'You look so beautiful!'

Wait till Nathan sees me, I whispered to myself. *Wait till Nathan sees me, and finds that I can resist him after all.* 'Dervla,' I said, 'what is Lady Beatrice wearing?'

'A red silk gown,' she announced, 'and the diamonds her husband gave her as a wedding gift. She looks very glamorous. But Maddie, you will make Lady Beatrice look *old* – which she is, she must be almost ten years older than you – and she will be so jealous . . . Oh!' She pressed her hand to her mouth almost comically. 'You'll never tell her I said that, will you?'

We giggled, and she made me turn round again, admiring me. But I suddenly stopped; because I'd realised that instead of her usual print dress she was wearing a black frock, with a white cap and apron. 'Dervla. You're wearing a maid's outfit. Why?'

She hesitated a moment too long. Then – 'Oh,' she said brightly, 'I said that I'd help the other staff tonight, serving the supper and so on, and Lady Beatrice agreed, because they're all simply rushed off their feet below stairs. Besides, it means I'll be able to see all the dancing and the beautiful dresses and everything – just like London, you know, Maddie?'

My own problems obsessed me. The fact that I would soon see Nathan drummed in my head. And like a fool I thought, *what mischief could she get up to, dressed like that*? 'You'd better go then,' I said. 'You'll be busy.'

And she hurried away.

I looked one last time in my mirror, then I picked up a gauze wrap and slid on a long pair of kid gloves. I fixed a smile to my face, and I went downstairs to stand at the

Duchess's side and greet the guests. I could see the men's eyes snapping towards me; I could see the women casting sidelong looks at me that were filled with envy. The Duchess introduced me to her friends in her loud, ringing voice; I think she hadn't quite taken in the flagrancy of my attire. Once, I heard her saying loudly to the elderly lady standing next to her, 'She is Lord Ashley's ward, you know. Her name is Marianne. Unfortunately she's French, and we all realise what the French are like, oh dear me yes. But we may be starting to make something of her at last ...' I think Lady Beatrice had told her that the red white and blue of the bunting represented the colours of the Union Jack.

I didn't care what the Duchess said or what people thought about me. I only knew that Nathan was going to be here tonight, and my emotions were tight and bitter. Nathan and Lottie and Beatrice. What would he say to me? What would I say to him? *Nathan, you lied to me – again.*

He would perhaps answer coolly, 'I thought that you didn't want any promises from me, Madeline. I thought that our relationship was about mutual pleasure, and nothing else.'

No commitment, he had once said about his relationship with Lottie. And I'd pretended to myself that what was happening between us – what was happening to *me* – was under my control, but quite clearly it wasn't.

I wandered around, smiling brightly and drinking champagne much too fast. I think I was vaguely aware that those extra servants Lady Beatrice had hired were in fact causing our own footmen and maids considerable annoyance since, as Nell had predicted, they didn't know where anything was and were getting in everyone's way. But most of the time, all I could think of was Nathan. Would he come to me with that smile of his and compliment me calmly on my looks? Or might Beatrice get to him first? I couldn't forget her gloating delight as she'd murmured, *He's so very well-endowed, as we ladies like to put it.*

I was drinking too much and flirting outrageously with the men who'd gathered round me. There was a professional photographer in the main hall, hired by Beatrice, with his arc lamp set up to take portraits of the guests, and I posed for him with two men I didn't even know, linking my arms with theirs and smiling as they offered me outrageous compliments.

I was immune to hurt, I told myself. But suddenly my hard-won composure was shattered – because Nathan had arrived.

I was at the Duchess's side when I saw him coming towards me, tall and quite devastating in a black, beautifully tailored evening suit that hugged his muscular, lean body so wickedly that all the women he passed turned to gaze at him, hungry-eyed. This was the man to whom I'd given my trust. This was the man whom I'd allowed, time and time again, to bring me to such excruciating pleasure that I couldn't imagine being intimate with anyone else, ever.

He was within a few feet of me now, and I felt the champagne pounding in my head. The Duchess was looking at him coldly. 'Mr Mallory,' she pronounced in the voice she reserved for people she considered beneath her. 'Such a surprise to see you here at the Hall.' She turned to me. 'Mr Mallory,' she explained tartly, 'owns some of the land adjoining the Belfield estate. And I certainly didn't invite him—'

'But *I* did,' interrupted a smooth female voice.

Beatrice had arrived. She was wearing a red silk evening gown, just as Dervla had told me, with long black kid gloves. Her diamond necklace and earrings glittered coldly against her pale skin, and her lipstick was as bright as her dress, but she didn't look as beautiful as me, and I could tell from the way her eyes hardened when she saw me that she knew it. She placed herself in front of Nathan and smiled up at him. 'My,' she said, 'Mr Mallory, you look elegant tonight. Will you dance with me?'

Oh, he was so handsome. In contrast to the formality of his clothes, his curly brown hair was only half-tamed and fell loosely from his temples; his angular face with its wickedly sensual mouth was for once smoothly shaved, but he was still my gamekeeper; he was still the man who'd taught me to shoot, and to drive, and . . .

To make love. He'd taught me, quite simply, that there was no end to the miracle of my sensuality when I was with him. In his arms I'd felt whole, and undamaged, but he'd betrayed me. *Nathan and Lottie and Beatrice.* Even now, Lady Beatrice was hanging onto his arm, eager to take him to the dance floor; I think all the women in the room were looking at him and wanting him, as I had done, but he was still looking at me. At my gown.

'*Mam'selle*,' he was saying to me softly, 'perhaps you will honour me with the next dance?'

Beatrice was watching me intently. I saw her hand on Nathan's arm tighten.

'I'm afraid I can't,' I said brightly.

'Later, then?'

'I'm really not sure. My dance card is so terribly full.'

His eyes narrowed. 'Very well,' he said, and left. With Lady Beatrice.

I had never realised that I could hurt so much. Smiling, but feeling icy cold, I wandered around, greeting the guests I already knew and being introduced to those I didn't. I was surrounded by admirers and inundated with invitations to dance, but I refused each one, and all the time I knew I was drinking too much champagne. Suddenly I caught sight of Archie Carstairs with a group of his rich friends; I saw Archie pointing at me and saying something, with that smirk of his, to his companions.

I lifted my head high and went over to one of the big windows to stare out at the gathering darkness. Suddenly a man's voice came from behind me. 'Miss Dumouriez?'

I swung round. It was Lord Sydhurst.

'You're looking very beautiful tonight.' His languid English drawl chilled me, and his eyes lingered on my breasts as if he knew they were naked beneath my gown. 'I was hoping,' he went on, 'that you would dance with me.'

I was already backing away. 'Actually, I find it too warm to dance.' I thought for a fleeting moment that I could see Nathan in the distance, but then he was gone.

Damn you, Nathan, I thought. Damn you to hell for what you've done to me. Then I realised Lord Sydhurst was coming nearer.

'If you're too warm,' he was saying silkily, 'then perhaps I could suggest taking you somewhere cooler?'

'Thank you, but no. And I should rejoin the Duchess—'

'But I really need to talk to you, you see. And I think we'd be better going somewhere a little more private for our conversation. Where we won't be overheard.'

I stood very still. *Private.* I allowed him to lead me to the conservatory, remembering every word he'd said the last time we were alone. *After all, you should know about whores. Since your mother was one.*

Had he sent that letter? Had he? Had he been in Paris, eight years ago?

It was almost dark in the conservatory, though outside the moon was rising above the wooded hill, and with a sudden twist to my heart I remembered Nathan saying, *The moon does strange things to animals as well as to people.* I stumbled a little in my high-heeled silver shoes, and Lord Sydhurst moved to steady me; I could feel his hands caressing my half-naked back and I jumped away, almost crashing into one of the lush potted palms that surrounded us.

He went to turn on a lamp. 'You are very beautiful,' he said to me, drawing near again. 'Even more beautiful than my memories of you at Lady Tolcaster's. Yes, it was truly wicked of His Grace to deprive London society of a little French temptress . . .'

I swung round on him, my blood heating. 'You sent me that letter, didn't you? You knew my mother . . .'

'I knew that Celine Dumouriez was a whore,' he said. Suddenly he gripped me and forced his mouth on to mine, his tongue sliding itself like a reptile between my lips. I tried to push him away, but he was grasping my arms, bruising them beneath my long kid gloves with his fingers.

'Come, now,' he was saying harshly, 'you can't pretend you got dressed like *that* –' his eyes greedily assessed my gown '– without wanting to play games. Indeed, I sent you that letter. And I have to assume – *anyone* would assume, with only one look at you – that you're on offer to the highest bidder, just as your mother was . . .'

I was struggling more and more frantically, but Lord Sydhurst was stronger. By now he'd forced me back on to a settee and was hauling up my dress, rucking the delicate fabric almost to my hips. 'Stockings,' he was breathing, 'stockings, but no panties – my God, you *are* a little tart, aren't you? Exactly as I thought.'

I was fighting him wildly by now, but suddenly he went so still that I could hear my own heart thudding. And I realised that he'd seen – at the top of my thigh – the mark that Nathan had made with the talisman. The falcon.

He was gazing at it in amazement. Once more, I struggled to get myself free from under him, and this time he drew back to stare at me as I staggered to my feet.

'Why the *deuce* have you got that mark on your thigh?' he marvelled.

'It's none of your business.' I was desperately smoothing down my gown, preparing for a fresh attack from him, but he just stood there, smirking as if at some private joke.

'Oh, Madeline,' he was saying, 'oh, Madeline. Really – how delightfully entertaining . . .'

He was sidling towards me again. I faced him, my eyes blazing. 'Stay away from me. Do you hear?' How idiotically stupid I'd been to wear this dress. How stupid to allow him to trap me in here.

I slipped my feet into my shoes, which had fallen off, and went on, 'If you mention anything at all about this encounter, Lord Sydhurst, I shall tell everyone how you tried to force yourself on me.' My voice was shaking and I hated myself for it.

'Really?' he said softly. 'Is *that* how you'd put it? Do you think for one minute – *Celine's daughter* – that anyone would believe you?'

With a gasp I swung round and began to walk from the conservatory, but as I reached the door I stumbled. I realised my heel had broken – *merde*.

'Madeline,' he called after me. 'There's something I've been meaning to ask you. Yes, I was in Paris, before the war. And I remember the Marquis de Valery. Do *you*?'

I froze, then turned to him slowly. The cloying scent of the tropical plants all around was hateful in my nostrils. 'The Marquis de Valery?' I echoed. 'Do you know, my lord, I've no idea who you're talking about.'

'On the contrary, I'm sure you do. For his death was notorious – he died during a party in a Paris mansion around eight years ago, didn't he? A mysterious affair, they say, and what is more—'

'You might like to know, my lord,' I broke in, 'that you have lipstick all down the front of your shirt.'

'What? *What*?' He backed away angrily, and for once I had the advantage; for while we'd struggled, while he'd held me hatefully close, I'd deliberately smeared my mouth on his clothing. He swore aloud and bent his head to examine the damage, while I walked as steadily as I could from the room. He'd known my mother. He'd known the Marquis. And he'd seen the mark of Nathan's talisman – but he couldn't know who'd put it there. How could he?

I carried on walking – limping – in those stupid silver shoes, out of the conservatory.

Chapter Fifteen

Once I felt sure that Lord Sydhurst wasn't following me, I pulled off my shoes and hurried down a side corridor in my long gown and bare feet. *No retreat*, I vowed. But I needed to change this dress – which I hated now – before returning to the party, and I needed different shoes.

Crossing another corridor, I almost bumped into two of the Belfield footmen, who were muttering to one another as they headed for the ballroom with more trays of champagne. 'Where the devil are those hired servants who are supposed to be helping us? It's all the French girl's fault. We wouldn't be having this wretched party, and the old Duchess would still be safely stuck in the Dower House, if it weren't for the French girl . . .'

I took a servants' staircase up to the east wing, hoping from there to get to my room without being seen. But as I turned at the top of the stairs, I saw that the door to the portrait gallery was wide open and a light shone from it. I stopped, mystified; I was even more so when I saw that someone in a maid's outfit was hurrying along from the other end of the corridor towards it.

It was Dervla. She hadn't seen me. She disappeared inside, leaving the door open, and I stood at the top of the stairs in the darkness, my headache drumming at my temples again. The portrait gallery was supposed to be closed off awaiting the repair of the plasterwork that had collapsed when those heavy paintings of the Duchess's son were hung. I couldn't understand why Dervla – why *anyone* – should be in there. Still carrying my shoes, I tiptoed towards the open door but then pressed myself quickly back into the shadows, because two people were coming out. One was the man who'd been taking photographs downstairs – and the other was Lady Beatrice.

'You must make it absolutely clear,' Beatrice was instructing him, 'that these photographs of the maid and the footmen have been taken in Belfield Hall, and nowhere else. You could get one of the stained-glass windows in the background, perhaps, or the big marble fireplace that *everyone* knows. And you're to use my camera, as we arranged. Do you understand?'

The photographer wore a suit but had removed his tie; he was already taking the box camera from Lady Beatrice and examining it. 'Whatever you say, my lady. I'll have to get the flash set up and move a few of the dust sheets, but once that's done, I'll get the job finished to your satisfaction, I promise you.'

'So I should think.' Lady Beatrice's voice was cool. 'I'm paying you a good deal of money, both for the photographs and for your silence. If one word of this escapes, I hope you realise that I can ruin your career.'

The man was relaxed in the face of her threats. 'Of course, my lady. But if you're worried about discretion –' he pointed towards the open door of the portrait gallery '– what about the little Irish tart?'

'I'll deal with her.' This time Beatrice spoke with utter contempt. 'As for the footmen –' she was handing him money as she spoke '– make it absolutely clear to them that this payment is not just for their services, but for their silence also. Now I must go back to the party, but I'll collect the camera from you before you leave tonight.'

'You'll be pleased, my lady.' He pocketed the money with a nod. 'Very pleased, I can assure you of that.'

She glided down the corridor away from me in her sleek red dress, back towards the main stairs. The photographer had returned to the portrait gallery – where Dervla was.

Dervla had often been in trouble in the past, but now I was truly frightened, because Lady Beatrice was involved, and had spoken of my friend with such contempt. I hurried towards the still-open door, with some idea of – of what? Of hauling her out? Why not? That photographer didn't frighten me as much as Beatrice did.

But when I got to the doorway I stopped, because what I saw next made me breathless with confusion and yes, with fear. The photographer was calmly giving instructions to three of the footmen Beatrice had hired; they were still wearing the black coats and breeches braided with the silver and red of the Duke's livery, but their white shirts were undone and hanging loosely to display their muscular chests. And the photographer had his arm round Dervla – Dervla, in her black maid's dress and white apron, with her blonde hair peeping from under her maid's cap and her face painted with cosmetics, as no maid's would be allowed to be painted.

The photographer was telling Dervla to sit on the walnut table by the far wall, close to the piano, and I saw her eagerly perch there, her eyes dancing. 'That's it, sweetheart,' he was saying. 'Legs apart, yes, let them dangle . . . My, you've got pretty legs. Pull up your skirt, so we can see your stocking tops – that's the job. Now, tickle yourself a bit with your fingers, darling, show us your panties . . .'

Dervla. Oh, Dervla.

The three footmen had come up to her now, and were kissing and fondling her, at the same time reaching to their trousers to free their heavy erections. Dervla pulled down her bodice, and one of them began to rub his phallus against her breasts. And the photographer was taking pictures. 'That's it,' he was urging. 'Yes. In your mouth now, love, yes, take him in as far as you can, and feel your own breasts, will you? That's the job. Now, how about turning round on all fours, up on the table, while one of the men lifts your skirt? Perfect. Just perfect . . .'

More games. My skin was icy cold. *More dangerous games.* I remembered Dervla singing and stripping in the servants' hall – arranged by Beatrice, witnessed by Beatrice. It was like my mother's parties all over again, and I almost heard the Marquis whispering in my ear: *People enjoy debasing themselves, Madeline. People are capable of doing anything – for pleasure, money, or both.*

The photographer was giving yet more instructions, telling Dervla to climb down from the table and kneel on one of the satin couches by the wall. She still wore her white cap and apron, but her black dress was pushed up around her hips, and she was smiling slyly at the photographer as one footman took her from behind, while the other two used her mouth in turn for their pleasure. I had wild ideas of stopping them all somehow, of running in there and dragging Dervla out, but at the same moment I realised that Beatrice was returning – and with her was Lord Sydhurst.

I ran barefoot back to the narrow servants' stairs and hurried another way towards my room; but I got lost, several times, in the winding dark passages, and I was gasping for breath by the time I reached my refuge, where I rushed to my bathroom and was sick from the champagne I'd drunk, vomiting into the washbasin until my stomach was empty and sore.

The years rolled back, and my childhood – my terrifying childhood – once more had me in its grasp.

I'd been so young when Babette had been made to leave. I'd been afraid of the night-time without her stories to comfort me, but my mother had started locking me in my room if I cried, though I would beg her not to. 'Please. Don't leave me in the dark. I'll be good. I promise I'll be good.'

I became even more afraid when the Marquis started to visit me. He whispered to me that I would be put in prison if I did not let him do exactly what he wanted, or if I ever tried to tell anyone about his visits to me. I stopped eating, and I would shake whenever he came to the house. I was less than ten years old.

I like to think that my mother had no idea of this. She still made me dress up and curtsey and pass round dishes of sweetmeats whenever her friends visited in the afternoon or early evening; whenever *he* visited, which was often, for he had, after all, provided my mother with the house. If my mother was holding one of her midnight parties I would be in even more dread, because then the Marquis would come to my bedroom. It was no use for me to pretend I was asleep – he was stronger by far than I was, he was resolute. He would grasp my hand and pull me from my bed, dragging me out to the galleried landing, in the shadows, to look down on them all.

'You like watching, don't you, Madeline?' he said the first time, his hand gripping my thin shoulder. 'I know that you spied on Babette and me.'

I'd shut my eyes. I was terrified. To this day, I don't know how he'd realised that.

'If you close your eyes,' he went on calmly, 'I shall keep you out here, for however long it takes, until you *do* look properly.'

So I looked, and I could see all the people below, in a mass of colour and movement that was horrifying to me. Often the party guests were in fancy dress, or masked, which only added to my terror. They would be drinking, they would be dancing; but then they would start doing other hateful things that I refused to look at – the things I had seen Babette doing with the Marquis, and more. The Marquis would see that I had closed my eyes, and he would shake me until I opened them.

After a while the Marquis would take me back to my bedroom, and that was the worst of all. Often I tried to run, but the door would be locked and he would throw me back on the bed, and as I huddled there I would hear him unfastening himself and then he would say: 'Say it. Say it, Madeline.'

That was when I had to get to my feet and make a low curtsey. 'My name is Madeline, and what can I do to please you?'

Already fully aroused, he would take my hand and press it against his flesh, making me tend his needs. I used to feel dizzy with nausea and shame; I hated what he made me do, but he told me it was my fault, because I tempted him into it all, he said; he told me the devil was inside me. *Please,* I would say. *I'll be good. I promise I'll be good . . .*

I'd thought, in my childhood, that all men were like him. I thought all mothers were like mine.

The Marquis often praised me afterwards, and it was he who gave me that bracelet. I wished I had it again now to ease my anguish, as I was sick again and again in my bathroom at Belfield Hall. With the noise of the party below reverberating in my ears, I sponged my face and tried to steady the turmoil of my mind, thinking that I should have protected Dervla from this madness; I should have guessed. I thought in desperation, *I must speak to the Duke.* Could I tell him what Beatrice and Dervla had done? Perhaps not, but I could warn him, at least, what was going on; I could beg him to come home, *now.* And I would use the phone in the library – no one would be in there tonight. Hurriedly I found the piece of paper with his number on it, then I pulled on a different pair of shoes and set off down to the library, still in my blue satin ballgown. I'd taken my long kid gloves off to be sick, but now I wanted them on again, to cover the livid bruises on my arms from Lord Sydhurst's assault.

I'd had no reason to visit the library at night before, but I remembered that the light switch was outside the door, because the workmen who'd installed the electricity had been ordered not to damage the room's oak panelling. I turned the lights on and hurried inside, making for the telephone, but then I froze, hearing the voices of some of the servants: Robert and Richard. I pressed myself back against the near wall as their footsteps drew closer, then stopped – right outside the library door.

'Look here,' Robert was saying angrily, 'those so-called footmen have disappeared to God knows where, yet they've left the lights on all over the place, even in the Duke's library. What business did they have in here, anyway?' He turned the lights off, then slammed the door shut. 'It should be locked,' he went on, 'with so many strangers around. Chaos. Absolute chaos. No wonder half the staff are on the brink of handing in their notice . . .'

Already plunged into blackness, I now heard a key being turned. *Oh, no.* I ran to the door, rattling at the handle and calling out; but Robert's voice was fading away down the corridor. My throat began to tighten, my lungs to squeeze. I wrestled with the door handle again, but to no avail. *Please don't leave me in the dark . . .*

I can't recall how long I was in there. I remember that I stumbled across to the windows, desperately wondering if I could get out that way, but I couldn't find a catch to open them. I tried the door one last time, but it was no good. I would have to ring the bell and summon a servant, though already I could imagine their shocked faces and the whispering. *She was in there, alone in the dark. All alone . . .*

Then I heard a key turn in the lock. The door swung wide open, the lights blazed and Nathan stood there. 'Madeline,' he exclaimed. 'What, in God's name, are you doing in here?'

I could barely speak. 'I – was looking for something. The lights – the door . . .'

He strode across the room and he held me. I tried to break away, but he wouldn't let me go. My breath still came in short gasps, my heart hammered.

'You're not running from me this time, *mam'selle.* Dear God, I've been looking all over for you.'

There was something in his eyes that made me unsteady again, but I tried to fight him, remembering Beatrice gloating over him. *Dear Nathan, he went through a very wicked patch, you know* . . . 'No,' I tried to say. 'Don't touch me. Don't you dare to touch me . . .'

He let me go and I saw his face grow darker. *He* was angry with *me*? 'My God, Madeline, what's all this? You didn't return my phone call today. You virtually turned your back on me earlier tonight. Where have you been? Why are you hiding from me?'

I'd stepped backwards, my fists clenched. 'You came as Lady Beatrice's guest.'

'I accepted her invitation, yes.' He had gone very still. 'Because it seemed the only way to see you again.'

Oh, God, if ever I'd needed strength, I needed it now. He looked so devastatingly handsome with the soft light playing across his beautiful features, and his black evening suit outlining the perfection of his lean, power-ful body. '*Mam'selle?*' he said gently. '*Mam'selle?*' He reached out one finger and stroked my cheek; he tilted my chin so I had no alternative but to face him. *Oh, Nathan . . .*

Any minute now, he was going to kiss me. Any minute now, he was going to hold me. My whole body was drenched with tension, simply yearning for him. He repeated steadily, 'Why wouldn't you talk to me on the telephone? What have I done?'

I drew a deep, deep breath; I tried to stand as tall as I could. 'Beatrice has been telling me things. About you, and she, and Lottie. In London . . .'

He looked different all of a sudden. His jaw tight-ened. 'I see,' he said. 'Can we talk?'

'I don't think that there's very much to talk about.' I met his gaze and made an effort at a shrug. 'It's really quite simple, Nathan. I've been learning a lot about you, while you were away and since Lady Beatrice moved in. Are you going to deny that you once had affairs with both Lottie and Beatrice? At the same time?' My voice broke again a little. 'You could at least have warned me. This is too much, Nathan. Too much.'

I saw his eyes darken almost to black. 'At least give me a chance to explain.'

I stepped jerkily away. 'Spare me, please. You explained about Lottie, but I'm no longer in the mood to hear yet more sordid details of your past.' I was already walking towards the door, but he blocked my path. I raised my chin. 'Are you going to let me go? Or would you prefer me to beg you – on my knees?'

He tightened his fists, like a powerful animal coiled with tension. '*Listen* to me. It was after the war, in London. I was drinking too much, I was invited to too many of the wrong kind of parties. Those times, with Beatrice and Lottie – all of it ended within a matter of months. And none of it meant a thing . . .'

There was more, but I hardly heard, I was hurting so much. I couldn't get Beatrice's voice out of my head. *What do you like best about Nathan Mallory, I wonder? His rather wicked good looks? His skill? His stamina?*

'Madeline.' He was speaking very earnestly. 'Madeline, have you listened to what I've been saying?'

'You're good with words,' I said. 'But what about your affair with Lottie?' I poured scorn into her name. 'So it didn't mean a thing, you've just announced – yet you continued to see her, up here in Oxfordshire?'

'Lottie and I continued our relationship, such as it was, for a while. But I told you about Lottie, didn't I?' He spoke with strained patience, as if explaining something obvious to a stupid child.

Already I was turning to the door again. 'Not good enough, Nathan,' I said calmly, though my heart was thudding against my ribs. 'Clearly I'm naïve. But I've had enough of being made to look a fool.'

Just as I started to push my way past him in complete and utter despair, he reached to lift my hand to his lips and press kisses to it with a fierce hunger that made me start to tremble again. 'Please,' he said in a low, desperate voice. 'Please, Madeline. I'm the one who's been the fool. Because I never imagined – I never dreamed – how very, very much you would come to mean to me.'

I was shaking my head. 'How can I know that what you tell me is true, Nathan? Don't you realise that I've never in my life been able to trust *anyone*?'

'What can I say?' He held me close and was cradling me tight. 'I need you to trust *me*, Madeline. You're so alone, yet so brave. You're wonderfully, wildly beautiful. And I can't bear the thought of any man but me ever touching you . . .'

Suddenly he lifted my arm and I realised with a sinking heart that my long glove had slipped down to my wrist, revealing the livid bruises inflicted by Sydhurst's grasp. Nathan's eyes blazed with concern. 'What in God's name have you done to your arm?'

'It's nothing. Really . . .' My voice was threatening to break again.

He tugged down my other glove, then looked at me sharply. 'These are finger marks. Who did this to you?'

I pulled my gloves up again and shrugged. 'That was from earlier this evening. You can blame an overeager dancing partner with a ferocious grip.'

His eyes narrowed. 'You expect me to believe that?'

'I bruise very easily.'

'Oh, Madeline' he said. 'Oh, Madeline.' He put his hands around my waist and gathered me to him, not with lust but with overwhelming tenderness. Still I tried to resist, I tried so hard, but it was so good, to be in his arms . . .

Suddenly he held me away. 'Can I take you up to your room, and see that you're safe there?' He must have seen the look almost of fear in my eyes. *No. No. I won't let you humiliate me again.*

He went on, 'I promise with every ounce of integrity I have left that I won't try to make you do anything you don't want to do. This damned party. I would have hunted you out earlier, only—'

I shook my head in disbelief. 'You were too busy fending off your female admirers?'

'Oh, no.' Suddenly his eyes sparkled with mischief. 'You've actually got completely the wrong idea.'

What? He'd put me through all this – and he found it amusing? I felt my emotions threatening to overflow again, and I started towards the door. But he called, 'Madeline. *Wait*. You see, I had a fight with Archie Carstairs, out in the courtyard.' I turned slowly to face him, my eyes wide. 'Oh, yes,' he went on, his mouth twisting into a smile. 'The real thing this time. We almost followed the Queensberry Rules – in fact quite a few men came out to lay bets on us. I won, of course.'

'But why—?'

'Carstairs made an ill-advised comment about you,' he said softly, taking my hand again. 'Within my hearing. Foolish of him.' Then he pulled me right into his arms, and cradled me against him. 'Please, *mam'selle*. Please accept my very sincere apologies, for not having been here for you when you needed me.'

'*No*. It's foolish of you to apologise. You went to London for something important, Nathan. To try to save your estate—'

'Enough,' he chided softly, wrapping one strong arm round my waist and tilting my chin up. 'Nothing is more important than you. *Nothing*. Do you understand?

I closed my eyes. He'd fought for me. He said that he

cared . . . *Be careful,* my inner voice warned. But some-how, it was as if all my anguish, all my loneliness was melting away, and I was smiling up at him like a stupid creature. I forgot Beatrice, I dismissed Lottie – he was mine now, he'd said so, he was mine. Maybe I was still light-headed from the champagne I'd drunk earlier but, whatever it was, I was deliriously happy to be in his arms again.

'You really hit Archie Carstairs for me?' I breathed.

'For you. And I'd do so again,' he said seriously.

I melted inside. Drawing my finger over his lean, square jaw, his beautiful, sensual mouth, I whispered, 'I'm not trusting you yet, do you understand? You must not count your hens before they're hatched.'

His dark eyes danced with sudden laughter. 'Oh, *mam'selle*, I find you irresistible. I've wanted you from the very first moment I set eyes on you . . .'

And so I was his again. Oh, God, I was shameless – I almost dragged him upstairs to my room.

Chapter Sixteen

I'd scarcely locked my bedroom door before I was running to him and he was holding me, his mouth colliding with mine. Nothing mattered except him, nothing at all. I was gripping the lapels of his jacket, and his tongue was delving into my mouth until heat and a delicious yearning filled me. My breasts were pressed hard against his chest and I felt that if I didn't get more, I was going to die right here in his arms.

I wanted so very badly to trust him, you see. The sound of the party floated up to me as if from another world, another time. He looked at my bed and hesitated, but I pulled him to me again. 'Please,' I said quietly. 'Make love to me, Nathan. I'm begging you.'

I thought he was still uncertain, and I was plunged into despair again, so I struggled out of my flimsy dress until I was naked except for my silk stockings. I knelt on the floor before him, bowing my head and putting my hands on my parted thighs, offering myself to Nathan, the only man I'd ever wanted, or would *ever* want.

I heard him make a sound of desire, low in his throat. He pulled me up; he was kissing my face and naked breasts, running his hands with feverish hunger over my hips. 'Madeline. You are brave, you are beautiful, and above all, you're mine—'

Someone was knocking at the door. *Merde.* 'Ma'am? Are you in there?'

Oh, no. Harriet's voice. She was knocking again, louder. I shoved Nathan under the bed – we were both smothering laughter – and I hauled on a silk dressing robe, then hurried to open the door just a fraction, pretending to cover a sleepy yawn. 'Yes, Harriet? What is it?'

She peered at me. 'I guessed that you must have retired for the night, ma'am, and I wondered if you needed me to help you out of your clothes, or anything?'

I suspected that she was wild with curiosity, because I'd disappeared long before the party was due to end. I really hoped she couldn't see how my hair had been rumpled by Nathan's hands, how my lips were swollen from his kisses. 'No,' I said lightly, 'I'll be fine, and I'm really so, so tired, Harriet. Goodnight!'

I locked the door and leaned back against it with a sigh of relief, then Nathan was scrambling out from under the bed, and I was in his arms, and we were laughing. 'Tired?' he was whispering. 'Oh, I hope not.'

Already I was unbuttoning his shirt, tearing it from him, and the sight was utterly glorious. I adored the sculpted muscles of his chest, I adored the way his black trousers hugged his strong thighs, and I couldn't get enough of the scent of his hair, the scent of his smooth, sun-browned skin; I loved everything about him. Our mouths were still locked as he drew me back with him to my bed.

His hands were already tugging off my robe, casting it aside and skimming my legs above my stockings, and

I let my own hands rove freely beneath his loosened shirt, hungrily raking the smooth skin of his lovely, hard-muscled back. I could hear my own ragged gasps as my heart pounded, and I squirmed eagerly on the silken counterpane, because he'd braced himself above me, spreading kisses from my throat to my naked body and drawing my nipples into his skilled mouth, each in turn. 'So beautiful,' he was whispering. 'So beautiful.'

'My breasts are too small,' I moaned.

'Believe me, they're exquisite,' he said huskily. 'Like you, *mam'selle.*'

I drew a sharp breath, because he'd slipped his hands beneath my hips and brought my body up against his erection – I could feel it through his trousers. Liquid heat trickled through me, down *there*. Oh, my. 'Nathan,' I whispered. 'Please – *more*.' Splinters of hunger shot directly to the base of my belly, to where he rubbed his arousal against me. I whimpered beneath him, my breath coming in short mewing gasps as his mouth moved back to my mouth and his tongue delved and thrust deliciously – oh, I was going to explode.

I grasped his shoulders, feeling his muscles bulge – I'd never felt so needful, so wet. I wanted to undo his trousers, but then his hand was *there*, between my legs, and I melted – oh, God, it was wonderful, because he knew exactly what to do, how to arouse me to fever pitch and beyond; his hand was finding the exact place where I burned for him, writhed for him, and he was stroking that place with the hard pad of his thumb while plunging his fingers into me almost urgently, and at the same time his teeth were dragging at my breast . . .

'Are you sure you want me?' he said through his teeth. He was pressing kisses to my hair now; his eyes were dark. 'Are you sure? Now that you know so much – too much – about me?'

Beatrice and Lottie. Anguish spiked my blood – how could I compete with them? But then, I told myself, hadn't he said they were nothing to him? Wasn't he showing me, in the most delicious way possible, that they were nothing to him? Now it was up to me, and my happiness lay almost within my grasp. I laced my hands around his neck, pulling him close, breathing in the heady male scent of his smooth skin. 'I've become rather fond of my gamekeeper. *Mon garde-chasse.*' I nuzzled his jaw with my lips. 'I cannot resist the way that he talks to me, and kisses me, and – *oh!*'

My heart raced feverishly as he tugged me into his arms, sat on the edge of my bed with his feet planted on the floor and turned me on my front so I was sprawled over his strong trouser-clad thighs. He began to rub his hand over my bottom and spank me tenderly, then he was pulling me round to sit on his lap, his breath rasping as he ran his palms over my silk stockings and garters. My naked skin felt deliciously sensitised against his warm, strong body, and my thighs fell apart; I placed one hand with a sigh of pleasure over his chest, then I began with almost ferocious determination to tackle the buttons of his trousers.

'*Mam'selle.* Slowly.' Laughing, he eased me from him and stood up. 'Let me do it. It's a little awkward.'

Indeed, he was so hot and hard that I felt my mouth go quite dry. *The size of him. The strength of him.* Then he was completely, wonderfully naked, and joining me on the very bed where I'd longed for him, so often; I shuddered with pleasure as his arms enfolded me, and his muscular frame was hard and warm against my breasts. I gasped as I clung to his broad shoulders, as if he were the only solid object in my world, and oh, God, I felt sheer lust pump sweet and sharp through my veins, I felt my loins rear towards him as his lips moved to my neck. 'Little *mam'selle*,' he murmured, 'I've been driven crazy with wanting you since I've been away, do you know that?'

I nodded, desperate. 'Me too.'

'Now, I'm going to make love to you.' It was a delicious promise. 'I'm going to kiss your sweet little aristo mouth, and give you pleasure until you're screaming with delight.'

His hand travelled down to feel my wetness again, then he was kissing my lips, teasing and tantalising, and he slipped his fingers inside me once more so I gasped, conscious of his erection rearing dark and heavy against his taut belly. 'Please,' I whispered. 'Oh, please. Don't stop, Nathan, I beg you—'

He froze. 'I've told you, Madeline. I don't want you to beg any more.' He was smiling still, but his eyes were dark and intense.

'But – the talisman? Should I get the talisman? It was your gift—'

He cut in sharply, 'I don't want you to beg me, or to use the talisman, ever again.'

'Then I won't,' I whispered. 'But Nathan, please. I cannot wait.'

He smiled slowly. 'Then the waiting's over, *mam'selle*.'

I was moaning with delight as he eased himself inside

me. His hips were so sleek and powerful as he thrust, and my lower muscles clenched darkly as I clung to him in helpless passion. He went still suddenly and I whimpered my protest, but it was only so that he could heave my legs around his waist, and soon my tremors of pleasure were turning into something much stronger. Soon I was arching up to meet his rhythm, relishing it when he slid so deep within me that I could feel no space between us.

His pace quickened, his breathing grew unsteady and the tension inside me built until the pounding of Nathan's body sent me over the edge. I felt a surge of excruciating pleasure wash all around me, and as I soared and shattered he still moved deeply, steadily inside me, his dark eyes intent, until my ragged breathing started – just – to return to normal.

Then he slowly withdrew, his own pleasure uncompleted, and – *oh, my.* I quivered anew at the sight of his phallus, dark and thick and moist with my juices. His hand closed urgently around my wrist as I began to move away. 'Jesus, Madeline,' he said, his patience evidently strained. 'What are you trying to do to me? Can't you see . . .'

I sneaked a sideways peek at him. 'I'm not going far, Nathan, I promise. I'm just – getting into position.'

I heard him catch his breath harshly as I crouched beside him on the bed and started to kiss him, beginning with his flat brown nipples and powerful chest. *Oh, what a gorgeous body.* All mine. All mine. My lips followed the delicious path down his hard-muscled abdomen; I used the velvety tip of my tongue to lick and stroke, and I heard him gasp, I felt his hands entwine themselves in my hair – *'Jesus, mam'selle.'* I kissed his hard, honed flesh all the way to his navel and beyond, I kissed the lovely trail of gold-brown hair that led to the place where his erection reared, so spectacularly.

I wrapped my hands around its thickness. I licked its crest slowly, luxuriatingly. I sat back on my knees, moistening my lips and batting my eyelashes at him.

'Madeline. Mercy, for God's sake.' There was delicious laughter in his voice, but desperation too.

'Did you show *me* any mercy earlier, *monsieur le garde-chasse*?' I asked him provocatively.

'No,' he grinned, 'but you certainly enjoyed it.'

'And so will you, *monsieur*,' I murmured. 'That is a promise.'

He emitted a full-bodied groan as I let my hand slide around the heavy pouch of his testicles, then I heard him groan again as I sheathed my teeth and took him in my mouth – *oh my, the power of him, the strength of him*. I licked around his most sensitive place; he called out my name and grasped at my hair with his fists, and I slid my mouth down and sucked and sucked, taking him as deep as I could. At long last he shouted out his ardour as he pumped his seed deep and warm and salty into my mouth.

Heat suffused every inch of my body. He held me again tenderly, and I knew that being in his arms, breathing in the scent of his skin, was the best feeling in the world. We lay on the bed, tangled in one another's limbs.

Sleepily I heard the sounds of the party coming to an end. Voices were raised in farewell out in the courtyard, followed by the noise of vehicles moving off into the darkness of the night. We sat up against the pillows, Nathan and I, and we talked to one another as we'd never talked before. He told me about his lands, and how his father had worked so hard alongside his tenants to try to save the farms when the contaminated water supply had first started to affect them; but it was no good: all the cattle died or had to be destroyed, and the financial restrictions imposed during the war had ended all of his hopes. Then Nathan told me how his father had been strongly opposed to the war, in fact so vociferous in the speeches he'd made throughout the county that he'd been sent to gaol.

My heart went out to both father and son. 'How brave,' I said quietly. 'How very brave of him. And –' I hesitated '– it must have been difficult for you. Since he suffered for opposing the war, whereas you were in the army—'

'I wasn't in the army,' he said. 'I never told you that. I didn't go to France to fight.'

'But you said—'

He turned to me. 'I went there as an ambulance driver.'

Oh. And everything was tumbling into place. In Paris, I'd heard people talk about the men who drove the ambulances, at the Front. *Those ambulance fellows. They won't fight, but it's not out of cowardice. You should see them bringing in the wounded, under shellfire and bullets and even poison gas. You'd think they were mad, but really they're heroes . . .*

'Don't try to make a hero out of me,' he said, guessing my thoughts. 'I was only doing what had to be done. But the things I saw there, Madeline. The suffering. The inhumanity . . .' He drew me closer, stroking my hair, and I gazed up at him, my heart full.

'Your father must have been proud of you, Nathan. And so glad when you got safely home.'

'My father died.' His eyes were expressionless again, but I heard the pain of loss in his voice. 'While I was in France.'

'Oh,' I breathed, my fingers tightening around his. 'I'm so sorry—'

'He died shortly after his release from gaol,' he went on. 'He'd caught pneumonia in there and never recovered. By the time I got home he was dead, and I realised that the estate he'd left me – and the house – were, through no fault of his, almost ruined.' His eyes were hooded, unreadable once more, and I felt a quiver of the old unease. But then he drew me to him, and smiled his wonderful lazy smile. 'So,' he went on, 'instead of being a gentleman of leisure, I had to become a farmer, and yes, a gamekeeper too.'

'But you stayed in London for a while.' *And you amused yourself with Lottie and Beatrice.* Inevitably my thoughts were darker now.

'I did,' he said steadily. 'London was a strange place after the war – a little like Paris, I imagine. Those of us who'd been involved in the fighting felt guilty to have survived, and we were angry with those who'd seen nothing of the bloodshed, or were wilfully blind to the suffering the war had caused.'

He hesitated, then began stroking my hair. 'There were parties in London – strange parties, parties where the normal rules were broken. That was where I met Lottie and Beatrice. But after a few months we went our different ways, and I can honestly say that I hadn't seen Beatrice for at least two years when I noticed her outside Oxford station and brought her here. And Lottie – I told you about Lottie. I believe she's gone off on her lecture tour around England. She's also found someone new to amuse her – a visiting American professor who's writing a long, long book about British stately homes.'

No more Lottie, trying to get her claws into my man. But . . . 'You know,' I said, trying to speak casually, 'I suppose it has occurred to you that marrying someone as rich as Lady Beatrice would be the solution to all your financial problems, Nathan?'

'You're joking, I hope? She's a snake.' He was still stroking my hair, but his voice had become harder. 'And believe me, *marriage* isn't what she would want from me – she's aiming far higher. Don't forget she was once destined to be the Duchess here, until her husband died. She hasn't yet got over her disappointment.'

'Do you think she wants to marry another aristocrat?'

'Definitely. It's not long, after all, since she was using her wiles to try and trap the new Duke into marriage.'

Despite the warmth of his body next to mine, I was suddenly feeling cold. 'You mean – she wanted my guardian?'

He hesitated. 'More than that. You didn't know?'

I shook my head.

He took my hand. 'I thought you'd have heard – the gossips had a field day. In fact Beatrice and your Duke had a very brief affair once, years ago, when she was married to Lord Charlwood. Lord Ashley – as he was then – had no idea that he would one day inherit the title. He ended their liaison, to Beatrice's chagrin – but later, once he became the Duke, Beatrice tried again. He rejected her, and she's never forgiven him.'

Something was turning unpleasantly in my mind. *Beatrice. Beatrice and the Duke . . .*

But I was in Nathan's arms, I was deliciously sleepy, and I pushed my half-formed thoughts aside. So stupid. Something else that I cannot forgive myself for.

I woke again, early. The sun wasn't yet up, the house was silent and, when I reached out for him, Nathan wasn't there. I sat up, my heart thudding.

He was standing by the window with his back to me, dressed in his white shirt and those smoothly fitting black trousers that clung to his lean hips. He'd pulled the curtains back to gaze out, and as he slowly turned, the sight of the grey light of early dawn shining softly on his features was quite heart-stopping. My breath caught in my throat and I felt myself melt with longing for him all over again.

'Nathan.' I pushed my hair back from my face. 'How long have you been awake?'

He smiled at me from across the room. 'I decided I'd better leave before the servants are up and around. Don't you agree?'

'Of course.' But I felt bereft at the thought of him going. I didn't want him to go, ever. As if knowing it, he came to sit on the bed beside me and gathered my sleep-dazed body in his arms. I curled against him: oh, what now? What now?

I hadn't imagined it possible for him to look more beautiful than he had last night. But I loved the dark stubble that now shadowed his face, and I needed him to kiss me again, so very much. As if reading my thoughts he said, 'Madeline, I want to stay with you more than anything. But, you know, I really have to go. I'm leaving for London again, in a few days.'

'*Again?*' I was pulling myself up. 'Oh, Nathan. I completely forgot to ask you. Did you manage to get the loan you needed?'

'I've – almost – arranged a loan against the value of my land,' he said, 'which would mean that I can restore the house, and perhaps make some of the land workable once more. But I have to meet more people yet, in the City. Bank managers, accountants.' He pressed a kiss to my forehead. 'I've a few jobs to do around the house over the next day or so, before I go. But as soon as I'm back, I'll be in touch.' He held me close. 'Will you trust me this time, Madeline? Please?'

I nodded, but a huge lump was forming in my throat. He rose to his feet, pulling on his black dinner jacket, and I watched him with steady eyes. 'Someone might see you leaving, Nathan. Or hear your car.'

He shook his head. 'I parked beyond the gatehouse – I'll walk over there, and no one will see me. I'll ring you as soon as I return. Mr Villiers, remember?' He came over to press my fingertips to his lips, and was gone.

And I sat there, terrified by the strength of my feelings for him.

Chapter Seventeen

Somehow I slept again, but I woke before eight to see Dervla entering my room. Those photographs – oh, God, those photographs.

As I pulled myself out of bed, searching for my dressing robe, she hurried towards me. 'Oh, Maddie.' I saw that she was trembling. 'I did something very stupid last night . . .'

And she told me what I knew already: that Lady Beatrice had asked her to dress as a maid, then pose in the portrait gallery with the hired footmen, for the photographer. She broke off at that point, and when she began again her eyes were brimming with tears. 'The things that I did, Maddie – they were wicked. I'm so ashamed.'

I felt cold. 'Why did you do it?' I said.

She was weeping openly. 'Lady Beatrice offered me money – she said it would be like a game. So I agreed to let her dress me up, to look like Sophie—'

This time I felt as if I'd been punched hard. The breath left my body. 'Sophie?' I interrupted. 'The Duke's Sophie?'

'Yes. Yes. That's why I was wearing that maid's outfit – it was what Sophie would have worn, when she worked here. Lady Beatrice told me that I looked like her, you see – I was the right age, with blonde hair. It was her camera. She made it sound fun, but now I'm *afraid*, of what she made me do.' She was sobbing again.

I was remembering the party down in the servants' hall. The singing. The mockery of Sophie. I started to whisper, '*Why?*' but then with a flood of nausea I remembered Nathan telling me how badly Beatrice had wanted to marry the Duke, and how angry she'd been that he'd rejected her. *She's never forgiven him*, Nathan had told me. Now I could barely speak. 'And those footmen?'

'Oh, Maddie. Those men weren't servants *at all*. In London they get paid to entertain rich people at private parties, doing – things like that. They told me they'll do anything for money—'

'You realise, don't you,' I cut in, 'that Beatrice will try to use these photographs to destroy Sophie?'

Dervla gazed at me, horror-struck. 'Oh, no. I'm so sorry, Maddie. I honestly didn't realise what Lady Beatrice meant to do, and I'm so very ashamed.'

Her tears were flowing fast again. I held her and I soothed her, but my mind was reeling. I should have guessed last night what Beatrice intended. She would indeed make use of those photographs – she would reveal their existence to the press, perhaps, claiming that they were of Sophie, taken when she'd worked here at Belfield Hall. Or Beatrice might decide to circulate them amongst her friends, no doubt trusting that the lurid talk they'd incite would make any kind of reunion between Sophie and the Duke quite impossible. I was seared again by my memory of the two of them together at the Duke's house, and how in love they had looked.

'Think, Dervla. You said the camera was Beatrice's – where would she keep it? You're her maid, you must surely know.'

She was trying to dry her tears. 'It – it should be in her private sitting room still. Lady Beatrice left it on the sideboard there, last night, before she went to bed – I saw it when I helped her to undress.'

'So it will be there this morning?'

'I think so. But Maddie, she'll notice straight away if the camera vanishes—'

I interrupted her. 'When will she be expecting you to come to her?'

'She told me not to bring in her tea tray before nine.'

'Then don't,' I said. 'Will her door be unlocked?'

Dervla's eyes widened. 'Yes. But Maddie, what are you going to do?'

'You said that she offered you money. Has she paid you?'

'No.' She shuddered. 'And I don't want it now.'

'You *must* ask her for the money, or she'll suspect something. And as for the camera, leave it to me.' My patience was running out. 'Now, off you go.'

As soon as she'd gone I got dressed, then made my way swiftly along the corridors to Beatrice's suite. I stole silently into her sitting room – and stopped when I realised that her bedroom door was half open, with clothes lying scattered around the floor in there.

Lady Beatrice lay naked, asleep on top of the

crumpled covers, in the arms of her lover – Lord Sydhurst. I shrank back, all my senses recoiling. *The camera. Concentrate on the camera.* I scanned the shadowy sitting room and saw it on the sideboard. After opening it up – oh, how my hands shook on the catch – I pulled out the film, replaced the camera on the sideboard and hurried away, closing the door very softly. I crept downstairs to drop the film into one of the huge waste bins at the back of the house. Which was a suitable end for it, I thought rather shakily.

By the time I arrived in the dining room for breakfast, the Duchess was sipping her tea and describing the party in lavish detail to Miss Kenning. 'It went so exceedingly well,' she was pronouncing in her loud voice. 'Sir Anthony and Lady Carstairs told me that there hasn't been a party like it in Oxfordshire since the ones that my husband and I used to hold before the war.' The Duchess's eyes fastened on me as I took my seat. 'Didn't you think it went well, Marianne?'

Madeline. My name is Madeline. I thought of all last night's hideous events: Dervla and the photographs, and Lord Sydhurst's veiled insinuations to me about the Marquis de Valery. Then I thought of Nathan, and my breathing became calmer. 'It was a wonderful party,' I answered quietly.

Twenty minutes later, Beatrice came down to join us, looking groomed and sleek. 'Madeline.' She gave me her cool smile. 'You disappeared rather early last night. I do hope you enjoyed yourself as much as the rest of us did.'

'I developed a slight headache,' I said.

'Really? Such a pity.' She helped herself to toast while I ate my own small portion of breakfast and felt my spirits rising. I'd destroyed the film – and even if she suspected me, what could she do about it? And Nathan had said that he would be back for me.

But on that very same day, my stupid hopes of happiness with Nathan were brought to an end – by Lottie.

The Duchess had gone up to her room to rest after lunch – the party had exhausted her, she kept telling Beatrice and me, as she consumed a very hearty meal of pea soup and roast beef – so I seized the chance to get away from Beatrice for the afternoon and went out for a walk in the gardens with Miss Kenning. But a summer thunderstorm was brewing, and we could see the heavy clouds gathering to the west.

'Thunderstorms bring on my migraines,' Miss Kenning reminded me. She seemed very distressed, and once we were back in my sitting room, she told me that she wanted to leave Belfield Hall.

'Leave? But Miss Kenning—'

'I'm so sorry,' she whispered. 'So sorry.'

I made her sit down, and my mind was whirling as she began to give me her reasons, but they were none of the things I feared. Instead she blurted out that she had a sister in Yorkshire, whom she hadn't seen for many years, but who was now very sick, and she really felt she ought to go to her.

'Of course,' I said. 'Of course you must.'

'And you don't need me now, do you?' she persisted

anxiously. 'Now that you have the Duchess to chaperone you?'

I almost smiled; Miss Kenning's idea of chaperonage had allowed me an almost unlimited amount of freedom. 'You're right,' I said. 'But I'll miss you.' And I meant it. She talked a little more, about how sorry she would be to leave me and Belfield Hall, and then she retreated to her room.

She'd not been gone for long when there was a knock at my door. It was Mr Peters. 'Lady Beatrice hoped that you would join her and Miss Towndrow for afternoon tea, ma'am,' he announced.

'Miss Towndrow? Here? But I thought . . .' I thought she'd gone. Everyone had said that she'd gone.

'She arrived while you were out, ma'am. She and Her Ladyship are in the conservatory.'

I didn't want to join them in the slightest. I hated Lottie, I hated Lady Beatrice. But I thought, *I can deal with this, now that I have Nathan on my side. I can deal with anything . . .*

'Tell them I must change first, Mr Peters, after my walk,' I said to him.

'Very well, ma'am.'

I changed my clothes slowly, touching my throat and breasts, remembering Nathan's lips there last night, missing him so much already. I pulled on one of my plain skirts and a high-necked blouse and went downstairs at last to the over-warm conservatory, hating the smell of its hothouse flowers, hating the memory of Lord Sydhurst assaulting me in there. Outside the rumbles of thunder were drawing closer and the sun had gone behind the clouds.

'Madeline!' Beatrice rose to greet me. 'Of course, you've met my dear friend Lottie, haven't you?'

'Several times,' I answered. Lottie, red-haired Lottie with her pale green eyes, looked as calm as ever. *My dear friend.* I felt cold again, even in the heat of the conservatory, realising it was quite possible – inevitable, almost – that Lottie had been using her visits to Belfield Hall as opportunities to spy on me for Beatrice.

'I was telling Lottie,' Beatrice enthused, 'about the wonderful party last night. Such a pity she missed it.' One of the housemaids brought us tea and buttered scones, but I merely toyed with my cup as Beatrice and Lottie talked on and on about the party, and about London.

'Of course,' said Beatrice, turning to me, 'you were in London for a while last year, weren't you, Madeline? Staying with Lady Tolcaster, I believe. But then, you poor thing, you were exiled here to Belfield . . .'

I put my cup down abruptly, knowing she would have heard this from Lord Sydhurst. 'I chose to come here,' I said. 'I wasn't happy in London.'

'And you're happy here?' Beatrice arched her elegant eyebrows.

'Yes. Aren't you?'

She laughed. 'Oh, there's one thing to be said in Belfield Hall's favour – without a doubt it replenishes one's eagerness for London life. And of course I realise, as Lottie does, that the countryside has its attractions.'

She meant Nathan, of course. I knew that. They talked on and on, including me only occasionally in their conversation, until Mr Peters came in to announce in his ponderous way that there was a telephone call for Lady Beatrice.

I was about to seize the chance to get away, but Lottie moved swiftly over to sit by me, in that conservatory that smelled of palms and warm earth, and she said, 'I realise that you're becoming rather obsessed with Nathan Mallory, Madeline. He is extremely attractive, isn't he? But you're only eighteen, and bound to be still a little naïve – so I think you should know that you're only a very small part of his life's ambition.'

I rose and went to stand near the windows. Heavy drops of rain were starting to fall on the terrace outside. I said, 'I don't particularly want to discuss Mr Mallory with you.'

She stood up too. 'Oh, but I think you should. You see, Nathan knew you were coming here, to Belfield Hall. And he made his plans accordingly.'

I swung round on her. 'I really don't wish to listen to any more of this.'

I was already making for the door, but she moved swiftly to block my way. 'Madeline, I assure you, you ought to listen – for your own sake. There's something you should see.'

What? I almost laughed. 'Have you some more letters you want me to translate?'

'No. Oh, no. This time, I want to take you – to the Duke's chapel.'

Looking back later, everything after that had a sort of dreadful inevitability to it – like watching an object fall to earth from a great height and being sure exactly where it was going to land.

I knew that Lottie had spent some time researching the history of the chapel; according to Miss Kenning it was one of the oldest rooms in the house, with a notable stone altar and carved oak panelling that dated from the seventeenth century. There was a high gallery for the family to occupy when they were in residence, while the servants sat below them on rows of seats to listen to the daily morning service. As I entered the chapel with Lottie, I suddenly pictured Sophie sitting there with the other maids years ago, so young and so shy. I remembered Harriet telling me how they'd all thought her too proud, because she spoke well and loved to read books.

I guessed that Sophie must be kind and good as well as beautiful, whereas I was none of these things. I was a burden to the Duke my guardian, and forever marked by my own dark past. I didn't understand why Lottie had brought me here, but she wasted no time in making her purpose clear. Leading me straight up to the stone altar, she pointed to an embroidered silk banner draped across its full width.

'This is an historic artefact,' she told me. 'It was made almost a hundred years ago by the then Duchess of Belfield's seamstresses as a gift for her husband, and it shows as clearly as any map how Oxfordshire was divided in those days amongst the great landowners. Here –' she was pointing as she spoke '– are the holdings of the Duke of Belfield, consisting of thousands of acres of farmland. Do you see how the seamstresses have carefully embroidered the sheaves of wheat, the sheep and the cattle? And you'll see the Belfield crest – the three plumes rising from a ducal coronet – embroidered at intervals all around the Duke's boundaries.'

She moved to one side, still pointing. 'Where the Duke's lands end, you'll see that his neighbours' estates are represented in just as much detail. Now, here is the area I want you to look at, Madeline. Whose lands do you think these are, adjoining the Belfield boundary to the south-west?'

I didn't want to look, but I found myself gazing at the intricate needlework and realised she was pointing at Nathan's estate – the Mallory lands. Her green eyes were fastened on me all the time.

'You know those acres are Nathan's, don't you, Madeline? You'll see a representation of his family home – which is half-ruined now, of course – over here. And you'll see his lands marked, according to whether they were used for crops or livestock – cattle mainly. But look closer, do; because you might see something interesting, on that rather charming animal embroidered right in the middle of the Mallory estate . . .'

I saw it. I stepped back, my heart thudding. She was pointing at a brown and white cow, almost naïvely stitched, like a child's drawing, with something black embroidered on its flank.

It was a falcon's head, in profile.

'I think you've seen it before,' she said softly.

I whirled round to make for the door, only to see that my way was blocked – by Beatrice. I must have let out a low exclamation, because Beatrice folded her arms and said, 'I guessed you might be in here, the two of you.' She nodded towards Lottie. 'And I really think, Lottie, that for Madeline's sake you ought to continue with your story.'

Lottie turned back to me, as I stood frozen. 'Perhaps you'll understand now,' Lottie began calmly again, 'about the black falcon. It's been used for decades for branding the Mallory cattle, and you have a mark that's very similar – don't you? – in a most private place.'

My lungs were so tight I could scarcely breathe. *Oh, God*. How did she—?

She answered my unspoken question. 'Lord Sydhurst told Beatrice, and he told me as well. He thought we would find it amusing, which of course we did – all three of us.' From the corner of my eye I could see Beatrice smiling as Lottie went on, 'How does it feel, Madeline, to be branded like livestock?'

My mind was spinning. I remembered Nathan tenderly imprinting the bird on my skin. *Do you mind, mam'selle? Do you object to being mine?* The falcon's eyes slanted up at me, knowingly, chillingly, and Lottie's green eyes gleamed with triumph. I was cold, so cold suddenly. I thought I could hear the drumming of steady rain against the high windows, and I told myself, *Stay calm. Don't waste energy in fighting her*. But there was worse to come.

'Nathan hates the Belfield bloodline like poison,' Lottie went on, 'because the old Duke had his father sent to prison for preaching against the war. And it's always been rumoured that the old Duke proceeded to ruin the Mallory lands by deliberately contaminating the water supply, though it could never be proved.'

I was backing away towards another door, one that led outside, but once more Beatrice forestalled me and moved swiftly to bar my way. Lottie laughed. 'Come now, Madeline. How can you bear to leave before the end of my story? The best is yet to come. As you'll have realised by now, I think, Beatrice and I got to know Nathan extremely well in London after the war. Poor Nathan – he was very bitter in those days over what had happened to his father, and he took refuge in decadence; we all did. Oh, the parties! The champagne and the cocaine! But then Nathan left London and came back to Oxfordshire – to the ruins of his father's estate – because he knew that *you* were coming here.'

I reached to twist my bracelet, but of course it wasn't there.

'Nathan never told us why he was so interested in you,' Lottie went on. 'Not in so many words. But Beatrice and I guessed, from the way he talked about you, what his intention was – to seduce you and humiliate you, which is precisely what he did. Doesn't the brand prove it? For then he would be able to tell the Duke exactly what he'd done to his precious ward. What you'd *allowed* him to do to you.' She smiled coldly. 'After all, you made it easy for him. He's a very attractive man, and you must have practically fallen straight into his arms. I could see the change in you whenever I came here. So *very* amusing.'

It all made such terrible sense. My surprise, when Nathan and I first met in the woods, that he'd known exactly who I was. The talisman he'd given me – with the cattle brand on it. The way he'd used it to make love to me; the way he'd marked my thigh with it.

It's to show, Madeline, that you're mine, he'd breathed as he rolled the ink across my skin and kissed me until I was desperate for his lovemaking. His revenge. Nathan's revenge.

Surprisingly enough, it was Beatrice who put a temporary end to my torment by saying in her cool clear voice, 'Lottie? You've made your point, and I'm finding this place damnably cold. Shall we go?'

She cast one last, thoughtful look at me, then left the chapel arm-in-arm with Lottie. Their work was completed, and I wanted to sink to my knees before the altar and bury my face in my hands. *Oh, Nathan. Oh, my gamekeeper.* I'd been betrayed, one way or another, many times in my life, but this was easily the hardest treachery I'd had to bear, because I'd actually, stupidly thought he was beginning to feel something for me.

Perhaps he *was* starting to care, I thought blindly. But that could not make up for the fact that he'd set out to debase me, for the simple reason that I was in the care of the Duke, who symbolised everything Nathan hated. I put my hand to my forehead, trying to endure the pain, trying to work out what I must do; already knowing what I must do.

I hurried upstairs to my room and, using a pumice stone, I scrubbed that brand from my leg with hot water and soap until my skin was sore. Then I pulled on a coat, slung a leather bag over my shoulder and went out – seeing that, as was often the way with summer storms, the heavy clouds had moved swiftly onwards and the sun was glittering on the lawns that surrounded the Hall. Eddie was in the courtyard, carefully polishing the Duchess's Rolls-Royce with a chamois cloth. He stopped as I drew near and I told him that I wished to take the Duke's smaller car – the Ford – for a drive. 'That is, if you don't need it for an hour or so, Eddie.'

He gasped. 'I didn't know that you could drive, ma'am.'

'I can,' I said, 'I assure you. And His Grace told me that I could use it any time I wished.'

He believed my lie. The car had an electric starter, thank goodness, and by some miracle I managed to move off without stalling the engine while Eddie pushed back his peaked cap and gazed after me, looking dumbfounded.

Chapter Eighteen

As I'd guessed, Nathan was at work on his old house. I'd stopped the car a little distance away so he wouldn't hear me coming, then I walked up the narrow lane with my bag and entered the courtyard. Nathan was high on a ladder with his back to me, reaching to mend a section of guttering and whistling softly to himself. The hot July sun had made the air humid after the storm, and he'd stripped off his shirt; my breath caught, because he looked so glorious. For a moment I gazed at the way the powerful muscles of his back and shoulders flexed sleekly beneath his tanned skin. And my heart had never ached so badly.

Couldn't I ignore what Lottie had said? Couldn't I pretend that what she'd told me was a lie? No. Because in my heart of hearts, I knew it had to be the truth.

He must have heard my footsteps on the gravel as I came nearer, because he looked round and his face lit up. 'Madeline.' He came quickly down the ladder and across the courtyard to take me in his arms. 'I've missed you all day, *mam'selle*,' he said, softly pressing his forehead to mine. 'Missed you badly. How did you get here?'

'I drove,' I told him calmly. 'I borrowed the Duke's Ford. I've left it down the lane.'

He grinned. 'Good for you. No near-collisions with trees?' I shook my head. He went on, 'I thought you would be kept fully occupied by the Duchess today.'

'I needed to see you *now*,' I said huskily, drawing my finger down his naked, muscled chest, touching his flat brown nipples and gazing up at him.

'It's as well, then,' he breathed, catching my hand, 'that I've almost finished my jobs for the day.'

'Fortunate for me, indeed.' *Oh, Nathan. Two can play at this wicked game.* I lifted his hand and pressed it to my lips, letting my tongue's tip dart out to caress his palm.

With a low growl, he reached for me. He swung me up into his arms and carried me inside, where he kissed me, and as our mouths collided, the sheer raw intensity of the feelings he aroused in me was so strong that for a moment I couldn't help myself thinking: *Nathan, I don't care what you've done. I need you. I need you so badly . . .*

I fought those feelings down. I let my fingers dig into his shoulders and I kissed him as hungrily as ever, my mouth every bit as greedy as his, my tongue stroking his every bit as boldly. But now I was declaring in my own way, *Look what you're giving up. Look what you've thrown away.*

He retreated a little, his eyes almost black with desire. 'Madeline. Oh, Madeline.'

You've thrown me away. Hooking my arms around his hard-muscled back, I pulled him close again. Pride was driving me. Revenge was driving me. A broken heart was driving me.

Suddenly Nathan pushed me onto the old couch in the corner, then tangled his fingers in my dark curls and kissed me again. My arms locked around him, roving the satiny skin of his back; our tongues and bodies entwined, we kissed as if we'd been parted for months, and his every touch was as skilled and nerve-shatteringly perfect as always. My emotions were at melting point. I was so desperately angry and hurt – as hurt as I'd ever been in my life – but my anger stoked the fire of need within me that was already white-hot.

He was running his hands up and down my slender legs now, finding the tops of my stockings. My own hands slid over his glorious chest as he leaned over me, and I saw that his eyelids were half-lowered as he gazed hungrily at my body. Then he was unbuttoning my blouse, he was ripping away my lacy brassiere, he was fastening his silky-hot mouth over first one breast then the other.

I tried to hate him, and I couldn't. When he started drawing my nipples out with his teeth, my head fell helplessly back and my hips squirmed as hot, liquid pleasure pumped through my veins. I trailed my mouth over his lovely, lightly stubbled jaw; I undid his breeches and closed my fingers around the glorious velvet length of his erection. *The last time. The last time.* As I caressed him, he dragged my panties aside and then entered me in a single, driving thrust that had me crying his name aloud. He was hard and full and pulsing, and for a moment I was afraid again, as I always used to be, of his power.

Suddenly I reached out to grip his waist, I swung my whole body round, rolled him over and landed on top of him, taking advantage of his surprise. He was still deep, deep inside me – but now I was in charge.

I sat up, kneeling fully astride him on the couch, gazing down at him. 'Beg,' I said softly, moving myself until I heard him groan. 'Beg, Nathan.'

He was laughing, but his dark eyes were hazed with pure desire. 'Oh, *mam'selle*. Time for your games? Very well. Your wish is my command.'

I didn't smile back, but drew my hips up carefully until I was only enfolding the last inch of him. Oh, he was beautiful. So utterly desirable. With my hands I pinned his muscled arms down on either side of the couch. 'Beg,' I repeated softly.

Nathan Mallory had at least three or four times my strength. Of course, he could have thrown me on my back and taken me there and then. But he'd realised that something had altered in our relationship, that the balance of power had somehow shifted.

'Beg,' I repeated, as I began to slowly move myself up and down his engorged shaft.

He moistened his lips. 'Please, Madeline.' His voice was thick with need.

I stilled again, high above him. 'Tell me how you feel about me, Nathan,' I said. 'I'd really like to know.'

His eyes widened – I could see the disquiet there openly now. But he said, carefully, 'Madeline. No other woman has ever made me feel the way you do. I need you, *mam'selle*. You mean so much to me—'

'Enough,' I cut in, because I was desperate myself, I'd been afraid to move or even breathe in case my own need became too much for me to control. But now I could hold on no longer. I sank onto him again – *oh*. And the feeling of him, driving incredibly deep and thick within me, was so shockingly good that I rose again, sank again; his hands were greedily fondling my breasts as I rode him, and he was thrusting hard to meet me, grinding himself against me with unerring skill. He was reaching to touch me, at the tender, tiny knot of nerves that craved his firm fingers – *damn you Nathan, for knowing exactly what to do, always* – and as tingling pleasure began to take hold of me, I couldn't help but moan his name aloud.

I twisted my fingers in his hair and pulled his head up to mine as I locked my mouth to his, twining my tongue with his while he pounded into me. We kissed through my choked gasps and through his tortured groans, until in a final frenzy he pulled himself out, turned me onto my back and pumped his seed over my belly, then buried his mouth in my sex, using his tongue to bring on a climax that roared through me and left me sated. Tenderly he kissed me on my lips, while running his hands over my hips, my thighs. So gentle. So unbearably gentle . . .

Then – 'The mark,' he suddenly said. 'The falcon. It's gone.' He'd become very still. 'Madeline, you must have scrubbed it away. You've made your skin sore . . .'

He saw everything in my face, I think, before I spoke a word.

He lay there, and watched tensely as I climbed down from the couch and walked over, naked, to my shoulder bag. With my back to him, I swiftly drew out what I'd put in there – a piece of sponge, a tiny phial of indelible ink and the talisman. With the sponge I smeared some ink across the talisman, then walked back to him, knelt beside him and pressed it against his naked flank. I blew gently on the small black falcon image I'd made on his skin, and his eyes never left me.

I looked at him at last. 'It's dry now,' I told him. 'It will come off eventually. But you'll have to scrub hard.'

Then I drew myself up and dressed. He rose from the bed too, slowly pulling on his breeches and boots and shirt. He listened as I told him why I'd come to him for the very last time. Why I would not be seeing him again. But of course, he knew that already.

I drove back to Belfield Hall in the Duke's car, feeling hollow inside, because Nathan hadn't denied a thing – how could he? He'd just gazed at me when I told him what Lottie had said, about his plan to revenge himself on the Duke by seducing his young French ward.

'I regretted my intention,' he said quietly when I'd finished. 'As soon as I began to get to know you, I came to care for you, Madeline. I thought you needed me, perhaps. And after that, I wasn't thinking of revenge at all.'

My distress was tearing me apart all over again. 'But you were intending revenge at the start, weren't you?' I cried. 'Wasn't that why you made me beg for you? Wasn't that why you used the talisman on me, why you branded me as if I were – some *animal* you owned? So that you could gloat and laugh to yourself each time you saw it?'

My voice almost broke then – oh, it would have been so easy to let the tears fall, because I knew that he would gather me in his strong arms, and kiss me, and make everything all right again.

But it could never be all right again. I believed him, yes, when he said that he'd come to regret his plan of revenge – I understood now why he'd told me not to beg, not to use the talisman. I even believed him when he said that he cared for me. But it was too late. He knew it as well, because instead of answering my questions, he bowed his head.

'I'm not proud of what I intended,' he answered quietly at last. 'But revenge is a powerful motive, possibly even more powerful than hate. If it's any consolation to you, I despise myself utterly for what I've done. And I won't blame you if you find it difficult to forgive me—'

'Good,' I broke in. 'Because you've just about summed it up, Nathan. And I'm leaving you now, because I've said everything I needed to say.'

'*Madeline*.' He'd come closer to hold me by my shoulders. 'Don't go. I know you must hate me. I know that I've been a bastard—'

'Again, your words, not mine. But I won't argue. Now, will you take your hands off me, please?'

He did. I walked towards the door, still hoping against hope that he would come after me, stop me forcibly and beg me again to stay with him. But he didn't, of course. Though I heard him calling out clearly and strongly, 'If you need me, I'll be here for you, Madeline. Remember it.'

I got the car safely back to Belfield Hall – much to the relief of Eddie, who'd been watching out for me, I think – and headed straight for my room. As ill-luck would have it, Harriet caught sight of me. 'Oh, ma'am,' she exclaimed, 'they've just started serving dinner, and Lady Beatrice, Miss Towndrow and the Duchess are all waiting for you—'

I interrupted. 'Tell them I'm not hungry, will you?'

'Would you like something served in your room, ma'am?'

'No. Thank you, Harriet.'

I just wanted to be alone. But that wasn't possible, for less than an hour later Mr Peters knocked at my door, and with an extremely grave face told me that a telegram had arrived, to say that the Duke had been injured, badly, in Ireland.

I closed my eyes. *No.* Please, no.

'There's been an explosion, ma'am, in Dublin. There's been fighting and all kinds of trouble there. But they've brought him back to London—'

Oh, my dear, kind guardian. 'So he was well enough to travel?' I was clutching at any kind of hope.

'Yes, ma'am, and he was insistent that he return. But since then he has developed a fever, and his doctors are deeply concerned about him.'

'I must go to him.' I didn't hesitate.

'Ma'am, he will be well cared for—'

'He's my guardian, and I owe him a great deal, Mr Peters.' I was already looking around my room, planning what I must take. 'Will you enquire about trains to London for me?'

'Ma'am – are you really quite sure?'

'Indeed I am. Completely sure.'

He bowed his head and left. Mrs Burdett came up soon after that, to try to dissuade me also, but I brushed her objections aside. Of course I had to go to him. He was the kindest and best man I had ever met – he had accepted his responsibility for me without hesitation, before he'd even set eyes on me – so I would do whatever I could for him. Then Miss Kenning came hurrying up to me, so upset to hear the news about the Duke. 'Oh, Madeline. I'll come with you to London, shall I? I really cannot leave you now . . .'

'It's all right,' I said to her gently. 'Miss Kenning, you must continue with your plans to go to your sister. I'll be fine.'

Dervla came rushing in, moments after Miss Kenning had left. 'Please,' she begged, 'can I come with you to London as your maid, dear Maddie?'

I soothed my poor, calamitous friend, as she told me how she'd asked Lady Beatrice for the money she was supposed to be paid for the photographs '– just like you told me to, Maddie, so she wouldn't be suspicious!'

But Lady Beatrice had refused. 'I don't see why I should pay you,' she'd said to Dervla. 'After all, you enjoyed yourself, didn't you?' Then Lady Beatrice had told her she was a slut.

'And she dismissed me, Maddie!' Dervla was weeping noisily. 'She told me to get out of her sight, and to leave Belfield Hall, but I've nowhere to go, unless you take me with you!'

I told Dervla that of course she could come to London with me – what else could I do? Beatrice couldn't attempt to discover who had stolen her film without revealing her own part in the affair; but it would certainly be safer if Dervla was well away from Beatrice's reach. Gradually Dervla grew calm, then began to be excited at the thought of seeing London again. But after she'd gone, I went over to my bed and sat there, pressing my hands to my face. *Nathan. Oh, Nathan. I'm going to miss you, so badly*.

I began to make a list of everything I would need to pack. Finally I went to fetch my pistol case from its hiding place, and opened it carefully to examine once more the weapon that Nathan had taught me to use – because I would be taking that with me, too.

Chapter Nineteen

In fact it was three days before I could depart, since a landslip on the line meant that all trains to London had to be cancelled. In the meantime, Lottie left for Oxford and Lady Beatrice went off immediately after, saying she was going to stay with Lord Sydhurst, making me wonder bitterly what new mischief they were concocting between them. I'd seen her only once since the episode in the chapel, to tell her that I intended to employ Dervla as my maid. She'd raised her eyebrows and said that it was up to me, of course, but her words held a world of contempt. Later Dervla and I had watched Lady Beatrice driving off from my bedroom window, and I saw that my friend was shivering.

The news that the Duke had been injured raced around Belfield Hall, and many of the maids were openly weeping as they went about their work. 'Oh, ma'am,' they kept saying every time they saw me. 'His Grace will be all right, won't he?'

'Of course he will,' I reassured them. 'They wouldn't have made him endure the journey from Ireland if he had been in any danger.' But I wanted to say instead, *How should I know?* All I knew was what Mr Peters had told me: that he had developed a fever, and that his doctors were very concerned.

The Duchess was the only one who brushed the news aside. 'Oh, Ireland,' she said haughtily. 'Nothing but trouble has ever come from there. And Lord Ashley was foolish to allow himself to be caught up in the politics of the place.'

On hearing her say that, I found it difficult to remain in the same room.

When I told her that I was going to London to be with my guardian, for the first time I could remember she was lost for words. 'And what is the point of that, pray?' she finally managed to say.

'If there is anything I can do for His Grace,' I responded quietly, 'I will do it. He has been most kind to me.'

She hardly spoke to me again. But as Eddie loaded my luggage into the Duke's Daimler on the morning of my departure, I realised that some of the servants were waiting by the main door for me, and Robert spoke for them all. 'When you get to London, ma'am,' he said, 'will you tell His Grace that we're all thinking of him?'

'Of course. I'll give him your good wishes,' I promised.

'Thank you, ma'am. Good luck, ma'am!'

It had begun to rain, so I hurried towards the waiting car under a big umbrella with Dervla at my side, aware of them waving me off mournfully.

As the train rumbled away from Oxford, sending out clouds of steam and smoke, it was Nathan who filled my thoughts. I had to keep reminding myself that before he'd even met me, he had planned to use me to avenge the wrongs that the old Duke of Belfield had done to his father; but going over it all again was like twisting that tight emerald bracelet on my wrist, scouring anew the old scars, making them raw again.

The rain drummed steadily against the windows of our compartment, which Dervla and I had to ourselves. Miss Kenning had left yesterday to take the train to Yorkshire, fretting as much as anyone about the calamity that had befallen the Duke, although I'd done my best to reassure her, promising that I would write to her as soon as I could to let her know how he was.

'I'll miss you, dear Miss Kenning,' I said as I hugged her. And now Dervla was my sole companion: Dervla, who as we sat in the carriage picked nervously at the fabric of her skirt until, in sheer exasperation, I put my hand over hers to stop her.

'Oh, Maddie.' Dervla turned to me, her eyes damp with tears. 'It's so *good* of you to take me to London with you. And those photographs. I was so *stupid* . . .'

I was beginning to wonder if I might regret my decision. 'Well,' I said wearily, 'the photographs are gone. It's over now.'

We sat in silence for a while, then Dervla reached for her bag to draw out a clean handkerchief – but as she leaned across the seat, I suddenly glimpsed an inch or two of an exquisite lace-edged silk petticoat showing beneath her skirt. I breathed, 'You are still wearing the things Lady Beatrice gave you.' I felt cold. 'You're still wearing them. My God, Dervla . . .'

She had gone quite white. I reached up to bring down her suitcase, and wordlessly I unfastened it. Then I tugged open our window by its leather strap, and despite the rain gusting in, I pulled out Dervla's silk lingerie and stockings and I threw them out of our compartment, all of them. I closed the window, shaking with emotion, as Dervla sat huddled and silent.

'What else did you let Lady Beatrice do to you?' I said at last.

She glanced at me and began to stammer. 'She – she sometimes liked me to share her bed. And she liked to watch me and Lord Sydhurst—'

'You and *Lord Sydhurst*?'

'She liked watching us in bed together,' she whispered. 'And Lord Sydhurst gave me gifts – chocolates, and scent. It was so exciting, for a while. I honestly didn't mean any harm, Maddie!'

I put my hand to my forehead. 'Dervla,' I said slowly, 'you could have done a great deal of harm. You know that, don't you?'

She threw herself into my arms, bursting into sobs. 'Maddie, I'm so sorry. So very sorry.' I sighed and held her. Yes, Dervla had been a fool, but I had been even more of one, with Nathan. And God, I was paying for it now.

Dervla rambled on with her apologies, but I was hardly listening, because I'd suddenly realised that there was one thing that I could retrieve out of all this chaos. I'd lost Nathan, but then, I'd always known I didn't deserve happiness. The Duke and his Sophie did. I would do my best to make sure they achieved it. I would reunite them – somehow.

★　★　★

By the time our train had drawn into Paddington station, I felt as if grimy, smoky London had me in its grip once more. A porter took our luggage and led us to the line of taxicabs. 'Please take us to Hertford Street,' I told the driver. 'To the Duke of Belfield's home.'

I had already telephoned the Duke's housekeeper, Mrs Lambert, to tell her my plans, and though she'd been as warm to me as ever over the phone, she'd sounded so anxious. 'His Grace will be glad to see you,' she assured me. 'But you need to be aware that he gets tired very easily, although the doctors and nurses are taking excellent care of him, day and night.'

Day and night. Doctors and nurses . . . I told myself that it only meant he was in safe hands – if he'd truly been in danger, he would surely be in hospital. But I'd felt fresh fear at her words. As the taxi rumbled through London's busy streets, Dervla was still sobbing quietly into her handkerchief; whether because of my scolding, or because of the loss of her precious underwear, I didn't know. I managed to keep up a façade of calm as we alighted from the taxi, but when Mrs Lambert opened the door looking pale and drawn, my heart contracted. 'How is His Grace?'

'He is progressing well,' she said quickly. 'But . . .'

And then, I realised that someone else was sweeping into the hallway behind her, in a cloud of familiar scent – musk roses and patchouli. 'Madeline! Madeline, my dear! Mrs Lambert told me you'd decided to come to London!'

Lady Beatrice was here. Completely ignoring Dervla,

she glided towards me with her arms outspread – and the shock was as great as anything I'd yet felt.

One of the Duke's footmen had appeared to collect our luggage from the taxi, and while Mrs Lambert was giving him instructions I turned swiftly to Dervla. 'Go upstairs with the footman, will you? You can start unpacking my clothes.' I'd deliberately avoided Lady Beatrice's outstretched hand.

A maid was waiting to take my coat and hat, but as soon as she'd gone Lady Beatrice interposed herself between me and any chance of escape. 'You've had such a long journey, Madeline,' she said in her sultry voice. 'You really must be ready for a little refreshment. Mrs Lambert –' she turned to the housekeeper '– I would like some tea to be served to Miss Dumouriez and myself in the first-floor parlour, immediately.'

'I wish to see the Duke,' I said. 'That's why I came.'

'Oh, but he'll be resting.' Beatrice's voice was full of unctuous concern. 'He'll most certainly be glad to see you – but not just now. Shall I lead the way to the parlour?'

I was tired from my journey, and emotional at the thought of the Duke lying injured in his room upstairs, but Lady Beatrice was as calmly determined as ever. I noticed, as I followed her, that she was wearing a long cream silk cardigan embroidered with red flowers, over a red silk sheath dress; she looked exquisite and hateful.

Once in the parlour, she beckoned me to a settee by the window then took a seat herself so that she was facing me, and said softly, 'I really thought, you know, that I ought to be in charge of looking after the Duke.'

I remembered everything Nathan had told me about her and my guardian. *He rejected her, and she's never forgiven him.* Looking directly at her, I said, 'I cannot imagine His Grace wishing to be in your care. When did you get here?' Like everyone else at Belfield Hall, I thought she'd gone to stay with Lord Sydhurst in Newbridge.

'Oh, I drove down two days ago,' she said casually. 'I have a house in Grosvenor Square, so it's very easy for me to be a constant presence here – which is absolutely necessary, because, you see, poor Ash has been very ill.'

My heart suddenly lurched. 'Is he – is he in danger?'

'I think they let him travel too soon. He was injured by the debris from the explosion, and he's lost a good deal of blood, but I've arranged for the best doctors in London to visit him – it really is the least I could do.'

I stood up. I said, 'You are no friend to him, and you know it.'

Her perfect eyebrows arched. 'Be careful, Madeline,' she murmured.

I ignored her. 'I want to see him, *now*. He has others who can look after him apart from you, servants who are completely devoted to him.' And all the time I was thinking, *He needs his Sophie. He needs his Sophie.*

Beatrice remained calmly seated, but her eyes narrowed in that catlike way of hers. 'You seem to think you have it all worked out. But you are no doubt feeling emotional after your journey. And before you start raising objections to my presence here, I think I really ought to mention something that might have been preying on your mind – *considerably*.' She leaned forward. 'You thought that you'd got rid of those photographs of your friend Dervla, didn't you?'

I felt as if ice-cold liquid was being trickled down my spine.

'You got rid of the wrong film, I'm afraid,' she went on softly. 'And so I've still got the photographs. The film you stole was one I'd just put in, and it was unused. My photographer had already removed the film that *you* wanted – and he's developed it for me. With most satisfactory results, as it turns out.'

'How do you know that it was me who took it?' I'd found my voice at last.

She chuckled softly. 'Who else would go to such trouble? Dervla will have given you some fabricated story, and you decided to take action; but now, all that matters is – I've still got those photographs.'

I sat down again. The lamps in here suddenly seemed too bright, and Beatrice's scent – oh, how I hated that strong scent she wore. She had her handbag at her side, and as she reached for it and pulled out a large envelope I watched, mesmerised. She extracted the contents and came to sit next to me on the settee. She showed me those hateful pictures, one by one.

There was Dervla, posing in her black maid's dress and white apron, with her blonde hair peeping from her white cap. Dervla again, sitting on that big table in the portrait gallery, with her feet dangling and her legs obscenely apart as she fondled herself, her mouth wide open with pleasure. Then came the ones with the footmen. *I agreed to let her dress me up, to look like Sophie . . .*

Beatrice was holding them out to me in silence. Oh,

God. They could not have been more explicit. I pushed them back to her, trying to keep my voice steady as I said, 'So? You have some photographs of a rather foolish maid-servant, having fun at a party. No doubt she deserves to be dismissed – oh, but you've already done that, haven't you?'

'And you've brought her here as your maid, Madeline.' She was shaking her head, her eyes gleaming. 'Rather foolish of you – and equally foolish was your attempt to steal the film from me. Presumably your motive was worthy, if naïve. You knew that Dervla, dressed like this, indulging in obscene games in one of the most recog-nisable rooms in Belfield Hall, could easily pass as Sophie when she was in service there.'

'If you make those photographs public,' I said calmly, 'I shall tell everyone that it's Dervla. And Dervla will tell everyone too, because you don't have her in your power any more.'

She'd been lighting a cigarette in a long tortoiseshell holder, but now she leaned forward, amused. 'My dear Madeline. By the time I've circulated these photographs to the press, do you think that any self-respecting jour-nalist with an eye for a story would want to listen to a single word you say? Believe me, I know the newspaper-men. They'd much rather listen to *my* version of the story behind the photographs – especially if I were to pay them very generously and remind them that Sophie went on – however briefly – to entrap no less a person-age than the Duke of Belfield.'

I was fighting down panic, and she knew it. 'It could be *anyone* in those pictures,' I argued. 'Any fair-haired girl, dressed as a maid . . .'

My voice trailed away as she reached into her envelope again and passed me a newspaper cutting. 'That's Sophie,' she said.

I looked silently at the grainy black and white picture of Sophie standing outside a theatre – in New York, I guessed – looking so gracious, so lovely as she smiled for the press. I glanced at the headline. *English songstress makes it big on Broadway.*

Beatrice was right – the resemblance between Dervla and Sophie was strong enough for Beatrice's story to be immediately believed. The press would surely pounce on the photographs of Dervla with delight, and the salacious rumours about Sophie would spread everywhere, while the Duke of Belfield was in no state to fight their lies.

I gazed at Beatrice, hating her. She regarded me thoughtfully, drawing on her cigarette. 'You think me devious and scheming,' she said. 'But I really have to defend myself, you know. I *could* say that I had Ash's true interests at heart; because I wished, all along, to ensure that he didn't ruin his entire life by marrying a scullery maid.'

The scorn she'd poured into those last two words enraged me. 'What if she *deserves* his love? What if he cannot live without her?'

'So you're hoping that they might be reunited? My, you really are a little romantic, aren't you?' She smiled – I shall never forget that smile. 'And so am I, at heart. In fact, I've had an interesting thought, Madeline. It's occurred to me, you see, that you yourself might be able to persuade me not to use these photographs.'

My heart was thudding. 'I don't understand.'

She leaned closer and tapped my hand. 'It's simply a matter of keeping my options open, always – and I'll explain the details to you, all in good time.' She glanced at her watch. 'But now, I have an appointment with my couturier in Bond Street. We'll talk again, very soon.'

She left me and I sat there feeling dizzy and afraid.

I went slowly up to my room, where a distraught Dervla was unpacking my things and putting them in untidy heaps all over the place, then picking them up and depositing them somewhere else, clearly as alarmed as I was to see Beatrice here. 'Oh, Maddie,' she kept whispering. 'I can't believe it. I thought we'd got away from her.'

I said little, but as I changed out of my travelling clothes, Beatrice's words were hanging over me like a thundercloud. *It's simply a matter of keeping my options open, always.* Then I went downstairs to find Mrs Lambert, who was in her sitting room talking to James, the Duke's loyal valet and chauffeur, and despite my desperation I felt a flash of gladness because at least these two were utterly devoted to the Duke.

'Her Ladyship is trying to take over, ma'am.' Mrs Lambert had been weeping, I saw. 'She hasn't stopped interfering since she arrived two days ago – giving orders to the doctors, the nurses, everyone.'

'But they stand up to her.' That was James's calm voice. 'And Dr Grandersleigh has been His Grace's physician for years.'

'Does Lady Beatrice actually stay here overnight?' I had carefully closed the door.

'No,' said James grimly, 'she returns to her own house in Grosvenor Square in the evenings. But she's back here every day.'

I nodded. 'I'd really like to see my guardian, if possible. Though first, please will you tell me exactly how he is?' Beatrice had outlined his injuries, but I didn't feel I could believe a word she said.

Mrs Lambert explained that a bomb had gone off in Dublin. 'It was in the city courthouse, and the Duke was close by, you see, ma'am. The doctors in the Dublin hospital had to operate to remove the debris from his wounds, and afterwards they advised him to stay there and rest – but he insisted on coming home, and by the time he'd got here, a fever had set in. You'll find him very tired from all the medicines.'

After that she took me straight up to him, though we paused a moment in the Duke's sitting room, where my eyes flew to the desk stacked with documents. 'He's not trying to deal with any of the business of the Belfield estate, is he, Mrs Lambert?'

'Not at all. Mr Fitzpatrick came back from Ireland with His Grace, and he set off for Belfield this morning to check that everything there is in order.'

In order? With the Duchess in charge? But the old Duchess was the least of my problems now.

Already Mrs Lambert was opening the door to the bedroom – and at the far end the Duke lay in his bed, slightly raised by pillows. His eyes were closed, and my heart sank, because he looked so pale. On one side of the room was a table that was laden with bowls and implements and bandages; the air was filled with the pungent smell of disinfectant. A nurse in a blue uniform and a white starched headdress was sitting on a chair at his side, but she rose quickly as we came in, and she perhaps saw my shock, for she said in a gentle voice, 'You must be the Duke's ward. Please try not to worry about him – the worst is over, and he just needs to build up his strength. He's asleep, but if you wish to sit beside him for a while, then please do.'

Oh, my poor guardian. A sheet had been pulled up almost to his shoulders, and he wore pyjamas, but I could glimpse the thick bandaging across his chest. Mrs Lambert left the room quietly, so I took the chair at the other side of his bed and my emotions tore through me. I looked swiftly up at the nurse. 'May I touch his hand? May I speak to him?'

'Of course.'

I took his hand that was scarred from the war and whispered, 'Your Grace. It's me. Madeline.'

And I saw his lips begin to curve in the smallest of smiles. He turned his head in my direction, then he half-opened his dark blue eyes. 'Madeline,' he said, almost in wonder. 'How are you?'

I wasn't sure whether to laugh or cry at the fact that this ever-thoughtful man who'd been so gravely injured was asking *me* how I was. 'I'm very well, Your Grace.' I tried to smile back. 'I really wanted to see you. To find out if there was anything at all that I could do . . .'

I realised that the nurse had tactfully gone off to measure some medicines, and the Duke was gripping my hand.

'Sophie,' he said. His voice was barely audible. 'I need Sophie.'

That was all – then his eyes closed again. *Oh.* I blinked away some hot tears and sat by his side, unable to move.

The nurse asked me if I would stay for a little while. 'He looked happy when he saw you,' she said. 'You don't appear to disturb him, as some visitors do.' I wondered if she meant Lady Beatrice and I felt afraid again, but I was more than glad to stay by my guardian's side, and as the minutes ticked by I looked around, gazing at his bookshelves, remembering how Mrs Lambert had once told me that his Sophie used to read poetry aloud to him. Then James came in and I rose to go, but he stopped me and said in a low voice, 'Lady Beatrice is back, ma'am. She's in the library.'

Feeling chilled again but full of fresh resolve, I went downstairs, finding Beatrice just putting down the telephone in the library as I entered.

'I've seen the Duke,' I said to her flatly. 'Sophie must come to him. Someone must send a telegram to New York, to tell her that the Duke needs her badly. I will do it, if necessary—'

'And what about those photographs?' she broke in. Her voice was silky-smooth. 'I think you should imagine the consequences for everyone if Sophie returns to her Duke's side, and those pictures have been circulating all around London.'

I faced her steadily. 'I've imagined the likely consequences already. You told me that you were willing to make some kind of bargain with me, and I've come to you because I want to know what that bargain is.'

She glided to a chair. She began to explain – and I realised that perhaps my worst ordeal was yet to come.

Chapter Twenty

There, in the Duke's library, Lady Beatrice told me that her intention was to present me to her elite circle of fashionable friends. 'I want you to be noticed in London, Madeline. I want you to become all the rage, in fact.'

My heart was thudding. 'You must know that last summer, my entry into society was hardly a success. I hated the other debutantes and they hated me.'

'Ah.' She was lighting a cigarette. 'Lady Tolcaster is a fool, and from what I've heard had no idea how to handle you or make the best of you. In the end, she banished you from her house, didn't she? I heard the story from Sydhurst, of course. But that was because you cast her two ugly daughters completely into the shade, and no wonder – good heavens, even their father's fortune can't buy them presentable husbands.'

She inspected me again, and my blood ran cold under her scrutiny. 'You're very pretty,' she went on thoughtfully. 'You don't try particularly hard. But if you took more care with your clothes, and enhanced your face with make-up as you did on the night of the Duchess's party – you could be a sensation.'

I remembered how Lady Beatrice had pandered to Dervla's vanity by giving her expensive clothes to wear and painting her face, and I fought to conceal my revulsion. 'I'd appreciate it if you'd be a little more explicit,' I said.

'Very well.' Lady Beatrice walked over to the window, then swung round to face me. 'Here's my bargain, Madeline. If you'll promise to do as I say – to make an impression as my *protégée* in the circles I move in – then I'll send a telegram to Sophie and tell her that the Duke needs her. In fact I'll do it tonight.'

'But I could do that. What about the photographs?'

She drew on her cigarette. 'Keep your promise, and I'll destroy both the photographs and the negatives in front of you. Break your promise, and I'll use those pictures to full effect, believe me.'

Her words curled around me as threateningly as the smoke from her cigarette. 'You say that you want me to make an impression in the circles you move in. But how will you judge that I've become – a success, as you put it? How can you measure my success?'

She sat close to me and explained. She told me that she would present me to her friends at a private party – a charity ball – in three weeks' time, before all of fashionable society began to leave London for their country homes for the remainder of the summer.

'That's all you have to do,' she concluded calmly. 'Although I might take you out to the occasional minor social event beforehand, by way of preparation. And in the course of the crucial evening, I'll destroy the photographs in front of you, Madeline.'

I didn't believe, of course, that she'd told me everything. I didn't believe for one minute that it could be so simple, and I had absolutely no way of knowing that she would keep her word. But one thing was for sure – I couldn't afford to turn her offer down.

'If I agree,' I said, 'do you swear that you will destroy *all* the photographs?'

'I do. I'll also send a telegram to Sophie, tonight, by telephone – and I'll send it in your name. You can be with me when I make the call. Of course Sophie will have to cancel her forthcoming New York engagements and arrange her sailing, which will take her a little time – while you, Madeline, will have three weeks in which to prepare yourself.' Beatrice smiled at me silkily. 'Well?'

I agreed. Of course, I agreed, though I felt cold with apprehension. But she sent a telegram to Sophie that very night, and I told myself, *I have already lost Nathan. What else have I got to lose?*

For the next few days I didn't see Lady Beatrice at all, and I was aware that Mrs Lambert and the rest of the household revelled in her absence. 'Perhaps we've seen the last of Her Ladyship,' Mrs Lambert said hopefully. But I said nothing, because I lived in hourly expectation of her summons.

Meanwhile I settled into my apartment in the Duke's Hertford Street house and Dervla, as my maid, had a small room next to mine. She was quieter than she used to be, and I should have been suspicious about it, but I wasn't. 'Lady Beatrice hasn't finished with us yet, Dervla,' I warned her. 'And we must be very careful of her. Do you understand?'

'Yes,' she whispered. 'Of course, Maddie.'

The wet weather that had prevailed when we arrived in London had almost immediately given way to several days of heat; in fact the sun was so relentless that the plane trees wilted even in the shade. During that time of waiting, I sat with the Duke in his bedroom every morning and every afternoon.

Sometimes he asked me to read to him from his books of poetry, or perhaps an article from the daily papers; but I noticed that after a while James would come in, and I soon realised that his entry was a signal that I had been with my guardian for a little too long. As I made my departure I would whisper to James, 'I'm so sorry. I didn't mean to tire him.'

James's few quiet words always reassured me. 'Not at all, ma'am. You're doing him a world of good. He's been sleeping far better at nights since you came.'

I wasn't sure how much my guardian remembered of what I'd told him on the telephone, or if he recollected at all that first the Duchess and then Lady Beatrice had moved into Belfield Hall. But one afternoon, he touched my hand and said, 'Last time we spoke, you were worried about the Duchess. I hope you've heard that Mr Fitzpatrick has gone to deal with her.'

I nodded. 'I wasn't sure, at first, if she had your permission to be there. I should have telephoned you, straight away—'

'It's all right,' he said quickly. 'Not your fault.' He smiled. 'Once she's decided on something, it's like stopping a steamroller.'

I didn't mention Beatrice, and I hoped he had forgotten her.

But he hadn't forgotten Sophie. I was sitting in his bedroom one day after lunch when I realised that the Duke was becoming disturbed, almost feverish. His blinds were drawn against the bright sunlight, but the heat was nevertheless making him uncomfortable, I could tell. The nurse had gone downstairs to prepare a cold drink for him, and I'd got up anxiously to go and look for her, when the Duke caught my wrist.

'Sophie,' he was muttering. 'Sophie.' Perspiration sheened his brow.

I clasped his scarred hand and leaned close to him so he could hear me. 'I swear that I'm doing everything I can to bring her to you. To make her yours, Your Grace.'

His breathing became easier and he lay back against the pillows. His eyes had closed again, but I heard him whisper, 'Thank you.'

Later that afternoon I went to find James, to ask him if he would move a gramophone I'd noticed in the downstairs parlour up to the Duke's sitting room. I followed, carrying some records under my arm, and as soon as James nodded that all was ready I put the first one on the turntable.

Through the open door I could see the Duke lying in his bed, his bandages starkly white beneath the neckline of his pyjamas. His eyes were closed, and I had my hand ready to stop the record in an instant if need be; but as the sweet melody filled the room I saw his eyes gradually flicker open in surprise and pleasure.

I walked through to him to sit on my usual chair by his bed. 'This is Sophie's latest record,' I told him.

Now listen to me, sweetheart, 'cause since I met you
My friends all say I'm crazy, don't know what to do.
Can't sleep at night, can't think, can't dance,
Just wander around with my mind in a trance.
All I'm thinking is, Where are you?
'Cause I'm breathless – just breathless for you.

After that I played her songs to him often. Being with my guardian made me happy, because I felt useful; but after I'd left him and gone to my room I would feel heartbroken all over again. I would try to make some sense of Dervla's chatter as she tidied my dressing table or saw to my clothes or gossiped about the Duke's beautiful house and his staff. I'd quickly realised that any remorse she should have felt was submerged by her excitement at being back in London – during that first week she was forever rushing to the window to gaze at the cars and people outside. Neither did the heat appear to trouble her, though I found the dusty air of London oppressive.

When she'd gone I would gaze out of the window too, but I would be thinking all the time of Nathan and how he'd betrayed me, and Sophie's beautiful songs would make me hurt all over again. Because I'd loved him, you see. I'd loved him, so very much.

Then Lady Beatrice rang to give me my instructions.

She told me over the telephone that I was to go to her house in fashionable Grosvenor Square that evening at six. 'We've so much to see to, Madeline,' she said briskly. 'You need to be fitted with clothes. You need to be groomed to perfection.' She paused. 'I really hope this is not too much to ask.'

I bowed my head, thinking of the photographs and of my guardian lying on his sickbed, longing for Sophie. 'What about Dervla? Should I bring her with me?'

She almost laughed. 'Good God, no.'

She told me she would send her chauffeur Christopher for me in her Rolls-Royce, and with that she ended the call. I had to explain to Mrs Lambert and James where I was going, of course; I saw James's face darkening, and Mrs Lambert looked upset. I offered some paltry explanation, I think – I told them that Beatrice had offered to show me a little more of London – but of course, they couldn't understand why I was going there and I could tell that they were disappointed in me.

Dervla's eyes widened when I explained where I was going. 'Tell me all about it, Maddie, won't you?' she pleaded. 'You'll find her clothes and her house and everything simply wonderful—'

'Dervla,' I said, 'next you'll be telling me you wished you still worked for her.'

She looked abashed. 'Oh, no, Maddie. Never.'

As soon as I arrived at Grosvenor Square, Lady Beatrice took me up to a bedroom suite on the top floor – I instantly hated its opulence. 'This is for you,' she told me. 'You can sleep here whenever you wish.'

I went very still. 'I don't see why I should ever need to stay.'

She shrugged. 'The offer is there, always. And look –' Beatrice was opening the wardrobe door '– I've bought some clothes for you. From Paris.'

She pointed to a luxurious display of day gowns, evening gowns and stoles, with shoes to match each outfit. Beatrice took my stunned astonishment for delight. 'Oh, Madeline,' she exclaimed, taking my arm. 'We are going to have such fun, you and I.'

I drew away from her as if her touch scalded me.

After that first night Beatrice sent her chauffeur for me most evenings at around six, and I always insisted he drove me home later, for the thought of sleeping under Beatrice's roof horrified me. She didn't argue with me, but she talked constantly about the fundraising ball that she and her friends would be holding; she seemed obsessed with it and with me, and night after night she would send her own personal maid, Margaret, to help me take my bath and style my hair. Then Beatrice herself would come in to watch me trying on the various gowns she'd bought for me.

Margaret, I remembered Dervla saying, had been Beatrice's lady's maid for many years, though she'd stayed behind in London when Beatrice came to Belfield Hall. Harriet had mentioned her almost with fear. *Thank goodness she's not here*, she'd said. Margaret was more than a maid, I soon realised – she was almost Beatrice's confidante. I would stand motionless as Margaret held up one ballgown after another against me, while Beatrice walked around saying, 'No. Not the dark blue, Margaret. With Madeline's black hair, it's too sombre. The pink might be better, I fancy. Or the jade green . . .'

But first, of course, came the expensive lingerie, simi-lar to the garments that Dervla had revelled in, only far more luxurious, and all this preparation took hours. I submitted silently as Margaret helped me into the silk brassieres and panties, the stockings and gossamer petticoats, but I kept thinking, *This was what Dervla let them do to her.* Those photographs of her posing in the portrait gallery at Belfield Hall haunted me.

I think Beatrice liked to consider me as a plaything, a possession. As for Margaret, I was beginning to understand what Harriet had said about her – quite simply, she frightened me. Her face was narrow, her eyes dark, and she had a small scar on her left cheek. She'd quickly noticed that I was scarred too, spotting the old silver marks on my wrist when she bathed me even though I'd tried to snatch my hand away. Margaret had said softly, 'So you like to punish yourself, Madeline? You enjoy – pain?'

I said nothing, although my heart hammered. I lifted my head and waited for her to bring the towels so I could dry myself – but I knew she would run straight to Beatrice with this news.

By day I would spend hours with the Duke, reading aloud to him or listening to Sophie's records with him as the nurse sat by the window, reading or knitting but always watchful. Sometimes the Duke would talk a little about Sophie. 'You saw her in that turquoise dress, didn't you, Madeline? She wore it often, because she knew that I loved her in it. She looked beautiful in it, didn't she?'

'She *is* beautiful, Your Grace,' I said. 'And she is on her way to you, now.' Yesterday a telegram had arrived from Sophie, who was about to set sail from New York

– Tell him I will be with him, very soon. Tell him I think of him, always.

He smiled at my words, but then his eyes became shadowed. 'People will talk, when we are together again. Their opinion means nothing to me, but you are my ward. I'm afraid that they might be cruel to you, Madeline, out of spite—'

I leaned close, and I whispered. 'Please do not worry about me. I cannot wait to see Sophie either. I will be happy if you are happy.'

I'd realised early on that Christopher the chauffeur was one of Beatrice's lovers. One evening, she'd told me to come straight to her room as soon as I was ready and dressed. 'Margaret will show you the way,' she said casually. 'There's no need to knock.'

When I went in, Lady Beatrice was standing with her hands flat against the wall to support herself, wearing nothing but a black silk kimono – and Christopher was there. He was fully clad, but his trousers were unfastened. He'd pulled her kimono up around her hips and stood behind her, pleasuring her fiercely while she cried out, very near to her extremity. But she looked over her shoulder at me and smiled, and I knew then that she'd intended me to see all of it: her sleek, naked hips, Christopher's thrusting erection: *everything*.

At first we ate alone at her house, Lady Beatrice and I, waited on by her silent staff. But after the first week we began to go out, as she'd promised. We dined in splendour at the Ritz one night, and the night after that at the Dorchester, with a select few of her female friends, and I realised Beatrice had been quite right when she told me that her companions were nothing like the people I'd met when I was being chaperoned by Lady Tolcaster.

At the Tolcaster house, I'd been surrounded by girls who were always closely guarded. Now, I was with a different type of woman – all of them were rich, needless to say, and many of them had titles – and there were no innocents here. Most of the women were married, but they often spoke with scorn of their wealthy husbands, and with pride of their various lovers.

All of them regarded me, Beatrice's protégée, with curiosity, amusement and, yes, jealousy; because Lady Beatrice and Margaret had, in that short time, transformed me. My clothes were only a part of it. On the evening that she planned to take me out for the first time, Beatrice had brought her own expensive hairstylist to my room to have my dark curls trimmed and shaped into a fashionable bob, and Margaret had seen to my make-up. By the time they'd all finished, I scarcely recognised myself, for with my scarlet lips, and pale face powder, and kohl'd eyes, I looked – 'Stunning,' breathed Lady Beatrice.

On the Monday of my second week as her protégée, we dined early at her house, then Lady Beatrice told me that we were going to meet her female friends at a small hotel in Chelsea, where a private show was to be given by some dancers. Chelsea was considered to be daringly beyond the fashionable limits, and Beatrice's friends were buzzing with excitement as they waited for us in the bar, their cut-glass accents giving their origins away as they sipped martinis or champagne. Some of them, I'd realised, were habitual users of cocaine, taking it like snuff from tiny, enamelled boxes they kept in their clutch bags.

Beatrice herself always drank a large glass of chilled champagne before Christopher drove us to the evening's venue, and she would insist that I have one too. She also offered me Christopher, saying, 'You must be so frustrated, my dear. After all, you're not a virgin, are you? I find his services take the edge off my appetite, so that I can be a little more discerning later on.'

This was really how she used to talk to me. This was how she talked to all her women friends.

On the night that we went to Chelsea, I'd had a larger than usual glass of champagne – I must have sensed what was in store. With Beatrice's hand on my arm, we followed her friends downstairs to a private room. I was wearing a sleek cream gown, I remember, with narrow shoulder straps and a plunging neckline. It was hot down there, and it took me a while to get used to the dim lights and the haze of cigarette smoke. A jazz band played in the far corner, though at first the musicians could hardly be heard for the cacophony of voices.

While we waited for the dancers to come on, some of Beatrice's friends had gathered around me and one, whom I'd not seen before, exclaimed, 'But she's the Duke of Belfield's ward, surely, Beatrice, darling. When the Duke recovers and hears that she's joined our set, there's bound to be a scandal—'

'Leave it to me, Sybil,' Beatrice said calmly. 'I know what I'm doing, believe me.'

When the dancers arrived, six young men in tuxedos

and six girls in short dresses, they performed dances from America – the cakewalk, the turkey trot, the one-step. The men were athletic, often lifting the girls high or swinging them round, and I began to realise that Beatrice's friends knew them by name, pointing and talking about them casually. 'Oh, there's dear Benjamin,' the one called Sybil exclaimed gleefully. 'The third from the right – see? Darlings, I had him at the Ritz last month – the *best* bedroom! – and my husband footed the entire bill, though the poor fool didn't have a clue.'

By the end of the evening, several of Lady Beatrice's friends had left in taxis with the men of their choice. 'My dear,' Beatrice said when she saw me looking, 'my friends will do anything to relieve their boredom.'

She thought I was shocked, though of course I wasn't. I was more than usually quiet as Christopher drove us home, though.

'A fit of the sulks, Madeline?' Beatrice enquired in her hard, bright voice. I could see from the glitter in her eyes that she was angry with me. 'You could at least pretend to have enjoyed yourself. I'll expect a better performance from you on the night of the charity ball.'

A fresh shiver ran through me. What exactly was she planning? And whatever she intended, could I really trust her to destroy those photographs? At least another, particular fear of mine had not materialised – I had been afraid that in Beatrice's company I would meet Lord Sydhurst again, but of him there had been no sign.

My resolve remained intact – until one evening when Christopher brought me home a little earlier than usual and I found Dervla searching my room.

Chapter Twenty-one

Dervla told me everything, then. How at Belfield Hall, the day after the party, Lady Beatrice had made her confess that I had stolen the film. How Beatrice had forced Dervla to work her way into my favour again – and had ordered her to spy on me in London.

'She said she would get me into trouble, if I didn't get you to take me as your maid.' Dervla was scrubbing tears from her eyes. 'Please, Maddie, don't be angry with me.'

Dazed, I stared at her. 'When she first hired you in London – did she realise, Dervla, that you and I used to be friends?'

Dervla wept again. But I got her to tell me, eventually, that her story of the employment agency had been a lie – she had in fact worked for a while as a waitress in a smart London restaurant, and had caught Beatrice's eye there because she pronounced the names of the French dishes with such fluency. After that Beatrice had talked to her more closely, and had discovered how we'd been at the convent at Nantes together, how Dervla had been my closest friend. Lady Beatrice had hired her as her maid instantly.

I was beyond anger – I was in despair at my own

incredible stupidity. I said, 'I can't believe that I was foolish enough ever to trust you. What have you been searching for in my room?'

She hesitated. 'Lady Beatrice asked me to see if you'd received any letters from Nathan Mallory.'

What? I clenched my hands. 'Why?'

'She – likes to know everything,' she stammered.

'Well,' I said, 'I'm no longer in touch with Nathan Mallory. You can tell her yourself. You can go and work for her again. Because you're certainly not working any longer for me.' I was already holding open the door.

'You want me to leave – *now*? In the middle of the night?'

'You can wait till daylight. I'll tell Mrs Lambert that you've had to go and stay with a sick relative. Or something. Oh, and if you *do* go and work for Lady Beatrice, please make sure that I don't have to see you at her house, will you?'

She was weeping. 'I'm sorry. I'll go, of course. And Maddie, this charity ball that Lady Beatrice is taking you to—'

'Yes?'

'Be careful,' she whispered. 'That's all.'

I didn't see her again. By then I knew I had to spend only a few more evenings at Lady Beatrice's house before the ball, but my apprehension was soaring; I hadn't needed Dervla's warning to know that Lady Beatrice was capable of almost anything. I hated those evenings, from the moment Christopher came to the Duke's house at six to collect me to when he brought me back a little before midnight. I hated the way

Margaret would bathe me with a sponge and scented soap, and finger my skin as I lay tensely in the water. 'So pretty,' she would murmur. 'So very pretty.'

On the night of the charity ball, I had just taken my bath when Beatrice came into my bedroom. I was sitting in front of my dressing table clad in a silk kimono like the ones Beatrice loved, and the gown I was to wear lay on the bed behind me – it was made of rose-coloured silk, with silver sequins on the bodice and a silver girdle to tie round my waist.

Margaret was arranging my hair with great care when Beatrice entered. 'We'll soon be ready, my lady,' Margaret told her. 'She'll be the star of the party, no doubt about it. She'll have all the gentlemen bidding through the roof—'

And that was when I began to realise what was going to happen. That was when all my fears, all my suspicions, gathered and erupted.

'*Bidding*?' I spun round on my chair, knocking over a tiny scent bottle. 'Bidding? What are you talking about?'

Beatrice dismissed Margaret from the room.

She explained that it was customary, at this annual party, for her women friends to take turns to bring a girl of their choice to be auctioned amongst the many rich gentlemen guests who were invited. 'It's for charity,' she said calmly. 'I told you. This year it's my turn, and I'm bringing *you*.'

'But what are they paying for?'

She shrugged. 'Oh, a dance or two. The pleasure of your company.'

A dance or two . . .

I realised Beatrice was still speaking.

'Really, Madeline,' she was saying, 'these annual parties of ours are such fun! It's quite straightforward – you'll go under the auctioneer's hammer tonight, we'll raise some money for a worthy cause, and those photographs will be destroyed. I know you've no intention of letting me down. Of course, it is just possible that whoever acquires you might insist on a more intimate encounter, shall we say, in return for his money . . .'

The voice of my childhood echoed in my brain: *My name is Madeline, and what can I do to please you?* Who would be there? Who would be bidding for me? Her friends? Lord Sydhurst? 'No,' I said, starting to get to my feet. '*No.*'

'Remember the photographs, Madeline,' she said, and I saw her smirk of satisfaction as I sank back into my seat. 'Oh, and by the way, we're allowed to send invitations to extra guests. I wonder if you can guess who I'm inviting?'

I felt the blood pounding in my head.

'I'm inviting Nathan Mallory,' she went on. 'Yes, he's in London – still desperately trying to raise money for his beleaguered estate. Dear Nathan. We used to have such fun, he and Lottie and I . . .'

She must have seen the colour draining from my face. Then she left my room and Margaret came back to dress me, but I stood up, almost pushing her aside. 'I must make a phone call,' I told her.

The old scar on her cheek pulled her mouth into a

sneer. 'Not to the Duke, I hope? That really wouldn't be wise.'

'Not to the Duke. But I need a telephone, *now*.'

She led me in silence down to the telephone in the main hall, and though I knew very well she would be listening, I phoned the Duke's house and asked for James.

I was put through to James's office, where he answered me coolly. He and Mrs Lambert were of the same mind, of course – neither of them could understand why I was in thrall to Lady Beatrice – but at least they'd not told my guardian about my constant visits to Grosvenor Square, and I was grateful to them for that.

'James,' I said. 'There's a man called Nathan Mallory, who owns a small estate in Oxfordshire. I'm not sure if you've met him?'

'I have met him, ma'am.'

I pressed on. 'I think Mr Mallory is in London, James. I don't know where, and I know this could be difficult, but please, will you see if you can somehow find him, and tell him – tell him not to come to the charity ball tonight?'

There was silence at the other end of the phone. I knew that James kept a meticulous record of every call he made or received on a notepad in his office, and I pictured him writing my message down. At last he said, 'I'll do my best, ma'am.'

'Thank you, James. Thank you so much.' I ended the call and sat very still in Beatrice's magnificent hall.

I'm doing this for the Duke and Sophie, I told myself. *For the Duke and Sophie.*

Then I let them prepare me. I tried to convince myself that Nathan wouldn't dream of coming anyway, but I could imagine his scorn if – *when* – he learned that I was involved with Beatrice again. Did that matter, after what he'd done to me? After he'd planned to use me for his own revenge against the Duke? Yes, it did. It mattered and it hurt more than anything.

Beatrice gave me champagne, and I drank too much of it; I was so weary of battling her. Then Margaret removed my kimono and brought me a new set of lingerie to wear beneath the rose-pink gown: a brassiere made of black satin trimmed with tiny pink silk roses, and lace-edged panties of the same fabric that squeezed and caressed my most intimate parts. Wordlessly I put everything on: the long gown with its silver girdle, the pendant diamond earrings that Lady Beatrice had insisted I borrow; and finally Margaret, careful as ever, put more kohl around my eyes and painted my lips a vivid pink to match my dress.

'Is this enough?' I asked them both. 'After tonight, am I free?' I was feeling dizzy with champagne and sick with despair.

Beatrice parted my gown's deep cleavage and adjusted the flimsy cups of my brassiere; I recoiled at her touch, although I couldn't help but be aware of how my tender nipples stiffened and rose to her caress. Finally she fastened a tight diamond bracelet around my scarred wrist, then she looked at me and said quietly, 'It will be enough, after tonight.'

The charity ball was being held at the exquisite Belgravia home of one of Beatrice's friends. By the time we arrived the house was bright with lights, and music echoed loudly from the lively band in the grand salon. But once our wraps were handed to the hovering footmen, Beatrice led me not to where the guests were gathered, but along the hallway to a back room.

Margaret was in there, waiting. 'Watch her carefully,' Lady Beatrice instructed her, and left. I looked around, seeing that a fire was burning in the hearth despite the warmth of the night. Several bottles of champagne stood in buckets of ice on the table and Margaret was already handing a glass of the pale, sparkling liquid to me.

'This is where the gentlemen pay to see you in advance,' she told me. 'This is how it's done, every year.' I thrust the glass aside. 'You'd better calm yourself,' Margaret went on. 'They'll be in soon, to inspect the goods.'

She went to open a different door from the one I'd come in by, and I stood very still as the men outside began to saunter into that room: men of all ages, all in formal evening attire. Those men gazed at me, stared at me and talked about me as if I wasn't there. I began to twist that bracelet on my wrist, but I told myself, *This cannot be worse than anything you've already endured. Think of the Duke and his Sophie. Remember the photographs. By this time tomorrow, it will all be over . . .*

Lord Sydhurst came in. As he strolled up to me, the other men left the room – and even Margaret moved away as far away as she could. 'Madeline,' Lord Sydhurst said. 'I've been looking forward to this evening.' He touched my cheek, and as I recoiled he laughed. 'You do realise, don't you, that I can outbid everyone here? That means you'll be mine for the whole night. How interesting to see you following in your mother's footsteps.'

I felt my senses reel. *Anyone would assume, with only one look at you – that you're on offer to the highest bidder, just as your mother was.* He'd said that to me when he had me trapped, during the Belfield Hall party. *I cannot do this*, I thought wildly. *I cannot do this.*

'And just in case you're still thinking of trying to run,' he was saying softly, 'I really must tell you that I know everything that happened on the night that the Marquis de Valery died. You see – I was there. And I saw you kill him.'

Then he left me, and except for Margaret I was alone. I sank into the nearest chair, and I gave way to despair.

When I was a child, the Marquis, my mother's lover, had explained to me that I would be put in prison if I did not let him do exactly what he wanted or if I ever tried to tell a soul about his visits to the house in the rue Saint-Honoré that was, after all, *his* house. I almost stopped eating, and I would shake every time he came through the door.

My mother still made me dress up and curtsey and pass round dishes of sweetmeats whenever her friends visited in the afternoons. Whenever *he* visited. But soon she started complaining about me to everyone when I was in the room.

'Little Madeline is becoming so thin,' my mother exclaimed one day, 'thin and sulky.'

The Marquis had glanced in my direction in a bored

sort of way, as if what he'd done – taking away my innocence, making me hate myself – meant nothing to him
at all. 'Buy her something,' he suggested. 'Buy her a
kitten.'

So she did, and I loved my kitten – I called him Pepin.
But one night when I was ten, and my mother was holding a fancy-dress party with the guests all in masks, the
Marquis came to my room. He was wearing a full-length
white Roman toga and a mask painted black and gold,
and he took my hand, thrusting Pepin, whom I was
clutching, to the floor. Then he led me out onto the
landing, to make me watch my mother's party.

I think the knowledge that the war was shortly to
break out made my mother's guests that night lose what
few inhibitions they had; and the wine did the rest.
There was a troupe of acrobats there to entertain them,
lithe young men and women who were dressed in short
Grecian tunics, and after they'd finished their tumbling
tricks, the lights were dimmed and they began to copulate, in front of everyone.

I'd jerked my head away, but the Marquis gripped my
arm and forced me to watch while my mother's masked
guests – they were so drunk – began to copy the antics
of the young tumblers, kissing and fondling one another
and engaging in sexual acts in corners.

I bit the Marquis's hand to make him let go and ran
to my bedroom. He charged after me – he had been
drinking heavily, like the others – and stumbled over my
sleeping kitten. Swearing, he snatched Pepin up, but
Pepin scratched him – and the Marquis strangled him
and threw his limp little body to the floor. I think I was

hysterical; I ran from my room in my nightgown, carrying Pepin, who was still warm. 'I will tell the *gendarmes*,' I sobbed. 'I will tell them what you've done.'

Though it was well past two by then, the party had not abated, but I was beyond caring. The Marquis caught me on the landing, at the top of the wide staircase; he threw Pepin aside and tried to drag me back to my room, but I kicked and struggled, pushing at him until all at once he tripped on his toga and tumbled down the stairs. He lay at the bottom, all of a heap; he had broken his neck. Every single one of my mother's masked guests had turned to stare, and I stood at the top of the stairs, petrified with fear.

One of the women started screaming. My mother, who was dressed as Marie Antoinette in a white wig and a hooped gown, hurried upstairs to grasp my arms and shake me. 'You fool, Madeline. You stupid little fool.'

And then a masked man clad in an old-fashioned army officer's uniform climbed the stairs also and moved my mother aside. 'That isn't the way to deal with the matter, Celine.' He spoke with a slightly foreign accent – English, I thought – and I saw, through the slits in his mask, that his eyes were unusually pale.

He advised all the guests to depart, and to remain completely silent about the evening's events. After some footmen had carried the Marquis's lifeless body away, the masked man in the officer's uniform turned to me and said in a low voice, 'Of course, it's quite clear what happened, you little fool. *You* caused his death.'

'No. No,' I cried. 'The Marquis kept coming to my room. He did things, and he killed Pepin—'

'You pushed the Marquis down the stairs,' he pronounced. 'You are a wicked child, a whore in the making, and a murderess.'

I gazed up at him in terror – was he right? *Had* I killed him?

'If you ever say one word about the Marquis,' he went on, 'if you tell *anyone* your made-up stories about what he did to you, you will go to prison or the madhouse for ever.'

My mother was at his side, still wearing her mask. 'You killed him,' she hissed at me. 'You killed him.'

I shrank away, shaking – *it must be true, then. It had to be true.* I was cold, so cold, and no one came to my side, no one else spoke to me, but I saw the man in the uniform take my mother's arm and speak to her reassuringly. My mother was very beautiful – have I said that? She was so beautiful that she made men mad for her – they would say anything, do anything for her.

The man with the pale eyes became her new lover, but shortly after that the war began, and I never saw him again – I guessed he had returned to his homeland. Afterwards my mother never mentioned that evening, or the Marquis – except to tell me, in her cold, clipped voice, that his death had been reported to the authorities as an accident. By then she was completing her arrangements to have me sent to the Convent of the Sacred Trinity in Nantes, to keep to myself the knowledge that I was responsible for a man's death.

I'd known, from the moment I'd received that unsigned letter at Belfield Hall, that my past was catching up with me. What I hadn't known was that Lord Sydhurst was the man in the officer's uniform who'd taken charge on the night of the Marquis's death; I hadn't recognised him, because he'd been masked and I had been a child, a terrified child. I'd had no one to turn to, and when I was told that I was a murderer, I believed it.

On meeting me in London at Lady Tolcaster's last summer, Lord Sydhurst must have realised exactly who I was. He'd been playing games with me all along, with his letter and his insinuations, and he wanted me, desired me just as he'd once desired my mother. This evening, the charity ball, offered him the opportunity he'd been waiting for, and I could see no way out. After he'd gone, I was alone in that back room except for Margaret; I asked her for a glass of water, but when she came back she had Beatrice with her.

'Drink more champagne,' Beatrice ordered me.

'No.'

'One more glass of champagne, Madeline. And then you can watch me dispose of the photographs.' She pointed to her jewelled evening bag. 'I've got them – they're in here.'

Though it made me dizzy and sick, I drank the champagne and she nodded approval. She drew those photographs out of her bag, together with the negatives, and walked over to the fireplace to start throwing them onto the flames, where they hissed and melted in the heat.

'I keep my word, you see,' she said. 'And now it's time for you to keep yours.'

I cannot look back on that evening without remembering the horror and the shame of it; so I shall pass quickly over how I had to stand at Beatrice's side, in front of those enthralled and hateful guests in their evening finery, while Beatrice put her hand on my arm and smiled around at them all with pride.

There was a master of ceremonies, a small, sprightly man in a tailcoat, who stood on a podium and read aloud from a parchment he'd unrolled that listed all my supposed attributes. 'Here we have Lady Beatrice's protégée, for our charity auction – a young lady of striking beauty, as you can see. She is of French origin, and an aristocrat by birth – her father was a baron, and her mother a star of Paris society during the war years . . .'

Lies, all lies – my mother was a whore and my father unknown. But everyone gazed at me with rapt attention as the man on the podium went on, 'This young lady is truly exquisite, as we've all observed. She is compliant. And she belongs to the highest bidder, ladies and gentlemen – for the next twelve hours. Let the auction begin!'

I stared ahead of me at the darkness beyond the lights, turning Lady Beatrice's diamond bracelet on my wrist. I was thinking, *It will soon be over.* The photographs had been destroyed. After tonight, I would escape from Beatrice. I would leave London, leave England for ever . . .

I could hear their bids. Twenty guineas. Fifty. A hundred . . . *What?* Were these people crazy, to spend such an amount on a few hours with me? No, they were just fabulously, recklessly rich, and a kind of wildness had infected them all, I think – I had seen it at my mother's house, amongst people who had always had everything that money could buy, but who still wanted more.

I could endure it, I resolved fiercely. The photographs

had been destroyed. I *would* endure it, for my guardian and Sophie's sake – or so I thought, until I realised that, as he had threatened, Lord Sydhurst was leading the bidding. He had made an offer of two hundred guineas, and the other bidders were shaking their heads; Lord Sydhurst was moving closer to me. *No.* I could not do this . . .

Then the double doors swung wide open – and Nathan arrived.

Chapter Twenty-two

Everyone had turned to stare as the doors crashed back. Nathan stood there in his shabby coat with his tie undone, yet still looking, to my eyes, so very beautiful.

'Two hundred and fifty guineas,' Nathan pronounced.

'Three hundred.' Sydhurst's cool voice floated across from the other side of the room. The bidding started once more. Again and again Lord Sydhurst raised his offer, only for Nathan to come back with a higher bid still. I was briefly distracted as I glimpsed Beatrice move to Sydhurst's side, whispering something; but at almost the same moment Nathan made a bid of five hundred guineas – and all eyes were on Lord Sydhurst, who shook his head, looking furious. I saw Nathan write out and hand over a cheque – *oh, Nathan, how can you afford it?* – then he came for me, and his eyes were so hard and so cold. 'Madeline,' he said harshly. 'What the hell are you doing? Sydhurst? *Beatrice?*'

'Nathan,' I began. 'I'm so sorry. That money – you—'

He cut in sharply. 'Let's get you out of here. Then you can embark on your list of excuses – though I warn you, my patience is wearing thin.'

Nathan took my hand, with no gentleness, and swept

me past the avid onlookers. I was trembling with tiredness and mortification. But it wasn't over yet, because Beatrice grabbed me just before we exited the room and managed to hiss in my ear, 'Oh, Madeline. You've done so well – better than I could have believed possible. You've raised a wonderful amount of money for my charity, and my friends are wild with envy. And as a completely unexpected bonus – you've ruined Nathan Mallory.'

She was still smiling as Nathan dragged me away. My brain was reeling. Nathan. Oh, Nathan. He'd no doubt raised all that money to try to save his estate, but now he'd lost it. Beatrice had perhaps wanted him to come so he could witness my humiliation, but when he'd entered the bidding and driven it so high she'd decided to let him ruin himself. Why? As revenge, perhaps, because he so clearly preferred me to her?

I was exhausted and overwrought as Nathan led me away from that place. He wrapped me in his coat, as he'd done on the hillside above Belfield Hall on the night we first met; for one brief moment I was in his arms, but this time there was no gentleness in his touch. Yet I still wanted him so much, with his tie undone and his thick brown hair all awry as if he'd been running his hand through it again and again. I wanted him so much, but he despised me – I could see it in the harsh set of his gorgeous mouth, the wildness in his dark eyes. He said tightly, 'What's your address at the moment, Madeline? You'll have to update me. Are you living at the Duke's house? At Lady Beatrice's? Or wherever your latest adventure happens to take you?'

Outside, the heat of the evening had diminished and a hint of mist curled around the bright street lights. I clutched my arms across my chest and bowed my head, simply hurting. *Not fair,* I whispered to myself. *Not fair.* But what else could I expect? He thought I was worthless, and he was right, I'd always been worthless. I'd tried to warn him of that.

I tilted my head up at last to meet his hard gaze. 'I'm living at my guardian's house in Hertford Street,' I said. 'I suppose I could ask you to give me a chance to explain, about tonight. But you never were very good at giving me a chance to explain, were you, Nathan? Come to that, you were always rather late with the truth yourself.'

For a moment, some stark emotion broke through his utterly bleak expression and he lifted his hand to let his knuckles drift across my cheek – oh, the need I felt for him! The sheer longing. But then his mouth was a thin line again, and he looked at his watch.

'It's two in the morning,' he said tersely, 'and I don't imagine I can take you back to your guardian at this hour.'

I shook my head – *no*. Everyone would be asleep, and my arrival, however quiet, would disturb someone in the house, somewhere.

'You'll have to come back to my place.' He thrust his hand into his pocket, drawing out his keys. 'It's very small, but I do have a spare bedroom.'

That message was clear enough. I shrugged. 'Why not?' I said, but I was hurting so very much inside.

This man had intended using me for his revenge

– he'd admitted that. But for a few moments, when he'd wrapped his coat around me, being in his arms and breathing in the familiar, enthralling scent of his skin and hair had been all I wanted . . . No, that was a lie. I wanted more – I always did want more, where this man was concerned.

His old, battered car was parked a little way down the street. I'd loved that car, and had so many memories of the happy times we had had in it, of his patience and humour as he taught me to drive . . .

He opened the car door. 'I rent a house in Poplar, in east London. I'm afraid it's rather below your standards.'

I looked at him. 'Oh, nothing's below my standards,' I said. 'I thought you'd have realised that by now.'

In fact, after the hateful opulence of Lady Beatrice's house I found that entering his little home was like returning to some well-loved place, because everything about it – his books, the ready-laid fire in the sitting room, the way his few belongings were so tidily kept – reminded me almost unbearably of the gamekeeper's cottage.

After lighting the fire, he went through to the tiny kitchen to make us both tea – I could see him from where I stood, boiling a kettle on a single gas ring. When he came back, he told me to sit down.

That money he'd paid for me. I sat on the very edge of a chair and put aside the mug he'd brought me, then I clasped my arms across my breasts. I still wore his coat over my shoulders, but it wasn't fastened and I was desperately trying to hide my rose-coloured gown's shameful cleavage. 'Nathan. The five hundred guineas. I'll pay you back, somehow. You must sell my emerald bracelet – that will help. And—'

He hissed out an exclamation – a warning, I realised – and my heart sank even further. He sat too, but on the other side of the room, and his posture was tense. 'Drink your tea,' he said. 'And then we'll both get some sleep. I don't think I particularly want to talk at the moment about the almost unbelievable mess into which you've got yourself.'

His dark eyes blazed across at me and I thought in despair, *I shouldn't have come here. I was a fool to have come here, with him.*

'So now you feel free to despise me,' I said calmly. 'Do you know, Nathan, I almost preferred it when you were using me for revenge.'

He raked his hand through his hair and put his mug down hard on a nearby table. 'Good God, Madeline—'

'Answer one question for me. Why did you rescue me tonight?'

'*Why?* Do you really have to ask?'

I shrugged. 'I imagine you're taking great pleasure in thinking me guilty of every vice under the sun – because then your own abominable behaviour to me is quite neatly cancelled out. Isn't it?'

He exhaled sharply and said in a cold, hard voice, 'I had to make some rapid decisions, when I arrived at that party and saw you at Lady Beatrice's side, for sale. And I came to the following conclusion. I decided that if you really wanted to put yourself up for the highest bidder, then I was damn well going to have you. Nobody else, Madeline. Nobody else.'

He'd got up from his chair and was walking steadily across the little room towards me. Something in the set of his powerful shoulders and the slant of his hard mouth made me jump for the door, but he was too quick for me. Dragging the coat – *his* coat – from my shoulders, he devoured me with his eyes – then his gaze flew to Beatrice's diamond bracelet.

His fingers closed around my wrist. 'Who gave you this?' His teeth were clenched. I tried to pull my hand away, but he lifted it up with a grip like steel and with his other hand unfastened the clasp using swift, deft movements. 'It was Beatrice, wasn't it?' He threw it to the floor. 'Another damned bracelet that's too tight for you. God damn it to hell, Madeline – you've been using it to punish yourself again. I shall send the wretched thing back to her tomorrow . . .' His hand closed around the fresh, livid scars that were now exposed on my wrist, and when I made an attempt to free myself he swung me into his arms. 'I've paid money for you,' he stated. 'I've bought you for the night, *mam'selle.*'

At the harshness of his words, a torrent of emotions poured through me. *No. Not like this. Please, not like this.* 'I'll pay you back. I've told you I'll pay you back, Nathan! Now, let me go . . .'

But he'd kicked open the door into the narrow hallway and started carrying me up the stairs. 'Never.'

'Nathan.' I was struggling to get free from the iron grip of his embrace – I hated him, hated him for doing this. 'Damn you, Nathan – put me *down.*'

'In good time.' He was at the top of the stairs now, where I glimpsed a tiny room to my left, bare of furniture; but he was already moving on to shoulder open another door, then he'd switched on the light and we were in his bedroom. He carried me over to the bed and dropped me there.

'I've put you down,' he announced. And as I tried to pull myself up, he pinned me to the narrow bed – in fact he knelt astride me – and started unfastening the girdle of my evening gown. Then he ripped the garment itself apart, inch by gaudy inch, and I saw his face tighten dangerously as he realised what I was wearing underneath.

The black and pink brassiere that cupped my breasts. The tiny black panties, starkly circling my hips and running down to barely cover my sex.

I struggled to get away from him, feeling his eyes burn into my brassiere, beneath which my stiffening nipples were already treacherously yearning for his fingers, his mouth. He pinned me down again, with an oath; I closed my eyes in despair.

Then – *what*? My eyes flew open again. He was flexing the silver cord of my gown; he was using it to tie my hands to the iron headrail of his bed . . .

'Nathan.' This time my voice was trembling. 'Nathan – what are you doing?'

He carried on securing the knots, so that my arms were splayed out and stretched behind my head. Aghast, I struggled in vain to pull myself free. '*Nathan . . .*'

'I've decided,' he pronounced calmly, 'that I want you, and you want me. As I said – I came to that party

287

and I bought you, because I cannot bear to see any other man on earth lay a single filthy finger on you.'

I lay very still, while my heart thudded wildly against my ribs. But then I jerked myself frantically away, swivelling my hips so that I got my feet to the floor, pulling with all my might at the cord that bound me. Its grip was relentless.

Shaking his head in rebuke, Nathan clasped my bottom and heaved me squarely back onto his bed – and all the time there was a dangerous gleam in his eyes. Before I could clamp my legs together, his hands slid swiftly from my knees up the insides of my thighs, his palms flat against my skin; his thumbs hooked the lace of my panties aside, then parted my slick flesh, feeling my wetness, sliding steadily up and down. Acute desire curled in my belly; my blood was on fire. I closed my eyes, desperate with longing, desperate with shame.

'No. Keep your eyes open,' he chided. 'And you will see just how sorry I feel for you, *mam'selle*.'

Not like this, I wanted to say. *Please. Not like this*. But it was too late. I tried to swivel myself aside again, but he pinned me down with his firm hands. I jutted my chin. 'Just tell me first, will you,' I breathed, 'who you're getting your revenge on this time, Nathan. Is it me? The Duke, or Lady Beatrice? Or is this your wretched idea of *amusement*?'

He silenced me by pressing a hot, hard kiss to my lips. Then he got to his feet, his expression dark and unreadable in the shadows, and began stripping himself, exposing his lean, muscular body to my full view.

His spectacularly *aroused* body. Oh, my.

Pinioned as I was, I tried desperately to suppress the melting longing that surged through me – but my need for him only increased. By the time he arched himself over me, I stopped breathing – stopped *thinking* – as the heavy weight of his erection brushed across my tender abdomen, as his muscular chest caressed the sensitised tips of my breasts, which leapt to his touch with a yearning that all but overwhelmed me. I gave a gasp of shock that turned into a series of moans as he pressed kisses to my neck.

'Does *this* feel like – amusement?' He moved against me, his voice rough with desire. 'This isn't amusement. It isn't revenge either. It's called wanting you. Needing you.'

My head was spinning and my pulse thudding as he lifted my hips, knelt between my legs and licked there, rasping with his tongue, circling me until I was almost on the edge. Gazing at me steadily, he moved up my body and entered me with such a strong, such a breathtaking thrust that he drove every coherent thought from my mind. He cupped my chin to make me look up at him.

'Can you feel me?' he growled. 'Can you feel my desire for you, Madeline?'

I cried out 'Yes. Yes!' I longed to grasp him closer, but the cord held me and my wretched captivity only intensified my desire – oh God, I was his, and only his. Inside me he felt so big, so hard, so shockingly male, and my whole body craved him so much that my breathing was coming in short, desperate gasps.

He drew my nipple into his mouth, half-biting it, and

fresh pleasure seared me. Then he moved his hips, almost withdrawing his steely erection from me so I cried aloud, but he swiftly slid deep into me, again and again, and each thrust sent rolling waves of pleasure all through my trembling body.

He lifted his head. His beautiful eyes were dark with passion and his wicked mouth full of sensuality. 'You,' he was breathing, keeping me on the brink. 'I need *you*, Madeline.'

I tried to say, *You don't. You can't.* But then I couldn't say anything at all, because I could feel my body rising to grasp at the pleasure he was offering with each strong stroke. For a moment, his eyes burned into mine as he arched over me, then he kissed me deeply, his tongue masterful; he drove into me and ground himself against me, and I was consumed by an explosion of pleasure so pure and so intense that I couldn't breathe, I couldn't see – my world simply flew apart, and my hips shuddered against his as my raging climax rolled through me. Only when I lay limp and my breathing grew steadier did he pull out and ease himself between my lips, to pump his seed into my mouth, and I swallowed it down greedily, licking and sucking – *he thought me a whore, so I'd use a whore's tricks on him* – then I lay breathless and dazed.

He touched my cheek in the silence that had fallen, and I realised that a tear had squeezed its way out of my eye. *Merde.* I did not want him to see what he did to me. He untied the cord swiftly and gathered me in his arms, so I couldn't help but nestle against his naked chest, and he said, 'I meant it, Madeline. I don't want anyone to have you but me. Ever.'

If he *did* mean it, he was a fool. 'Nathan,' I said. 'I will ruin you. I *have* ruined you, after tonight.'

His gaze met mine calmly. 'Nobody ruins me but myself. And I've managed to do that quite well on my own. I want you to give me another chance, Madeline. To give *us* another chance.'

I began to speak, but my throat dried. *Nathan, my past is wretched and shameful. You don't want me. I cannot let you want me.* I desperately needed to say it all, but I couldn't find the words. I saw his eyes grow colder.

'I'm not rich enough for you,' he said. 'Is that it?'

I felt as I had when I was a child, curling away into my helpless corner of misery, and he drew his own conclusion. Rising from the bed, he started pulling on his clothes, handing me one of his clean white shirts to wear for what was left of the night. And he said, 'Whatever you think to the contrary, I will always be here for you. Always.'

I lay in his bed when he'd gone, hugging my arms across my chest. Where was he? In the tiny spare room I'd glimpsed, sleeping under a blanket on the floor? He preferred that to sleeping with me? Of course he did. Yet already, I missed him so much. He'd asked me to give him another chance, but only because he could not bear for anyone else to touch me. He thought I was a whore for allowing Beatrice to sell me off tonight. I'd thought that I could trust him; could even, some day perhaps, tell him about the scars and shattered innocence of my childhood; but I knew better now.

I must have fallen asleep at last, because I woke with

a start at six when he came in. He was dressed, and in the soft morning light he looked so like the Nathan I used to know that I wanted to reach out, and pull me to him, and . . .

'I'll take you back to the Duke's house,' he said flatly. 'Can you be ready in ten minutes?'

Chapter Twenty-three

I slipped into my guardian's house using my key, managing to avoid the servants, who I knew would already be busy about their morning tasks. Once in my room I ran a bath and afterwards dressed in an old, plain gown, brushing my hair and tying it back in a ribbon. I didn't go down to breakfast – I wasn't hungry. I was, quite simply, in despair.

Mrs Lambert – who assumed, I was sure, that I'd stayed at Lady Beatrice's house for the night – brought me a tray of coffee at ten and spoke to me coolly. But a little before lunch she came up to me again, to tell me that there was a telephone call for me – from Lady Beatrice.

I was studying the newspaper that I'd collected from downstairs, to see if there was anything the Duke might like me to read to him. I looked up and said, 'I really don't want to speak to her, thank you. Would you tell her so?'

Mrs Lambert's stiff expression was replaced by one of surprise. 'Very well, ma'am. But—'

'Please tell her not to ring me here again,' I said.

Mrs Lambert went hurrying off, and I thought that I'd seen a look of wonder and relief on her face.

With Beatrice's chauffeur no longer calling for me at six every evening, I had more time to be with my guardian. He still spent most of the day in his room, but he was usually up and dressed for his breakfast by nine, and Dr Grandersleigh, who made twice-daily visits, assured me that he was making an excellent recovery. I was so very glad. The Duke started teaching me to play chess, but sometimes he would break off to talk about Sophie and her voyage across the Atlantic. We often listened to her records, and I would remind him that every day brought her nearer to him.

As for James, I didn't find out if he'd contacted Nathan before the charity ball – I never asked. I avoided him, but sometimes I thought I saw him watching me. I tried not to think about Nathan, because it hurt too much; but instead, I thought about Sophie. When she did return, I wanted everything to be perfect for her, so I spent hours with Mrs Lambert, seeing to the rooms that had been hers when she lived here with the Duke last year, choosing new bedlinens and curtains from the samples the furnishing stores sent us. Each day went by slowly for my guardian, and slowly for me. But at last Sophie came home.

I'd been with the Duke in his parlour, playing chess, but I was even worse than usual, despite his tactful advice, because my mind as ever was filled by my yearning for Nathan. I missed him terribly. I had to remind myself that he despised me, and rightly so. *Why, then, did he ask you to give him another chance?* a tiny voice kept tormenting me. I had my answer ready: he couldn't bear the thought of anyone else touching me. He still wanted me, but the cure for that lay in my hands. All I had to do was to tell him of my past, and he would discard me for good.

I stared at the chessboard, angrily blinking away a sudden tear. Now I couldn't even remember which way a bishop moved – *merde*, how stupid could I be? The sound of a vehicle pulling up outside the house was almost a welcome distraction – I assumed it was a delivery van, or perhaps the doctor arriving early. But then I heard Mrs Lambert's glad cry of welcome, and I glanced up to see a look of almost painful expectation on the Duke's face.

There were light footsteps on the stairs, light footsteps in the corridor, followed by a sudden silence, as if someone was hesitating. Then the door opened and Sophie was there, looking exquisite in a pale green taffeta jacket, a matching dress and high-heeled cream shoes. She quietly stood there, gazing at her Duke.

'Sophie,' he breathed, and held out his arms to her.

'Oh, my love. My darling love.' And she ran into his embrace.

I tiptoed from the room, quietly shutting the door.

The Duke's recovery was swift, now that his Sophie was here. At first I kept my distance, but Sophie was so sweet and friendly to me, always. 'He tells me that you have taken such good care of him,' she said. 'And how could I forget that it was you who sent me that telegram?'

I said nothing, of course, about Lady Beatrice, but I was warmed by their happiness, and I was touched by the way she often confided in me. One day she explained to me that she'd gone to New York because she'd thought she would cause him harm. 'I realised from the beginning that he was expected to marry someone of his own class,' she confided. 'I never stopped loving him, ever – but I expected almost daily to hear that he was betrothed, and I – I would have accepted it. I tried to prepare myself for it.' She looked down at her hands, then up again at me, swiftly. 'When I received the telegram, and realised that he'd been hurt, so badly, what could I do? I always said that I would give up my career the moment that Ash needed me. And he does, more than ever.' Her voice was soft with wonder. 'He tells me that times have changed. *Everything* has changed.'

My heart was bright with gladness. 'You're going to marry him?'

'Of course. You're the first person I've told. He's asked me – and I've said yes.' She took a few steps across the room, took my hand and began to sing softly:

> *Can't sleep at night, can't think, can't dance,*
> *Just wander around with my mind in a trance.*
> *All I'm thinking is, Where are you?*
> *'Cause I'm breathless – just breathless for you.*

I sang the last words with her, and I hugged her. 'I'm so very happy for you,' I whispered.

Her face grew more serious. Still holding my hand, she said, 'Dear Madeline, you've changed since I saw you last year.'

'I'm a little older.' I laughed.

'Yes, I know. But it's not just that. Has something happened to you? Have you met someone?'

'I thought that perhaps I had,' I whispered. 'But I was wrong.'

'I'm so sorry. But are you sure that it's over?'

I lifted my face to gaze steadily at her. 'Absolutely sure. Besides –' and I tried to make my voice light '– one wedding at a time is *quite* enough for the staff to cope with, don't you think?'

Later that evening I heard low music coming from the Duke's rooms. Someone had left the door ajar and the gramophone was playing one of Sophie's songs – 'All I Want is You'. I peeped in, and saw that they were dancing cheek to cheek – she was in his arms, and he was softly singing the words in her ear. I allowed myself to feel jealous, but not for long, because I was so truly glad for them.

Because the wedding plans were taking up such a great deal of Sophie's time, it wasn't as difficult as I'd thought it might be to get my guardian to myself. One afternoon when Sophie was downstairs with Mrs Lambert, I knocked on the door of the Duke's sitting room and went in to find him seated at his desk. He was working, but he turned round and gave me his usual warm smile. 'Madeline. I feel that I've been neglecting you.'

'Not at all. Your Grace –' I hesitated ' – may I speak to you about something that might surprise you a little?'

He pushed the papers on his desk aside, and gave me all his attention. 'Of course. You can speak to me about anything at all.'

'Have you heard of Mr Mallory? Nathan Mallory?'

His eyes widened. 'Yes. I have, as it happens. Why do you ask?'

'I've known him for a while,' I said in a rush. 'I met him while I was staying at Belfield Hall, and I happened to discover that his family estates – his grazing lands – were ruined when the local water supply became contaminated. Mr Mallory helped me once, Your Grace, in a difficult situation . . .' My voice trailed away.

'Do you want to tell me more?' prompted my Duke gently. 'About this difficult situation?'

I was put up for auction, by Lady Beatrice. Nathan rescued me, but once again he's broken my heart . . .

'I don't think it's necessary to tell you more,' I said quietly. 'But I was wondering if it was possible for you to somehow help Mr Mallory to restore his farmlands. All his tenant families had to leave, and I know he hated them losing their livelihoods and their homes.'

'But this is incredible!' the Duke exclaimed. At first I was dismayed – but then I realised that my guardian was smiling. 'Madeline,' he went on, 'look at these maps.' He pointed to some plans laid out on his desk, and he explained to me that Mr Fitzpatrick had recently arranged for the sealing-off of a faulty conduit that had been discovered on the Belfield estate. It had been leaking poisoned water, he told me, from some ancient mine workings into Nathan Mallory's land.

'What really worries me,' my guardian went on, 'is that Mr Fitzpatrick said it looked as if the conduit was deliberately damaged, years ago. I'm only sorry that it's taken so long to address the problem – and I'll do everything I can to help Mr Mallory get his estate and his farms back into working order. Are you still in touch with him, Madeline?'

'No,' I said quietly.

'But you'll be glad to hear all this, and he should know it himself, very shortly – Mr Fitzpatrick is writing to him with the news. Oh, and by the way –' his gaze was steady '– Mr Fitzpatrick has also informed me that the Duchess has now moved back to the Dower House. Mr Fitzpatrick had a few words with her – discreet words, I'm sure – but she informed him that she preferred to live in a household where *the old values are still appreciated.*'

I could almost hear her saying that, and I coloured slightly. 'I'm afraid it was my fault entirely that she came to Belfield Hall.'

He shook his head. 'Nonsense – I'm only sorry that you were put in such a difficult situation because of my long absence.'

'You did what you had to do,' I said earnestly. I felt a great rush of affection for this man, who had always been so generous to me, and whose sense of justice was so strong – so very strong, in fact, that I'd never once heard him utter recriminations against the men responsible for the explosion that had injured him.

'They thought they were fighting for their country's freedom,' he'd once told me when I'd hesitantly asked him about it. 'And God knows, the Irish have suffered centuries of injustice. We can only hope that they come to see the ballot box as the way forward, rather than civil war.'

Now, as I got up, I hugged him – I couldn't help myself. 'I'm so glad,' I whispered, 'for you and Sophie. She's beautiful and kind, and you both deserve every happiness.'

I ate my evening meal as usual with my guardian and Sophie. As usual, I left them early so they could be together and wandered along to the library, where I tried to read but instead got lost in my memories of Nathan.

Suddenly the door opened and James came in. His manner towards me had been distant lately, but not tonight. He looked distracted. 'I beg your pardon, ma'am,' he said. 'But I wondered where you were. You'd left the dining room early, and you weren't in your room ...'

I rose slowly. Did he think that I'd gone to Lady Beatrice's? 'James,' I said, 'why are you so worried as to where I am?'

And he told me that ever since the night of the charity ball, Nathan had rung him, almost every day, to check that I was safe.

I sat down again. Nathan was ringing James, about me? My lungs felt tight, my pulse was racing. I didn't under-stand. I beckoned to James to sit down also and said, 'I think you'd better tell me more.'

And he did. He explained that he'd known Nathan during the war. 'We were in the ambulance service together,' he told me. 'Afterwards, we lost touch. But when you telephoned me that evening, ma'am, and asked me to tell him not to come to the charity ball, I found out – by ringing other friends who'd been with us in the war – that Nathan was in London, and I got his number.'

I sat very still, trying to absorb all this, all the implications. *The ambulance service. They knew each other.*

'I gave him your message, ma'am – though I gather he didn't take any notice of me. And since then – you must forgive me for not telling you – Nathan has rung me here most days, as I said, to check that you're all right.' He hesitated. 'So you have no plans, to go out tonight?'

'None whatsoever.'

I thought that I saw him let out a sigh of relief as he left the library. Feigning complete calmness, I waited until I heard his footsteps die away; but then I paced to and fro, thinking: *This was no ordinary check on my whereabouts. He looked alarmed. He asked me if I had plans to go out.*

Guessing that James would have gone to join Mrs Lambert in her sitting room, as he usually did once the evening meal was over, I hurried along the corridor to his office, which was indeed empty. Switching on the light, I went straight over to the table where the telephone stood, knowing that beside it would be the notepad on which he wrote the details of every call he made or received. Listening always for the sound of his footsteps, I picked it up and swiftly read: *8.15pm. NM rang. The Grosvenor Chapel, South Audley Street – at 9pm. Check Miss D.*

I replaced the notepad carefully. It looked like an appointment. Had someone told Nathan that *I* would be there this evening?

I knew the Grosvenor Chapel – it was only a brief walk away. Hurrying up to my room, I proceeded to dress in the dark, drab clothes I used to wear at Belfield Hall, then I crept down the back staircase of the house and out by the servants' door. Light rain was falling as I quickly walked along Hertford Street towards South Audley Street and the Grosvenor Chapel. I was trying my best not to panic. Had someone rung Nathan, or sent him a note purporting to be from me?

There were few people around at this hour, and when I reached the chapel, the neighbourhood appeared deserted. But then I heard muffled sounds from the churchyard, and hurried round the side of the building to see two shadowy, burly men kicking at something in the near-dark. It was a man, on the ground, and I glimpsed his face as he struggled to get up. It was Nathan. And someone in a black hat and coat was hurrying away – Lord Sydhurst.

I think I almost threw myself in front of him. 'Stop them. Stop those men – they must be yours. Call them off, or I'll raise the alarm, I'll run for help—'

'You won't,' he cut in. 'Or I'll tell everyone I witnessed you killing the Marquis all those years ago, at your mother's party.'

My blood froze. *You are a wicked child, a whore in the making, and a murderess* . . . I felt the old, sick fear – but then I saw, from the corner of my eye, that Nathan was trying to get up, and those men were starting on him again. 'Tell everyone,' I said quickly. 'I don't care. But call your men *off*.'

Sydhurst stared at me, then turned to his men and

called out, 'Take him round the back. Out of sight.' To my horror I saw that they were dragging Nathan's body by the arms, into the darkness behind the church – *he must be unconscious*. I let out a low cry as I suddenly felt Sydhurst's hand grip my shoulder. With his other hand he'd caught my hair, hurting me; he was slowly forcing me to my knees on the damp ground.

'Damn you,' he said softly, 'you weren't meant to be here. But now that you *are*, I'll have a little entertainment from you, I think, before I proceed to give Mallory exactly what he deserves for outbidding me at that auction.' I'd started trying to rise; he wrenched me to the ground again. 'A little amusement, for old times' sake. Say it. Say what you used to say, at those parties in the rue Saint-Honoré.'

The London drizzle had begun to fall again and I was cold, I was on my knees; above all I was terrified for Nathan, whom I could no longer see. 'My name is Madeline,' I said in French, in a low voice. 'My name is Madeline, and what can I do to please you, *mesdames et messieurs?*'

'Again,' he rasped. 'Again.'

'My name is—' Then I was upright, and I'd pulled out my pistol from inside my coat – the Ruby pistol that Nathan had taught me to fire. I'd sprung away from Sydhurst, and I was aiming it straight at his chest.

'Madeline?' I could see the terror in his eyes now. 'Madeline, be sensible. Besides, you cannot possibly know how to use that gun—'

'I do,' I said. My voice was quite calm. 'Believe me, Lord Sydhurst, I do.' As he moved slowly towards me, I steadied my grip; my finger was about to squeeze the trigger. But suddenly I heard footsteps, and there were four men closing in on us – including James, who had seized Sydhurst and was wrenching his arms behind his back until he cried out in pain. I staggered away, my legs suddenly unsteady, and felt hands on my waist – I struggled and twisted round to see Nathan, smiling down at me. There was a cut on one side of his face, from which blood trickled, but his eyes gleamed with humour.

'*Nathan*. Oh, God, I thought . . .' I was beginning to shake.

'I was playing dead,' he explained. 'Waiting for my chance. James has brought three of his ex-army friends along with him, and they're dealing with Sydhurst's men at the back of the church.' Carefully he took my pistol from my grasp and as he examined it his eyes grew darker. 'It's loaded. And the safety catch isn't on . . . Were you actually going to use it, Madeline?'

'Of course,' I said steadily. 'What else?'

Exhaling sharply, he disarmed it and put it in his pocket, then he held me. Simply held me, in his arms. And I thought, blindly, *I'm just going to stay here – for ever. Please, let me stay like this for ever . . .*

Still holding me, he swung round to James. 'Let Sydhurst and his brutes go free.'

'Nathan?' James still had Sydhurst's arm twisted tightly; there was perspiration on Sydhurst's face. 'You're sure?'

'Quite sure. You've given them a taste of what's to come, if there's any more trouble.' He turned to me. His hair was rumpled, there were bruises on his cheekbones and jaw as well as that cut, but he was safe. That was all that mattered. He was safe.

Then he said gravely, 'I heard everything that Sydhurst said to you, Madeline.'

And, heavy-hearted, I prepared myself to tell him the truth.

Chapter Twenty-four

Nathan had left his car close by and he drove me to his little house in Poplar, while James headed back to Hertford Street, promising to ensure that no alarm was raised over my absence. I bathed Nathan's poor face and helped him to change his shirt. The bruises on his ribs were livid, but he claimed nothing was broken.

'Sydhurst clearly wanted revenge over that auction,' Nathan mused as I pressed a cold cloth to the cut on his cheek. 'Beatrice must have ordered him not to bid any higher. And he decided to get his own back on me.'

We were sitting on his small settee before the fire. I rinsed the cloth in a basin of cold water at my side and lifted it to his face again, but he put his hand over mine to stop me. 'How did you know, Madeline? That I was going to be there, and Sydhurst too, at the Grosvenor Chapel?'

'James—' I began.

'He didn't *tell* you?' I saw his anger flare.

'No! That is, he was only checking to see that I was still in the house, and safe. But I made him tell me that he'd known you, in the war. And because of his questions, I was suspicious.' Quickly I told him about James's note, left by the telephone.

Nathan frowned. 'I rang him because I'd just received a message, supposedly from you, asking me to meet you in South Audley Street. I doubted that you'd written it, but I couldn't afford to take any chances, so I decided to go there straight away. James promised to turn up too, but neither he nor I had counted on you arriving – armed and lethal.'

My heart was turning over as I continued to bathe his bruises. *James was a little late*, I was thinking. Nathan must have read my thoughts, because he went on, 'Don't blame James. It was my fault that I gave Sydhurst's brutes a chance to use their fists and their boots on me. I'd arrived early – in case I'd totally misjudged the message, and you were there after all.'

You could have been killed. I swallowed down the lump in my throat and gazed at him. 'Nathan, I'd never realised you and James were friends.'

'We lost touch when the war ended, and James went into the service of Lord Ashley. Then James rang me out of the blue with your instruction that I wasn't to go to the charity auction – and so, of course, I did the exact opposite of what you'd asked. I decided I had to attend, and James agreed with me. I certainly have a great deal to thank him for and Sydhurst should be grateful to him also.'

I was mystified. 'Lord Sydhurst? Why?'

He gave his glorious smile. 'Because James's arrival stopped you from doing Sydhurst serious damage with that pistol of yours.' He took the damp cloth from my hands, then put it to one side, stretching a little so I could see where beads of moisture were trickling down his lovely, sculpted chest. I didn't want to talk – I just wanted to kiss him, and more. But I knew what was coming.

'Now,' he said softly. 'I want you to tell me, Madeline, about the Marquis.'

Of course. He had heard what Sydhurst said. I gazed up at him with despair racking me. 'Nathan. I don't *want* you to know about my past. Whatever your feelings for me, whatever we've shared, you cannot *afford* to be involved with me.'

And he said, very quietly, 'It's because of my feelings for you that I need to know the truth. *All* of it. You have a great deal to forgive me for – my original intentions to you were despicable. But I'll only know that I've begun to make recompense if you trust me enough to tell me about your past. My life is not worth living without you.'

Disbelief pounded through my veins, but I said, as calmly as I could, 'It was a different matter on the night of the auction. I thought you felt pure scorn for me.'

'We'll come to that later. I'm waiting, Madeline.'

And so I told him.

I told him how the Marquis had forced me, when I was a child, to watch my mother's decadent parties, then locked me in my bedroom and made me satisfy him. The look in Nathan's eyes almost frightened me. 'Did he take your virginity?'

'No. Not that. He made me use other ways—'

'The bastard.' His teeth were clenched. 'The bastard. So you lost your virginity during your escapades at the convent?'

I shook my head.

'In Paris, then, after you were expelled?'

'No.'

His eyes widened. 'Then – where?'

I breathed, 'You took my virginity, Nathan. In your cottage.' *You were my first, my only man.*

He raked back his hair, looking utterly confounded. 'So your reputation—'

'I cultivated it.' I gazed at him squarely, because there was no hiding any more. 'I let people think that I'd behaved wildly. It was the same when I came to London. My reputation held most people at bay. It kept me safe.'

He took me in his arms and kissed me, so tenderly. 'I will keep you safe from now on. I swear that I will keep you safe. If this Marquis wasn't already dead, I would go to Paris and kill him myself – slowly.'

Still holding me tightly, Nathan talked me through it all again, and told me at last: 'You are not a murderer, Madeline. You were a terrified victim, a child trying to protect yourself against a grown man. No court in either France or England would find you guilty of murder, and Sydhurst knows it.' Gently he brushed a lock of hair from my cheek. 'To think, that you've carried the burden of the Marquis's death with you, all this time. Oh, Madeline . . .'

I was shaking inside. 'Don't pity me. I don't want your pity.'

'You won't get it,' he said. 'I love you, so much.'

I turned to him slowly, in utter disbelief.

'I love you,' he repeated.

'But you despised me on the night of the auction, and rightly so—'

'I was an ignorant fool,' he said bitterly. 'But I know now what happened, Madeline. I know now about the photographs. I realise how Beatrice used them against you, and believe me, I shall never forgive myself for not realising it earlier.'

Again, I was astonished that he knew, but he gave me the answer in one word. *Dervla.* James, Nathan told me, had always been suspicious of Dervla, and after the auction he tracked her down. She'd confessed to James about the photographs taken at Belfield Hall. 'She told him,' he explained, 'that you only agreed to that auction to protect Sophie. I'm just sorry that I didn't learn about it until afterwards. After I'd treated you so despicably.'

I was shaking my head, trying to absorb all this. 'I hated that auction.' I still felt utterly wretched. 'I hated you seeing me like that.'

'Hush,' he said, 'hush. I've told you – I understand now, and I'm the one to blame, not you.'

We talked, then, for so long. I told him how I'd tried to get rid of the film the morning after the Duchess's party, and thought I'd succeeded, but had in fact failed. I told him how dreadful it had been to come to London and find that Beatrice still had the photographs. 'I think the worst moment,' I said quietly, 'was when Beatrice told me that she'd invited you to the charity ball. I couldn't bear for you to see me like that, so I asked James to stop you. But you still came. You bought me—'

'How could I do anything *but* buy you?' He cupped my face and smiled down at me wickedly. 'You looked quite divine in that pink dress. And presumably you managed to get the photographs?'

'Beatrice destroyed them in front of me.' I was still anguished. 'But only at a terrible cost to *you*, Nathan. The five hundred guineas you paid for me—'

Nathan silenced me by kissing me again. 'I want you to know,' he said, 'that I would pay ten times that to hold you safe in my arms.'

Then he confessed so much to me. He told me how he had been bitterly resentful over the fate of his pacifist, idealistic father and the decline of his estate. He told me about his dream of a socialist government, and his anger for the poor, who deserved better jobs and a better future – but he felt that he'd betrayed his father's ideals with the life he'd lived in London after the war, mingling with people like Beatrice and Lottie. And since then, he'd been struggling to save his inheritance.

I caught my breath. Didn't he know about the Duke's plans to redress the wrong done to his father's lands? If not, then I'd say nothing – yet.

But I had to say something to the man I loved so much. I had never seen him lay himself bare like this before, and his despair tortured me.

'You must not despise yourself, Nathan,' I urged, taking his lovely face gently in my hands, carefully avoiding his bruises and making him look into my eyes. 'Think of how you've worked to restore your house and estate yourself. And some day –' I chose my words carefully '– you might be able to bring life back to those tenant farms.'

'Impossible.' He shook his head. 'All I've done is to raise people's hopes falsely. I'm not worthy of the trust people have put in me.'

I held him tenderly in my arms, feeling wonderfully strong suddenly – because this time, *I* was the one helping *him*. 'No,' I said. 'No, you're good, you're the bravest and most honest person I've ever met. And I have complete faith in you.'

'Even after what I did to you?' he asked wonderingly. 'Using you for revenge? I betrayed you wretchedly.'

'You told me how much you regretted it. And Nathan –' I was pressing kisses to his chest '– I simply adored the talisman.'

He drew me to him and kissed me so sweetly, so intensely. Then he brushed his lips against my wrist, where my scars lingered. 'It strikes me,' he said, 'that you feel you deserve pain and punishment. You carry a great weight of guilt on your shoulders, yet I cannot see why. I want you to let me heal you. To love you. Please, will you promise to give our relationship a chance?'

I clasped him to me. 'You've made my life worth living again, Nathan,' I whispered. 'You've made me whole again. But – you must think carefully about any sort of commitment. Don't you think Lord Sydhurst will try and tell people about my past?'

'Sydhurst wouldn't dare. After all, what was he doing at that party where the Marquis died in the first place?'

I gazed at him, speechless.

'Think about it for a moment. He was a British government minister – you didn't know that? – in Paris on the eve of a disastrous war, and he was indulging in debauchery at a notorious nobleman's party.' Nathan's eyes narrowed in scorn. 'Sydhurst wouldn't want anyone knowing about that – and convincing you that *you* murdered the Marquis was the best way to keep you quiet. He'll be terrified now that you might break that silence, so trust me, he'll keep well away from you. He won't dare to say a word about you or your past.'

I felt that most fragile of emotions – *hope* – starting to pulse slowly through my veins. 'Will you press charges against him? For setting his men on you?'

He shook his head. 'Not worth it – though if he ever comes near you again, I'll make sure he's sorry.' He gazed at me. 'I love you, Madeline. I need you, so very much.'

'And I love you.' I nestled in his arms. 'More than I can say.'

I saw the hunger in his dark eyes, wild and wanting; I felt the same hunger, in the deep clenching of my abdomen, in the warmth that was melting my breasts. I think I breathed his name, then we were in one another's arms, our mouths and tongues melding, my cheek scraping deliciously against his stubble as I pressed myself against him, needing to feel his hard body against mine.

He groaned and pushed me away, but only to deal with the buttons of my garments. I felt my bones dissolve as he dropped his mouth to first one breast and then the other, suckling my nipples until I thought I would explode with ecstasy. I was reaching for him, my finger-nails raking his back, relishing his firm muscles; he pushed my hands aside, but only to unfasten his waist-band, then he pulled me close again and I felt his heavy erection hot and thick against my abdomen.

'Nathan – your injuries!'

'There's no better cure,' he said breathlessly.

Still sitting, I leaned back on the settee, parting myself for him, and he knelt over me, soothing me, caressing me until I felt his hardness enter me in a surging thrust. I ached for completion, yet he held me there suspended for what seemed for ever as his tongue ravished my mouth – until he drove with his loins and ground himself into me, again and again. Because I was already on the brink, my climax came in a giant wave, building and intensifying until there was no way to go but to be lost in the storm of my release.

I held him tightly in my arms, drenched with pleasure and peace. *My gamekeeper.* He loved me, and he was mine. Afterwards he kissed me, and told me all the things I'd always thought I was not, murmuring that I was good and brave and kind, until I pressed my hands to my face and said, distressed, 'No, I am not, I am damaged.' But he took my hands away and kissed me until I couldn't speak at all, then he said huskily, 'Please, Madeline. Please do me the very great honour of being my wife.'

My emotions reeled. 'Oh, Nathan . . .'

He was holding me closer. 'Think about it, I beg you,' he murmured softly. 'But not for too long. I need your answer soon, *mam'selle.*'

314

Epilogue

Belfield Hall, four months later – December

It was three in the afternoon on Christmas Day, and Belfield Hall was bustling with activity. A service had been held in the chapel that morning, offering a spell of calmness; but afterwards the preparations grew ever more frantic, because at four o'clock the many guests – the Duke's Oxfordshire friends, neighbours and tenants – would start to arrive with their families. There were gifts for the children to be arranged beneath the tree, and Cook, I knew, was fretting terribly downstairs over the elaborate supper menu.

'Poached salmon with lobster sauce, minced venison croquettes, veal *fricassée*, apricot jelly with champagne blancmange – oh, my goodness me,' she could be heard wailing to anyone who happened to be in the vicinity of the kitchens. Mr Peters had already made the footmen polish the silverware twice, and now he was creating the usual fuss over getting them to bring up the finest wines from Belfield's vast cellar to the dining room. I was helping Mrs Burdett with the final decorations, reassuring her that the reception rooms looked beautiful, from the boughs of holly hung on the high picture rails to the big candles garlanded with ivy and red holly berries.

Yesterday morning, Nathan had worked with Robert and Will to hoist a twenty-foot pine tree in the entrance hall. When it was finally secure, Robert climbed a ladder to hang a multitude of gilded wax fruits, glass baubles from Germany, miniature toys and rainbow-coloured sweets from its branches, while the housemaids clustered eagerly below to offer advice, Harriet being the loudest of them all if Robert put anything in the wrong place.

Afterwards Nathan came to stand by my side, smiling down at me. I stood on tiptoe, seizing the opportunity to whisper, 'I love you, Nathan. But you've got pine needles all over your collar!' I started picking them off.

'Surely you know that it's considered good luck to decorate the Christmas tree?' He pressed my hand to his lips. 'Although I've had all the good luck I could wish for, Madeline, since you came into my life.'

'You sound,' I answered wickedly, 'as sugary as the icing on Cook's special Christmas cake.'

He grinned back. 'Sweet words but true, *mam'selle*.'

Oh. I shook my head at him in mock reproof, but could I have been any happier? I didn't think so.

Nathan had to leave after that, but he'd promised me that he would be at the Hall in time for the party. And now it was Christmas Day; I was labelling the gifts for the children, and laying them carefully under the tree, so I was one of the first to see him when he arrived a little after three, with a big cardboard box under his arm.

He came up to me and kissed my cheek. 'Electric lights, for the tree,' he murmured, tapping the box. 'I drove into Oxford yesterday evening, to collect them. Only Robert knows.'

Robert was clearly delighted to be in on Nathan's secret. Swiftly he brought in his ladder again and the two of them set to work, with Robert following Nathan's instructions and climbing nimbly to secure the chain of tiny light bulbs around the tree's branches, while the other footmen and the housemaids gathered round, frowning. 'Bits of green glass, strung on wire,' scoffed Betsey. 'What's all that about, for goodness' sake?'

'Wait and see,' Robert called down to her with a knowing air, while I watched Nathan, who'd disappeared round the back of the tree to fix the plug into an electrical socket.

When the lights came on, everyone gasped in delight. Indeed, the effect was magical, with all those tiny, sparkling bulbs shimmering on the glass ornaments and tinsel. Robert looked as pleased as if he'd invented them himself. 'Mr Mallory ordered them,' he pronounced as he came down his ladder at last. 'They've come all the way from America, they have.'

Nathan was at my side again, his arm around me, and I leaned against him. 'You're always full of the most delightful surprises,' I murmured up to him.

He grinned, and I could tell that he was as satisfied as anyone with the tree. 'We aim to please, *mam'selle*,' he said, his embrace tighter. 'Always.'

But the tree was no longer the centre of attention, because one of the housemaids came scurrying in. 'He's here! I think His Grace is here! I saw the lights of his car, in the distance . . .'

The whispers flew around the house and servants were running to gaze out of the windows. 'The Duke is here. With his Duchess!'

From all corners of Belfield Hall, from outside too, they hurried to the entrance hall and lined up: Mrs Burdett, Mr Peters, the housemaids and scullery maids, the footmen and bootboys and grooms, all waiting for my guardian and his new Duchess to enter their home. For the Duke and his Sophie had been married in London two months ago, at St Margaret's church in Westminster. I'd been one of six bridesmaids, and the Duke had looked so handsome, Sophie so beautiful in white lace and satin. They had sailed to the south of France on honeymoon, staying on in that mild climate for several weeks in order for the Duke to regain his health completely, but now they were home at last.

Robert and Will – oh, no, Robert had pine needles on his coat, Mr Peters would be horrified – were already swinging open the big doors, and standing stiffly to attention as the Duke and Duchess of Belfield came in. My heart lifted to see the Duke looking so well and his Duchess so radiant. After handing his overcoat and hat to Robert and greeting him by name, my guardian spoke to all of the servants – not just Mr Peters and Mrs Burdett, but the footmen and the maids as well. The maids were gazing awestruck at Sophie, who looked shy but serene in a dark blue velvet coat with a sable collar and a matching velvet hat.

On the day of her wedding, she had confided in me

that one of her few remaining doubts about marrying the Duke lay in the possibility that the staff would be reluctant to accept her as the mistress of the house, since she had once been a servant there herself. But their awe and admiration as they curtsied to her was only too evident. 'Your Grace,' they all breathed. 'It's truly good to see you here, ma'am.'

As I'd told Sophie in London, the Duke was held in such high regard that the staff couldn't help but be delighted by her, especially when they saw how very much the Duke loved her. Now, at Belfield Hall, her home once more, I led Sophie upstairs to her private rooms, and the minute that she had me to herself, she hugged me close and whispered, 'Do you know, Madeline, I didn't realise that I could be so happy.'

Nathan had asked the Duke for my hand in marriage the very morning after our encounter with Lord Sydhurst. He'd driven me back from his house in Poplar to Hertford Street, where James had tactfully kept the news of my overnight absence from everyone but Mrs Lambert; then Nathan had come in with me, to ask my guardian if he could speak with him privately. Nathan was calm, but I felt as nervous as I'd ever been, and I'd waited with increasing anxiety in my little parlour while the two men were closeted in the Duke's study. But after a while Sophie came tiptoeing in to me.

'Oh, Madeline,' she breathed. 'I saw him. Mr Mallory. You love him, don't you? James was telling me how honourable he is, how brave he was in the war – and he's so handsome! I'm very, very happy for you!'

'The Duke might say no,' I whispered. 'I'm only eighteen, and he might make me wait.'

'I really don't think he will. I know how much Ash wants you to be happy. My dear, you *deserve* to be happy.'

We'd hugged each other and talked about Belfield Hall, and Sophie's memories of it, until at last the Duke came to my room with Nathan to tell me that our marriage had his complete approval. My guardian also took the opportunity to explain to Nathan about the plans he'd made with Mr Fitzpatrick, to resolve the matter of the old mine workings that had leaked poison into the Mallory lands for years; I gathered the Duke had offered Nathan money by way of reparation, and though Nathan had refused, he gladly accepted my guardian's offer of teams of hired workmen to help clean and restore the river and the streams that irrigated his estate.

Nathan and I had decided to get married after the New Year, at Eastertide, perhaps – quietly, in the village church at Belfield. He bought me a beautiful sapphire engagement ring – 'To match your eyes,' he told me – and in the meantime his priorities were his estate and his house. I'd moved back into Belfield Hall after the Duke's wedding, but to be truthful I spent most of my time with Nathan, driving with him into Oxford to find old furniture at markets and sales, helping him in the garden of his house if the weather was fine or decorating inside if it was wet. Because we were betrothed, everyone at the Hall seemed happy to turn a blind eye to my lack of a chaperone – in fact Nathan often came to pick me up from the Hall in his car, and though Mr Peters was cool towards him, Nathan had Mrs Burdett twisted round his little finger. 'Such a charming young man,' the housekeeper would declare, rather pink and flustered after he'd flattered her, while all the house-maids were open-mouthed with envy of me.

Nathan had sold my emerald bracelet, and I suggested that we use the money to have electricity installed throughout his house sometime soon. But meanwhile, as the dusk gathered I loved to go round lighting candles everywhere, then sitting with him in the drawing room while his two dogs sprawled happily before the log fire. Those days and evenings were more than precious to me, because by talking over my hateful past and exam-ining my raw hurt, Nathan helped to heal the mental scars left both by the Marquis and my mother's neglect.

'Worse than neglect,' Nathan exclaimed in anger. 'She must have known what was happening to you – yet she did nothing to protect her own daughter!' But by assuring me that none of it was my fault, Nathan gradu-ally made me whole again, and happy in a way I'd never dreamed I could be.

'I shall be like the old Duchess once we're married,' I teased Nathan merrily one afternoon as we climbed the stairs to his bedroom to make love. 'I'm almost tempted to say that I don't want electricity, I don't want any – *modern gadgets*. Just candles and lanterns and log fires, like your cottage, Nathan.' And in his bed, enfolded in his arms, I would imagine that I could hear the chatter of children's voices – a little Nathan, perhaps, with his father's curling brown hair, or a daughter who would adore her father and be loved in turn, who would never suffer the unhappiness and torment that I had suffered.

Nathan reminded me, of course, that the old Duchess was the Dowager now. As my guardian had told me, she'd moved from Belfield Hall back to the Dower House, only to fall into a towering rage the instant she heard that the Duke was marrying Sophie. She had attended the grand London wedding 'only because one must.'

But on the afternoon of the Christmas Day party at Belfield Hall, to which all the Duke's tenants and neighbours and their children were invited - she appeared.

The first guests had begun to arrive at four, and the Duke and Duchess stood in the decorated hall to greet them, while I stayed at Nathan's side in the background, enjoying the aura of happiness that enveloped my guardian and his bride. The Duke was surrounded by well-wishers, and many a gently envious glance was cast at Sophie, who wore a long gown of pale turquoise with a cream cashmere stole, and a necklace of diamonds that had been the Duke's wedding present to her. Before long the doors were closed on the darkness outside, and the party was under way, with the musicians playing festive tunes and the children excitedly examining their gifts, while the footmen proffered trays of champagne, lemonade and mulled wine.

But an hour or so later, the big front doors swung open yet again – and in swept the Dowager Duchess.

The staff were horrified – I could feel their acute tension as she marched into the festively decorated entrance hall. 'Look out – the old witch is back,' I heard Harriet mutter to Betsey. The musicians stopped playing; the children fell silent. The Dowager Duchess – dressed all in black as usual – took one look at the Christmas tree, her lips pursed; then she walked further in, and the Duke came steadily towards her, his arm still around his wife.

She looked them both up and down and addressed Sophie first. 'So,' she said. 'This is your first Christmas at Belfield Hall.'

There was a dreadful silence, because of course it wasn't. All the staff and most of the guests knew that Sophie had been a maidservant here, for years. Then the Dowager went on to pronounce, 'And may all your days here be as happy as this one.'

The Duke, with a smile on his face, reached for a glass of champagne and handed it to her. 'To the health and happiness,' he said in his clear voice, 'of the Dowager Duchess.'

'To the health and happiness of the Dowager Duchess.' All the guests raised their glasses and the party began again, even more noisy and merry than before.

I looked at Nathan, who'd drawn me aside. 'I don't understand,' I whispered. 'I knew she'd been invited today, but I never thought she would attend – no one did. She hates my guardian. She hates Sophie.'

Nathan grinned. 'Keep up with the news, Madeline. There's a good reason for that smile she's fixed to her face today. Your guardian received a great deal of acclaim for his contribution to the peace settlement in Ireland – and amongst his admirers is the Prince of

Wales, who has also been completely charmed by the Duke's Sophie. In fact the Prince has announced his intention of visiting Belfield in the New Year – and the Dowager Duchess isn't going to miss out on the prestige *that* will bring her amongst her cronies. So there's a temporary truce.' Nathan had already taken my hand and was leading me towards the staircase. 'But that's quite enough about *her*. Go and get your coat, will you, *mam'selle*? I want you,' he murmured with a wicked smile, 'all to myself.'

In the darkness we hurried through the park like mischievous children and climbed the hillside to the clearing where I'd first met him. Down below us sparkled the lights of Belfield Hall, and in the distance I thought I could hear the sound of the foxes.

Our breath misted in the frosty air, but he had his arm round me, and I was warm. He was leading me to the cottage with that dark smile on his face; he was opening the door and drawing me close, already unbuttoning my coat and pressing kisses to my face.

I was aghast and delighted. 'Nathan – *now*? But the party . . .'

My voice faded as he covered my mouth with his, tracing my lips with his tongue and licking delicately until they parted. I felt his gentle fingers on my breasts, tantalising, caressing, and delight pierced me. I wrapped my arms around his neck.

'You were saying something about the party, *mam'selle*?' he whispered.

'It – can wait,' I gasped. 'Can wait – *oh* . . .' He was feathering kisses over my face and jaw, and I was melting. Holding my waist with one steely arm, he led me in, and the room was warm after the cold outside; I realised that embers still glowed in the hearth and I spun round on him accusingly. 'Nathan?'

'I lit a fire earlier,' he said, his fingers already seeking the fastenings of my garments. 'I knew, you see, that I would want you all to myself at some point during the festivities. I need you, so much.' He took me in his arms and led me to his bed; he made love to me and I to him, my beautiful gamekeeper, both of us sinking at last, after a fierce explosion of joy that all but consumed us, into one another's arms.

He woke me with sweet kisses. I mumbled his name – a complaint, because I didn't want to move – but he was adamant; he was dressed and gently stroking my cheek. 'Madeline? Sweetheart? It's time to go back to the party, I'm afraid. They might just be starting to miss us.'

The party at the Hall. Oh, no. I was on my feet, I was pulling on my dress, stumbling into my shoes. Nathan laughed, helping me. 'I thought,' he said, 'you miscreant, that we ought to be back at least for the carols around the tree. Or, you know, people might talk. Might say that I was using dastardly tricks, kidnapping you, forcing you into marriage.'

'They'll say you're going to make me live in a house without electricity. Without servants,' I teased. 'When I could have picked from suitors by the dozen in London, and gathered a title or two, and been driven around in a Rolls-Royce instead of your battered old car.'

He drew me into his arms. 'If you didn't look so incredibly happy, I might be seriously worried, you know. Because all of that is perfectly true.'

'Oh, *Nathan*.' I reached up to stroke his hair back from his forehead, feeling raw emotion tighten in my throat at the sudden vulnerability in his eyes. 'You need never worry about my love for you. Never. Ever. Believe me, please.'

He took my hand and kissed it, caressing with his lips the place on my wrist where the old scars had all but healed. He drew my arm into his. 'Your future is mine,' he said quietly. 'And I am yours. I want you to know that, always.'

I reached to kiss him tenderly.

'Back to the party?' His voice was sweet and husky.

'Back to the party,' I said. And we walked down the path to Belfield Hall. Together.

Find out how Sophie and Ash's story began, in
the provocatively romantic novel by

Elizabeth Anthony

ALL I WANT IS YOU

An innocent girl
1920. Seventeen-year-old Sophie is a scullery maid at
a large country house, Belfield Hall, but what she truly
desires is to dance on stage in London.

Caught up in a dangerous game
Glamorous Lady Beatrice offers her assistance, though not
without an ulterior motive. A new heir – the seductively
handsome Lord Ashley – is about to arrive at the Hall: a
man that Beatrice will do anything to ensnare . . . even if
she has to exploit her young maid.

Of forbidden passion
What she doesn't know is that Sophie has met Ash once
before. And as Lady Beatrice's devious plan unravels,
Sophie has two choices: refuse to be a mere plaything for
the man she loves so desperately, or give in to the thrill of
unimaginable sexual pleasure . . .

Out now in paperback and ebook

HODDER